The Assassins'
Lover

a tale of the demon world

EMMA HOLLY

This story is a work of fiction and should be treated as such. It
includes sexually explicit content which is only appropriate for
adults—and not every adult at that. Those who are offended by
more adventurous depictions of sexuality or frank language
possibly shouldn't read it. Literary license has been taken in this
book. It is not intended to be a sexual manual. Any resemblance to
actual places, events, or persons living or dead is either fictitious or
coincidental. That said, the author hopes you enjoy this tale!

This book contains mf, mm and mmf scenes.

cover photos: Klubovy, ccaetano

DEDICATION

To my readers, who make it
possible for me to do what I love.

CONTENTS

1: HAPPY BIRTHDAY, PRINCESS

Today was Katsu Shinobi's thirtieth natal day. She'd heard such milestones upset Human females. They were considered "on the shelf" once they hit the third decade mark. Given that her race could expect to live centuries, at thirty Yama were scarcely adults. Consequently, it was not the weight of the years she'd experienced that lay heavily on Kat, it was the years she had left to go.

Her natal day was the one day she and her father always spent together. They'd share a pot of Imperial White at her dead mother's favorite teahouse, then reminisce with pleasant stories over platters of savories.

Because that was not to be this year, Kat closed her rim-to-rim silver eyes and tipped her lovely face to the morning sun. She reminded herself she had reasons to be thankful. She might be exiled, but she was safe and her enemies far from her. The Human world, so encroaching in other places, had made few inroads here. Ever since the Humans discovered a hidden Yamish city forty years before, Kat's people had put up with being called demons. She supposed it natural her race would seem infernal to the more primitive Humans; they'd barely invented electric power, after all. Also natural was the fascination the other race's emotions held for her kind. Human energy affected Yama like a drug—something sensible people avoided. This province where Kat had been banished lay far from the peninsula that connected Yamish lands to those of Humans. The area was less novelty-loving than the capital. As a result, it remained culturally unconfused.

1

Perhaps just as important, spring had reached Ningzha. The sky was a bird's egg blue, and the scent of cherry blossoms lent a kiss of sweetness to the soft air. The lush walled garden in which she sat was an ode to nature and the landscaper's art. Dragonflies flitted from bloom to bloom, their colors as carefully selected by the master gardener as a princess's party gown.

"Cousin Kat!" cried the very voices she'd been hoping to avoid today. "Why are you hiding all the way out here?"

Quashing her dismay, Kat turned on the rustic bench to greet her three female relatives. The girls were fifteen, seventeen and twenty, all blessed with the ruler-straight blue-black hair that was the Yamish ideal. Their ankle-length silk robes—only two layers in this nice weather—boasted the latest fashionable hues: lemon, lime and orange, as it happened. All her cousins were pretty; Yamish genetics rarely left room for ugliness. They were not, however, as elegant as their youth led them to believe. Jules, for one, should have eschewed anything to do with yellow, no matter how popular it was that season.

"Good morning, cousins," Kat said calmly. Her overgown was a less fashionable but flattering bronze, the color suiting both her milk-and-roses skin and the antique brass undernotes in her black hair. Satisfied with her appearance if not her prospects, she smoothed the silk neatly down her thighs.

"Is it true?" Jules demanded, her flush betraying an undignified excitement. As the eldest daughter in her family and of marriageable age, she merited a pair of guards. The two males who accompanied her this morning were not the House of Feng's shining best. This was probably due to Jules being the eldest daughter of a junior branch of that illustrious family. Though tall and muscular, the guard to Jules's right had eyes in slightly different shades of silver. The one to her left was marred by a strawberry birthmark stretched along one cheekbone. Presumably, the imperfections had no bearing on their competence. Certainly, they were too professional to react to Kat's quick perusal of their persons.

Rather, they almost didn't react. The one with the birthmark, whose face was as smoothly sculpted as a statue, shifted the merest bit in his parade stance. Kat pulled her gaze from his otherwise handsome features with a small effort.

"Is what true?" she responded to her cousin.

"Did Prince Avel's eyes turn black for you at his dinner? Did Aunt Miry exile you because she was hoping Cousin Mara would snag him?"

Both claims were accurate. Prince Avel had displayed the involuntary ocular reaction that signified sexual and genetic compatibility, without which no blue blood's marriage could be sanctioned. Other classes might find spouses where they liked, but royal genes—and royal libidos—were demanding. Producing heirs required close matches. It was also true that Kat's stepmother had hoped to catch the prince for her daughter. Neither of these facts, however, were politic to acknowledge.

"What did your mother tell you of the matter?" Kat evaded.

"She said it must have been a trick of the light, but I don't believe it. When that other prince's eyes turned black for you last year, Aunt Miry sent you away then too. I think she's annoyed your mother passed better genes to you than she did to her own daughter. People still remember Miry 'discovering' her royal blood."

Kat remembered this herself, for it had caused quite a stir. Mara's birth nine months after Miry's marriage should have put the whispers to rest for good. A prince couldn't get a child on a nonroyal. Sadly for Miry, her daughter's inability to attract a mate resurrected the wagging tongues. Now people claimed her line wasn't royal *enough*.

"Aunt Miry says you're coarse," Jules's middle sister, Jade, piped up—in what she must have thought was a superior tone. "She says your pheromones call to so many princes because you don't have a perfect mate."

Not as confident as her older sister, or as respected as Katsu, Jade was prone to envy. Because Kat knew this and remembered what it was to be seventeen, she answered the girl gently. "I imagine that could be true. Not every princess has one ideal husband."

"Aunt Miry says I will," Jade declared.

Her little sister, Joy, was young enough make a rude noise. She was also smart enough that, when Jade spun to face her, she'd retrained her countenance to proper Yamish stillness. Kat had to tip her chin down to hide her smile. Once her amusement was under control, she looked up. To her surprise, the handsome guard with the strawberry birthmark was gazing directly into her eyes.

Perhaps he was as shocked to be caught staring as Kat was to be stared at. The circumference of his pupils jumped wider. Kat blinked, then he did, and then both of them looked away. Kat thought the other guard might have glanced sharply at his partner, but managed to control herself enough not to check. Her thighs were dangerously warm, and her face threatened to become so. It simply wasn't done to connect with servants in a personal way. She wished she hadn't noticed how good looking the guard was, in spite of his facial flaw. His shoulders were positively monstrous in his gray fighting robes. He'd been bred to be strong, of course, but it was too, too trite for unattached Yamish females to develop yens for their protectors.

Kat had her quirks, but she trusted being trite wasn't one of them.

"We've planned a boat ride on the lake," Joy said, thankfully oblivious to Kat's struggle. The girl was bouncing just a little on the balls of her jeweled slippers. "We're hoping you'll join us."

"Do say you will," Jules seconded more moderately.

Kat rose from the bench she'd intended as her sanctuary. The lake was an easy walk outside the garden's wall.

"It would be my honor," she said. Maybe she'd have been more peaceful without the girls' company, but she was fond of them, and her youngest cousin was a very likable wild thing. Joy didn't have much longer to be irrepressible: two years, at the outside, after which she'd settle into being a well behaved young lady. Today, that inevitability made Kat reluctant to miss a minute of her effervescence. In truth, it made her a little sad.

It had been too long since Kat herself had been inappropriate. In the deep dark privacy of her mind, she sometimes thought it would be fun to live as freely as the primitive Humans.

True to form, Joy ran ahead of her sisters, her expensive gown trailing damply in the flower dotted grass. To Kat's surprise, and a little to her discomfort, the handsome guard fell into step beside her. He was very tall—at least a hand span above her own royal height.

"You don't travel with an escort?" he commented quietly. His gaze was on Jules's back—where indeed it belonged. As was also right, his partner guard walked by the other girl.

Kat should have had an escort. She was the eldest daughter of the Shinobi clan. Regretfully, her stepmother had resented her from the start. At first, the cause was the respect with which Kat's father and the House retainers regarded her. Later, it was her father's failure to leave off honoring—if only occasionally—his first wife's memory. When Katsu's greater appeal in princely circles became apparent, distaste turned into hostility. Kat saw little use in complaining to her father. He wasn't unhappy in his second marriage, nor was Miry the sort to change her behavior for anyone. She'd simply have become slyer, and Kat preferred her enemies out in the open.

"Bringing an escort would have caused my House an inconvenience," she said aloud. "I'm sure no harm will come to me here."

The guard said nothing, though he did glance at her again. He walked an arm's length away, his strides shortened to match hers. She supposed his question could be professional. If she had no guard, he might be expected to protect her. Though this was the likeliest explanation, she couldn't deny her skin tingled on the side of her body nearest his. Annoyed by her lack of discipline, she sought to push the sensation from her as they reached the reed-fringed bank of the sparkling lake. Two light rowboats were tied to the wooden dock. Their lack of a power source increased their picturesque appearance. This boat ride, evidently, was to be an old-fashioned exercise.

"You're in my boat," Joy announced to Kat. "You too, Hattori. We'll trounce Ciran and the others with no trouble."

Hattori seemed to be the name of Kat's walking companion. He bowed to Joy as if she hadn't committed a breach of etiquette by not calling him Citizen.

"As you wish, Princess Joy," he said gravely.

Joy giggled, and the back of Kat's eyes actually stung at the merry sound. If she was this emotional, maybe her uncelebrated natal day *was* affecting her. Both guards stepped into the rowboats to steady them, their highly trained grace barely causing the hulls to slap against the water. Nimble as an elf from a Human story, Joy hiked up her gown and hopped into Hattori's boat without help. Then Hattori held his hand politely out to Kat.

It was natural that their eyes would meet, but not that her heart would start beating faster. Hattori's pupils were more enlarged than before, like ink shining in his molten silver irises. Kat put her hand in his and he clasped it firmly. His skin was warm, his palm callused from sword play over most of its surface. She couldn't help imagining that roughness sliding over her breasts.

"Princess," he said low and huskily.

She nearly stumbled at the gravelly sensual sound. He had to catch her elbows to help her sit without falling. When he released her, confident she wouldn't capsize the boat, his narrow nostrils flared.

Kat's hand fluttered to her throat before she could stop it. Hattori had an erection. She didn't dare look at it directly, but the engorged shape had altered the fall of his fighting trousers. The knowledge of his arousal ran through her veins like fire, swiftly heating the soft flesh between her legs. The wetness Hattori had probably scented grew. She was more affected—more aroused, to be frank—than she'd been for Prince Avel at his dinner.

With the slightest hitch in his movements, Hattori lowered himself to the seat that faced hers. He'd be rowing backwards while she and Joy rowed ahead. From the tiny flickering grimace of his facial muscles, Kat concluded sitting down was uncomfortable. The glimpse she'd caught of his genital bulge suggested he was endowed as well as erect, perhaps approaching the size of a royal male. The men of her class were the most prodigious of all Yama: longer, thicker, and so addicted to sex when they were in heat that they literally lost all sense. The lower classes didn't experience rut, but if Hattori's organs of procreation were as large as a royal's, his pain might indeed be considerable.

Kat's desire to steal a longer look was shamefully strong.

"Grab your oar," Joy twisted around to urge her from the front of the boat. "We need to be ready when Jules says go."

"We're not racing," Jade insisted with icy seventeen-year-old scorn.

"Oh let's," Jules pleaded, causing Jade to frown at her older sister's betrayal. "I'm not too old for a bit of fun. And if our boat wins, I'll give you that diamond hairpin you've been pestering me to borrow."

Pretty jewels were Jade's weakness, which Joy could not fail to know. "Race," the youngest Feng daughter chortled, her fist pumping the air with delight. "Race, race, race!"

Both the guards nearly smiled.

"Around the rock and back," Jules said, laying out the rules. "First one to touch the dock again claims the prize."

The guards, Hattori and Ciran, wrapped their hands around their oar handles, each in the center position of their respective boats. Ciran's shoulders were as broad as Hattori's, though his overall physique was leaner. Both guards looked a good deal more purposeful than the girls, who had one oar to the men's two.

"Ready," Jules said, her voice vibrating with anticipation. "Set . . . *go!*"

They set off with a lot of splashing, but not much momentum.

"In synchrony," Hattori instructed, as if Kat and Joy were students. "Dig your oars into the water at the same time as me."

Joy was laughing so hard she was gasping, but their crew still coordinated itself first. Suddenly they were shooting forward at an impressive clip.

They weren't the only ones to find this breathtaking.

"No!" Jules cried. "After them, my hearties."

Kat suspected her cousin was mangling the Human phrase, but it hardly mattered. The empress's ridiculous Human Fiction Channel, approved for broadcast six months ago, provided all any of them knew of pirates—or manual boats, for that matter.

"Arrhh," she growled in same spirit. "Look sharp, or you'll walk the plank!"

The lake wasn't very large, and they were almost to the ornamental boulder Jules had named as the turning point.

"Rock," Hattori said, nodding to show he'd spied one to his right under the water.

"Rock!" Joy crowed, mistakenly assuming he meant to exhort her on. She dug in her oar and struck the very obstacle Hattori had been warning her about. The collision of stone and paddle unbalanced her. Quick as thought, the guard reached back and grabbed her waist sash to keep her from falling out. Unfortunately, his speedy reaction startled Joy even more. Her weight swung

7

wildly as her arms pinwheeled. Caught unprepared, Kat found herself catapulted over the side.

The lake was little better than ice melt this time of year. The cold shock of the water closing over her was succeeded by a sharp crack against her skull—probably the rock that had started the trouble. Kat inhaled water, which her body tried to expel before she could surface. Choking pulled more water into her, but her legs wouldn't kick her upward because her gown had tangled around her calves. Her hair was doing the same to her face and neck, like a nest of weeds strangling her. She heard a splash, and a vise seemed to seize her ribs as her vision narrowed to one gray spot. The fear that gripped her couldn't be described. She was only thirty. She wasn't prepared to die.

She returned to consciousness with her head safely above water and her throat raw from coughing up half the lake. Hattori was behind her, towing her toward the shore, his hold a warm and reassuring band beneath her shivering arms.

Kat thought she'd never felt anything so lovely.

She didn't have long to enjoy it. Horror assailed her as she spotted the sinking nose of the overturned rowboat.

"I can swim," she gasped, trying feebly to do it. "Please make sure Joy is all right."

Given the circumstances, Hattori might be forgiven for snorting out a laugh. "Your cousin is halfway to the dock already. You're the one who passed out with her scalp bleeding."

"Oh dear," Kat said. They were going to be in so much trouble.

♦

Hattori carried Kat up the path to the unoccupied stone guesthouse that overlooked one end of the lake. She was dripping like the Humans' horrific loch monster. What had been a mild spring day became dead of winter now that she was soaking wet. As she shuddered in Hattori's arms, the guard's striking face turned grim.

"Curl closer to me," he said harshly.

Kat couldn't disobey the order. She felt better as soon as she gave in and clung to him. Despite his own dunking, Hattori's body was fever warm, already starting to dry his clothes. He made a sound as her face snuggled to his throat where his now limp undercollar left bare skin. If her closeness pained him, he wasn't shying away from it. His nose was against her cheek, smelling her.

Jules used her thumbprint to key open the guesthouse's faux wood door. In actuality, the entrance was solid plasteel, as secure as a diamond safe. The interior maintained the rustic pretense, though of course it had the standard amenities.

"I'll find blankets," Hattori's partner said.

"Find some for Joy," Kat reminded through chattering teeth.

Hattori's arms tightened around her. Rather than release her, he sat in a big leather chair with her in his lap. The heat in the guesthouse had been shut off, the exposed wood framing of the slanted ceiling only visually cozy.

"I'll activate the power grid," Jade volunteered.

"I'll find the first-aid kit," Jules said.

"You should be seeing a physician," Hattori muttered under his breath. "You might have a concussion."

They were alone in the dim stone-lined room. Hattori didn't move, just closed his eyes and hugged her to him—as if grateful she was alive. Kat doubted she'd ever been held like this even as a child. The upper classes didn't believe in displaying affection. Hattori's arms were big, his muscular thighs like iron under her. Throwing appropriateness to the wind, she pulled her shivering legs to her sodden chest. To her amazement, his lap was hotter than the rest of him. She shifted in surprise, and the skin of his eyelids tensed.

"Are you all right?" she asked softly.

His lashes lifted, his pupils huge. His gaze was glassy enough to be drugged.

"Sorry," he said, even more quietly than she had. "Everything about you does it for me."

She blinked at him, her body proving it did have heat in it. As she stared, lips parted for her quickened breathing, the guard's erection lurched under her bottom. The wet silk she wore was thin, and there was no mistaking his hardening. In truth, she wasn't certain he'd been completely soft in the cold water.

She tried to speak but didn't know what to say. She had one hand flattened on his chest, and his heart thudded strongly against her palm. The tip of Hattori's tongue came out to wet his upper lip, exposing the dark forked marking that had inspired Humans to label their race demons. Yama considered showing one's lamril a sexual display. Probably Hattori was just nervous, but Katsu's cheeks heated with a flush anyway.

That was a signal he couldn't miss.

"Princess," he whispered in soft longing.

"We are in so much trouble," Jade moaned mournfully from the door.

Kat started guiltily, though she doubted her cousin had noticed what was transpiring between her and the guard.

With a slump that would have done a sullen young Human proud, Jade switched on the smokeless gel burning fireplace. As the blue flames rose, Ciran reappeared with an armload of green blankets. Unlike his partner, he was perfectly dry.

"I can take her," he said to Hattori. Hattori shook his head tightly.

Close as she was, Kat saw the meaningful look that passed between the men. Did Ciran guess what Kat's presence in his partner's lap was hiding, and if so, did he disapprove? If he did, he wasn't going to press the issue. With a face as uninformative as a royal's, he bundled blankets around them both. The heavy wool felt delicious, and Kat's shivers relaxed at last. Her head fell to Hattori's muscular shoulder, causing him to let out a silent sigh. She was almost too comfortable to notice when Joy padded into the room in her own blanket. With her wet hair draggling around her, she looked closer to five than fifteen.

"You're bleeding again," she announced, coming to a halt in front of the chair.

"I could stitch her up," Ciran offered. A hint of unsureness colored his professional tone. "Or possibly a doctor would be better."

"*No*," the Fengs said in a hasty chorus. As if to emphasize their preference, Jules handed Ciran the first aid kit.

"If Father heard what happened, he'd dismiss you first and ask questions later," Joy explained. "You need to hole up here until Kat is healed. Jules can say she decided Kat should have you as guards instead. She can tell Mother she got tired of looking at Ciran's funny eyes and Hattori's funny face. Mother's certain to believe her. We don't mind how you look, but she's snooty about those things."

"Your father might be justified in firing us," Hattori said slowly.

"Pshaw," Jade scoffed. "Joy would have taken that boat with or without you, and Kat would have gone with her. Joy is her favorite. What if they'd fallen in when you weren't there?"

"I *am* stupid enough to have gone rowing by myself," Joy confirmed cheerfully.

"Kat ought to have a guard," Jules added with older sibling finality. "Just because her stepmother is a viper doesn't mean our family should pinch credits. I'll get new ones, and Kat can borrow you."

All the Feng sisters seemed to think the question settled—the prerogative of princesses, Kat supposed. Less sure, and perhaps unused to being defended by teenage girls, Hattori and Ciran exchanged another look. Under her now warm bottom, Hattori's cock continued to throb. Under the blankets, his right hand patted her side.

It was a strangely gentle gesture, as if he were an old friend of hers.

"It would be better if we didn't risk separation," Ciran agreed carefully, "which might happen if we're dismissed."

Kat thought this an interesting warning, though no one else noticed it.

"It's decided then," Jules said. "We'll tell Mother and Father that Kat's feeling sulky on account of being sent away from the prince. We'll convince them she doesn't want to inflict her low mood on us."

This excuse was closer to the truth than Kat wanted to dwell on. If her stepmother had her way, she'd die unmated.

She wasn't the only one who fought a grimace. Jade cursed as her tiny pocket communicator buzzed to signal a call. She dug the walnut size crystal out of her inside sash pocket.

"Balls," she said, checking the readout that was now projected into the air. "It's Mother."

The three girls hustled out of the guest house, where they could ill afford to be seen by the miniature holocamera. Kat heard them arguing about how far Joy needed to stand to be out of view.

Their girls' departure shifted the mood. They were three adults now, if not precisely three equals. Ciran looked at Kat. His eyes weren't funny, they were beautiful. One was silver-blue while the other was touched by gold. Kat felt dizzy staring into them. The guard was calm, but she sensed him measuring her.

It was an unusual look for a social inferior. Though Yamish age could be hard to judge, the way he studied her gave the impression that he was older . . . or at least more worldly.

"I wouldn't do anything to harm either of you," she promised. "You probably saved my life today."

A smile broke shockingly across Ciran's face. Kat gasped, because full-grown Yama—low or high—simply didn't expose their feelings this way.

"You won't harm *us*," he repeated humorously.

"Yes, yes," she said, recognizing that she'd been mocked. "I'm sure you two are dangerous characters."

Ciran's smile faded to a wry glimmer. "You've no idea how dangerous we are . . . and we'll try to keep it that way."

♦

Fortunately, the first aid kit included a small surgical stitcher. Hattori continued to hold her while Ciran closed the sluggishly bleeding gash at the edge of her hairline. Kat was proud of herself for not making noise or squirming. After her impromptu surgery was over, Hattori patted her again, then carried her into the large shower room. He seemed willing to help her undress, but Kat drew the line at that.

"I won't faint," she swore as she pushed him out. "I'm only staying under the water long enough to warm up."

His eyes glowed with the intensity of his interest, which he seemed less able to conceal now that the girls were gone. "You make one noise and I'll be by your side, princess."

His words sounded more like a warning than a promise of rescue. Kat shivered in response, but not unpleasantly.

The sound he made on seeing her reaction was very close to a growl.

She shouldn't have been surprised that the steaming spray took little time to thaw her. What was surprising was the nervousness she felt when she emerged—warm and dry once more in a silk bathrobe. She'd been with men before. The premium royals placed on emotional restraint didn't extend to sex. In that arena, they were inclined to indulge themselves, males especially being driven by their hormones. The lower classes were reputed to like sex too, but Kat had never indulged with them. She'd heard rohn males could ejaculate any time they wanted, instead of only at the height of their cycles. Unlike royals, they didn't need a biologically suited mate to achieve a wet release.

She admitted she'd entertained a fantasy or two around that topic. It seemed so abandoned for a man to spill when he pleased, though perhaps it robbed their climaxes of suspense.

She shook her head at herself as she wandered into the now empty living room. She had no business contemplating the different classes' sexual habits. She wasn't planning to seduce Hattori, no matter how willing he was to succumb. She pressed her lips together, searching the room for signs of where her supposedly assiduous bodyguards had gone.

So much for Hattori leaping to her rescue if she uttered a sound.

Her irritation at their absence pointed up her arousal. The flesh between her legs felt swollen, both tender and hungry. Evidently, her body had its own ideas about what she ought to do.

She heard the faintest murmur behind her, where a hall led to two bedrooms. She followed it, assuming the men were there. One door was ajar. Overcome by curiosity and built for stealth like most Yama, she crept silently to it.

She wasn't sorry she'd been quiet. The tableau she found was unexpected—and too personal to walk in on. Ciran and Hattori were standing very close together in front of a small window. Wisteria shrouded the thick security panes behind them, the alarm wires forming little diamonds inside the layers of glass. Despite the foliage, the sun penetrated brightly enough to light their profiles. Ciran looked troubled, while Hattori seemed a shade angry. One of Hattori's hands rubbed up and down his own chest. This wasn't just an unYamish gesture, it was unguardlike too. If her people had a deity, it was self-control.

"You can't give in to this," Ciran was saying. "You have to fight your attraction."

"I can't help the way I'm reacting. It's as if my body recognizes her."

"You'll give yourself away. You'll endanger both of us."

13

"I know that," Hattori said with clearly fraying patience. "I'm telling you I can't help it."

The hand that had been rubbing his chest slid down to between his legs. He was still hard, the bulge his fingers closed on larger than Kat had imagined a rohn could get. Perhaps he'd meant to prove his point to Ciran by underscoring how stiff he'd grown. If so, the grip did more than he'd intended. He squeezed the shape that pushed out his gray trousers, gasping for air as pleasure made his spine roll.

"Don't." Ciran clamped Hattori's wrist and tried to pull it away. "You're going to make it worse."

Abruptly Kat realized how raggedly the second bodyguard was breathing, how his fighting trousers had arched up from his groin. Tingles of surprised excitement swept down her spine. Unable to wrest Hattori's grip away from his cock, or to stop the knuckle-whitening massage it was engaged in, Ciran shoved his hand under Hattori's between his thighs. As shocked as Kat was by this change in tactic, Hattori gasped at the cupping pressure around his balls.

This was a favorite caress of royals, because their seed stored up between cycles. Giving their sacs a good, deep rubbing helped relieve tenderness. Kat had never been with a prince in rut, but her experiences with them at other times had familiarized her with their general preferences. What she hadn't known was that rohn would also enjoy this, but perhaps some pleasures transcended class. Ciran certainly was proficient at the trick—not to mention extremely bold. As Hattori spread his legs wider, Ciran edged his chest to his.

They stood as close as lovers about to kiss.

"Let me try to bring you off," Ciran said. "Maybe you're not too far gone."

Hattori's head fell back as Ciran's fingers kneaded him. His ready acceptance of the help suggested they'd done this before. The pressure Ciran used was strong enough to have the tendons in his wrist cording.

"I'm . . . pretty sure . . . it's too late." Hattori's voice was strained by his obvious urge to groan. His own hand still tugged his shaft, though he was careful not to interfere with the aid his friend was supplying.

"Still," Ciran said throatily, "if there's any chance you could spill . . ."

Something snapped in Hattori. Without shifting his right hand from its apparently crucial task, he started tearing at the tie to his outer robe. Before he could even fumble, Ciran used his free hand to help.

Evidently, Ciran wasn't that much more sensible than his friend.

"Yes," Hattori said, his chest heaving up and down beneath his undertunic, his fight for oxygen frantic now. Waves of heat flooded Kat's body. As one, the guards reached for his trousers. They were too impatient to undo the drawstring. As they yanked, the waist caught the head of Hattori's erection. He hissed through his teeth. Ciran pulled harder, and the monster won its freedom.

At the sight of it, Kat bit her lower lip. Hattori's vein-girded cock was as thick as a woman's wrist and as dark as if it were sunburned. Blood pumped through its tissues in heavy surges, the marvel so stretched the head was strafing Hattori's ridged abdomen.

His phallus was as regal as any emperor's.

She didn't blame Ciran in the least for falling to his knees like a worshiper. Somewhat to her disappointment, he didn't pull Hattori's trousers down all the way.

She supposed this didn't matter to Hattori. He could see what he wanted to. His hands fisted in Ciran's hair, his fingers getting a firm grip on the blue-black locks. Ciran's hair only reached his shoulders, but it was long enough to steer with.

"Lick it," Hattori whispered. "Squeeze me and lick the top."

Ciran licked him with the flat of his tongue, wetting him with saliva as he surrounded Hattori's scrotum with both his hands. Ciran didn't seem to mind when Hattori thrust the slickened knob in between his lips. He let it in and sucked him harder, pulling deeply enough to hollow his cheeks. Coupled with the firm kneading of his sac, this was more than his fellow guard's control could withstand. Hattori shuddered and urged him closer, biting his lip until it whitened. If he'd been royal and Ciran had been his mate, he'd have been spurting kith by then. Saliva contained triggering hormones to draw the aphrodisiac substance free.

"Wetter," Hattori urged, his head arching back as his hips rocked forward. Ciran widened his jaw and took him, but the change didn't help. "Shit. I don't think I can come."

Ciran released him, resting his brow on Hattori's hip. "Your balls are pulsing," he said, his fingers still working them. "They feel to me like you can."

The growling noise Kat had heard before rumbled in Hattori's throat. "Fuck Muto Feng. Fuck him and his experiments."

Kat didn't know what any of this had to do with the ruling prince of the House of Feng—not that she was going to ask.

"Shh," Ciran soothed, kissing Hattori's shaft—a futile bid for comfort, if ever there were one. His cock had already received too much stimulation. At this point, its skin was so red it glowed.

Unable to resist, Hattori steered the swollen head back between the lips that tormented it. He swallowed a groan as Ciran swallowed him.

"Fate take it," he swore. "I don't want you to stop."

Ciran didn't want to stop either. He sucked him inward fearlessly, sounding as if he were getting him as wet as he could. Ciran was making soft eager noises, his bobbing motions impressively loose and swift. His ease could only be the result of a lot of practice. Imagining how he'd gotten it, Kat pressed trembling thighs together. To her, watching Ciran give such skillful head to his friend was incredibly erotic.

The skin of Hattori's penis shone with spit each time it pulled free of Ciran's lips, its shaft swelling strangely thicker in the middle—not just from the veins but the flesh itself. The organ looked like it was ready to burst and Hattori like he very much wished it would. He'd been watching Ciran work, the way most males would, but his eyes now screwed shut in agony. Kat was so caught up in their drama, she'd begun to hold her breath.

Her lungs let it out again without warning, and both men froze at the sound.

"Shit," Hattori said, catching sight of her first.

Ciran let go of him and turned. "Princess . . ."

"I'm sorry," she said, retreating with her face aflame. "I shouldn't have spied on you."

Hattori moved so fast she let out a very unYamish shriek.

Before she could stop him, he had her by the wrists, pinned back against the wall just outside the bedroom. Every inch of his violently aroused body blazed heat at her.

"I won't tell," she promised, squirming under his weight. He hadn't yanked his pants up, and his cock remained bare. Considering how wound up he was, she guessed he couldn't help grinding against her. Even through her robe, she could feel his prick hadn't shrunk any. Between that and her voyeurism, she was embarrassingly wet. "I know it's none of my business!"

"Do you even know what you stuck your nose in?" Hattori demanded.

That forced her addled mind to think. He didn't mean having sex with a fellow guard. Fraternizing might be considered unmanly in some quarters, but it wasn't against the law.

"Your genes," she burst out. "Someone spliced royal genes in you."

"And she guesses it in one," Ciran observed drolly.

This was more problematic. Their culture's survival depended on the social strata staying distinct. Guards were selectively bred, and that included genetic adjustment. Giving them upper class traits, however, was prohibited. Commoners weren't even supposed to know what upper class traits were. Knowledge was power, and daimyo preferred to reserve that for themselves. On the other hand, what top-ranked royal thought he had to obey the rules? A prince like Muto Feng wouldn't think twice about experimenting for his own benefit.

Then a new thought occurred to her. If Hattori had royal genes, something more than strong attraction might be unfolding here.

"Are you going into heat?" she asked curiously.

Hattori's fingers tightened on her wrists. "Halfway there," he growled, apparently familiar with the term. "Just enough to bung up my normal responses."

"You're responding to me," she deduced. "I triggered this reaction."

Hattori blew out his breath on a sigh. He released her wrists a moment later, though he didn't move otherwise. Maybe his body wouldn't allow him to. He braced his palms on the wall instead, doing a kind of arrested push up in front of her. He was looking down at her breasts, at the tightened thrust of her nipples against the silk bathrobe. Despite the evidence of her interest, he didn't press closer.

"I know you didn't mean to wind me up, princess."

His eyes rose to hers and held there, the expanded black of his pupils nearly swallowing his irises. Staring back at him, Kat felt unexpectedly shy. He was just a man then, not her inferior.

"Could I help?" she asked, trying to control her flinch when his body jerked. "Obviously Ciran has some genes that yours are fond of, but maybe his profile isn't close enough."

Hattori gawked at her for a moment. "You want to help me get off?"

"Some people would say I owe you."

Hattori shook his head firmly. "Saving you was my job."

Kat swallowed, her tongue curling out nervously. Hattori's eyes darkened at the sight of her lamril. He looked like a prince with his gaze gone so close to black. The thinnest rim of silver was all that circled his pupils.

"Admit you want him," Ciran advised. "He won't accept your offer unless you do."

He seemed calm—watchful maybe but not like the thought of her wanting his friend bothered him. The mystery intrigued her. Who were these men? What were they to each other?

"I do want him," she acknowledged, though she blushed for the confession. She looked back at Hattori. "It's like you said. Everything about you does it for me."

He moved as if afraid to scare her, one big hand coming up to conform itself to her cheek. His thumb smoothed her eyebrow around its arch. Simple thought it was, the contact tingled powerfully through her skin. "I doubt I'll be what you're used to."

"Who says what I'm used to is what I want?"

His lips curved slightly. "Would you let Ciran join us?"

"I don't need to—"

"Yes," Hattori said, cutting off his friend's demur. "You know you like it when we share a woman. I'd like you to share this one, if she's agreeable."

Kat would have felt shut out if Hattori's hips hadn't settled on hers just then. His bent knees evened out their heights, pushing between her thighs to brace his weight on the wall. He rolled his pelvis to her, the motion luscious and arousing as it squeezed the living heat of his erection into her mound. He sighed with pleasure and she did too. He felt so good it took a moment for her brain to turn over. When she spoke, her voice was husky.

"You and Ciran have been together a while."

Hattori was dragging his smooth-shaven cheek up and down her neck. "Fifteen years. Since we were assigned to the same dorm room at the Feng palace. Ciran's talents saved my sanity more than once."

He turned his head to lick a bead of sweat from her collarbone. The wetness of his tongue shook her knees. Fearing she'd lose her balance, Kat clutched his broad shoulders. "He's very fond of you."

Hattori hummed his agreement against the crook of her neck, then stiffened and drew back. "He likes women too, Kat. You don't have to worry about that."

His hands slid to her waist as if he couldn't stop touching her. Kat realized this was the first time he'd used her name.

"It's true," Ciran said from closer than she expected. "I guess you could say I'm omnivorous."

Hattori's diminishing self control cut short the debate. No permission beyond a lack of protest would be required from her. Abruptly breathing harder, he tugged the tie of her robe loose. When her front was bared, he took half a step back to look at her. Kat knew she was pretty, maybe even prettier than most. Her breasts were high and pointed, her limbs graceful and firm. When Hattori's gaze ran over her curves, she truly felt beautiful. She let the robe drop from her shoulders.

"Princess," he said, her title a word of praise.

He surprised her. He reached for one small breast with two hands, molding it higher as his thumbs rolled its painfully tight nipple. Ciran stepped next to him, shoulder to shoulder, and began doing the same thing. They were one person in their dexterity. Both were hard, both gentle, both blessed with the swordfighters' calluses she'd dreamed of touching her. Kat's nerves took about two seconds to overload. She cried out as the men bent to kiss her nipples. Their lips molded around her, their tongues flicking the aching nubs in identical rhythms. The simple sight of their hair mingling together made cream run from her body.

This was a fantasy she hadn't known she harbored. She wanted to memorize every detail to replay later, but the myriad pleasures were too much for her blurring brain. Their strong hands held her as she began to thrash.

"I can scent her," Ciran gasped against her breast. "She smells of lilacs and cinnamon."

Hattori moaned at the reminder of what he already knew. "Lift her for me," he said, his voice almost too thick to decipher. "I need to take her now."

His eyes were completely black, his muscles shaking with a fine tremor. Kat was shaking too but not as subtly. She was so ready to be ravished she needed new words for it.

"Step forward, princess," Ciran instructed.

She stepped and the second man moved behind her, between her and the wall. Hattori uttered a longing sound. Plainly, this was a scenario he enjoyed playing out.

"Twine your arms around his neck," came Ciran's quiet instruction.

Kat complied, then jerked as Ciran's hands took a firm grip on her rear end. His skin was almost as hot as Hattori's. "His clothes . . ."

"We don't have time to take them off. It's enough that you're naked."

Was this true, or was it part of the men's mutual fantasy? Kat didn't have breath to ask. Ciran was lifting her and so was Hattori, his hard hands gripping her thighs to spread them around his hips. He was narrow here compared to his shoulders, but wide enough to stretch her groin muscles. She twitched as his juddering length met the wet pulsing of her folds. Her sex was smooth, as was the fashion, and the slide of those satiny surfaces against each other made her spine dissolve. Hattori's breath rushed out of his lungs loudly.

"I've never done this before," she blurted. "I've never taken a man in heat. No male ever spilled in me."

Hattori's Adam's apple bobbed. Like most of his gender, he liked staking claims. "I'm going to flood you," he rasped. "If the Fates allow it, I'm going to drown you in seed."

She was going to drown him herself. Pressed tight behind her, Ciran reached between them to shift his friend's rigid cock to the right angle. Hattori shuddered as the flaring head found her drenched entry.

"You burn," he breathed and began pushing.

Kat hissed at the instant bliss of his penetration. Ciran added his strength from behind. Like Hattori, he'd shoved his trousers under his cock, his shaft and balls squashed against the curve of her ass. Though he wasn't as big as his partner, his blood beat faster. Maybe it was fickle to enjoy that, but Kat couldn't help herself.

Despite the assistance she was receiving, getting Hattori in her wasn't easy. He was very thick and there was a lot of him to engulf. His breath whined out when he was halfway, sweat rolling like liquid diamonds down his temples.

"I can't," he said, the muscles in his jaw clenching. "I'm trying to make myself smaller, but I just can't."

Most Yamish males could contract or expand their erections at least somewhat. This was under normal circumstances, though. No sensible royal female expected her partner to constrict himself when he was in heat. Instincts more powerful than he was didn't allow for that.

Feeling for him, Kat stroked the side of his worried face. "Don't try. Just go as far as you can."

"I want all of you, Kat. I want my cock all the way inside."

His guttural admission almost made her smile. She pressed her lips to the strawberry mark that was supposed to mar him, then brushed her mouth softly over his. A small, resonant sound broke inside his chest. To Yama, kissing was more intimate than sex. Married couples didn't always do it, but Kat wanted to with him. She licked his lips with her lamril, causing them to tremble and part for her.

"Yes," he sighed. "Oh please, yes."

Their mouths sank into each other, tongues reaching deep and stroking, the fit immediate and welcome. Kat's arms wound tighter behind his neck. Doing this felt illogically right to her. He tasted like some sweet tangy wine she'd been waiting all her life to drink. They hummed their pleasure into each other's throats.

Perhaps sensing her relaxing, Hattori gathered his muscles and thrust his hips at her. Ciran did as well, his mouth open on her shoulder. Their coordinated efforts gained Hattori another inch into her.

"Fate," Hattori moaned, drawing his tongue out only to push in and suck again. "Oh princess, you're paradise."

His hands ran over her body, as if he wanted to memorize her. His rocking thrusts continued, gradually working him deeper. His movements weren't hard, but they were getting harder, so she supposed the female essences in her cream were having an effect. Neither he nor Ciran seemed to mind bumping each other's hands as they caressed her. She could tell the inadvertent touches excited them, and their excitement excited her. Ciran only hesitated when his big hard palm fanned her flat belly. His fingertips were inches from where his friend entered her.

Sensing it wasn't her the guard hesitated to reach for, Kat drew one hand down from Hattori's neck. She smoothed her fingers over Ciran's.

"Ring him," she said. "Rub his cock where he can't shove it inside of me."

Ciran did it. Both men must have enjoyed this, because the pressure of the big hot bodies on either side of her increased.

"Shit," Hattori hissed.

Ciran had taken her suggestion one better. He was twisting his thumb and two fingers around the base of his friend's erection, as if it were a jar in dire need of unsealing. The men found this game as thrilling as she did. Hattori heaved at her, groaned, then set his feet and did it again.

Her body was too excited to resist the extra force. He was in her then, penetrating her completely but for the ring Ciran's fingers formed. She and Hattori both moaned loudly. The head of his penis was squashed to the end of her. It amazed her that she could feel it, that she had nerves to register this deep intrusion. She couldn't remember feeling this with other men. Hattori seemed to relish the sensation. His hands clamped around her bottom, like he'd stay right where he was forever.

Kat knew he wouldn't. No matter how good he felt, his body was incapable of remaining still. As if to prove it, he ground ferociously into her for about five heartbeats.

"Fuck," he snarled and let loose with all his might.

Ciran couldn't shove then. All he could do was protect her from being battered against the wall. She gave thanks the females of her class were resilient. Hattori's thrusts were glorious: long, thick, with that wonderful extra swell in the middle of his shaft. The added pressure did things to her sexual nerves, things she hadn't known them capable of. She gasped for air as a quick orgasm struck like a lightning bolt.

She knew she'd just gotten him wetter.

"Again," Hattori ordered, his hips working like he wanted to paint every cell on his cock in her essence, and from every possible angle. "Princess, do it again."

Ciran grunted, his muscles straining stiff as stone behind her. His cock strafed up and down the curve of her ass. From the feel of it, he was very close to going with her. Hattori must have recognized the warnings.

"Don't come," he said harshly. "You know where I want you when you spill."

Ciran cursed but stopped rubbing himself against her so hard and fast.

Brief though it was, the exchange opened a window to their sexual preferences. Hattori liked being fucked, and truly it was no wonder, if his experimental genes were doing what she suspected. Royals had kith glands piggy-backed on their prostates. In the later stages of heat, they craved few things more than having both well pounded. If nothing else, the predilection pushed the upper ranks to erotic adventurousness, whether through toys or additional partners.

"Do you itch yet?" Kat asked, unable to contain the intrusive question.

"Like I'd welcome a regiment back there," Hattori admitted ruefully.

"Has your kith ever risen?"

Hattori jerked his head *no*. Now that she was looking for signs, she noticed he was squeezing his ass together each time he thrust into her. "It just . . . feels like it should."

He groaned as he treated her—and himself—to an especially lengthy plunge. "Sorry," he said. "Don't think I can talk anymore."

She let him focus on his pleasure; let him focus on hers, if it came to that. He knew how to make her come, and Ciran knew how to help. She didn't think she could have stopped them even if she'd been inclined to. Too many fingers were finding too many sensitive spots. She lost count of her orgasms though, strangely, none prevented her from wanting more. Each time she grew creamier inside, Hattori's efforts became more crazed. She wondered if they ought to stop. If he couldn't come, maybe continuing would be cruel. The arousal of males in rut could rise indefinitely, but—without release—might not recede for days. Hattori hadn't even had a dry orgasm, which normally he'd have done.

Then, all at once, everything he did slowed down: his breathing, his thrusts, the long, low moans that escaped from him. He was driving into her just as hard, but he was *really* paying attention.

"Fate," he breathed, his eyes nearly rolling back. "Ciran."

Ciran kissed the back of her neck. "That's my cue, princess."

Hattori had lost his strength to hold her, or maybe he just wanted his weight powering into her from above. As Ciran slipped out from behind her, Hattori lowered her to the polished wood of the guesthouse hall. They lay at a slant, because the hall was too narrow to accommodate their height. The hardness of the floorboards couldn't lessen the pleasure of being ravished in this new position. Ciran watched them revel in it as he tore off his clothes. She was glad he wanted to be naked. His body was hard— and more dangerous looking than she'd foreseen. Pale thin scars marked the lean muscles of his chest.

"Wait," she panted as he prepared to kneel.

He looked at her. Despite the thick hot organ being drawn so deliciously in and out of her, she was caught again in the spell of Ciran's bicolor eyes.

"Let me kiss your cock," she said. "Let me do for you what you did for him."

Ciran didn't expect that, and neither did Hattori. His tantalizing thrusting slowed even more.

"You want to suck me," Ciran verified.

Kat didn't understand his doubt—unless the women he shared with Hattori somehow failed to notice him.

"Yes," she said. "I want to, and not just to thank you for the pleasure you've given me."

Hattori didn't add his opinion, maybe because he couldn't speak. Instead, groaning, he tipped her up until they were coupling on their knees. This position had new charms, but his head turned to his partner, gesturing Ciran closer with a jerk of his chin. Hattori's pulse drummed visibly in his neck. Kat could think of only one reason why this would be.

Hattori was looking forward to watching her fellate his friend. Happy to oblige, she smoothed her hair neatly behind her. That earned her a twitch from the organ inside of her.

Without taking her left hand from Hattori, she let her right smooth over Ciran's hip. The tensing of his tendons enchanted her, the hair-trigger responsiveness of his nerves. In return, Ciran laid a hand on her shoulder. His light clasp moved with her as Hattori's rolling thrusts rose and fell.

Clearly anticipating going weak in the knees, Ciran braced his second palm on the opposite wall. "He can't stop while you're doing me. He's too far into arousal."

Kat sensed this wasn't a complaint. It wouldn't have been for her either. They'd happily work around Hattori's needs.

Ciran sucked in a breath as she leaned to him. She licked his cock just for pleasure, tasting his sweetness and swirling around the head. Beads of pre-ejaculate welled from its center, which she found rather flattering. His penis trembled, so she took him.

He slid into her mouth like steel wrapped in satin, hot and thick and just long enough to give her a sense of accomplishment. Evidently wanting more control over her, Ciran's hand moved from her shoulder to cup her skull.

"Oh that's nice," he said, guiding her to him as he thrust carefully. "Kat."

She loved the way this pair said her name. "Ciran," she murmured around him, and thrilled to his small shudder.

Excitement building, he pushed farther into her mouth. Hattori's breathing quickened as Ciran went in and out. His hands squeezed her hips, ensuring she didn't stray too far from his thrusts. Instinct told her he wished *he* were licking Ciran.

"You're as good at that as he is," he gasped.

She wasn't. No one could be. Nonetheless, it couldn't be denied that the second guard was having trouble holding back his climax. The noises he made were broken, his guiding fingers stiff. Sucking him harder felt wonderfully mischievous.

Hattori seemed enthralled by his friend's struggle. "It's usually him going down on me. I never knew he'd look like this."

This was reason enough to ring her lips beneath Ciran's rim and focus some good licks there. The taste of him grew stronger, the fluid that wasn't seed yet increasing in volume. She held tighter onto his hip, some deep part of her longing to make him forget himself. He groaned at the intensification of her tongue's pressure.

"Enough," he said breathlessly, pulling free of her. His cupping hand slid down the side of her hair. "Thank you."

Hattori's fascinated gaze was locked on Ciran's exceedingly upright cock, at the evidence of her suckling shining bright on that taut flushed skin. As if the sight were too much to bear, he closed his eyes and turned back to her. His arms hugged her close as he buried his face against her shoulder.

He almost looked frightened by what was coming.

Kat didn't think that was true, though he trembled and held her tighter as Ciran moved into place behind him. No, what caused this big, lethal man to vibrate like a tuning fork was that he needed this so much. He was vulnerable—not only to Ciran, whom he knew and trusted, but also to her. Yama didn't fancy being vulnerable, and guards liked it even less. Ciran smoothed Hattori's hunched shoulder muscles and tucked himself close to him.

"She licked me," he whispered next to Hattori's ear. "You're going to feel her essence on me when I push in."

If Ciran meant this as a warning, it didn't prepare his friend. Sound rattled in Hattori's throat at the first intrusion. Apparently, her genetics suited him, sensitizing his anal passage as Ciran pushed into it. His spine stretched, his mouth, his breath coming hot and ragged on Kat's neck. He caught her hips to him in grips of iron. He couldn't thrust now, or at least he couldn't withdraw. Her cream had bespelled his cock, and he lusted after her depths too much. Helpless to move other than squirming, he had to rely on Ciran to push him over that final edge.

Ciran wasn't shy about exercising power. His lean features hardened with purpose, each strong thrust targeting the aching gland his friend hid inside. Over and over, his drives massaged it, his angles shifting but not the force he used. Kat could only imagine how that smooth swollen crest would feel. Hattori moaned with pleasure, straining desperately for climax. When the extra thickness in the middle of his shaft pulsated, Kat's desire coiled in sympathy.

"Almost," Ciran rasped.

And then Hattori began to go.

She felt his face twist against her shoulder, felt the sudden liquid heat shoot inside of her. Hattori let out a muffled shout and ground his glans crazily deeper. He must have craved the extra friction, but the pressure so deep within her sex triggered a fierce climax.

The effect of her added wetness was dramatic.

"Move," Hattori begged like he was dying. "Both of you, move faster."

She and Ciran obeyed, humping him wildly from either side. It didn't matter that they weren't in synch. Hattori writhed between them, gasping, seized by more ecstasy than he could handle . . . or get enough of.

"Never," he choked out a minute into it. "Never like this before."

On and on, he abandoned himself to it. This much seed must have been storing up for cycles, and understandably Kat was a partner he was eager to take full advantage of. He flooded her as he'd promised, but she loved the messiness of it. The profound relief he was displaying moved her, his intensity catching. She was no more able to stop climaxing than he was. Somewhere in the middle of the madness, Ciran groaned and went over too.

He pressed his face to Hattori's shoulder, his hands clamped on Hattori's heaving pectorals. The contortions of Ciran's expression suggested he'd needed this release as much as his lover.

Seeing this satisfied a tension Kat hadn't known she had.

When all of them were sated, she sagged in Hattori's lap. The men weren't as flattened as she was, but they hadn't been coming since the start. Hands ran soothingly over her, mouths pressed by turns to her skin. Though these men were strangers, she'd never felt so cared for. If it were an illusion, she didn't want to know. Perhaps they understood the yearning. Two male sighs echoed in her ears.

"There's a prince-size bed in the next room," Ciran observed to no one in particular.

There was, and Hattori carried her to it, only staggering slightly as he went. He lay down with her in his arms, then drew one hand down her front and tucked it between her thighs. She suspected he liked the feel of his seed marking her. Kat didn't mind. She could shower later. For now, she was too relaxed.

His other arm made a perfect addition to the pillow.

Close as they were, her hand rose naturally to Hattori's face, tracing its smooth carved lines. He lay on his left side, and the pillow hid his birthmark. The perfection of what remained was new and interesting.

Hattori's eyes crinkled as he pretended to bite one curious finger. "You all right? No headache or dizziness?"

Kat's eyebrows quirked. "Now you're asking me about signs of a concussion? After you introduced me to your personal earthquake?"

"I checked your eyes when I pinned you to the wall earlier. Your pupils weren't uneven."

She remembered how blazingly angry he'd been—and how blazingly aroused. "You're a man with great powers of concentration."

A cloth dropped to the carpet beside the bed. Though the platform was sturdy, it creaked as Ciran's weight descended on the mattress. Hattori's gaze flicked watchfully to his friend's approach. Kat didn't think the reaction was jealousy, more like he wasn't certain Ciran would be welcomed.

"Your stitches didn't strain while you were blowing me," Ciran said.

Hattori made a sound that could have been a chuckle. "That I didn't notice. I was too busy watching the show."

Ciran grunted, sighed, and snuggled up to the lower part of Kat's body. His head rested on her side above her waist, his groin finding a comfy home against the back of her legs. He'd tidied up with the cloth he'd dropped. His smooth lax penis was warm and clean. The carefulness of the action struck her. When it came to sex, these men knew how to please a woman. They were as skillful as they were passionate. That being the case, the intimacy of cuddling—and whether she'd like him doing it—had to be what he was insecure about.

Kat moved her hand to rub Ciran's side. He butted her shoulder blade with his silken hair, a hunting dog asking soundlessly for more praise. Thinking he deserved it, Kat reached back to stroke his head.

"You're so sweet," Hattori said in a marveling tone.

Kat snorted, unconvinced that what she'd done with them fell under that term.

"You are," he insisted, and again came that note of the tentative. "Sweeter than either of us scarred blades deserve."

Kat thought before she spoke. She knew their previous assignments couldn't all have been as innocuous as guarding her cousins, but neither could she believe them undeserving of kindness. Deep down, she knew they were good men.

"You showed care for me," she murmured. "And for my cousins. And each other."

"You see," Ciran teased his friend from her side. "You and I are sweet too."

Hattori laughed, soft but unmistakable. He petted the long straight locks that had fallen across her breast, not arguing any more. The niggling tension in all of them released.

"Happy natal day," he murmured.

Kat lifted her sleepy head from his arm. "You know about that?"

"Princess Jules instructed her sisters not to mention it this morning. In case it bothered you."

Overcome by emotion, Kat hid her face in his shoulder.

"Good present?" Ciran suggested, wriggling higher to share the pillow. His long arm draped her companionably. She was glad he'd decided this wasn't presumptuous. When his fingers started playing over Hattori's bicep, her smile broadened. Hattori must have felt her mouth curve. He let out a low and satisfied rumbling sound.

"The best present," she felt bold enough to confess. "In fact, this year's gift was so good I might have to open it again tomorrow."

Hattori's cupping hold on her breast tightened. His thumb fanned warmly over her nipple. "All summer, princess," he corrected. "We three are going to get to know each other much better."

"Much, much better," Ciran emphasized.

Kat's bright grin couldn't be contained. Surely no exile had ever been as nice as this one.

2: FIFTEEN YEARS EARLIER

Some guards took longer than others to face the central truth of their existence: They weren't people, they were things and—as things—they were expected to do what they were told.

When the captain of Hattori's unit called him to his stark black office, Hattori didn't ask questions.

"Go to that address," the captain said, waving toward the small scroll he'd handed him. "Your client will recognize you. Do what's asked of you and return."

Hattori unrolled the digital parchment. The address he found inside was that of a teahouse in the Forbidden City's outermost reaches. The place was as far from the palace quarter as one could get without tunneling through the wall. Hattori was fortunate he knew the area. He'd triggered the data scroll's self-destruct when he opened it. No more than ten seconds had expired, and the missive was disintegrating into ashes atop his palm.

"Take the Bullet," the captain said, referring to the imperial city's underground high-speed train. "If you're not carrying your ops kit, collect it first. You're expected within the hour."

The captain's stony eyes pinned Hattori's, daring him to object. They both knew why refusal wasn't an option. Hattori bowed, wiped his ashy palm on his winter weight fighting trousers, and backed out of the room. He didn't bother asking if Prince Feng had personally approved the job. If it required his kit of assassin's tools, Muto's involvement—or lack thereof—wasn't information he'd be entrusted with. Hattori wasn't officially a Feng employee; the

House's tax rolls listed him as an independent contractor. All the same, he'd been their de facto possession since before he was born—as had the surrogate who'd given birth to him.

Don't think about that, Hattori told himself, repressing an instinctive shiver at a sudden blast of cold air. He'd stepped into the wintry throughway behind the complex where the House of Feng's security lived and trained. He sincerely doubted his birth mother knew he was there, or the controversial nature of the children she'd been carrying. For his part, he'd never met her, nor heard a soul speak her name. That being so, there was little point in either resenting or pitying her now.

Because his ops kit was already on him, he trotted to the nearest maglev entrance, the frost-laden air gathering in a nimbus around its illuminated blue indicator post. The Bullet train was reserved for government employees and security personnel. Ordinary civilians walked, cycled, or—if they were feeling flush—bought dispensations to hire floating palanquins. Aristocrats ruled the sky with their aircars; the rest of the Yama were forbidden from looking down on them. At the moment, Hattori didn't care two credits about the inequity. The train would take him where he was going without attracting notice. He was no stranger to flying in any case. Someone had to pilot those useless royals to their parties.

He was ahead of schedule, so he exited the maglev at Goldfinch Way, one stop short of the teahouse. Last week's snow blew in crystalline eddies along the street. He was blocks from the city wall, but the barrier loomed over the humble brick shops and apartment houses like a leviathan, so tall it needed radar to warn off aircars in bad weather. Though the wall appeared to be black granite, it was plasteel and loaded with electronics inside and out. Before he got off the train, Hattori had keyed on the jammer that was hooked to his weapons belt. His presence still might be seen, but it couldn't be recorded.

His destination, the blandly named Good Fortune Teahouse, blocked the end of an alleyway. As he slipped down its shadows in his unremarkable dark gray robes, Hattori kept one hand on his charge-knife and all his guard senses on alert. His only apparent company was the city's notoriously hardy squirrels, which didn't mean no one watched from the roofs above. If they watched, their job wasn't to attack. Hattori reached the teahouse unharmed.

Because he was taller than most rohn, he had to duck to enter the bright red door. Once past the threshold, the place smelled of sesame noodles and real aged wood. Though it was dim, he'd trained his eyes to adjust quickly. He picked out his client instants after arriving.

She was young and beautiful Miry Oryan, wife to equally young but less beautiful Tudou, who owned a modest chain of aircar appliance stores. Both were daimyo but not royals. Hattori recalled gossip he'd overheard: that Miry Oryan was ambitious and regretted her strictly horizontal marriage. With his own eyes, at a party he'd been detailed to guard, he'd seen her flirting with the House of Shinobi's recently widowed head. Lady Oryan was one of Hattori's master's particular female friends, as welcome at Prince Feng's table as in his bed. Taken together, the pieces added up to a single sum.

Lady Oryan was in the market for a Yamish divorce.

He went through these calculations without allowing any to reveal themselves in his expression. Miry Oryan was dressed in plain gray tunic and trousers—no cosmetics, no jewels—as if she thought she could pass for a common maid. Any half-competent royal guard would have recognized her. Their survival depended on knowing all the players. Then again, the lower classes frequently knew things the upper ones didn't guess. Guards too often had no more reality to their masters than a painted support column.

Unwilling to betray that he recognized Lady Oryan, he stood where he was until she spotted him.

She did so a moment later, gesturing him to her table with two fingers. Lunch had ended, and the third-rate teahouse was not crowded. The décor was both worn out and traditional, with low wood tables and "lucky" red floor cushions. Hattori tucked his large body onto the cushion opposite Lady Oryan. Given how susceptible he was once aroused, he girded himself against responding to her beauty. Physical distraction was the last thing he needed now.

"You should pour for me," he pointed out as she brought her steaming cup of tea to her mouth.

She looked at him over its rim as coolly as if he were a bug. He waited for her to realize he'd spoken the simple truth. A woman of his class neglecting to serve a male drew attention. If she wanted to preserve her disguise, she'd have to take the daimyo nightstick out of her ass.

"Fine," she said crisply, filling a second pale blue cup before sliding it across the scarred wood to him.

She must have ordered the finest leaves the teahouse stocked. The jasmine infused green was smooth and fragrant. Sorry he wasn't there to enjoy it, Hattori drank half and set it down.

Lady Oryan studied him with barely hidden displeasure, her gaze lingering on the misshapen stain that stretched over his left cheekbone. He'd noticed the disfigurement offended low-ranked aristocrats more than royals—the result of their own feelings of inferiority, he supposed. Their staring no longer affected him. Better they should be misled by appearances.

"Well, I suppose you're rough enough for the job," she said by way of breaking the silence. "I'm told you're reliable."

He inclined his head in uninformative agreement. He suspected she knew he had reason to be that way.

Lady Oryan turned her empty cup in a seemingly aimless circle, her fingers slender and feminine. He was momentarily—and unwillingly—hypnotized. Her nails were pampered, her skin as perfect and smooth as cream. She obliterated his fascination with a scorpion sting wrapped in sweet honey. "Conditions at Winter Prison must be barbaric this time of year."

Hattori's gaze widened and rose slowly. Was the infamous correctional facility where his brother Haro was being held? Security had their own underground intelligence network. Though he'd tapped every source he could think of since the night his brother was dragged away by Imperial Guards, Hattori had come up dry. His heart knocked faster behind his ribs. Winter Prison was located in the bleak northwest, within the arctic zone. Life behind its high tech walls was reputed to be brutal. Lady Oryan had tossed out her observation casually, as if it meant nothing. Stymied, he examined the patterns of her aura, an inborn rohn skill he wished he were better at. He read something in her energy that intrigued him, but not whether her words were true. The obvious explanation was that she wanted to ensure his compliance. Of course, simultaneously misleading him with disinformation wasn't unthinkable.

"Yes," he said carefully. "I'm certain Winter Prison isn't a place I would want to be."

The corners of her mouth gave a tiny twitch. "One's stay could be made easier. With blankets or better food. Even in prison one can suffer less or more."

Hattori's hands fisted in his lap, the tightness of their clenching making his knuckles ache. His brother was worth a thousand aristocrats, maybe a million. "I assure you," he said, striving desperately to sound calm. "I do not share my brother's squeamishness concerning assignments."

"Goodness, you have a brother?" Lady Oryan pursed her lips with ill concealed amusement. "I had no idea."

Hattori drew a lengthy breath to quell the rage bubbling up in him. "Do you have a target you want me to see to?"

The humor in her face fell away. She pulled a data scroll from the inner pocket of her plain black sash. Like the data carrier his captain had given him, the special parchment was designed to self-immolate. Unlike the first scroll, this contained a great deal of information. He had sixty seconds after breaking the seal to memorize the details of where and when the hit should transpire. The logistics seemed well thought out, though he'd prepare for contingencies. As he'd expected, the target was Lady Oryan's young husband.

"Can you do it?" she asked.

"Yes," he said, his voice harsher than he wished.

"And it will look like a heart attack?"

"Yes."

She stared at him, Yama to Yama, for the first time. Her youth was written across her face, determination warring with the nervousness in her eyes. That nervousness, along with the knowledge that his incarcerated brother would have preferred he refuse, prodded him to speak.

"Are you certain you want me to proceed? There's no undoing a job like this."

It wasn't the proper question for making her reconsider. Her delicate jaw hardened. He knew then she was a true dragon lady in the making. "I want it over with."

She said this as if she had reasons she could not delay. They weren't his business any more than the rest. Hattori nodded and rose, forcing her to look reluctantly up at him. His stomach was tight, but it didn't show.

"I'll take care of it at once," he said.

♦

Yama loved to gamble but not to pay taxes on winnings. Tudou Oryan's favorite off-the-books betting parlor was on the Ring Line, six stops past the exchange point nearest the teahouse. Like most such places, it possessed a number of hidden exits, the better to allow its customers to escape Imperial Collection Department raids. The ICD cracked down harshly on tax evaders, especially those from the lower ranks of aristocrats. One of the secret doors had been left unlocked for Hattori, by someone he'd probably never meet. He used it to access a tobacco scented rear hallway. His soft-soled cloth boots made no noise on the floor at all.

Once inside, the boisterous rattle of porcelain tiles told him Pig-Rooster-Ox was the game in play, bets being placed on how many of each animal would turn up following the toss of a canister. Calculating the complex odds required an aristocrat's intellectual capacity. Though far from stupid, Hattori abstained from games of chance. Getting out of bed in the morning was gamble enough for him.

An unwatched break room supplied him with a stained maroon waiter's tunic. Thus disguised, he slid unnoticed into the crowd. The main betting room was large. Rice wine flowed by the liter while groups of excited men gathered around circular baize tables. No windows lit the space. What light existed was artificial and heavily muffled with red silk shades. Hattori picked up a serving tray and began clearing empty wine cups from here and there. He spotted Tudou in a noisy back corner. The daimyo's face was too indecisive to be handsome, his build just a little soft. The sweaty flush that colored his features suggested he was winning.

Hattori hoped he was enjoying it. He expected Lady Oryan viewed his choice of entertainment as an unnecessary risk to an already insufficient annual income.

To him, the right and wrong of it couldn't matter. The poison he needed was on a metal thimble, which he slipped from his ops kit onto his finger. Once he'd removed its protective cover, he had to be careful not to touch anyone. Tudou let out a shout as he threw the minimum amount of roosters to keep control of the tiles. Other gamblers were pressed around him, drawn close by his winning streak. Hattori reached through the bodies and beneath Tudou's queue, where his skin was bare and vulnerable. He squeezed Tudou's neck as if congratulating him.

If anyone had seen him do it, they'd have thought his behavior inappropriate for a waiter. Fortunately, no one—including his victim—turned. The result of Tudou's next roll was too vital to let anything distract them.

It was done then. Hattori set down his laden tray, dropped the thimble back into its fake sweets wrapper, and tossed both into a wall trash bin. That taken care of, he walked calmly from the room. His borrowed waiter's tunic was returned to its hook, where his outer robe had been hanging. He exited by the same hidden door he'd used to enter. As he shut it behind him, distant cries of alarm rang out: Tudou's "heart attack" commencing. In two minutes, he'd be dead. In four, the poison that caused it would have disappeared into his normal blood chemistry. In all likelihood, the gambling parlor's owners wouldn't call a physician immediately. They'd wait until their other customers vacated the premises. Miry Oryan would suffer a tiny scrap of scandal over her dead husband's hobby, for which she'd be pitied. After a decently brief period of mourning, she'd be free to marry again.

He'd heard Sanjiang Shinobi had a fifteen-year-old daughter. With an heir in place, he might be willing to marry a nonroyal aristocrat, especially if—as rumored—he'd come up empty in his search for a second genetic match. Miry was probably convinced he'd propose, or why resort to murder? With luck, the little princess would enjoy her new mother. Hattori had grown up in a state-controlled rearing center, with apathetic, overworked caretakers. Even Miry Oryan had to be a step up from that.

All's well that ends well, he thought acidly.

He was surprised to find his hands trembling. He'd killed twice before: once in self-defense and a second time on another assassination for Prince Feng, an embezzler his employer had wanted to make an example of. Neither occasion had left him sweating and cold like this.

Discovering Haro thought life was sacred had weakened him.

Hattori ground his molars together and continued walking through the seedy neighborhood he'd escaped into. With every bone and sinew, Hattori cherished his twin brother. Haro's morals, however, were a luxury only one of them could afford.

"And barely that," he murmured to the frost-rimed street. Haro wouldn't be alive if he wasn't so valuable a hostage for Hattori's good behavior.

He is alive, Hattori swore to himself. That he had to believe or go mad.

It probably wasn't necessary, but he took a circuitous route back to the Feng palace. Riding one way and then another, he transferred on and off the various Bullet lines. He also walked a fair distance, maybe as much as five miles, while the pale winter sun set behind the Forbidden City's high dark wall. No one followed him. The night settled cold and quiet, the stars a hazy blur beyond the reach of the Yamish capital's lights. He should have been calming, but his body felt increasingly out of sorts as he inhaled and blew out the icy air. Perhaps too much adrenaline pumped through him. Certainly too much regret.

He reminded himself what daimyo did to each other wasn't his concern. He couldn't have saved Lord Oryan by turning down this job. Another guard would have accepted it before Prince Feng had time to snap his plump fingers. Tudou would still be dead, and Hattori would have lost what little leverage he had to protect his twin.

Life was what it was. It wasn't his responsibility to change the fundamentally unjust nature of the universe.

He let out his sigh before stepping back inside the Feng guard complex. The combined dormitory and training center was two floors high and a whole city block in length. Bird-wing eaves overhung the spiraling green dragons that formed the front pillars. Prince Feng maintained a force of a hundred here in his main palace, and this wasn't overkill. His ruthlessness in business, coupled with the various dynastic squabbles he'd manipulated in his favor, had earned him enemies.

Possibly one of them would kill the prince one day. Hattori doubted even that would improve his fortunes more than marginally. His usefulness as an asset would be the same to any royal who inherited his contract.

Ignoring his weary muscles' protest, he ran lightly up the steps to the dorm room he'd formerly shared with his brother. He lifted his hand in preparation to press the palm lock, only to realize the door was open.

Another guard was emptying a duffle on Haro's bed, sorting out items it contained. He looked up as Hattori stopped dead on the threshold.

Hattori recognized the man. His name was Ciran, and they'd faced off a time or two on the practice mat. He was a good fighter—quiet, controlled, and fast. Though they'd never spoken outside those matches, Hattori knew Ciran specialized in the kind of assignments he'd been getting more of lately. The other guards tended to avoid him, perhaps sensing he was more dangerous than them. His blue-black hair fell straight and loose to his wide shoulders. The length was close to breaking regulations; only daimyo wore their hair long. But maybe Ciran wasn't worried about enemies catching hold of it. Like Hattori, he had a genetic anomaly: one silver-blue iris paired with another in silver-gold. The unruffled manner in which he met his stare said he had no interest in concealing the flaw.

He'd arrived at the palace six months before, from where no one knew. Of the few facts Hattori had dug up about him, that was the most suspicious.

"Sorry," Ciran said, his smooth face expressionless. "Two new recruits were put in my room. The captain ordered me to shift here."

Hattori was surprised he'd bother to apologize, curt though the offering was.

He nodded and turned away, his nape prickling as he removed his ops kit and weapons belt. Stowing their contents in his unadorned black bureau required only a fraction of his mind. With the rest, he wondered if Ciran was there to spy on him. Did Prince Feng fear Hattori would devise a plan to break Haro out of prison? Or perhaps it was Hattori's concealed anomalies his employer wanted information on. With his brother's help, Hattori had done his best to hide them, but maybe he hadn't succeeded. Because Haro hadn't suffered from the same handicap, they'd assumed his sexual complications had arisen by accident, the unplanned side effect of too much tinkering. Then again, maybe Hattori's royal gene load hadn't been inserted just to give him a strength advantage. Maybe Muto Feng wanted his super soldier to have a chink in his armor.

The springs of the second bed creaked as Ciran stretched out on it. Hattori gritted his teeth and stripped off his outer robe. He needed a shower, and he wasn't any more at risk naked than he was clothed. An excess of modesty was likelier to raise eyebrows.

"So," Ciran said as Hattori grimly shucked his boots and trousers. "The Oryan job. I thought for sure they'd give that to me."

Hattori stared at him over his shoulder. He didn't ask how Ciran knew about it, or why he'd volunteered that he did. The guard lay on his back in the light gray trousers most of them slept in. His upper torso was bare, his lean hands folded on his concave stomach. Pale white whip marks, too numerous to count, crisscrossed faintly golden skin. His muscles looked like they'd been layered on with a trowel, not an ounce of fat visible. Ciran's strange eyes glinted as they met his.

"I know," he said, his wide mouth assuming the slightest curve. "Everybody thinks I don't talk, but that's because they won't talk to me. I'm hoping *you* won't be afraid."

"Because I kill people too, you mean."

"Because you can thrash my butt on the practice mat. And because these"—he pointed his index finger to each of his eyes in turn—"don't make you too nervous to look at me."

"I have my own mark," Hattori said gruffly.

"So you do," Ciran agreed, after which he actually grinned at him.

Disconcerted by the display of teeth, Hattori stalked into the bathroom to shower. If Ciran was a spy attempting to gain his trust, he was going about it strangely.

♦

Ciran hadn't been bred to be an assassin; he'd simply developed a knack for it. His genetic blueprint, designed and implemented at Muto Feng's behest, had been meant to enhance his charms for bedplay. He had a look most royals favored, a strength and a stamina. His libido had been ratcheted up beyond the norm, guaranteeing he'd be interested in having quite a lot of sex quite a lot of the time. Thankfully, he had no trouble ejaculating. In that way, his physiology was typically rohn. Despite this mercy, his early twenties had been torture, a blur of desperate couplings that never satisfied his bone-deep desires. At thirty, the itch remained, but he was more in control of it. He could go without, if it suited his purposes.

While he listened to the automated shower go on, he closed the bicolor eyes that had been an inadvertent result of Muto's experiments. Muto professed to like them, but the prince had eccentric tastes. Broad ones too, encompassing men, women, and all the combinations thereof. For close to a decade, Ciran had been his favorite pet, kept in pampered splendor in a secret mansion west of the capital. The upside to the isolation was that Muto hadn't been obliged to share Ciran with his wife. Muto was no prize, but his wife Erymita was repellent—a too inbred royal with limbs like a pink spider. Ciran would not have liked pleasing her, though he had no doubt he'd have tried.

Every Yama's fate was written in his chromosomes: his class, his looks, his deepest desires. If he wanted to escape them, he had to fight very hard.

Ciran had fought, training his body and his mind. Favor by devious favor, he'd established that he had other, more valuable talents than those he used in bed. At first, this had been a hedge against Prince Muto losing interest, but soon enough he'd come to enjoy his sideline. Ciran might have been born a pillow boy, but he'd turned himself into a sharper and much more dangerous blade. He was still a pet, but he was a pet who wielded the power of life and death.

What he hadn't predicted was that, with every job he executed successfully, he became increasingly uncomfortable to keep close. Muto visited less and less and finally not at all. The offer to transfer him to the guards had been an obvious farewell. *The separation will be best for both of us*, Muto said. For once, Ciran had known his employer wasn't lying.

Not only wasn't Muto lying, he'd undersold the truth. The lives of palace guards were regimented, but from the day of Ciran's arrival, joining them had felt remarkably like freedom. Ciran had peers to interact with, not just servants or superiors. He could sleep with whom he wanted, and refuse any he did not. He had days off, and they were not filled with boredom. He could even—if he chose—let himself fall in love.

Muto would have been astonished to know he wished that. Without question, Ciran had read too many Human romances. Nothing struck him as more delicious than giving his heart away. He'd wept buckets while reading *Physician Zhivago*, forced to ice the unexpected damage the tears had wreaked on his eyes. The experience had been so cathartic he'd thought he might enjoy crying for himself, should the occasion arise.

He laughed under his breath at the thought of it, at least until the shower jets shut off. The body dryers whirred. Ciran turned his head on the pillow without thinking. The washroom's door was a replica of an old-fashioned rice paper screen. This heavy modern version was milky glass and metal, but it did slide aside on tracks. Hattori pushed it open and strode out naked.

Long years of concealing every scrap of emotion were all that kept Ciran's jaw from unhinging. He'd known Hattori's body had to be good, but not that he'd look like this. The guard was huge. All over huge. And perfectly proportioned, his limbs and muscles as graceful as they were powerful. His packed shoulders were massive, his hips appealingly narrow. He didn't remove his hair like most royals did. A thin black haze shadowed him here and there. His legs were long enough to dry Ciran's mouth.

They, however, weren't what had his pulse ticking so rapidly in his throat.

Hattori's balls were the size of peaches, and his prick hung as thick and lengthy as the famous Plaza of Justice statue of a long dead emperor's horse. Rohn liked to rub the horse for good luck, the practice so common the statue's bronze genitalia had to be repaired periodically.

Ciran felt a bit like *his* genitalia were being rubbed. Hoping he hadn't been staring too obviously, he forced his eyes to Hattori's face.

"I cleared Haro's things from the supply cabinet," his new roommate said. "There's space for yours now."

Ciran's brain was still emblazoned with the sight of Hattori's swinging cock. His shaft had been thicker in the middle, as if it would swell larger there. "You didn't have to do that."

Hattori jabbed his legs into sleeping trousers. "These quarters are yours now as well."

He lay down on his back, and Ciran turned to him on his side. The dormitory floor was clad in imitation wood, done up to look like mahogany. Two meters of the planks stretched between their bunks. Ciran tried to ignore the fact that his own cock wasn't completely soft.

"I liked your twin," he said, "though he never did fight dirty enough."

Hattori didn't react except to press his lips together. "Lights off," he said, and the room plunged into darkness.

Resigned to making no further progress, Ciran closed his eyes. The other bed creaked as if Hattori were restless. To Ciran's surprise, he spoke. "My brother didn't like fighting dirty. He said it felt too much like cheating."

Ciran absorbed the information, unable to agree but savvy enough not to say so. "Do you know where he was taken?"

Hattori twisted around on his mattress. "Do you?"

"Ah," Ciran said, suddenly understanding. "You think I was sent to spy on you."

"No one knows where you come from. Or who you worked for."

Ciran wanted to laugh but didn't. "My answer wouldn't reassure you."

Hattori said nothing, just breathed into the silence. The sound suggested he was irate.

"Very well," Ciran said. "I was Muto Feng's secret pillow boy."

"What? You can't have been. The way you fight . . ."

Ciran found himself grinning. "I learned from a retired Dragon Way master. Prince Feng didn't want his pet to get bored or fat."

"What retired master?"

"Thelonio Ping."

Hattori whistled, low and admiring. "Thelonio Ping trained the previous emperor's guard." He fell silent, but this time it didn't seem angry. "Was it bad? Being Feng's pillow boy?"

"Not always," Ciran admitted. "I minded being loaned out sometimes. I couldn't say no to anyone."

The sheets on Hattori's bed rustled, evidence of his weight shifting. "The last time we went to the pillow house, you took three girls."

Though closely regulated, guards weren't expected to be celibate. If they had no personal arrangements, the palace sponsored weekly trips to the pillow house. Ciran hadn't failed to notice Hattori always went through more partners than anyone, and always left them looking pleased with themselves. It was one more reason the guard had caught Ciran's eye.

"I like choosing for myself," he said. "It gets my juices up."

"I didn't mean that. I meant you like women."

"I *also* like women," Ciran clarified.

Hattori didn't respond to that. His reaction could have been anything from repelled but polite to secretly interested. Ciran would have settled for on the fence, but Hattori turned to face the wall with his back to him. "I need to sleep," he announced.

He didn't sleep, though, to judge by his breathing. He lay awake like Ciran, whose nerves were too wound up to relax. He'd maneuvered himself into this situation, though the clerk who changed the room assignment likely didn't realize he'd been nudged. Almost since Ciran had first seen him, he'd been attracted to Hattori. The infatuation had seemed too silly to pursue, but gradually he'd come to believe the guard was not only an attractive cut of meat but a kindred spirit as well. Like his missing brother, Hattori had a heart. Unlike Haro, his conscience didn't cripple him. He was fair to his fellow guards without ignoring the precepts of survival. His sexual appetite was another plus, Ciran having a substantial one of his own to see to.

Butterflies danced inside his stomach at the idea of them seeing to each other. Ciran wasn't used to being nervous, and wasn't sure what to make of it. Could this fluttering be the start of the kind of love Humans wrote about, and—if it were—was he prepared for it?

You have the freedom to do this now, he reminded himself. *If you want to risk falling on your face, it's entirely up to you.*

With that thought running through his mind, Ciran fell asleep smiling.

♦

Hattori's sexual cycle wasn't consistent like a royal's, though there were signs to warn him his heat approached. It began as a general restlessness in his body, followed by sore and full testicles. He'd have aching, full blown erections—often dozens of them a day. Sometimes they'd throb for hours without going down. He'd have difficulty spilling when he grabbed a bit of privacy to rub one off, and even more difficulty curtailing masturbation once he'd begun. The need for release overtook every thought. Worst was when his anal passage started itching. The implements he'd found to ease himself had been creative, but ultimately none satisfied.

The best he could hope for when rut was on him was that it wouldn't last the full five days.

When his brother had been around, he'd covered for Hattori if his concentration wasn't up to carrying out his duties. That safety net was gone, though Hattori had been lucky the last three months. He'd had one short heat, which hadn't been extreme enough to preclude him working it out in the pillow house. If his rut wasn't too severe, the girls simply thought he had stamina. As long as he was careful to not to hurt them, they enjoyed the strenuous bed sessions.

This morning, he'd known his good fortune had run out. His waking erection had been immense, his balls heavy and hurting with the extra load they'd stored up. He'd given himself six quick orgasms in the shower, but nothing had come out. Finally, he'd resorted to binding his engorged prick against his belly, to prevent the others from noticing. He'd been trounced in every practice bout he'd fought, though it was hard to care.

To add insult to arousal, tonight was his section's scheduled trip to the pillow house. He knew he didn't dare join them. The way he felt, the things he needed, he'd pound half the girls to mincemeat.

He tried to exhaust himself with a long session of private training. He ran the obstacle course, climbed the rock wall, and punched his hands into sacks of beans until his body should have dissolved in sweat. Nothing helped. He was barely even tired. His body wanted what it wanted, and this sort of exercise wasn't it.

Finally, when he was certain the rest of his group had left for their night of debauchery, he returned to his room. Unexpectedly, Ciran was inside reading on his bunk.

"Why are you still here?" Hattori was startled into asking.

Ciran lifted the Human book to show him, an odd artifact printed on real paper and bound between cardboard squares. Members of the lower classes weren't supposed to read novels. Human stories were judged too liable to stir emotions, which rohn weren't believed able to handle. Apparently, Prince Muto had bought his former pet a dispensation. Ciran kept at least ten novels locked in their room's wall safe.

"*Pride and Perspicacity*," Ciran said. "No matter how many times I read it, I'm still confused. I don't understand why that girl Lizzie doesn't jump Mister Darcy the day they meet. I think I need more lessons in Ohramese."

Ohramese was the language most Humans spoke. Hattori barely knew a dozen words, and was impressed with Ciran for reading these books in their native tongue. He fought the temptation to express respect. He had urges sometimes to let down his guard with Ciran but didn't feel he ought to trust the impulses. Instead, he shrugged off his outer robe and mopped his face with it. Ciran watched him in that way he had, calm but focused, as if he were the first person who'd ever truly looked at him. It unnerved Hattori, but part of him liked it. His own brother hadn't made him feel this *seen*.

"Why keep reading it if it confuses you?" he asked.

"Because Human culture fascinates me. Doesn't it fascinate you?" Ciran sat up, swinging his long legs around the side of his bunk. His chest was bare, every line and shape of it elegant. The bandages that bound Hattori's long-erect cock tightened and grew hotter. For a moment, he couldn't remember what Ciran asked.

"I don't know," he said when his brain recovered. "I suppose they do. Humans stumbled onto Narikerr right around the time I was born."

"You're twenty-five?" Ciran asked.

Hattori nodded, inexplicably embarrassed to have told him.

"I'm thirty." Ciran touched his thumb to his bare breastbone. He had no hair there, possibly because his royal partners had preferred him smooth. Against his will, Hattori swallowed convulsively. "All this time, I thought you were older than me."

"Sometimes I feel like I'm a hundred," he blurted. A flush started in his chest at the indiscretion. Despite the warning, he couldn't stop the blood from rising to his cheeks.

Ciran's expression changed when he saw it. He was smiling, but his beautiful eyes were sad. "I'm sorry. You and your brother cared for each other more than most Yama get a chance to."

"Haro was stupid. Defiant. He got himself into that trouble."

Ciran didn't argue, just looked at him with melancholy-amused eyes. An anger Hattori couldn't control swelled in him. Why did Ciran have to be the one person who understood what he'd lost?

"Why aren't you at the pillow house with the others?" he demanded.

Ciran's faint smile faded. "I thought I'd keep you company."

"Me."

"Yes."

Ciran rose, and Hattori had the abrupt impression that his roommate was stalking him. His every movement was as sinuous as a cat. He stopped a hand's breadth away, causing hot chills to crawl up Hattori's spine.

When Ciran spoke, his voice was husky. "I saw how you woke this morning, how hard you were and how huge. I know you tried to find release in the shower and that you didn't succeed. I've spent time with royals. I've witnessed them in heat. I'm pretty sure I know what you're dealing with."

"I'm not royal."

Ciran laid his palm on the heaving center of his still sweating chest. Hattori gasped at how exciting the light touch felt. His cock was pounding like a gun volley.

"Muto played with your genes," Ciran said, "just like he played with mine."

"He changed yours?" Hattori was so aroused he could barely breathe. He could barely think, if it came to that. The idea that Ciran was aware of his problem delighted his gonads to an extent that he had trouble remembering the knowledge was dangerous. He knew his pupils had swollen. The room's low light was suddenly too bright. "What did his scientists do to you?"

"Someday," Ciran said, "when I'm not so desperate to fuck you, remind me to tell you what I found in my secret file."

"You're . . . desperate?"

Ciran's eyes were dark, the difference in their colors emphasized by the change. "They increased my sex drive. I can control it mostly, and I have no trouble ejaculating, but when I promise you couldn't wear me out, I'm not bragging."

Somehow Hattori's hands had found their way to Ciran's waist, where trim hard muscles dove into his sleep trousers. His skin was hot, but Hattori wasn't ready to stroke it. He'd never been with a man, never thought about it except in passing. If he were honest, Ciran made the thought go slower before it disappeared. He'd been making it do that ever since he'd moved in. Until now, he'd thought Ciran couldn't tell.

"Do you want me?" Ciran asked. He wasn't as tall as Hattori and gazed up at him a few inches. "If you don't, I'll leave you alone. I should tell you, though, I know a lot about pleasing men."

Hattori shuddered, his fingers tightening in an involuntary spasm. Ciran seemed calm, but a tiny muscle twitched in his lower lip. Hattori wanted to lick it, and maybe bite it too. A stab of pain shunted up his cock as it tried to swell even more. The faintest ripping sensation told him his bindings were giving out.

"I want you," he admitted, the words a growl, "but I haven't had sex with a man before."

Ciran's lamril came out to wet his lip. "Could I kiss you?"

Hattori groaned and kissed him instead.

It was the kiss of a lifetime: wet and strong and so deep Ciran might have been trying to crawl down his throat, tongue first. For a second, Hattori tried to fight how much he loved it, but that really wasn't fair. He'd jumped into this of his own free will. His body wasn't letting him back out anyway. Every inch of his skin was humming as he moaned and writhed and attempted to shove off his genital wrappings.

Ciran needed all his strength to pull his mouth free. "Let me help you with that."

His hands were much cleverer than Hattori's. Air hit blazing skin as Ciran dragged away the bindings. He cupped his balls, hot fingers rippling over their tenderness. His second hand gripped Hattori's cock, testing its hardness. Though he wasn't rubbing the shaft, the pressure was so well placed Hattori had a quick and very hard dry climax. His pained pleasure moan sounded like it came from a great distance.

"Shower," Ciran said. "I have a feeling this is going to get noisy."

Ciran pushed him there and ordered the spray full force, providing a masking sound. Too impatient to undress the other Yama, Hattori pulled him under the jets with his pants still on. He adored the way the cotton went transparent, the way Ciran's penis stood straight and long. He squeezed the length of him through the cloth, then fell to his knees to mouth him. Ciran let out a throttled sound.

"Too hard?" Hattori asked breathlessly.

The jets had plastered Ciran's blue-black hair to his face. He shook it back and forth in negation. "That felt good. I've just been wanting this too long."

With a care he wouldn't have believed himself capable of, Hattori eased the wet trousers over Ciran's hardness and down his legs. Ciran's cock vibrated with the blood in it, flushing darker as water rolled in streams down the swollen crest. Beneath that vision, his balls were red, like plums in their drawn up sack. Hattori had a second's hesitation, and then he sucked in the head and shaft.

Ciran groaned his name, so he must have done something right.

"Yes," he moaned, shoving deeper, to the very verge of his throat. Hattori forced himself to relax and let him do it again. The skin of Ciran's cock was as smooth as butter, swollen veins pulsing hard in it. "Yes, yes. Oh shit, don't do that just yet. Don't make me come. I don't"—he twisted, Hattori's curious tongue doing something he liked a lot—"I don't want to get too far ahead of you."

Hattori pulled back and sat on his heels shaking. Looking up at Ciran, watching him pant and shift with frustration was a pleasure he hadn't expected.

"There are cock sheaths in the cabinet," Ciran said roughly. "Lubricated. You can fuck me, or I can fuck you, whichever you think you'd like better."

To his surprise, both sounded good to him.

"You," he decided. "I want to fuck you."

Hattori found the sheaths and covered himself with one. He gave his balls a deep, thorough squeeze, knowing that helped him come. Ciran watched, his breath coming hard enough to cut through the roar of the spray. When Hattori completed his massage, at least for the time being, Ciran turned and laid his palms high and flat on the wet gray tile. The muscles of his back were stretched, his butt tense but inviting.

"Don't go easy," he said. "I'm a man, and you can be rough."

"I'm strong," Hattori warned.

"So are all the royals."

It there'd been a bowstring inside his penis, Ciran had just plucked it. Hattori moved closer and spread his cheeks, taking a second to admire his taut hindquarters. Ciran shivered as his tip touched the hole. Hattori brought his lips next to Ciran's ear.

"I liked kissing you," he whispered.

Maybe it was this that stirred Ciran's next shiver, or maybe it was that Hattori was entering him. Either way, all the tension ran out of Ciran's body at the same time. Ciran sighed a surrender as the resistance within him gave. Hattori was in him faster than he'd ever been inside a female.

Ciran's lean body writhed between him and the wall. "Fuck me," he moaned. "Do it now, Hattori."

Hattori pulled slowly back through the smooth, unfamiliar clasp—a pleasurable process for both of them. Ciran made strangled noises, his hips arching urgently back to him. "Do it," he repeated. "I want you to fuck me hard."

Hattori lost control so quickly it frightened him. He went at Ciran, and Ciran's moans changed from frustration to helpless enjoyment. His cries were hoarse, and he was difficult to hold still, but with the ecstasy searing through him, Hattori could hardly care. He came once, twice, his balls clenching tight without quite expelling their hot contents.

They dropped by mutual agreement down to their knees. Ciran leaned forward from the waist so his plunges could go deeper. Both Ciran's arms were braced on the shower wall. Hattori was pounding into him so hard he would have crashed into it otherwise.

"Keep going," Ciran panted. "I think you're getting there."

Hattori couldn't tell. All he knew was that this was both torment and paradise. He unclamped one hand from Ciran's hip to reach around for his cock. In a single heartbeat, his palm fell in love with how full and rigid he was, with how he pulsed and jerked as Hattori pumped his fist roughly along him.

"Don't," Ciran moaned, though the motions of his hips were definitely saying *do*. "Don't make me come."

"I want to," Hattori said stubbornly.

"Don't."

"You said I couldn't wear you out. One ejaculation won't finish you."

Ciran stretched his left arm back to rub his hip. "If I come, I won't be as hard as this. You'll want me hard when I'm pounding over your kingmaster."

The buried gland woke up at his words, like a match had been set to it. Hattori's need increased insanely.

"Fuck," he said, his hips speeding up.

Ciran's head flung back in approval. "That's it," he praised, voice shaken by Hattori's incredibly forceful thrusts. "That's it. Take one more dry climax, and then I'll fuck you. I can reach right where you want me. My dick is going to pound you like a damn piston."

Groaning, Hattori released Ciran's cock so he could grip both his hips again. He went full out and shouted as his next peak broke, the climax so hard it actually satisfied him for a few seconds.

Ciran pulled free of him, trembling. With limbs that weren't as coordinated as before, he scooted around to face Hattori. He needed the wall to support his back, but the pole that throbbed from his lap thrust admirably vertical. Despite this promising sight, Hattori saw they should have remained standing.

"I bruised your knees," he pointed out in dismay.

"Worth it," Ciran said, smiling. "Now." With an air of anticipation, he rubbed both hands down his muscled thighs. "If we move to your bed and the other guards come back, can you hold in your screams?"

Hattori's mouth stretched in its own tease. "I don't know, Ciran. Why don't we try it and see?"

♦

The bed was a stroke of genius, or so it struck Hattori. Plassteel rails lined its head and foot, allowing him to anchor himself. He needed that, as it happened. He'd been on his front to start with, but now he lay on his back. Ciran seemed determined to kiss and lick every part of him. It felt amazing, but it made him violently impatient.

"Are you sure . . . we have to do all this?" Hattori whispered, thrashing under him uncontrollably.

Ciran let the testicle he'd been suckling pop from his mouth. "If you want to spill, you need to be thoroughly stimulated, and your balls have to be warmed up."

"They're warm," Hattori moaned as quietly as he could. They hadn't heard any guards return, but they hadn't exactly been focusing on that. "You've got me so fucking hard. And my gland is itching like crazy." Unable to help himself, he ground his ass cheeks together and thrust upward.

Ciran smiled, licked two fingers, and shoved them under him. Long past embarrassment, Hattori immediately sprawled his knees wide and squirmed. Ciran's fingers didn't go as deep as he wanted, but every place they rubbed tingled with relief.

"Five more minutes," Ciran promised. "You haven't sampled my best skill yet."

The instant Ciran's mouth swallowed his erection he could have no doubt what his best skill was. Bliss rolled through Hattori in liquid waves. Down his cock they went, up his vertebrae. The palms that took a death grip on the headrail tingled—as did every one of his curling toes. Ciran's fingers still worked his anus, multiplying the pleasure of everything. Hattori could only gasp at the sensations he was experiencing. Ciran's mouth was strong, his tongue a cross between a muscled snake and a small hammer. When he wasn't tapping Hattori's cock, he was rubbing it, and he never stopped sucking. He found Hattori's sensitive spots and made each of them weep in turn. He drew patterns on his penis's head and just underneath the flare. Overwhelmed, Hattori was soon whimpering with enjoyment, the abandoned sounds impossible to restrain. His skin began to buzz from how wet Ciran was getting him.

"Good," Ciran panted, releasing his shuddering cock. "I think you're reacting to the hormones in my saliva. I think you'll be coming for real this time."

Hattori was shaking so badly he needed help rolling onto his front.

The feel of Ciran moving behind him and between his legs was more welcome than he'd known such an act could be. His body was very ready, easily giving way. Hattori's spine rolled as the other man entered, his breath sighing out of him. Ciran was hard but smooth as satin—and just thick enough to stretch hm. As promised, he reached the itchy pulsing spot Hattori most wanted.

"Slow," Ciran murmured against his neck. "Give yourself a chance to enjoy the ride."

That was a challenge, because his instincts urged him to twist and buck.

"I'll take care of you," Ciran soothed, running his prick directly over the center of the ache in him. "You don't have to be desperate now."

Hattori panted and arched, but he let Ciran have control. Ciran wasn't playing around now, wasn't teasing or trying to warm him up. His angle was perfect. He drove the bluntness of his cock into and over the crucial spot, his surging motions as steady as a machine. Hattori's excitement swelled along with his hope. His muscles began to tremble in a new way.

"Faster?" Ciran offered raggedly.

"Yes," he groaned. "*Yes.*"

Ciran dug his hand underneath him and curled it around his balls. He sped up as he squeezed Hattori, his thrusts suddenly intensely purposeful. Hattori knew he'd ejaculate then. His scrotum coiled under the pressure, and his scalp was tingling like it would lift off his skull. Ciran accelerated even more, his thrusts fantastically hard and just the tiniest bit uneven.

"Okay," Ciran gasped. "I'm going to come with you this time."

It was as if he could see inside Hattori, as if he knew exactly what was happening in his body. The thought was crazily arousing. Hattori humped the blanket like it was a woman, loving how the backward jerk of the motion drove Ciran deeper into him. Images of pillow girls flipped wildly through his mind.

"Fuck," Ciran groaned, and all the girls disappeared.

Ciran was spilling, and that at last triggered Hattori. His balls contracted, seed shooting up his cock like a plasma gun. It was a better ejaculation than he'd ever experienced: deep and strong and almost completely emptying him. He didn't scream, but his mouth opened like would.

One blissful minute turned the bed under him sodden.

"Ah," Ciran sighed, sagging down on him. He was breathing hard, his heart pounding like a drum. "You are some ride, Hattori. I thought you'd buck me right off you at the end."

"Sorry," Hattori said sheepishly.

Ciran hadn't been complaining, because he laughed. He pulled out with a muffled groan of regret. The bunk was narrow, so he still lay half atop him. His cheek came to rest on Hattori's shoulder, its sweaty warmth oddly comforting. His breathing began to slow.

Was he falling asleep back there? And did Hattori want him to? Sleeping together was an intimate activity, as intimate in a way as sex.

Ciran must have registered his tension. "Should I leave?"

Hattori thought for a few seconds. "No. You aren't bothering me where you are."

Ciran's expressive mouth curved against his skin. "Give me an hour," he said, "and we'll see if you can do that again."

3: THE PRESENT DAY

Muto Feng was missing for a year before Emperor Songyam declared him dead. The interval was neither typical nor unprecedented. Yamish law functioned according to force of influence as much as custom. Feng's body hadn't been recovered, and it wasn't possible to say if foul play accounted for his disappearance, but a prince that powerful wasn't likely to have run off to an island. Like most Yama, Ciran believed his former keeper breathed no more.

What was typical was that the moment his death became official, armies of lawyers sprang into action. Not only did various branches of the House of Feng submit competing claims to his estate, but so did many of the individuals he'd wronged. No longer inhibited by fear of the living man, they demanded reparations before the warring heirs received one credit.

Justice being what it was in the Forbidden City, Ciran wished them luck with that.

Two years later, the courts were still sorting out the tangle. In the meantime, Ciran and Hattori's life became very quiet. Erymita Feng, Muto's childless widow, had retreated to her family seat with a quarter of the palace guards—those who weren't considered too valuable to take. Another quarter of Muto's troops were detailed to protect the Feng lawyers, some of whom were receiving threats. Salaried employees—which didn't include the guards—scattered to other Houses as best they could.

All this left the once vital Feng palace a ghost town.

Some of the remaining fifty guards complained of boredom, but Ciran and Hattori knew enough to appreciate their leisure. They couldn't choose their next position like the paid employees. They were part of the estate. Had they tried to leave, imperial troops would have hunted them down. So they took their shifts patrolling the palace's empty corridors and filled the rest of their hours as pleasantly as they could.

Ciran fought a smile at how pleasant some of those hours had been. No previous period of his life had been this relaxed. Even during what he thought of as their summer of bliss with Kat, he hadn't felt this level of contentment. In those three halcyon months, Hattori and Kat had gotten too close for Ciran's comfort. They'd shared women before and found it exciting, but those females had been, at least for Ciran, interchangeable. Kat had seemed an individual from the start, a person with thoughts and wishes outside the ordinary run. Ciran had liked her—maybe even loved her, depending on how one defined that emotion. To see her and Hattori together, however, to witness them locking gazes and know that in that moment neither remembered him, had inspired a pang he hadn't minded leaving behind.

By the end of the summer, when Kat returned to her father's home, Ciran had feared the pair would try something reckless to stay together. Thankfully, they'd been realists. Princesses didn't elope with guards, and guards didn't risk their lives to keep bed partners. Katsu had shed a few tears on parting, perhaps even a few for him. What she hadn't done was try to convince either of them to fight for her.

Ciran had expected her to find some secret method to communicate with Hattori, but—truthfully—her silence was only evidence of good sense. She cared enough for Hattori to release her hold on him.

Whether Hattori released himself was another matter. Four years had passed since that summer, and Hattori still had the small lock of hair he'd stolen from her one night while she was sleeping. He kept it hidden in his ops kit—including from Ciran, or so he thought.

That amused even as it hurt. Who'd have thought Hattori would give his heart away? Ciran had believed himself the romantic half of their duo, but he'd been wrong. When Kat had gotten into trouble with her family, nearly a year after their goodbyes, he'd feared Hattori would lose his mind. For an entire week, his friend hadn't been able to tear himself from the evening vids, glued to the image of his lost beloved being arrested for a poisoning attempt on her stepsister.

She's being framed, he'd cried to the holo. *Someone has to speak up for her!* As if the testimony of a rohn could swing the court in her favor. Fortunately, Kat had been cleared almost as soon as she'd been accused, all charges dropped and the trial cancelled. She'd slipped from the public eye afterwards, for which Ciran had been guiltily grateful.

"That pawn isn't going to move itself," Hattori observed dryly.

His words returned Ciran to the present. They sat in one of the palace courtyards, surrounded by crimson maples and the bright wet song of a small fountain. Koi swam in its pewter basin, as tame as cats to the remaining staff. The season was late autumn with a snap in the air, though the sun still warmed their faces. Ciran and Hattori were playing chess, a Human game they'd come to enjoy.

"I'm thinking," Ciran said, looking up to smile—just a little— into his old friend's eyes. "I have a feeling I might beat you this time."

"If you think hard enough," Hattori said, a teasing note entering his voice, "you could mate me in four moves."

"No." Ciran studied the board to see what he'd missed. Four moves? He'd been thinking six. And leave it to Hattori to be so slyly pleased at the prospect of losing.

Both their heads snapped up at the sound of booted feet approaching. Ciran set his black onyx pawn back onto the board.

The four guards who'd filled the courtyard's points of entry were uniformed. Their livery was sage and silver, with oak leaves and acorns worked into loops of braid. Some dusty corner of Ciran's mind thought he ought to recognize the colors. Despite the guards' professional appearance, and regardless of what House they were from, Ciran was sure he and Hattori could take them. Fighting was one of the things they did extremely well together.

They'd risen to their feet as the guards arrived, instinct positioning them back to back on either side of the game table.

The leader of the intruders thrust out a beribboned scroll. "By order of Emperor Songyam, I instruct you to pack your belongings and come with us."

Pack their belongings? That sounded more serious than a mere summons.

"You aren't the emperor's guard," Hattori objected. "You're from the House of Shinobi."

His voice was dark, but underneath his suspicion was hope buried like a mine. Ciran suspected no ears but his heard its low ringing.

He should have known Hattori would recognize Kat's family livery.

"Your disposition has been decided," the lead guard said. "You're to report to your new owner."

The muscles around Ciran's spine tensed more than they had when the guards showed up. "We're both reporting to one owner," he clarified, wanting to know then and there if it wasn't true.

The head guard pulled himself ramrod straight. "Yes," he said grudgingly. "They're keeping you together."

♦

Together was better than apart—or Ciran thought it was.

"If it's her . . ." Hattori stuffed barely folded clothes into a duffle. His voice was low, repressed emotion causing it to vibrate.

"You know what people say," Ciran cautioned. "Kat went into exile after they called off the trial."

"Maybe she came out of it. Maybe she found a way to buy our contracts."

"I don't see how she could have. She's not the head of her family. Buying us from an estate that's still being settled would take a lot of pull."

Hattori zipped his bag and turned to Ciran. His expression was so troubled he could have been Human. "I know I'm letting my hopes run away with me."

"It's not wrong to hope."

His long-time lover let out a bitter breath. "Sometimes I think hope is all I have."

Ciran couldn't control his flinch.

"No," Hattori said, his hand immediately on Ciran's sleeve. "Whatever just crossed your mind, don't you believe it."

"Nothing crossed my mind."

"Ciran, no one will ever be the friend to me that you are."

The Shinobi guard appeared at the door. "Ready?"

Ciran slung his duffle's strap over his shoulder, very carefully not thinking that he was so much more than Hattori's friend. His movement had shaken off his partner's hand. Hattori gripped his bag by its handle, their every possession now packed away. As easily as that, their presence was erased from the room they'd shared for nearly two decades.

"Ready," Hattori said, nodding for their escort to precede them.

Ciran had found his first real happiness here, between these four bare walls. He forced himself not to take one last glance around as he exited.

◆

Hattori and Ciran were flown by aircar to a considerably different garden from the one they'd left. Still in the Forbidden City, this one took up most of the Shinobi palace roof. Glass that was likely weapons-resistant enclosed the plants, though the greenhouse panes looked delicate enough. Following instructions, they walked from the landing pad and entered the nearest door. Inside, the beds brimmed with dwarf versions of flowering trees, the crushed shell paths that curved around them forming patterns that reminded Hattori of math puzzles.

The soft, slightly moist air smelled of moss and earth.

Hattori curled his fingers into his palms, ordering his pulse to calm. Ciran was probably right. They weren't about to see Kat again. Kat had forgotten them—or would pretend to. She was royal, and they were not. Though he believed her feelings for him had been deep and genuine, the kindness of her nature had never trumped her intelligence. He didn't fault her for it; it was just how the world spun around.

His chest tightened when he spotted a white-gowned woman farther along the path. It wasn't Kat. Her hair was the wrong color, with undertones of midnight instead of antique brass. She was clipping pale yellow blossoms from one of the small trees, training it into a more controlled shape. Despite knowing the female couldn't be who he hoped, his heart didn't truly sink until she looked up.

Miry Oryan—make that Shinobi—was as beautiful as the first time he'd laid eyes on her. She didn't look older, simply no longer innocent. One glance told him the ice that smoothed her perfect features now went down to the bone. Her skillful makeup could not obscure the effect, no more than the diamonds glittering like dew in her intricately puffed-up and arranged hair. Twenty years later, the aspiring dragon lady had grown into her role.

"Good," she said, laying her shears on the rolling cart that sat beside where she was working. "I hoped you'd come without trouble."

"Princess Shinobi," Hattori said, bowing. Ciran joined him in the obeisance. They straightened in unison, shoulders back, hands clasped behind them as they waited to hear what was coming.

The princess linked her slim white fingers inside her trailing sleeves. Silver cranes glided across the silk with their wings outstretched, the embroidery as fine as an empress might wear. Both she and Ciran had slept with Muto Feng, but apparently without crossing paths. Her attention drifted over him to settle on Hattori. Him she remembered. The man who'd assassinated her first husband wouldn't have slipped from her memory banks.

"As you must have realized," she said, "Prince Muto was kind enough to leave me a small bequest, which the Courts of Estate have released to me."

There was nothing to say to this, not even that they were honored, because the princess wouldn't care if they were.

"You'll find me a fair employer," she continued, "as long as you fulfill your duties."

None of this explained why she'd called them here to speak personally. Hattori knew that was coming when her expression grew blander still.

"I trust you've received your brother's letters over the years."

He had: four brief notes, written in a crabbed but recognizable hand. Haro had thanked him for arranging for extra blankets and food, stated that he was well, and wished his brother the same. Uninformative though they were, the letters were—along with Kat's lock of hair—his most treasured possessions.

"I did receive them," was all he dared to say.

His voice was hoarse but even. He schooled his face to blankness as Miry Shinobi studied him. Ciran stood calm beside him, his steadiness steadying him. Hattori had shown his friend the letters, and Ciran knew what he'd done in exchange for receiving them. Their conversations concerning the devil's bargain had been as short as the notes themselves. Knowing his friend was aware that he still worried for his brother's safety was all he needed not to feel alone.

"Haro's twenty-year reassessment is coming up," Miry observed.

Heat like summer in the tropics flashed across Hattori's chest. He'd thought Haro was ineligible for parole. By defying Prince Muto's orders, he'd broken the guards' most important tenet. As a result, for nineteen years, Hattori had been missing the other half of himself, never feeling whole even when he'd been with Kat. The tension that gripped his body was unbearable, though he did his best to conceal it.

If Miry Shinobi was dangling this carrot, she wanted him and Ciran to do something terrible.

"Yes?" Hattori's question issued as a croak—no doubt to the princess's delight.

"You proved valuable to me once," she said. "For your brother's sake, I hope you can earn my gratitude again."

Hattori couldn't speak. His breath was coming too choppily.

"We'd be pleased to hear what you want," Ciran said serenely.

Princess Shinobi turned her painted smile to him. "I want someone dead, and I need it to look like an accident. Obviously, this accident mustn't be traced back to my new employees. You'll need assumed identities and discretion. This person isn't just daimyo, she's royal."

Ciran blinked rapidly for a few seconds, though he didn't react otherwise. Hattori was fortunate he was already breathing hard. If he hadn't been, he'd have gasped. He knew he and Ciran had just leaped to the same conclusion.

Kat must have been removed from her father's will. Her trial hadn't been canceled because her sire had defended her innocence. It had been canceled because she'd cut a deal, agreeing to exile instead of imprisonment. Such an arrangement would spare the

Shinobis a public scandal, and Kat would keep her freedom. As often as he'd obsessed about those events, Hattori should have guessed this was what happened.

Ciran's next words confirmed his thoughts were following the same track. "I hear your husband has been unwell," he said politely. "Thyrr's syndrome, isn't it?"

Miry showed them her gravest face. "One of the few diseases our scientists haven't been able to defeat."

"Sometimes the dying reconsider old decisions. They want to make amends with people they're estranged from."

"They do," Miry agreed, smoothing her beautiful white and silver gown down her slender thighs. "Thankfully, Prince Shinobi suffers no such indecisiveness."

Thankfully, my ass, Hattori thought. Miry wanted her daughter to inherit Kat's portion. Any threat to that, however small, had to be squashed.

"You'll need to name the target." Ciran lifted his fighter's palms to forestall protest. "You can leave the details to us, but we won't risk misinterpreting your wishes."

Miry narrowed her eyes. Hattori was certain her diamond-embellished sash was equipped with surveillance jammers. Nonetheless, she wouldn't relish spelling this out.

"Katsu Shinobi," she said at last, spitting it. "I don't want that creature setting foot in this house again. And don't use poison. That method wouldn't be suitable."

It wouldn't be suitable because she'd employed it once already.

"Done," Ciran agreed smoothly.

Princess Shinobi seemed taken aback by his readiness, despite having made the lethal request herself. Hattori watched her wonder just how dangerous her inheritance from Prince Feng was.

"We'll need operating funds," Ciran added. "And a general location."

"I'll see that you get both," Miry said faintly.

◆

Unsurprisingly, the princess wasn't housing her new possessions at her palace. Funded now, and soon to be supplied, Ciran and Hattori found a room at a boarding house. The shock of the day hit Hattori all at once. He sat on the side of one of the beds, watching

Ciran unpack his bag. Slumped over his knees, he rubbed the cup of one hand with the thumb of the other. Though he shouldn't have indulged the nervous gesture, he couldn't stop himself.

"You signed our death warrant," he observed, his voice coming from a cool distance. "If we're so ready to kill a royal, she's wondering what we'd do to her."

"She'd have killed us once the job was done anyway," Ciran said reasonably. "Reminding herself that she can—and probably should—will make her feel safer."

"Do you think she knows we've met Kat?"

"I'd say the chance of that is zero to none. She wouldn't want us anywhere near the assignment if she suspected."

Hattori pulled his thumbnail out of his mouth before he could bite it. "Fuck."

"Don't." Ciran abandoned his unpacking to come touch the side of his face. His eyes were the most compassionate Hattori had ever seen.

"How are we going to get out of this?"

Ciran shrugged. "Pretend to kill Kat, of course. And maybe stage our deaths as well."

"And Haro? Who'll protect my brother once I'm supposed to be dead?"

Ciran's mouth twisted. "I haven't figured out that part yet."

"Fuck."

Ciran made a clucking noise, his hands attempting to stroke comfort into Hattori's hair. "We have time to work through this. Have faith in that half royal brain of yours. And look on the bright side. At least we'll see Kat again."

"If she remembers us," Hattori said glumly.

Ciran laughed, the sound as dark as Hattori felt. "She remembers, my friend. Between the pair of us, we're unforgettable."

4: REUNION

The Yamish people were a northern race. Few corners of their lands were strangers to cold weather. The sub-arctic region known as the bleak northwest set standards that stirred shivers in all the rest. Surrounded by mountains and extending across a high plateau, this territory redefined frigid. In winter, temperatures of minus forty degrees were common, and minus eighty weren't unheard of. The elk and wolves could bear it, but only just. Yamish squirrels survived, as they did everywhere. Pine forests covered some of the highland, but gave up at the tree line.

Diamond miners liked the bleak northwest fine.

Once upon a time, before Yama or Humans crawled out of the primordial ooze, this area had been volcanic. The long-ago eruptions drove diamonds upward from the high pressure caches where they had formed. Now they nestled in carrot-shaped deposits known as kimberlite pipes. Up here, the pipes were rich enough to yield an eight-million carat harvest of high quality stones per year, more than worth the trouble of extracting them in this remote place.

Remoteness wasn't the only challenge miners faced. When the northwest thawed, as it did every spring, the plateau's marshland was too spongy to support roads. Mining on a profitable scale required huge machines, heavier than could be flown in by aircar. Companies were forced to rely on an ice road for large deliveries. Every winter this frozen highway was built anew, winding from mine to mine along a chain of lakes. Whatever the oversize equipment was, if the company didn't get it by spring, they'd have to do without for a year. The rohn truckers who drove here were legendary for their daring and their insanity. They helped make the people of the diamond lands the most colorful in the empire.

Love it or fear it, this was Katsu's home now.

The diamond lands were also her employer. For the first time in her life, Kat performed a job for which she was paid—two of them in winter. From nine in the morning to five at night, she labored with the Lucky Arctic Corporation crew, monitoring ice thickness and maintaining the ice road. From six at night to two in the morning, she ran her miner's bar. Working for LAC and the bar was exhausting, but she'd decided sleep and the dreams it carried were not her friend. Memories returned to her in slumber, particularly of one evening in Ningzha, when she and Hattori had stood together by the lake at sunset. Ciran had been laughingly trying to net a trout on the other bank, and Hattori had reached for her hand, not looking at her, just gently pulling their palms together. Even in dreams, the sweetness of the gesture inspired her pulse to skip. Four years later, she could recreate the exact texture of his fingers.

All in all, reminders of happiness once enjoyed were an irritation she could do without. So she kept busy and tired and was startled after a point to realize she'd become content.

Her stepmother would have been horrified to know how proud of herself she was.

Because Kat was royal, naturally she had a few secret irons in the fire. They also made her feel proud of herself.

Not the least bit secret, her bar was in the tiny town of Black Hole. In spring and summer, Black Hole was a fishing village. In winter, it was a rest stop a mile east of the ice road. Thanks to the shelf of granite on which it sat, even the heaviest forty-wheelers could layover here. Locals might not be rich enough to drape themselves in diamonds, but the personnel involved in digging them out ensured their businesses would thrive. Little restaurants and by-the-hour motels enlivened the town center. Elk meat was a local specialty, along with any sort of lake fish you could think of.

Kat's place, the Two Blades bar, sat on a wooded plot at the edge of town. It was a three-lobed black plasteel pod, as ugly as it could be but set solidly in the ground and not too hard to heat.

Inside, it was ugly too, everything in it factory made. One of the busboys had affixed glow-in-the-dark constellations to the rounded ceiling, but this had not improved the decor. What charm the Two Blades had came from the caliber of its liquor and its inexpensive but tasty food. The Shinobi family chef had gone into exile with Kat, refusing to work for that "viper" Miry if her favorite princess was banished. The decision turned out to be good for more than the miners' stomachs. The older woman's somewhat dramatic temperament blended in considerably better in diamond lands.

"We're low on rice," Rya told her now. It was early evening. The bar was half full, and they were writing up their next supply order at one of the back tables. "Also I'd kill for a shipment of fresh scallions."

Kat added them to the list, using the stylus on her handheld. Sadly, she couldn't tap a button and send the order off. Possibly due to interference from the northern lights, Yamaweb service didn't work out here. They received no holo broadcasts, either, unless they were shipped in on datachips—a special hardship for Rya, who was addicted to *What the Butler Saw* on HFC. At home, she'd used Kat's royal dispensation to watch the adaptation of the Human biography. Here, she had to wait six months for new episodes. It never ceased to grieve the chef that a primitive form of radio was their main method of communication, and even its reach was limited.

Some days Kat wondered if she'd gotten her idle wish to live like a Human—though at least she was spared corsets.

With half her ear, she heard the main door open behind her back. The last of the daylight entered, followed by a draft of cold air.

"Here comes trouble," Rya muttered under her breath.

Kat assumed the chef was referring to her would-be boyfriend, a striking looking but eccentric trucker who wore his shoulder-length hair in a hundred braids. Because Kat liked the man— probably better than Rya did—she turned to greet him. The two males she saw instead had her heart jumping to her throat.

They were dressed like truckers in heavy insulated black jackets, lug-soled boots, and loose-fitting one-piece black overalls. Their fur-lined hoods were thrown back, but wraparound mirrored glasses concealed their eyes. The glare of sun on snow could be blinding, so these items weren't just an odd fashion choice. Of the two men who wore them, one was very tall and the other only tall for a rohn. Their bodies stayed motionless while their heads turned to survey every shadow in the dim main room. She noticed they had their backs angled slightly toward each other. That wasn't a trucker habit. That was what soldiers did.

Her hand jerked with a nervousness she couldn't explain, sending her stylus rolling off the table onto the floor. She pushed from her chair, then forgot to pick it up. She was a mess, her lips chapped from working outside in the cold, her hair not combed since this morning. Her clothes were the plainest she'd ever owned: a blue wool pullover sweater and black trousers, the outfit as pedestrian as lower class Humans wore—and lower class Human males at that. She didn't know why that would bother her right then, or why her nipples tightened so emphatically.

And then, as one, the men pulled off their sunglasses.

It was Ciran and Hattori. Her body had recognized them before the rest of her. Inexplicably, Ciran's eyes matched in color, and Hattori had somehow covered his birthmark. Despite the differences, she couldn't be mistaken.

For three sweet months, she'd woken between those beautiful faces.

"Are you well?" Rya asked, still seated at the table.

"Fine," Kat said. "I'll . . . I'll just see what they want."

Hattori's eyes bore into hers like lasers as she approached. He stood about two meters inside the door, before the scattering of round blue tables began. He had no expression, and he didn't move except to lower the hand that had removed his eye gear. Kat wanted to run to him, to leap on him and kiss him and burrow under his coat until she reached skin. She thrilled when the subtlest wash of pink rose into his face.

She couldn't see it, but she knew that giant cock of his had just gone rock hard.

Her hormones responded with a swiftness she thought they'd lost their knack for. She opened her mouth to speak but was cut off.

"You serve food here?" Ciran asked.

His bored tone wrenched her gaze to him. He gave his head an infinitesimal shake, and light dawned belatedly. They were in disguise. She wasn't supposed to know them.

She cleared her throat and hoped her cheeks weren't red.

"We do," she said. "The best food in the territory."

"That table's fine." Ciran jerked his head toward an empty one by the wall. "Bring us whatever's already hot."

Kat pressed her lips together against the obvious response to that. As if he knew what she was thinking, Hattori ducked his head and smiled. Though she'd made a place for herself here, the sight of his curving mouth made her happier than anything had in a while. A thousand questions ran through her mind, none of them mattering.

"We have ginger fish on rice," she said, "with peapods and bamboo shoots."

She didn't wait to hear if that was acceptable. Black Hole was a small community, cut off from the rest of the Yamish world. Residents tended to speculate about their neighbors—if only to stave off boredom. Fearing her face would betray too much, she escaped into the kitchen section of her bar's three pods. With the frazzled remnants of her concentration, she dished up food and grabbed a teapot.

What were Ciran and Hattori doing here? Had they missed her? Did they have any idea how awfully she'd missed them? She regretted letting Hattori go more than she'd ever regretted anything; more, in fact, than she regretted letting her stepmother force her out of her home. Should she take the men's arrival as a sign that she ought to choose differently? Maybe rebel a little more?

With an inward lurch of dismay, she realized she'd grabbed three teacups to accompany the pot—as if she were going to sit down and chat with them.

Stop dreaming and pull yourself together, she ordered herself sternly.

She almost had her turmoil under control when she brought the tray back to them. Hattori took the plates off, but didn't look at her.

"Could we start a tab with you?" Ciran asked. "We'll be running the ice road all season."

Discovering she'd been struck speechless, Kat pulled a handheld from the pocket of her Two Blades apron. Both men pressed their thumbprints onto the scanning screen. Without the Yamaweb to connect to, no names came up. She'd have to radio for their credit status to the truckers main dispatch.

"I'm Sam Q," Ciran said. "And this is Harry Kim."

Kat acknowledged the eccentric names as impassively as she could. The bleak northwest was a wild frontier. Truckers often chose odd handles, including Human ones. "Citizen Q. Citizen Kim. I hope you enjoy your meal."

Her knees were stiff as she walked away. She sat down again across from Rya, struggling with and then giving in to the temptation to look back at the men. Hattori's gaze awaited hers, causing waves of heat to roll through every one of her cells. He averted his eyes a second before she could make herself.

"So-o," Rya said, her lower lip caught between her teeth to camouflage her amusement, "that's the sort of male who wakes Sleeping Beauty up."

"Maybe," Kat evaded, aware that denying the attraction would be futile. In the course of starting a business together, she and Rya had fallen into informal habits. It had been ages since the other woman called her princess. Though Kat preferred the more equal relationship, in that moment she'd have given a great deal to be spared the chef's teasing.

She didn't know how she got through the shift after that. Hattori and Ciran finished their meal and left without speaking to her again. She confused so many orders in the next few hours Rya told her to leave early. The blocky rough terrain vehicle she'd been issued by the LAC was parked out back in the employee lot. Shivering, because the air was frigid enough to cut her lungs, Kat went through her most reliable rituals for starting its cold engine. Almost to her disappointment, the maintenance truck roared to life on the second try.

Part of her felt like she shouldn't leave. What if the men returned to the bar later?

Aware that she probably should act normally, Kat navigated gently down the two miles of ice road that took her home. According to her instruments, thirty-six inches of frozen water lay between her wheels and the lake's early winter depths. That was plenty for safety, but the ice still crackled and creaked as she rolled over it. The sounds had been difficult to get used to when she first came here. Big trucks like the super wheelers made the ice groan like a wounded animal. Now her ears were so accustomed to the noises she could pick out the slightest change in the symphony. This was useful. Sometimes instruments, no matter how advanced, weren't quick enough to warn of danger. The LAC did their best to keep drivers safe, but occasionally trucks broke through and sank anyway.

At forty below, it only took seconds for the ice road to become the ceiling of a coffin.

Kat had the ice nearly to herself for this trip. One big rig grumbled slowly by in the other lane, returning from the mines with a small back haul. She pulled into her driveway with the tiniest rush of pleasure to have reached it unharmed again.

Her home was another prefabricated pod, brought to this side of Long Lake by one of the super W's she kept the road safe for every day. The snow that blanketed her pod's single dome improved its uninspired appearance, but not as much as the mammoth truck cab parked on its turnabout. The vehicle was light blue and unfamiliar. Ciran and Hattori must have figured out where she lived.

The engine was idling to keep it warm, thick white vapor trailing from its stack across a sky dotted with bright stars. As Kat stepped out of her RTV, the cab's door opened. Hattori jumped lightly down, followed by Ciran.

She couldn't move; she was so grateful to see them there. Hattori stared at her, his gaze intent, his handsome face lit by the truck's roof lights.

"Hey, princess," he said, and the spell that held her frozen melted in one heartbeat.

She ran and flung her arms around him, her face buried where his heavy coat opened at the neck. His skin was cold but recently shaven. She didn't care that she was squeezing him too hard for dignity. He was here, solid and real, and she didn't ever want to let go of him.

His arms joined hers in the tight embrace. Overwhelmed with joy, tears began to leak from her eyes.

"Shh," Hattori soothed, feeling them as he nuzzled her face. "You're all right, sweetheart."

He had no idea how much she'd missed him calling her that.

Behind her, another hand settled on her shoulder to rub it.

"Why don't we take this inside?" Ciran suggested. "You two might not be cold, but my manly parts are shrinking."

She let them in, but only after giving Ciran a quick hug too. He laughed at her as he returned it, his hold not quite as tight as his friend's.

Once they were inside, she felt self-conscious. Her house was far from a palace, just a big round room that combined kitchen, bedroom and seating, plus a bump-out for a small bath. Solar tubes let sun in during the day, but they were her sole windows. All her storage was built-in and utilitarian. Coupled with the fact that most everything was white, the place looked like a laboratory someone was camping in. Belatedly, she realized she hadn't made her bed that morning or folded it back into the wall. The rumpled mattress lay on a low platform, barely a foot off the floor.

Oh well, she thought. *At least the mess is homey.*

Both men looked around curiously.

"Warm," Ciran observed, rubbing his hands together.

"Let me have your coats," she said, remembering her hostess duties. They let her take them, the process awkward but desirable in that it would keep them there for a while. It was strange to see how much of them she remembered . . . and the little things she did not. Ciran was still lean, but his profile was sharper than she recalled. Hattori's height was closer to hers—she'd made him tower in her memory—but the scent of his skin was exactly what came to her in dreams. Finally, the men sat side by side on her two-person couch. Kat pulled the chair from her built-in wall desk to sit across from them. The men leaned forward over their knees, their shoulders straining the cloth of their coveralls.

Their huge boots dripped melting snow on her processed plastic and stone floor.

"Princess," Ciran began.

"Kat," she corrected.

"Kat," he agreed, his face softening. He was lovely; no imperfections to distract from his finely carved features. The shallow cleft in his chin had a charm she'd forgotten.

"I miss your real eyes," she blurted out.

70

He smiled a little less easily—and a bit more wryly—than she recalled being his habit. "I'm wearing contacts. We're keeping a low profile."

He looked at Hattori. She sensed them having one of their silent arguments over who ought to break bad news.

"I don't care who tells me," she said, "as long as one of you does."

Alarmingly, Hattori reached forward to take her hand. She couldn't mind the clasp of his callused fingers, just the thought that she'd need support.

"We're here on assignment, Kat. Miry Shinobi wants us to kill you."

That was less than delightful, but not a shock—and she didn't think for a moment they'd carry out the job.

"Why?" she asked. "I'm already exiled. What set my stepmother off?"

Hattori put a second hand around hers. "Your father is ill."

"Ill?" Her voice was abruptly rough.

"He's been diagnosed with Thyrr's syndrome. Rumor has it he only has a few months left. As near as we can guess, he's been rethinking his decision to disown you."

Kat pulled free of Hattori's hold. She wanted to stand, to pace, but wasn't sure her knees were up to it. One of the hardest things she'd ever faced was her father's willingness to believe she'd harm her younger half sister. She and Mara weren't close; Miry had seen to that, but even if Kat had hated her, she wouldn't have poisoned her. That sort of ruthlessness wasn't in her nature, which she'd expected her father to be aware of. As it turned out, she'd overestimated his faith in her.

"How is Mara?" she asked, perhaps not strictly on topic.

"Fine," Ciran said. "At least as far as we know. Still not married, though."

Mara's failure to attract a prince had long been a thorn in her mother's side—a weakness other royals couldn't resist jabbing at. They knew how badly Miry wanted her blood to be considered as blue as theirs.

Kat lifted her gaze to Hattori's. "I have to see him. I can't let my father die thinking I hate him."

"Kat—"

"I have to. I was always more disappointed than angry at his betrayal. I thought he should know me better, but sometimes fathers don't know their offspring. The evidence against me was strong."

Ciran's hand squeezed her knee. "I'm not sure we can get you to him. This situation is more complicated than it seems."

More complicated than her former lovers being sent to kill her? Kat looked at Ciran and then at Hattori. Hattori let out a quiet sigh.

"What aren't you telling me?" she asked.

To her amazement, tears rose to his breathtaking silver eyes. He swallowed but couldn't blink them back. "I have a brother. A twin. For nineteen years, he's been incarcerated in Winter Prison."

Kat had to stand then; had to walk away from them, though there wasn't much of anywhere to go. How could she not know he had a twin? Why hadn't he told her? They'd been so intimate in Ningzha, and not just physically.

Her cold storage was designed to fit into the curved kitchen wall. Desperate for something to do, she opened it, removing an assortment of leftovers to set on the white-countered eating bar. Luckily, Rya had prepared the food. It would be edible. She pulled three plates from the cabinet.

"There's more," Hattori said. He came to her, and her body reacted. The simple fact that he was close warmed her through and through.

"More?"

"I'm the reason this is happening to you."

Kat stopped dishing sesame noodles. "How can you be the reason?"

"I assassinated Miry Oryan's first husband. I freed her to marry your father."

Kat's brain went completely blank. Though she wasn't cognizant that she was thinking, she must have been. "Your brother," she said. "They threatened your brother so you'd comply."

"Killing Tudou Oryan was wrong. I despised daimyo then, but it didn't matter if every aristocrat in the world thought every other Yama's life was cheap. In my bones, I knew better. Worst of all, Haro wouldn't have wanted me to do it. They imprisoned him because he refused one of Muto's jobs. I can't even give myself credit for not wanting to do this one. I shouldn't have to be in love before I defy orders."

Kat couldn't help herself. She stroked his cheek where his birthmark had been. She felt no make-up, so perhaps he'd had a surgeon remove it. His new flawlessness wasn't calming him. If anything, her caress turned his eyes more anguished.

"I can't help being grateful you're not locked up," she said.

More practical than Hattori, though not less emotional, Ciran let out a huff of air. He pulled one of the plates closer. The movement broke their tension.

"I'm eating," he said. "This cold weather has me famished."

Though Kat wasn't hungry, she served herself and Hattori. She thought he might resist being fed, but guards burned calories like fire burned wood. They sat on the stools at her eating bar—she on one side and the men on the other—and ate together for a few minutes. The comfort of it was surreal. Because they were here, with her in her little home, everything was perversely right with her world. She didn't understand how three months out of her life had become so disproportionately important. By the time her stomach was full, she almost felt ebullient.

"Winter Prison can't be more than hundred miles north of here," she observed. To her surprise, the men gaped at her. Hadn't they thought of this themselves?

"Hattori and I are good," Ciran said slowly, "but Winter Prison is a fortress."

"Fortresses are only as impregnable as the Yama who run them."

Hattori's fork dropped with a clatter. "Did you miss the part about us being sent to kill you? About a contract being put on your life?"

"You and Ciran can find a way around that. Once you do, we really ought to think about breaking your brother out."

"*We* really ought to."

Kat viewed Hattori's horror with satisfaction. She'd been wondering if she needed to break more rules. What better reason was she going to get than this?

"Do you think I'm some fragile princess?" she asked. "I work the ice road, Hattori. People trust me with their lives. You said you love me, and I know you love your brother. I'm not giving you up again if there's the slimmest chance of avoiding it."

♦

No matter what their class, Yama weren't famous for frankness. Kat's claim that Hattori had said he loved her shocked him, though—looking back—he could see he had. The rest of it, her implied forgiveness, her willingness to help Haro, was too much to absorb. The single fact that nailed itself into his mind was that Kat didn't want to give him up. In spite of everything, she wanted to be with him.

Those months in Ningzha hadn't been meaningless for her.

As the realization sank in, his body grew more confused. He was aroused and adrenalized and hovering a millimeter away from either crazy laughter or mortifying tears. For four years he'd missed her like his own arm: four fucking endless years.

Ciran laid his hand gently on his back. "Are you okay?"

He wasn't sure. His cock was hard enough to smash bricks, and his heart ached just as badly. He felt like he would explode if he didn't take Kat that minute, but he didn't want to hurt Ciran.

He should have known his friend would sense his dilemma.

"Go ahead," he said. "I know you want to be with each other."

Kat made a little noise, drawing Hattori's eyes to her. She looked startled by Ciran's words, but not like she'd deny wanting him. Her cheeks were rosy, her pretty mouth just a bit swollen. Her lips were roughened by the cold, which didn't stop him from wanting to lick his way between them. Her lashes were so thick and dark the rims of silver around her pupils appeared to glow. The signs of her excitement were hammers to his own. His blood beat against his skin, suddenly too tight, too hot, too covered up to bear. Two spots on either side of his neck felt like they were burning.

"I'll wait in the cab," Ciran said.

He was already rising, already grabbing his boots from the mat Kat had set them on. As was usual for drivers here, they'd left the truck running; the engine iced up too quickly otherwise. Hattori knew his friend wouldn't freeze, but he nearly called him back all the same. It was simply . . . he and Kat had never made love alone. Ciran had always been close, participating in most cases. Hattori hadn't minded, or not hardly. Tonight, though, he didn't think he could hide his feelings. He needed Kat, body and soul. Her heart was the one his yearned for. That was something Ciran didn't want to know.

Before he could decide what to do, the weather seal on the door snicked closed.

Hattori slid off his stool and stood.

"Well," Kat said, rubbing her thighs nervously.

Hattori didn't wait for her to relax. He gripped her under the arms, lifted her up, and covered her mouth with his.

After all this time, her reaction jolted his senses. She melted against him, her hands sliding up his back in the firmest way. His whole body squirmed with pleasure, a low rough sound echoing from his throat to hers. Her kiss was open and wet, the slide and suck of her tongue strumming nerves deep inside his groin. He'd forgotten how tall she was, and what a marvel the closeness of their heights made kissing. The inside of her leg rubbed the outside of his, opening more of her mound to the urgent press of his erection. Hattori slid his palms over her bottom and clamped her close.

"Fate," he moaned, rolling harder. "I want inside you so bad."

Her chest went up and down with her quick breathing. Still in his arms, she peeled her dark blue sweater over her head. Underneath, a snug white shirt clung to her high small breasts. The undergarment was thin and stretchy, the dark tight press of her nipples unbearably erotic. He remembered how the little points tasted, how they felt rolling on his tongue. His lamril curled out to lick his lips, his gaze unable to rise higher. The rasp of metal teeth jerked him from his stupor. Kat was pulling his overall's zipper down.

"I want you inside me too," she said.

She slid her hand into the gap she'd made, finding and fondling his erection. Hattori wasn't in heat, but when her fingers curled tight and pulled up his shaft, the sensations were as amazing as if he were.

"You're as big as I remember," she said much more huskily.

Could any male mind hearing words like that? He kissed her, putting all his heart and lust into it. He had no words to express what he was feeling. Dying for a way to show her, he moved her toward the unmade bed he'd been trying not to stare at since they'd entered her home.

The thing was blissfully close. They tumbled onto it with her beneath him, and his pleasure at the impact made him cry out. Unable to wait an instant longer, he started to help her out of her black trousers. When that proved more challenging than he expected, he shoved up her snug white shirt and latched his starving mouth onto her left breast.

She arched like a bow, working frantically to push her trousers off by herself. He grunted in approval when she got them down to her knees, though he wasn't about to stop suckling her. Given more territory to play with, his palm compressed her silky-smooth pubis, cream and heat spilling wonderfully from her folds. Thinking that ought to be encouraged, he switched his mouth to her right nipple.

His sweetheart groaned loud and long.

"Take off your clothes," she panted, wriggling like an eel under him. "I want you naked on top of me."

Reluctant though he was to let go, he couldn't deny he'd enjoy all her skin on his. As she tore free of her undershirt and kicked off her trousers, he wrestled his coverall almost all the way off him.

The sight of her bare kept him from finishing.

"You're so beautiful," he sighed.

She was too thin now, but it didn't matter. She was herself: his sleek, smooth Kat with a harmony of curves and muscles that appealed to him on more levels than he could count. Her hands smoothed down and around his chest as he crawled forward and lowered himself to her. Being skin to skin was as wonderful as he'd anticipated. His weight caught his cock between them, its hardness cushioned by the satiny warmth of her abdomen. Her thighs were already parted to make a home for him. She spread them farther, wrapping her legs around him so that her calves slid over and caressed him.

His overalls were bunched at his ankles, but right that moment it didn't seem important to kick them off.

The wonder in her eyes was what mattered, the incredible ache that swelled outward from his cock to swallow his whole being. His prick pounded at the thought of having her to himself. She touched his face at the same time that he touched hers.

"I can't believe you're here," she whispered.

Humbled beyond bearing, he pressed his sweating forehead to hers.

"Take me," she urged. "I need to know this is real."

"I'm going to spill," he warned her roughly, "and probably pretty soon."

"Don't care, sweetheart," she said, smiling.

The small endearment winged fresh heat through him. Before, he'd been the only one to use it. Now he knew she'd remembered. As if they had one mind, both their hands met between their bodies to move his cock to the right angle. He wasn't certain, but he thought his fingers were shaking more than hers. Hers were definitely more exciting as they shifted him into place. They were warm and slender, and everywhere they touched buzzed with interest.

She sighed as his swollen crest settled against her slippery hot entrance. He couldn't wait then, not after all this time. The muscles of his rear and thighs gathered.

"You're snug," he hissed, beginning to squeeze inside.

She arched and tightened her calves. "There's been no one in my bed since you and Ciran."

He stared at her in surprise. A period of abstinence that long was unheard of for a royal.

"Don't tease me about it," she pleaded.

"Never. You honor me more than I deserve."

She gave him a small shy laugh—probably because he'd spoken so hoarsely—then hugged his ribs with her arms. "Come on, Hattori. It's been four years."

It had, and his hormones were reminding him of every minute they'd gone unsatisfied. He pushed more determinedly, then slid in so suddenly he gasped. The sensation of her heat and tightness was incredible. Her inner muscles rippled, and her cream tingled strongly as it coated his throbbing cock. Her essence made him hungrier for sensation and more appreciative of it. Fortunately, she was keeping pace with him.

She rocked herself to him with the power of her long lean legs. The pressure on the head of his prick heightened. The compression of those ultrasensitive nerves was so sweet his head flung back on a moan. It took a moment before he could straighten his neck again.

"Guess you still like that," she said with a breathless laugh.

He growled, working his hand under her bottom. "Let's see if I remember what *you* like."

She liked hard long strokes that hit her as deeply as he could go. To her, his length and girth were assets, so he didn't waste useless effort trying to shrink himself. A little struggle to drag in and out pleased her—as it did him. Being big gave him the sense of being her master, even if she was the royal.

Master or not, the ecstasy of those thrusts enslaved him. Every plunge sang through him, building both his relief and his excitement. How he'd lived without this he didn't know. He was grunting at the bliss of being inside her, but he knew she liked him noisy. She wasn't silent either. Her cries went up in pitch as her climax neared.

The sound of that was too much. His balls drew up and started pulsing like he was going to go in two seconds. He bit his lip, hoping the pain would delay the inevitable, but the trick didn't help. Everything they did felt too good. She was throwing her hips up his length and he was thumping right back at her. Her fingernails dug into his back as some object crashed from a shelf in her bed's alcove. His shaft swelled in the middle the way it did when he was really, really aroused. The increase in width pushed him even tighter against her walls. Streamers of delight climbed his spine.

He would have cursed if he hadn't been trying not to scream. As it was, his snarl was unstoppable. He had to go faster or he would die.

"Yes," she said, her head thrashing violently.

When her cunt clamped down on his cock, his seed simply exploded.

The ejaculation wasn't like the long, killing ones he had in his rut. This was a single mammoth kick of pleasure, followed by a few smaller contractions. As they faded, his cock began to soften inside of her.

"Shit," he said through his gasps for air. His body felt amazing, but he didn't think he'd lasted even five minutes. His only consolation was that she'd started coming first.

Kat pressed one fingertip to his lip. "You bit yourself."

"Sorry," he said. "I meant that to be better."

She laughed, the sound low and pleased, so he guessed she wasn't angry. "Roll onto your back. And don't let go of me."

He rolled without disengaging them. Kat pushed up until she sat with her long legs folded nimbly to either side of him. Her hair was mussed, spilling long and gorgeous over the front of her. Hattori slid his hands underneath the strands. Her breasts was small but perfect, and he loved the way he could cover them. Kat closed her eyes and hummed as he gently squeezed, rocking just a little on the saddle of his groin. When she laid her hands over the back of his, a lovely peace spread through him. He realized he'd been wanting this as much as the rest: simply to touch and know they were connected. For a long quiet moment, they sat that way.

"You're always exciting," she said once their pulse had calmed. "Whether you lose control or you keep it, you're a wonderful lover."

Her fingers glided down his forearms to the inner bend of his elbows. The nerves she stroked there stirred a tingle that set the tip of his cock twitching. Hattori knew Kat felt it, because she opened her eyes and smiled.

He suspected women had been smiling like that since the dawn of time.

"Can I take you in my mouth?" she asked. "Before you get too big to handle?"

The twitching of his glans became a stretching inside his shaft.

"Only if I can do the same to you."

"Deal," she said and pulled carefully off of him, grinning.

The smile was as much of an aphrodisiac as the rest. He was stiff by the time they'd wriggled into position along their sides. He realized they'd never done this before. It was a two-person game, and they'd always had Ciran to lend any extra hands. Maybe it was disloyal, but the newness of the act increased his eagerness for it.

Her pussy smelled like heaven as he nuzzled his face to it.

"You're not smaller anymore," Kat complained.

"Sorry," he said, sighing out his pleasure as she caressed his balls.

"Liar," she retorted.

She couldn't have been too annoyed. She took one testicle in her mouth, sucking it as her hands pushed and rubbed his shaft against his belly. He squirmed, immediately losing focus, because her saliva affected him even more than Ciran's. His fingers still searched out her pleasure spots, but his mouth was lost to a gasp for air. The pressure on his balls felt incredible. He bent his upper leg and rocked toward her, hoping this wasn't too aggressive. Kat hummed around his scrotum approvingly.

Then she kissed and sucked her way to the head of him.

He moaned as her tongue drew tingles around his flare. Around and around she went, until his slit wept with excitement. She dug the tip of her tongue in there. That pleasure was so sharp he couldn't help jerking. Kat pulled back to press her lips softly over him.

"Why do I love your taste so much?" she murmured.

She loved it because they matched each other, because Muto—may he rot wherever he was—had made a humble guard the prince of her hormones. No man could ask for a greater honor. Remembering that, remembering himself, he pulled her smooth thigh over his ear.

Tasting her hardened him even more, but Kat didn't seem to notice. To the delight of his inner conqueror, the flick of his tongue soon had her writhing in his grasp.

"No fair," she panted. "You're distracting me."

He settled in to distract her more.

"I'm going to make you come again," she warned as he increased his suction on her clitoris. "You're going to . . . shoot right into my throat."

Hattori chuckled against her, gripping her buttocks firmly as he commenced to combat her threat in earnest. She wasn't prepared for this.

"Oh," she cried, her pelvis twisting closer. "Oh. *Oh.*"

And then her mouth engulfed half of him. One hand pumped the base of his penis while the other massaged his balls. He didn't stop what he was doing, but continuing with much coordination was a struggle. They were locked in the fight together, jerking, sighing, and finally forgetting the competition except to give and get more pleasure. He loved the way her pussy welled when she came, the way they could hide their expressions even as their most intimate reactions were exposed. The contradiction might have been invented for Yamish lovers. Hattori didn't want the closeness to end, though of course it had to eventually.

"Let me turn," she pleaded, breathless from her last climax. "Let me pay attention to finishing you."

He was too wound up to argue. He released her, falling onto his back with his legs sprawled wide. Amazingly, his ankles were still caught in his black uniform. Kat moved between his thighs, gathering her long hair behind her neck as her head lowered.

"Wait." He shoved two pillows behind his back, not about to miss watching this.

Her lips curved, fingertips drawing up his exceptionally rigid length. "This is going to be fun."

Fun wasn't quite the word. *Devastating*, maybe, or *the most important relief on earth*. Her angle was better for him now, her strong tongue finding the sweetest spot underneath his crest. She was relaxed, and she took a lot of him, almost as much as Ciran. He groaned at the force she used. She wasn't trying to draw this out. She was sucking him tight and fast to his longed-for end.

His hands cupped the sides of her head, struggling not to pull her too hard to him. She made a sound, so maybe it was too much, but he was having trouble reining himself in. Possibly she sensed this. Her knees shifted, pinning his trapped ankles more securely. The impromptu bondage played an unexpected trick on him, twisting his excitement up to a level he couldn't control. He lunged at her from his pelvis, but she was ready. Her forearms slapped over his hipbones, her royal muscles restraining him. Even as she held him, her suckling on his cock strengthened. She was in charge then, and he thrashed helplessly.

Desire was draining the strength from him. He couldn't get free, and he didn't want to. Heat swelled, pushed, his climax abruptly inevitable. Fiery ecstasy streaked up his penis, then poured across her tongue.

The sound he made as it jetted was hoarse and primal: relief, surrender, maybe a note of mourning for the years they'd lost. She accepted all of it with a generosity he wasn't sure he deserved. She didn't let him draw free, but coaxed every drop of pleasure from him with the warmth and tenderness of her mouth. When he finished, she laid her cheek on his thigh, her ragged breathing fanning his fading cock.

No more than a minute later, she sat up with a groan. He thought she'd crawl beside him and snuggle; they'd always liked doing that. Instead, she swung her legs over the side of the bed and started pulling her trousers on.

Wondering why, Hattori rolled toward her and tugged the ends of her hair.

"Ciran," she reminded. "I don't want to leave him sitting in your truck all night."

Hattori bolted up guiltily.

"It's all right. You didn't mean to forget. I put other things in your mind."

"I'll get him," Hattori said firmly. "You stay inside and keep warm."

◆

Ciran had tried to prepare for this moment, for Kat and Hattori to lose themselves in their reunion. He'd ordered his sometimes selfish heart not to begrudge his friend happiness. Sadly, none of the lectures helped.

He hadn't expected to be literally left out in the cold.

He grew sick with envy as the minutes he sat drew out, finally gripping the seat so hard the polyvinyl began to rip. The muffled sound his voice made probably was a scream.

Before it completely faded, the door to the rider's side creaked open.

"Ciran?" Hattori climbed in and slammed the door behind him. "You all right?"

Ciran looked at him, everything he felt written in his eyes.

"Okay," Hattori said. "Stupid question."

He shoved his fingers worriedly through his hair. As easily as that, most of Ciran's hurt ran out.

"Forget it," he said. "I volunteered to wait out here."

"Kat wants you to come in."

Hattori should have minded that, but he didn't seem to. Maybe anything was fine when everyone loved you best. Ciran slid his hands around the steering wheel, forcing his choppy breathing to steady. Even with the heater running, ice crystals feathered inward on the windshield.

"Did you mean it?" he asked. "About killing being wrong?"

To judge by his expression, Hattori hadn't expected this question. "I meant it," he answered cautiously. "Unless you're killing in self-defense, I don't think it's justified."

"That means you think I'm unjustified. No one forced me to be an assassin."

"Why are you bringing this up now?"

"Just answer," Ciran said sharply.

Hattori stretched his arm along the seatback, his fingers touching the shoulder of Ciran's coverall. "I think you believe differently than I do. I think you follow your own sense of right and wrong."

"You think I'm not as good as you and Haro."

"I didn't say that."

Ciran snorted. "You didn't have to."

"Ciran—"

He shoved out of the cab before Hattori could make things worse. He didn't want to fight, and he was going to unless he got out of there. Hattori followed him more slowly, locking up with the radio-operated key.

Kat must have been listening for them. She opened the hatch to her home before they were close enough to knock. She wore nothing but a stretchy sleeveless white shirt and panties, but she waited there anyway. A flood of warm yellow light spilled around her delicate female form. Ciran ached to see how pretty and sweet she was. He couldn't blame Hattori for wanting her so much. She was a woman any man would be proud to be loved by.

"Hurry," she urged, starting to bounce from the icy air blowing in at her.

Ciran lengthened his stride so that he was inside before Hattori. While his friend sealed the door, he braced on the curving wall to tug off his boots again.

When he straightened, Kat's expression turned utterly dismayed.

"What?" he said, taken aback.

"Ciran," she exclaimed softly. "You look so sad."

He hadn't known that. He'd have hidden every scrap of feeling if he'd been able. To his surprise, Kat pulled him into a hug.

"I'm sorry," she murmured against his ear. "Ciran, I'm so sorry."

He wasn't certain what she was apologizing for. Maybe everything, if the way his eyes burned could be taken as a sign. He hugged her back, hiding his too bare expression in her long hair. It made no sense, but her sympathy was a comfort he could accept. It didn't sting his pride like Hattori's did. *He* was a block of darkness behind them, saying nothing at all.

"What will make it better?" Kat whispered. "Tell me and I'll do it."

He pulled back and met her gaze. She'd smoothed out her look of worry, and that calmed him—probably what she intended. He felt the old tender spot in his chest, the one that said maybe he loved her too. "A good night sleep wouldn't hurt."

"With us?"

She wasn't shielding her aura the way royals were trained to. Its edges touched his, gentle and tentative.

"With you," he said, "if that's where you want me."

"I do." She hesitated, and he wondered if she were going to suggest he join them for more than sleep. "I guess we all need to be up early."

"Crack of dawn," Hattori acknowledged, his own voice striving for casual. "We have to hook up our load first thing if we want to make our departure slot. You folks at the LAC are sticklers for scheduling."

Kat shook her head. "We're sticklers because the ice has to be babied. If trucks aren't dispersed just so, the road won't recover from the stress of their weights. Do I need to worry about the two of you driving?"

"We know what we're doing," Hattori assured her in a more serious tone. "If you hear about us pulling some rookie move, it'll just be for show. There's a method to our madness."

"Glad to hear it." Kat glanced at her rumpled bed, then toward the open door of her bath compartment. "I'm showering. You two do what you want about sleeping arrangements."

There wasn't much question they'd all be on her big mattress. Without bothering to discuss it, he and Hattori changed into sleeping trousers. They took their usual sides but left space between. When Kat returned, Hattori rolled onto his elbow and patted the middle spot. Kat crawled into it like a little tiger, unconsciously slinky. Hattori was behind her and Ciran to her front, lying on his side with his back to her. The sheets rustled as the other two spooned together. Hattori sighed like he'd set down a weight.

Then Kat's hand settled on Ciran's back.

"I'm glad you're here," she said, rubbing the rigid muscles between his shoulder blades.

His cock grew heavier at her touch, thickening from the surge of blood into it. He didn't turn to her, and she probably didn't guess she was having this effect. Ciran had a different sexual drive from Hattori: intense but not dramatic. Though his body would have been happy to find release with her, preferably more than once, he intended for his head to rule until his emotions were sorted out.

"Good night," he said, reaching back to pat her leg lightly.

Kat said good night as well and ordered the lights to shut off. Ciran didn't expect to sleep, but surprisingly little time passed before he sank into the peace of it like a stone. Evidently, the assassin in him felt safe with her.

If that wasn't ironic, he didn't know what was.

5: THE ICE ROAD

Kat discovered later that Ciran and Hattori had left their truck in front of her pod home deliberately. They'd counted on someone spotting it through the pines.

Locals knew Kat was a disgraced princess. Rya had made sure of that. Both their prestige in Black Hole was enhanced by Kat being an aristocrat, no matter what she'd been accused of. Daimyo habits being what they were, no one was shocked that she let herself be pursued by two men at once—even two men as rough as Ciran and Hattori.

Every morning for the next two weeks, their big truck followed her smaller one to LAC dispatch. Anyone who noticed was told they were making sure she arrived safely. Human sweethearts might have kissed in the parking lot, but even in the bleak northwest displays like that were thought eccentric. The men sketched waves through the windshield as their goodbye. Whenever their schedule of hauls allowed, they ate dinner at her bar. Kat took to joining them at their table, hiring a part-time waitress so service wouldn't suffer.

Their behavior wasn't flirtatious. They didn't speak much over the meal or interact beyond lingering glances and brief touches. Kat's stepmother Miry assuredly had a spy in town to keep an eye on her. News might be a challenge to relay to the Forbidden City, but eventually it arrived. Kat had no doubt every move she made was being watched as hungrily by Miry's proxy as it was by the rest of the residents.

Knowing this, it was better not be obvious. Twice Ciran and Hattori let themselves be pulled over for driving violations by LAC employees other than herself. The first time involved securing a chain improperly on a load. The second, they took a hill five miles too fast on the portage road. Anywhere else, the infractions would have been minor. On the ice, small mistakes could cost lives. Reports filtered back to Kat that "her" rookies weren't taking the safety rules seriously. One veteran trucker claimed Ciran actually laughed when asked to exercise more caution.

Kat coolly told her informant he must be mistaken. Then she set his plate of dumplings down hard enough that one rolled steaming into his lap. She was getting into her role for certain. Her sole regret was that the food hadn't been hotter.

Out of these small details the ground for their escape was laid. Kat could live with the prevailing theory that she'd gone man-crazy. Harder to stomach was people thinking Ciran and Hattori were irresponsible. When they were insulted, her bristling was genuine. The men also succumbed to this tendency. Two days earlier, while laying over at a rest stop, Ciran punched a local in the nose for suggesting Kat was letting her sexual organs rule her good sense. Though Ciran's response might have been extreme for their purposes, Kat was unaccountably touched.

She'd never had a male defend her honor before.

Like all fictions, the last page of theirs inevitably turned. Their final day at her house was an off day for all of them. Sleep was on the to-do list but hadn't been fit in yet—no surprise considering how wound up they were.

"You can't pack," Hattori reminded her unnecessarily. "Everything you value has to be left here."

He was sitting cross-legged on her bed in his sleeping trousers, his big bare chest impressive beneath its light shadowing of hair. Kat had noticed three people mussed the covers much more than one, a thought that heated her inappropriately. Ciran was in the truck, ensuring their emergency gear was secure in its secret compartment. From the beginning, he'd been considerate of her and Hattori's privacy—retreating either to the couch or outside when things became intimate.

Kat suspected he was trying to give them privacy today. Despite their precautions, what they were planning was dangerous. That they'd die in truth wasn't inconceivable.

Struck by that, Kat sat back from the low kitchen cabinet she'd been emptying of cookware. Looking at Hattori was a pleasure she didn't want to deny herself, though she did have one small complaint to air. "I wish you'd let me see that lawyer."

Hattori smiled very gently, an expression that never failed to tug at her. "You can't, Kat. It would make our accident look planned."

"I'm just worried about Rya. She's my partner, but she doesn't own a controlling share. What if Miry tries to claim the bar when I'm gone?"

"What would your stepmother want with a bar?"

"She might burn it down for spite. Rya took my side when I was banished. You can bet Miry hasn't forgotten that. Really, I should have thought to make her my heir already. It's only responsible."

"Fate, I love you," Hattori burst out.

Kat's mouth fell open, her cheeks gone hot. Hattori had almost said he loved her before, but that wasn't the same as hearing it flat out. Her entire body tingled, the powerful physical reaction momentarily befuddling her.

She hadn't known it was possible to be embarrassed and delighted at the same time.

"Sorry," Hattori said, his face reddening. "I shouldn't have—"

"No, no," Kat interrupted. "I . . . I feel the same."

The grin he flashed at her was brilliant and, though she was now blushing even harder, she couldn't help grinning back. He was so boyishly handsome it hurt her heart.

"I wasn't sure," he said. "I mean, I know you said you didn't want to give me up again if you could help it, but—"

"I felt it," she broke in, the words rushing out now that she was letting them. "Pretty soon into our summer in Ningzha."

"Me too." He laughed, relief in it. "I thought I was the stupidest rohn ever, falling for a princess."

"No," she said. "You could never be stupid."

Their eyes held, silver to silver. Kat felt as if her aura were getting brighter, as if it were spreading out in tiny particles to touch his. His face grew serious, his expression hot. His hands fisted in the covers that were gathered atop his lap. Kat was pretty sure she knew what was happening under them.

"Come over here and say that," he growled.

She couldn't laugh; he affected her too strongly.

"I can't," she said, her voice reduced to a husky whisper. "I've got something hidden behind these pots that really does have to come with us."

Her limbs trembled with arousal as she turned away and knelt to root in the depths of the cabinet for her prize. It wasn't hard to picture how she looked, on her hands and knees with her narrow butt in the air in nothing but white panties. Though she wasn't trying to tease Hattori, she also couldn't mind too much if she was. She'd never tire of knowing what she did to him sexually.

Even though she half expected it, he was on her so fast it stole her breath. He spared a second to squeeze the curves she'd been displaying so prominently, but that was all he delayed. She heard him muttering with impatience as he shoved his sleep trousers down; felt his fingers against her as he tugged the gusset of her underwear aside. Smooth wet heat pushed her folds open, drawing a moan from her. Then he grunted and plunged inside.

"I can't get enough of you," he confessed. "No matter how many times I take you, I still want more." His knees pushed hers wider, his aggressiveness causing her to gasp with excitement as he pulled back and thrust again.

She tried to say she couldn't get enough of him either, but his big hot shaft was powering in and out of her already, and the movement just felt too good. Though it might have been undignified to admit, this position was her pussy's favorite. His broad tip drove directly over such delicious places. Plus, he was being extra rough today. He usually tried to be careful, but perhaps he was thinking of the risk they faced, of maybe never doing this again. Her back arched hard as she had a quick orgasm.

"Ka-at," he groaned, his mouth hot on her shoulder.

He had one hand clamped on her hip and the other wrapped on the open cabinet's frame. That was one less hand than Kat wanted on her body.

"Let me," she said, squeezing the words between choppy breaths. She slapped her palms on the white plastic. "Trust me. I'm strong enough to brace us."

Apparently, he believed her. He cursed and let go, using his now free hand to cup her right breast. Two fingers squeezed and pulled out the nipple his palm massaged. His hips slammed into her like an oiled machine.

Luckily, she was too aroused to be embarrassed by the whimpers of pleasure this pulled from her.

"Go," he demanded, the order thick. "*Go*."

She came, and he made a sound like he was dying. Her orgasm was so strong it actually hurt—though in a good way. She knew her muscles had tightened around him.

"One more," she pleaded, loving what he did to her.

She wasn't sure he could last, but the idea that she wanted another climax certainly energized him. His powerful thighs jerked hers wider, no doubt craving more access. The entire bank of cabinets was shaking, her elbows locked to prevent them from bashing into its frame. If they did, they'd probably give themselves concussions. Hattori was really going at her, his muscles coiled hard as stone.

"You're so wet," he groaned, one callused finger rubbing half-on, half-off her clitoris. Despite his imprecision, the pressure was enough to propel her up to the edge again. His cock was pumping back and forth over one of her sweetest spots and simply pounding a second: the one at the very end of her passage that only he seemed able to stimulate. She bit back the wail that was trying to escape her, but she couldn't help growing creamier. That had its usual effect on him. As he worked his penis urgently in and out, the warning bulge in its center swelled, pressing wonderfully tighter against her walls. Kat trembled to feel it, but he must have enjoyed it too.

"Fuck," he swore, his groin slapping her faster yet. "You feel so good."

He pulled back, sucked in a mammoth breath, then drove in hard enough for her bones to reverberate. She felt his testicles jerk a second before he ejaculated, felt him grind deep into her sheath and shoot with a quiver that shook his frame. The sensation of those liquid bursts set her off—as if he couldn't take his pleasure without hers shattering.

The climax clutched her sex with pure ecstasy. She came like it was a seizure, arching up and forcing him to catch her against his chest. Her vision went sparkling white with the strength of it.

It occurred to her, distantly, that if their lovemaking got any better, neither would survive it.

"Kat," he murmured as she blinked sweat from her eyes. His arms were warm steel bands underneath her breasts. "You have no idea how much I love you."

She rubbed her cheek on his hard bicep, eyes closed, throat tight on her swallow. "Hattori," was all the answer she could get out.

The weather gasket on the front door shut with a muffled *thwup*.

"Sorry," Ciran said when their heads snapped around. "All finished out there."

Kat wondered how long he'd been watching before he closed the door.

She was temporarily incapable of standing, but Hattori pulled his cock free of her body while somehow managing not to groan. Kat consoled herself that he did have to grip the counter so he could rise. Apparently, his brain was functioning.

"Don't apologize for walking in on us," he said.

"Fine," Ciran replied tersely. "Don't apologize for wanting to be alone."

"Cut it out," Kat said, not needing to see their faces to know the stubborn looks they were trading. Sighing, she stretched up to grip the counter, but didn't have the strength to pull herself up just yet. "Ciran, you're officially invited to join us any time you want. For that matter, neither of you need my permission to do as you please on your own."

That silenced both men . . . at least for a few seconds.

"Kat—" Hattori began placatingly.

"I mean it," she interrupted, up to her knees at least. "I know you enjoy sleeping with each other. I guess it might make me jealous if you have fun without me, but that would hardly be the end of the world."

She tugged her shirt down and pulled herself to her feet, swaying for a moment before steadying. In his eagerness, Hattori hadn't actually undressed her. As she stepped around the eating bar, into view of the pair, she was as decent as any woman who'd just had a mind-blanking orgasm could be in her underwear. Their eyes flicked over her hard-tipped breasts in a male onceover they likely weren't aware of. The glance was flattering and—to her hormones—undeniably erotic. She told those unruly chemicals to behave. Despite their unconscious admiration, lust wasn't foremost in either of the men's minds. Ciran's mouth had pulled thinner, reflecting some emotion she couldn't identify. Hattori's eyebrows rose as Ciran's lowered. Evidently, her offer had surprised him.

She might not have planned to make it, and—Infinity knew—she might be impaired from postcoital bliss. All the same, she stood by what she'd said. She had no right to demand Hattori sleep with her exclusively. Ciran and he had been a couple long before she entered the equation. Whatever Hattori's precise feelings for his friend, they were far from casual. Then again, maybe that was the problem. Maybe Hattori wished his affections—and his attractions—were more focused.

Even royal males, who were nothing if not sexually open-minded, sometimes thought of desiring another man as unmasculine—especially when no woman was around to make it seem more acceptable. In the three months they'd previously been together, she and Hattori hadn't discussed these things. She saw now perhaps they should have. Hattori was still furrowing his brow at her. For all his intelligence, he wasn't prepared to untangle this sensual snarl. His frown of consternation was almost cute.

Unexpectedly amused, Kat crossed her arms and let one corner of her mouth quirk up. If it hadn't been inconsiderate, she was sure she'd have smiled outright.

♦

Ciran could see their little love triangle—such as it was—was entertaining Kat. For himself, he was too insulted to be amused.

Kat thought Hattori wanted to sleep with him because he *enjoyed it*, as if no deeper reason could exist. Not that Hattori had indicated there was another. Kat was the one who had *no idea* how much he loved her. Kat was the one who gave Hattori permission to sleep with Ciran even while denying he needed it. And how dare she say she *might* be jealous? That was offensive all by itself. Ciran deserved to be seen as more of a threat. As to that, he deserved to stir a little green-eyed fury on his own behalf. He wasn't some dispensable erotic partner, some replaceable convenience. She should have been jealous of Hattori for getting to bed *him*. Worst of all, most of all, he should have been invited to join them long before what was possibly their last night on earth!

Ciran could have continued his private tirade indefinately, were it not for the fact that he was hyperventilating with anger. He forced his breathing to steady, realizing—reluctantly—that he was being a little unreasonable. How could Kat and Hattori know he wanted to be included when he removed himself from their presence any time they shown signs of becoming intimate? Hattori hadn't declared his feelings for Ciran, but neither had Ciran enumerated his for him. He had reasons for that, of course: not wanting his heart irrevocably broken being just one.

He sighed and coaxed his fisted hands to uncurl. By the time it occurred to Kat or Hattori to look at him again, his ruffled feathers were more or less smoothed.

More or less wasn't quite good enough for Kat. She cocked her head sideways.

"Are you okay?" she asked.

"Fine," he said, taking a moment to unzip his thick black coat. "Everything in the truck is set."

"Ciran," she said, but he didn't want to get into this. Something caught the light on the kitchen floor, a welcome distraction to him just then. At first he thought the glint was a large piece of broken glass. It lay next to a dirty rag, as if it had fallen out of the trash. He stepped toward the shard, prepared to pick it up and protect Kat's bare feet.

Then he noticed just how brilliantly the glass was sparkling. Seen against the white stone and plastic floor, it was a pale sweet blue, the color of the sky in spring if the sky in spring had tiny rainbows jumping around in it like wild sparks. The radiance hypnotized him, drawing him a step closer. The thing was as clear as water and as big as a baby's fist. The pattern of its facets was both harmonious and gorgeous. More than mathematics had inspired the configuration. This was a magical sort of genius, not to mention a blinking fortune in a rock.

Ciran had never seen a stone so alive.

"Kat," he said, his voice echoing oddly inside his head. "Why is a giant diamond there on your floor?"

Kat spun around to see where his gaze was glued. "Oh," she exclaimed. "I almost forgot I wanted to pack that!"

Kat bent to pick up the bright treasure. For one illogical moment, Ciran couldn't comprehend how she had the nerve to touch it. That much beauty should have been nuclear.

"I'm calling her the Katsu Blue," she said, holding the stone at eye level between her thumb and forefinger. "Humans name important diamonds, so I thought I would too."

"Tell me you didn't steal it," Hattori breathed.

The question was incredibly impolite, but Ciran understood where it came from. The diamond was so spectacular it was difficult to imagine mere money buying it.

"Of course I didn't steal it," Kat said. "Though I suppose I bought the rough it was cut from on the black market."

"You suppose you did," Hattori repeated.

"Sometimes it's best not to question a deal that good. I did take a financial gamble, which I think makes going behind the diamond cartel's back less objectionable. The original stone had three tricky microfractures. I suspect everyone else the seller approached thought it would shatter on the wheel."

"But you knew a way around that."

Kat grinned at Hattori, the mischief in her expression impossibly endearing. "I smuggled it to a Human cutter I'd heard about in Yskut. He was nervous at first, and had to slice off a third of the carats, but by Fate he came through for me. When he gave it back, looking like this, I swear I nearly swooned. He told me he studied the rough for a week before he dared polish a window to look inside. Then he stared into that through his loupe for two more—'communing with stone's spirit,' or so he said. It took him six months to polish, with a faceting scheme he invented specifically for this stone, one he'll never be able to use again. Can you imagine a Yama doing anything so inefficient? It's no wonder Humans outshine us in every art. We're not insane enough to be that imaginative."

"No," Hattori agreed and sat numbly on one of her eating stools.

Since he was too staggered to ask the obvious, Ciran decided to. "What are you planning to do with that?"

"Sell it," Kat said matter-of-factly. "Use the proceeds to seed a new fortune. I know people think I let my stepmother beat me when I was banished, but I always hoped to go back and fight some day. The Katsu Blue is my ticket to returning as something other than a relative pauper."

"I'll say," Hattori murmured.

His tone brought the faintest flush up to her cheekbones. "Well, I know things are different now. There's our escape to think of. And saving your brother. I'd just like to believe that someday I'll get the chance to give Miry back a bit of her own."

"You wouldn't be royal if you didn't," Ciran said reasonably.

Hattori grimaced, but Ciran hadn't meant his comment as a judgment. He didn't think of revenge as a motive a person ought to be ashamed of. Naturally, Hattori's response was the one Kat paid attention to. She curled her fingers around the stone, hiding it.

"No one here knows I have this," she said, the set of her shoulders subtly defensive. "There's no harm in me bringing it."

"Of course there isn't." Hattori bent to kiss her brow, his big hands chafing her too tense arms. The gesture seemed well meaning but slightly stiff. Kat wasn't any likelier to miss that than Ciran was.

"I'm still a princess," she said. "Being disowned can't change that."

"I wouldn't want it to," Hattori said.

Though the glance Kat sent him under her lids was quick, Ciran saw she didn't quite believe him.

◆

The thought of the Katsu Blue buzzed in Hattori's brain like a bad tempered wasp. He knew he shouldn't let it but couldn't stop. After all they'd shared and with all they had yet to face, Kat was still contemplating reclaiming her royal life.

There seemed little chance she'd succeed, though money did cure a lot of ills for their kind. Perhaps a 500 carat, nearly flawless blue diamond could facilitate a return from the dead. Even supposing it could, she'd still be an outlaw, having aided and abetted Ciran and Hattori in—essentially—stealing themselves from Kat's stepmother. Should they succeed in freeing Haro, Kat would be criminalized beyond redeeming. Hattori had nothing to worry about. His only challenge would be doing whatever it took to preserve his hold on her heart. He could do that. At least he thought he could. Tonight, he wasn't as confident of anything as he liked.

Ciran was behind the wheel of their cab, driving to the Two Blades bar. Darkness came early this time of year, and outside snow fell heavily. Kat drove the prescribed two truck lengths ahead of them in her sturdy black RTV. The ice was moaning and crackling per usual, pulling Hattori's nerves tighter. Kat's red tail lights reminded him of baleful eyes as they illuminated the pelting flakes. Distinguishing the edges of the road from the endless white landscape on either side presented a true challenge. The air was misted as well as snowy, and reduced visibility forced their speed to a crawl. The ice road was monitored for safety by the LAC; beyond it, the thickness of the frozen layer could vary dangerously. Add to that the weight of their vehicles, and Ciran was abnormally smooth-faced—usually a sign that he wanted to hide something. He was a good driver, as good as Kat almost, despite having years less experience.

That bothered Hattori a bit. Part of him wished he were better at everything.

"About earlier . . ." he began, feeling guilty for his smallness. At the least, he could clear the air between them.

Ciran shot him a sideways glance. "Forget it."

"We didn't mean to hurt your feelings."

"You didn't."

"Do you want to have sex with me again?"

This time Ciran's look was longer but no less cool. "I can live without it," he said.

Now Hattori knew he was angry . . . and that he was missing a few pieces of this puzzle. "I know you've gotten used to you and I—"

"I said forget it," Ciran bit out, the flat of one palm slapping the wheel. Recovering, he drew a slow breath and let it out. "Let's get through tonight. Our focus needs to be on pulling off this performance."

"I'm aware of that, but if you—"

"No," Ciran said. "I'm in this with you and Kat. No second thoughts, just with you all the way. We're going to survive this, so let's get our heads in the show."

His hand was clenched on the gear shifter, but Hattori didn't reach forward to lay his own over it. Ciran's expression was too forbiddingly controlled for that.

"All right then." He returned his gaze to the snow driving thickly down in the dark outside. "Heads in the show it is."

♦

Kat stepped out of her RTV and looked around in satisfaction. The weather station's promised blizzard was underway. The Two Blade's lot was overflowing with unhitched cabs, the truckers who'd come as far as Black Hole waiting it out here to see if the LAC would close the ice road. If loads could be gotten to the mines, drivers would always try; they *were* paid per delivery. Despite the financial motivation, even the most profit-hungry drivers dreaded being stranded between rest stops. Idling trucks stressed the ice, especially loaded ones. The longer the super W's sat with their multi-ton cargos, the worse the stress became. No one wanted his haul—or himself—to end up on the lake bottom.

No one who wasn't them, that is. The idea was that, having publically seduced Kat close enough to kill her, Miry's assassins would now fall victim to their inexperience with extreme conditions . . . getting in over their heads literally.

Ciran and Hattori joined her in the parking lot, studying the foul weather much like she had. They didn't look as if they were thinking anything out of the ordinary, but Kat could sense their tension like tightened wires.

"Hey, Kat," hailed Rya's would-be boyfriend, Longsheng, he of the hundred braids. "What are you hearing from your bosses?"

"Same as you," she answered. "I'm not on call tonight."

Longsheng nodded, hunched forward in his jacket against the cold, and hurried into her bar's entry. He'd done her a favor once, and they'd become casually friendly—though not enough for her to confide in him now. She and her partners followed him without comment, their lack of any need to speak peculiarly comforting.

Inside was warmth and noise and the aroma of many well cooked meals. Kat experienced an unexpected pang. This was probably the last time she'd be in the thriving business she'd built from the ground up. Until that moment, she hadn't realized how attached to it she'd grown.

Longsheng wasn't the only casual friend she'd made. People greeted her as she and the men forged a path between the crowded tables: locals, truckers, harried employees offering a nod as they hustled trays to customers.

Hattori touched her shoulder when she shrugged off her coat, seeming to understand what she was feeling without making a fuss over it. They headed for the automated end of the bar, not only because there were open seats, but because the vending machinery would keep a record of exactly what they consumed. Kat braced herself, aware she had to get drunk for real. The less of this night they faked, the more inevitable its result would strike witnesses. It made her glad princesses had a high tolerance for alcohol.

"Kat," Rya exclaimed, the chef spotting her as she returned a tray of empty glasses to the bartender. Kat was dismayed to see her, not having prepared herself for goodbyes. Rya usually stayed in the kitchen, only pitching in out front when it was so busy it couldn't be avoided. For her part, Rya looked pleased to encounter her, her hands on hips and her eyes openly sparkling. "I expected you'd stay in tonight."

She wagged her brows once in the men's direction, indicating how she'd imagined Kat would be occupied.

"Busman's holiday," Kat said, stealing the phrase from a show on the HFC.

"Ha," Rya said, appreciating the reference. "Bet you couldn't get any farther in this weather."

"Nope," Kat agreed. "When you get a chance, could you send out three servings of elk stew?"

"Will do," her oldest associate said, disappearing from sight for what might be the final time.

"Drink?" Hattori offered, sliding a full cup to her.

The rice wine's heated ceramic flask had risen from the vending aperture in the bar while Kat was speaking to Rya. She accepted the tiny steaming cup from Hattori and tossed its contents back. Tears sprang to her eyes at its twenty percent alcohol content.

"Hit me with another," she said to her trusty assassin.

♦

Hattori should have known Kat would take the business of getting drunk seriously. She was pink-cheeked and swaying when she slid off her stool for the last time.

"Whoof," she said, dragging the back of her forearm across her mouth.

"Careful, princess," Ciran cautioned, catching her by the arm.

She pealed with laughter, a sound that carried—not coincidentally—most of the way through the bar. She needed help getting her arms back into the sleeves of her winter jacket, the pockets of which she patted in the universal gesture of searching for electronic keys.

At the nearest table, one of the older trucker's eyes narrowed. He was a veteran of the ice road, weather lines cut deeply into his face. "You're not driving," he said to her.

Kat pulled herself as straight as she could. "The road's not closed yet."

"As of ten minutes ago, it is." The trucker jerked his head toward the digital wall display, where the headlines for the current radio broadcast scrolled. Hattori would have bet money she already knew what it said.

Kat pouted at the display for a moment before she smoothed her face. "I'm an LAC employee," she enunciated, working on fastening her coat. It had a self-seal design, but that only worked if the opening was lined up, a task her fingers seemed incapable of just then. "We're going straight home. Only two miles from here."

"Take her keys," the trucker said to Ciran. "You're an idiot, but you look sober."

Ciran undercut this vote of confidence by breaking into a grin. "You hear that," he gloated to Hattori. "I look sober."

Miraculously, they got out of the bar without being stopped by other safety conscious patrons. Kat maintained her careful drunk impression all the way to the cab. Unfortunately, her inebriation wasn't as much of an act as he'd relied on.

"Balls," she said, bracing on the dash once they'd settled in the front seat with her between them. She breathed slowly and deeply. "Keep that window open for a bit."

"You all right?" Ciran asked, his worry not feigned at all.

"I have to be," she said, leaning back with a grim expression. "Drive out of view of the exit, and we'll switch places."

Ciran didn't argue. They'd already decided that—drunk or not—Kat was the best choice to handle this portion of their plan. With a grim look of his own, Ciran drove them past the reach of Black Hole's municipal street lights. The town was empty, everyone who wasn't huddled in bed at home having gone to Kat's bar. Once Kat took the wheel, they had a quarter mile of solid ground to cover before hitting Long Lake and the rutted entrance to the ice road. The deftness with which Kat eased the huge tires onto the treacherous surface told Hattori she probably was steady enough.

Adrenaline came in handy for clearing out drunkenness.

He admitted he wouldn't have wanted to be responsible for what came next. Between the mist of ice crystals in the air and the snow, they were approaching white-out conditions. His near-royal eyes could barely make out the distance their powerful headlights reached. The wind wailed around the truck eerily, joining the ice's uneasy song. In the warm cocoon of the cab, all their breathing came more quickly.

"Looks like everyone is off the road," Kat said. "Even the snowplows."

This had been their hope, so there'd be no chance of casualties but them.

Ciran shifted restlessly on the seat, now in the middle spot. When he spoke, Hattori sensed him working to steady his voice. "Where are you going to do it?"

"A half mile further. My instruments picked up a thinner stretch yesterday."

Hattori's heart commenced thudding in his chest. He'd been on risky ops before, so that wasn't his problem. His problem was that two of the few people he cared about in the world might lose their lives because of him. He'd assembled most of this mission's pieces. If he'd miscalculated and the other two paid the price, he wasn't certain he could go on.

Ignoring the fear reaction, he twisted around to detach a section of the cab's rear wall, revealing a slim hollow. Inside was a compact military submersible, flat at present, but capable of going three dimensional at the flip of a switch. Hattori had stolen it from an old contact who'd probably be court-martialed when it came up missing. Hattori regretted that, but hadn't dared leave a credit trail by trying to buy it honestly. In any case, even with Miry's funding, they couldn't have afforded anything near as good. The sub's technology was advanced—which didn't guarantee it would save their lives. That depended on Kat's knowledge of the ice and Fate.

For the first time in his life, he wished he knew a prayer to recite or someone to send it to. His hands were shaking as he pulled the submersible from its hiding place, laying it like a skimboard across their laps. Under its shadow, Ciran squeezed Hattori's thigh. It was a sign of Hattori's nerves that he welcomed the gesture.

"All right," Kat said. "I'm accelerating now."

Hattori knew why this was important. As the truck exceeded a certain speed, a wave would start to build up beneath the ice in front of the wheels, like a carpet pleating under a pushed weight. When the wave was big enough, the ice layer above it would burst, creating an opening for the cab to plunge through.

"Get the hammer ready," Kat said to Ciran, breathless now. "And the blood containers."

Kat must have sensed a change they could not. A second later, the ice made a noise Hattori never wanted to hear again, like a primeval monster being stabbed in the gut. The truck listed suddenly on one side, its frame shuddering.

"Brace," she gasped as the lake exploded in front of them.

They went under a good deal faster than he expected, their weight and acceleration catapulting them through the black water. The lights went out at the same time that the truck engine died, all its moving parts instantly frozen.

They drifted downward for a minute, then settled on the lakebed. If Hattori hadn't liked the noise of the ice before, he truly didn't relish the gurgling moans and crackles it let out as it refroze over them. Being underwater magnified every sound, and he had to grit his teeth to keep his response inside. He was more than a bit relieved when the electric torch he'd stashed under the seat agreed to light up. He checked the others' too-white faces, then set it on the dash facing them.

Fortunately for their purposes, they'd remained right side up and the cabin was indeed airtight. Without a word, they shoved the bench seat back to allow them more room to move. The submersible took five minutes to self-convert into its functioning shape. Hattori activated it and noted the time on his watch.

"We wait four minutes," he said. "Then Ciran takes the hammer to the windshield to make it look like we cracked our heads against it."

Ciran hissed out a curse. "That's assuming the safety glass lasts that long."

A tiny whining sent goose bumps prickling across his skin. He hadn't heard it initially, not above the clicking of the submersible's black ceramiskin carapace. A hairline fracture had appeared in the supposedly indestructible windshield. It had already crept six inches across the fogged surface.

"Shit," Hattori agreed, transfixed by the sight of the slowly lengthening fissure. A chill gripped his spine. Was that a bead of water seeping in from one end?

"It'll hold," Kat said. "I've seen safety shields survive cracks before."

She might have been lying, but her reassurance served its purpose. Hattori shook himself from his paralysis.

"I'm doing the blood," Ciran said, though strictly speaking it was early. He squirted it across the windshield and down the dash, one bottle for each of them. With the heater off and the icy lake all around them, the evidence of their "deaths" crystallized quickly. They'd drawn the blood from themselves over the last week, and it contained their DNA. The truck cab was too valuable to abandon. LAC Search and Recovery would try to winch it up. If they succeeded, local forensics would have something to identify.

When Ciran was satisfied with his artistry, he shoved the deflated bottles in his pocket. That done, Hattori checked the progress of the expanding submersible. The ringlike segments of its surface were three quarters erected.

"You could get in," he said to Kat.

She pulled a face but she wriggled around Ciran and bellied in. The sub was a long black ovoid, with a minimum of padding and a simple instrument panel in the nose. Hattori suspected it had been designed for illegal underwater espionage. The firms for at least two competing Houses were looking into the construction of submerged cities. But daimyo rivalries weren't his current concern. Instead, he noticed Kat peering at the dial on the hyper-compressed oxygen.

"This says it's full," she confirmed.

She looked shakier than before, her lips gone slightly blue from the increasing cold. Hattori didn't want to imagine what she was feeling. He hadn't forgotten she'd almost drowned in a lake before.

He didn't have time to comfort her. "Four minutes," he said to Ciran.

"You get in," Ciran responded, hefting the hammer.

Hattori climbed in and lay half atop their princess. Already the fit was tight. This was meant to be a two-man sub, and his height necessitated his knees be bent. He craned his neck to watch Ciran mentally gauging the force to use on the already cracked windshield. Hit it too hard, and he'd probably drown them. The torch was shining softly but directly into his face, his profile as sharp as if it had been chiseled. He caught his lower lip in his upper teeth. Its tremor made Hattori feel like he was invading his privacy.

"Four minute, thirty," Hattori said.

Ciran swung once, twice, three times in quick and powerful succession, aiming for the centers of his frozen bloodsplatter. A trio of spiderwebs appeared in the glass, two of them spurting water from larger holes. Ciran didn't need to be told to get into the submersible. He leapt in lightly, but was heavy enough for Kat's breath to whoof out of her. He pulled the lid over them and engaged the seal just as the truck gave a massive groan, some current causing it to tilt queasily toward one side.

"Crap," Kat said. "We better do this now."

She clicked her remote, and the driver's door blew open, inrushing water slamming them in the opposite direction. The small explosives in the hinges were a safety feature, though an overly optimistic one. Chances were, if a trucker had to use them, he'd simply die outside his cab instead it being his coffin.

To all their relief, the equalizing water pressure steadied the truck. Hattori shook the ringing from his ears as Kat wriggled out from under Ciran to ride his back instead. They were fortunate she was slender. With her mostly out of the way, Hattori could operate the controls.

"All yours, cap'n," Ciran said.

To Hattori's astonished ears, his tone was almost jaunty.

6: THROUGH THE JAWS

Now that she'd accomplished her part, there wasn't much for Kat to do aside from clinging to Ciran's back. She gave thanks she wasn't claustrophobic. She could only lift her head a few inches before it knocked the sub's disconcertingly flexible black skin. The material hardly seemed a sufficient barrier against the lake's dangers. There were rocks out there. Weeds waiting to strangle them. And who could forget the grumpy hibernating trout who'd resent being roused early?

When a laugh snorted out her nose—a tad hysterically, she admitted—Ciran squeezed the hand she'd wrapped underneath his chest.

"We're all right," he said. "Hattori knows what he's doing."

He seemed to. Almost too broad in the shoulder to fit beside Ciran, he was hunkered somewhat awkwardly on his elbows. His gaze was fastened on the enhanced sonar screen in the nose, his hands making quick adjustments to various controls. He'd told Kat earlier that both he and Ciran had memorized Long Lake's underwater topography. He'd meant to reassure her she'd get to safety no matter what, but she hardly liked the implication that either man might need a back up.

At least they'd made it this far. She was even warming up as their body heat filled the enclosed space. Her spine began to relax from its rigid state, and she let her face nuzzle Ciran's ear. Again, his fingers compressed hers comfortingly. It occurred to her that he was being far kinder than she would in his position.

She kissed his temple as a rush of gratitude swelled her heart. She didn't fight the emotion the way other royals would. Ciran deserved her thanks for being the man he was. In truth, he deserved her to love him too.

The thought had barely entered her mind when the mini-sub rotated without warning on its axis. She squeaked as Ciran's weight hit her body. Hers dropped onto his next, and a strident alarm went off. They spun around twice more before the dizzying motion stopped. Without thinking, Kat had flung a hand out to either wall.

"Sorry," Hattori panted, flipping a toggle to shut off the beeping. "Had to go around a curve. I think our weights need to be balanced."

Ciran didn't utter a word, just turned his head to give him a steely stare.

"Sorry," Hattori repeated more forcefully. "I've only driven this twice before."

Kat decided to pretend she hadn't heard that—any more than she'd seen the nervous sweat gleaming on his face. Afraid to move, she pulled her arms back in. Their winter jackets rustled as they wriggled into more stable positions.

"Try to slow your respiration," Hattori added. "Our oxygen will run out before our fuel."

"Wow," Ciran said, as snide as a character from the HFC. "That calms me down a lot."

Because his heart was beating more steadily than hers, Kat suspected his tone was meant to make her feel better. She peered between the men's heads toward the green viewscreen. A normal camera would have captured little in these black depths, but the sub's computer converted sonar data into images. She saw they'd entered a rocky trench, probably one of the fingers that led to Long Lake's northernmost reaches. Aquatic plants lined its ledges, not thickly, but enough to tighten her throat. Waving as they did in the current, they looked like spectral limbs beckoning them on.

"How much longer?" she couldn't help asking their driver.

"Until we run out of lake. So probably half an hour."

Half an hour was a ride on a palanquin. Kat was royal. Her nerves were hers to command. She told herself the time would pass like she was blinking.

◆

The next half hour was the longest of Kat's already eventful life. The alarm sounded twice more, for reasons Hattori either wasn't sharing or didn't know. The engine stalled when they accidentally sucked an adolescent trout into their intake, the loss of power temporarily shutting off airflow. Finally, they reached the spot Hattori had selected for their egress. He revved the engine, upped the draw on the power source, and rammed the ice above them.

The impact jarred her molars . . . and knocked a whole five inches off the thirty-inch ice layer.

"Okay," Hattori said. "I think we might have to do this a couple times."

Kat really, truly didn't want to know how much fuel remained.

However much there was, Hattori didn't hold back. He turned the dial to maximum for every one of his tries. On the fourth attempt, the sub shot out as if it were greased, sliding across the surface of the frozen lake like a puck from a shuttles game. This would have been great if they hadn't skidded onto a weaker patch. The mini-sub broke through it while Kat was clambering out. Frigid water poured over the open edge on the men. Luckily, the bottom was close enough to stand. Hattori and Ciran cursed but managed to pull themselves from the jagged hole.

"Don't let it sink!" Kat cried as the sub tipped behind them. "The lake's too shallow here. Someone might spot it."

"Stay," Hattori barked when she would have dashed to grab it herself.

She hadn't been able to bear the thought of their risk coming to nothing, but watching the men drench themselves as they wrestled out the ultralight wasn't her idea of fun. She wrung her hands so hard as they struggled that she nearly broke her fingers.

At last, they and the sub were on the lake shore. This area was past the tree line and into the tundra. The blizzard still raged around them, which would be good for covering their tracks if search parties flew over later in aircars.

The storm was less convenient when it came to figuring out where they were. Hattori had a global locator, which tended not to give accurate readings anywhere near the pole. As he turned this way and that, trying to get a fix, Kat closed her eyes. If she quieted her mind, she might retrieve aerial photographs she'd seen of this region.

"That way," she and Ciran said together.

Since they were pointing in the same direction, that way it was.

The large outcrop they wanted loomed out of the gale forty shivering minutes later. The rocks would provide shelter, in addition to hiding them. Though she hadn't suffered a dunking, icicles from the water vapor in her breath circled her fur-lined hood the same as the men's. The snow had drifted to their knees in places, forcing them to slog through it. Kat knew all of them were exhausted.

"This'll do," Hattori said, the clenching of his teeth from the cold making him a challenge to understand. "We can rest before we go on."

Kat didn't entirely fight back her groan at the idea of *going on*. "I know," she said when Hattori glanced at her. "We need to get as far as we can before we lose the dark."

He might have smiled. It was hard to tell with no light apart from the blue LEDs that were sewn, front and back, into their coat collars. Though the glimmers they emitted weren't bright, they helped them keep track of each other in the low visibility.

Without speaking further, Hattori jammed the ultralight they'd dragged with them into a snow bank, to serve as a windbreak. Then he and Ciran unzipped their jackets, not because they were crazy, but because the garments were designed to be unfolded and reassembled into a weatherproof pup tent. Once the shelter was up, Kat shook the snow off her jacket and crawled with it inside. The men came after, stiffer than she was from the cold. They had room—barely—to sit up and tug off their boots, which they put in a special pocket that would thaw them out without leaving big puddles.

The men stripped down to their thermal underwear, tucking their wet outer garments into more heat filament-lined pockets. The aroma of sweaty Yama expanded through the tent, a smell Kat discovered she didn't mind at all. In truth, it was comforting. She'd grown accustomed to both the men's chemistry.

"Ciran in the middle," she said when they would have put her there. "He got the wettest of both of you."

He was also thinner than Hattori, as well as lacking the advantage of the bigger guard's super recuperative royal genes. Blue-lipped and shuddering, he didn't protest as they covered him in her coat and pressed up against him to either side. Small solar-powered disks affixed to the walls provided enough light to see by.

"I th-think my n-nuts have shrunk inside my b-body," Ciran chattered out.

Hattori smiled and kissed his forehead, something Kat hadn't seen him do in a while.

"W-wouldn't mind a b-better kiss than that," Ciran quipped.

Hattori snorted and hugged him closer. "You'd break my teeth with your shivers."

Ciran's bravado wasn't fooling Kat. The chill of his flesh seeped into her everywhere. Too concerned for his well being to be self-conscious, she slid her hand into the waist of his thermal pants. This, of all places on his body, should have been warm. Worryingly, his groin was cool when she cupped it.

"G-good Lord," Ciran said, startling her with the Human curse. "Do you really think now's the time?"

"I don't care," she retorted, curving her fingers deeper between his legs. Ciran jerked but not away. "I'll get your blood circulating any way I can."

♦

Ciran could scarcely feel Kat's hand, which—considering what it was rubbing—was fairly strange. He did feel her breathing, wafting warmly behind his neck. Without analyzing why he wanted to, he turned around to face her instead of Hattori.

Her eyes rounded before he kissed her. Her lips were soft, her tongue hesitant but warm. He pushed his cold face to hers, urging her to respond, a muffled groan breaking in his chest. She caught her breath, then opened her mouth to him.

Liquid excitement rolled through his veins, the unexpected wave slow but sensual. His skin burned and tingled as it woke up. He kissed her harder, deeper, and the flesh she'd been so gently massaging began to swell—not just his cock but his balls enlarging.

He moaned, unable to hold in the sound. It had been too long since anyone had touched him, certainly too long for the needs he had. He supposed he could have masturbated. Watching, or even just knowing, that Kat and Hattori were going at it had excited him plenty. He'd refrained because taking care of himself had seemed humiliating . . . or maybe he'd wanted to be a martyr.

Whatever his reason, Kat's slow tight strokes were very welcome. He'd forgotten how strong her hands were, how she liked to pull and squeeze the parts she caressed. He had to leave off kissing her to gulp for air. In less time than he'd thought possible, she'd tugged him to the edge.

He drove his hands underneath her thermal shirt, loving the tightness of her nipples and the velvety sleekness of her breasts. She squirmed slightly in his hold, her own gasp soft but audible as her lips parted. Her thick-lashed eyes were open, her widened gaze locked to his. Her shining pupils were noticeably enlarged. They'd probably been nose to nose like this before, but he didn't remember it feeling so intimate.

There was a bond between them, apart from what they each shared separately with Hattori—a bond neither had acknowledged openly. Ciran loved that her hand was hidden inside his clothing, loved too, that the motion of her elbow said exactly what she was doing. The charm of simultaneously flaunting and keeping secrets was heightened by Hattori's cudgel of an erection throbbing behind his ass. He knew Kat could hear the shallowness of Hattori's breathing as easily as he. The confines of the tent magnified it deliciously. Her eyes flicked to the other man for a moment, then returned to Ciran.

"Faster?" she suggested, arousal making the word a rasp.

Ciran shook his head. "Put your other hand in there instead."

He could have asked Hattori to help out, but that wasn't what he wanted. His head jerked back against Hattori's shoulder as Kat did what he'd requested, his breath hissing with pleasure. The fingers of her second hand squeezed his testicles, the pressure she used skirting a perfect hairsbreadth away from pain. The sensation was a tightrope his former patrons had liked to walk. In their daimyo arrogance, they'd hardly cared if he enjoyed it—which he had scars to prove. That Kat knew she aroused him was betrayed by her now dark eyes.

She wanted to give him a thrill she thought Hattori wouldn't have a taste for.

This was a secret she was only sharing with him. In fact, this was a secret she might not have known herself. What they were doing wasn't considerate, and they both were reveling in it.

He wanted it to last forever: his arousal, Kat's, excluding Hattori from their play. Kat kissed his Adam's apple and made him shiver. Her hand dragged upward, palm surrounding and compressing his increasingly slippery glans. When she twisted that grip around him, right on the cap, tiny sparks shot up his urethra. Obliged to fight back his orgasm, he bit his lip and tightened his thigh muscles. Her eyes were on his again, drinking in his reactions. Ciran understood perfectly. He was afraid to blink, in case he missed something. Her grip released, her hand sliding down his thudding shaft. He was full to bursting, and her fingers ringed his base tightly. She pulled the cinch halfway up and then pushed down slowly. Again she did this, and yet again, curtailing the action at his midpoint, until every one of the nerves higher in his penis wept for her attention.

"If there were room," she whispered, sending hot chills streaking from his ear to his spine, "I'd squirm down your body and suck you off."

She did him in with her words. Well, that and the way her stroke abruptly squeezed up him all the way. Royal blood did more than give her a killer grip, it also increased her speed. She pumped him top to bottom, swift and hard, sensations sharp enough to scream over powering through his groin. He didn't scream, but he came in licks of lightning, the heat and force of his seed searing his still cooler than normal cock. He gasped at the intensity of his bliss as it shot from him. Relief he'd expected; relief this lengthy and cathartic, not as much.

She must have guessed how much he liked it. Her hand milked the contractions skillfully out of him. Finally, his erection began to flag and her grip loosened, her strokes caressing him gently now. The continued rubbing felt a bit too good. If she didn't stop, she'd bring him up again.

With some shock, he realized he must have gripped her when he climaxed. His fingertips were digging into her breasts, surely too tight for comfort. Ciran had been a pillow boy. He was accustomed to being the best lover in the room, the one who put everyone else's pleasure before his own. For the first time he could recall, someone had made him forget himself.

"Sorry," he said to Kat, forcing his hold to ease.

She gave him a feline smile, perhaps suspecting he wasn't truly remorseful. "Want another?" she offered.

His lingering erection tingled at the idea. He kissed her deeply, slowly, only pulling back when her heart rate picked up beneath his palm.

"I'd like to, princess," he murmured, lips brushing hers, "but coming that hard takes energy. For all our sakes, I think I'd better conserve my strength."

Her blush of response delighted him: that he could inspire it, and with no more than a compliment.

"Later then," she whispered shyly, which made him just plain grin.

"Well," Hattori said from behind him, his body stiffer than his studiedly casual voice. "Now that we're all warmed up, maybe we could sleep for a while."

Still smiling, Ciran pulled Hattori's arm close around his chest. If Hattori had more to say, Ciran didn't hear it. Two seconds after he closed his eyes, the former pillow boy sank into dreamland.

Though it wasn't the least bit true, he felt absolutely safe in that little tent with the storm blowing all around them.

◆

Guards and royals could travel fast, but a hundred miles in blizzard conditions was still a lot of ground to cover. The only living beings they encountered were a shaggy herd of elk, which they only noticed because the animals broke into thundering run.

Other than that, they seemed to have gotten away clear.

"Should have bought those maglev skis," Ciran grumbled midway through the third night.

Kat agreed, but there was no point in saying so. Plus, she was too tired to spare the breath. The storm system they'd been fighting for most of their journey was abating, but the snow it left behind was difficult to traverse. Add to that the thinness of the air at this altitude, and Kat was ready to drop. Only the knowledge that the men would halt if she did stopped her from giving in.

"Skis would have looked suspicious, and the maglev might not have worked anyway." Hattori's weary response came from behind her, since he was guarding their back trail. "I spent Miry Oryan's money on food instead."

The food was what every trucker kept in his glovebox: high energy, high protein snacks. Her cousin Jules Feng's father owned the firm that manufactured them. Every time Kat tore into the Gold Star wrapper, she recalled her summer with the sisters in Ningzha. Back then, she'd had no idea how complicated her life would get. Jules was the only member of the trio who'd kept in touch, in part because her husband—a savvy business mogul and unusually open-minded prince—provided her the means to occasionally smuggle a note to Kat on the sly. Last she'd heard, Jules was pregnant—always good news to a people who had trouble conceiving. The middle sister, Jade, was also mated, though less happily. Joy, the youngest, had held onto her ebullient ways. To her mother's horror, she'd become a holovid actress, specializing in impersonating Humans on the HFC. Jules claimed her littlest sister was talented, though—due to the scandalous nature of Joy's choice—she couldn't express her pride to anyone but her mate and Kat.

If word had reached them that she'd died, Kat hoped they weren't too upset.

"You all right?" Hattori asked from a few paces behind her. "We could rest if you need to."

They were crossing a broad plateau, their footsteps filling slowly behind them in the tapering snowfall. Leaving a trail didn't matter so much this far from Black Hole. They'd spotted a road to their east earlier, its presence given away by a lonely pair of headlights. The distance had been too great to make out what the vehicle was—besides a sign that they must be nearing their goal.

"I'd rather keep going," Kat said in answer to Hattori's question. "If you two don't mind."

In the lead, Ciran shook his head. Possibly tired of traveling single file, Hattori lengthened his strides to fall in by her.

"Haro used to love the snow," he said unexpectedly. "When we were growing up in the state rearing center, he'd drag me out of my cot in the middle of the night. We'd sneak past the guards and wander the city, watching it fall."

"I expect he's had his fill of snow lately," Ciran said.

"I expect," Hattori agreed.

Kat looked at him. His handsome face was calm, if a bit distant. He'd barely spoken of his brother since revealing that he had one.

Wondering if she should have encouraged him to talk more, she reached out to squeeze his gloved hand. He accepted her comfort for a few seconds, then let go of the hold.

She wasn't insulted. Many Yama wouldn't have allowed the touch at all.

"I can't imagine having a twin," she said. "My cousins were the closest I came to siblings."

To her surprise, Hattori laid his hand behind her shoulder, as if she were the one in need of soothing. "Sometimes," he said, "it's like being two people at the same time, as if your heart is beating in two bodies."

Kat had the oddest flash of knowing how that was.

A moment later, they bumped into Ciran, who'd halted ahead of them.

"I think I see lights," he said.

Now that he'd pointed it out, there *was* a glow on the horizon, the hint of acidity in its color suggesting the source was manmade. Kat's adrenaline surged, proving she wasn't completely done in.

"That's got to be it," Hattori said quietly.

They continued on toward the glow, silent but for the crunch of their boots through the snow layer. Kat suspected none of them knew what to say. They'd heard rumors of what they'd be up against, mostly stories to scare children. Even for the guards, who had a network to tap into, facts concerning their destination were challenging to come by. Now, at last, they'd see for themselves.

In her imagination, Kat had pictured Winter Prison as a fortress atop a hill, like a Human castle from one of their fairytales. Her breath caught in her throat as a valley and not a mountain opened before them.

The prison that sat in the bowl of land was a huge star-shaped structure with stark gray walls and snow-whitened roofs. A modest city had collected around the complex, reminding Kat of remora cozying up to a shark. Metropolis notwithstanding, by far the brightest illumination belonged to the institution whose defenses they'd come to penetrate. Blinding floodlights turned the empty exercise yards to day. Kat spied the glint of razor wire and weaponized lasers. In addition to this automated artillery, dozens upon dozens of armed guards patrolled the ramparts. In groups of five and six, they moved in black ant lines against the snow's white backdrop.

She was certain they wore the full complement of body armor—no doubt the latest version Yamish technology could devise.

She didn't have to look at her companions to know they were wondering how in Infinity they were supposed to get past all that. Even imagining they could, finding Hattori's brother among the prison population would be a task. A facility this size might house fifty thousand, or even twice that amount.

She'd had no idea their government had so many enemies.

"Well," Ciran said, feet spread wide and hands planted on his waist. "We've got our work cut out for us."

Hattori let out a sound that could have been a kind of laugh. If it was, it wasn't a happy one. His fist was pressed to his jacket in front of his diaphragm, very much like he'd been kicked there. Clearly, he hadn't been prepared for this.

No matter how stealthy he and Ciran were, they weren't breaking into that jail.

Kat had grown used to thinking of the men as unstoppable. Their stupefaction sparked the seed of an idea, necessity activating her royal intelligence. She closed her eyes and let that first spark call to another. She breathed slowly, smoothly, shutting out the world and trying to think of nothing while the deeper part of her mind— the part that wasn't conscious—organized her brainpower.

When she opened her eyes, her thoughts practically tingled in her brain. She knew she nearly had all of it.

"The front door," she said. "That's our only point of entry."

"O-kay," Ciran acknowledged, the pause in the word suggesting he might have bitten back a less polite response. "Any clue how we open it?"

"We get invited," she said, knowing her smile must seem ridiculous to the men. "And once we do, we have Haro delivered to us."

7: PRISONVILLE

The small snowbound metropolis that had grown up around the prison was known, appropriately enough, as Prisonville. Its name appeared on no maps—no more than the penitentiary's did. Winter Prison was designed for incarcerating "sensitive" prisoners, Yama whose crimes might embarrass important people if their details became public. Those trapped within its walls had, in most cases, been sentenced without a trial.

Not that Yamish trials necessarily resulted in justice.

From what Hattori could tell, the inhabitants of Prisonville were aware of this. They either worked at the secure facility or their livelihoods were inextricably tied to it. Young and old, they were a cynical lot, wryly mocking the inequities they saw around them . . . without the least intention of lifting a finger in protest. Then again, why should they? None of the power here belonged to them. As everywhere else, daimyo ruled Prisonville.

At Kat's insistence, they rented a four-seat snowskip from a shady looking vendor on the edge of town. Their bedraggled appearance didn't cause the bored clerk to bat an eye. Hattori inadvertently sucked air between his teeth when Kat pulled out a shiny black debit chip to pay. Fortunately, that early in the morning the clerk was sleepy as well as bored. Despite Hattori's reaction, he probably forgot their existence two minutes after their departure.

"That chip links to an untraceable account," Kat explained once the skip's titanium skis were skimming with breathtaking swiftness along a drab snow-filled street. She was behind the controls, having had previous experience with the elitist toy. She certainly looked at home with the icy wind blowing back her hair, once more a rosy cheeked female scion of privilege. Ciran lounged in the back behind the second windshield, seeming to enjoy the ride. Perhaps sensing Hattori's judgment, though not taking it seriously, Kat shot a twinkling glance his way. "The account the chip draws on is my secret pin money from before I was exiled. Trust me, Miry isn't the only Shinobi who can hide a financial trail."

"We have funds left," Hattori said, imperfectly masking his annoyance.

"Not enough for what I'm planning," she returned pleasantly.

With the unerring instincts all royals seemed to possess, she took no more than ten minutes to find the unfamiliar city's priciest hotel. Hattori supposed aristocrats had to sleep somewhere when they came to ensure the skeletons in their closets remained locked up. Though the Royal Arms didn't compare to to their palaces, it would do. Six stories tall and narrow, its front was smooth gray granite, the painted dragon frames on its snow-heaped windows both gaudy and weatherworn. Kat parked the skip like a crazy woman, slewing its nose onto the plascrete pavement under the lucky red awning.

"Don't scratch it," she instructed the surprised valet she tossed the keys to.

Hattori and Ciran were left to trail behind her as she strode, head high and nose in the air, to the small registration desk. One regal toss of her head made her travel stained jacket seem as elegant as mink.

Ciran chuckled softly under his breath. "This ought to be good."

Hattori was glad someone thought so.

"Give us your best suite," Kat ordered. She slapped her black debit tile on the polished counter, the single diamond in its center winking haughtily. That and its color identified it as a chip for a large account. "I don't care about the view as long as the bed is big."

The hotel employee's gaze flicked over the men. That he assumed they were Kat's subordinate lovers showed in his expression in subtle insulting ways.

"As you wish, Princess . . . Mahalawi," he said as the chip relayed her assumed name and presumably hefty balance to his data screen. "I believe our Emerald Suite is ready for visitors."

"We'll need a shopper," she tossed over her shoulder, already sweeping away. "Have one knock in an hour."

She didn't bother saying "please" or "if it would be convenient"—nor would the clerk expect her to. Nothing was inconvenient when it came to servicing royals.

The aged bellhop, his hair gone gray beneath his beaded silk skullcap, barely kept up with Kat's long-legged stride. He was lucky they had no luggage for him to haul.

"Tip the man," Kat said after the staffer opened the door. "And get us a chip key."

The chip key would save their thumbprints from going into the hotel's computer. In spite of Hattori's appreciation for her foresight, he bristled as he dug into an inner pocket for a few silver coins from their cash reserve. If the tip amount wasn't appropriate, the bellhop didn't complain. He bowed and retreated without a word.

In the short time this took to see to, Kat had disappeared into the bathing chamber. The sound of running water and the smell of bath salts told him what she was up to.

Ciran drew his attention with a soft laugh. "If you could see your face . . . She's putting it on, Hattori. She hasn't suddenly turned into a snow princess."

"I know that," Hattori said crossly. "She just slips into royal mode a little too easily."

"Proletarian snob," Ciran teased and began to remove his coat. "Why don't you join her? You'll feel better once you're both back to usual."

Ciran didn't seem upset, but Hattori narrowed his eyes at him. What did he mean by *back to usual*? Did he think that first night in the tent was an anomaly?

"You could join her too," he said, irritated by how hard it was not to sound grudging. "I know she meant what she said in Black Hole."

Ciran shrugged equably. "Someone has to wait for the shopper. If you two aren't out by then, I'm pretty sure I know what we need."

Hattori knew what he needed, and it wasn't falling in with Kat's risky plan. Regrettably, her idea was the closest they had to a workable strategy.

"Go on," Ciran said, shooing him. "Our princess might need someone to scrub her back."

Hattori opened his mouth, drew breath, but couldn't decide what he wanted to object to. He clamped his jaw shut instead. If Ciran wanted to shove him and Kat together, who was he to stop him?

♦

Too relaxed to move a muscle, Kat lazed like an empress in a bathing chamber that did its best to live up to the Emerald Suite's color theme. The slipper tub was vibrant green glass with inset heat filaments. Also green, a dazzling gloss lacquered the walls and the drying tube. Kat floated up to her neck in steaming hot perfumed water. The only sound was the drip, drip, drip of the 24-karat plated faucet and her own pleasured sighs. Perhaps it was shallow to have missed these luxuries, but it was nice to feel like a proper royal again.

Given that she hadn't wallowed like one in years, it was difficult to lift her eyelids when the chamber door opened.

Her visitor was Hattori, looking beautifully sulky even as he tried to seem impassive. He wore his creased traveling trousers and a thermal undershirt with the sleeves pushed up. Even in that humble garb, he was more attractive to her than a hundred jeweled princes. His amazement at her opulent surroundings was harder to conceal than his poor temper. Despite the hotel's shortcomings in other areas, management had splurged on the baths. Hattori's wondering gaze traveled from the green onyx floor to the golden fixtures, to the rock crystal chandelier that glinted softly down on her submerged body. She tried not to be insulted that for once her nakedness didn't have his full attention. Jaw agape, he finally dropped to the ivory footstool beside the tub.

"Are these real pearls?" he asked, running a finger along the fancy trim.

"Darling, in a second-rate outpost like this, I'm sure they're just cultured."

His dismay at her superior manner was so blatant she had to laugh. "Poor thing," she cooed, amused. "You really don't like seeing me play princess."

A scowl fought to make its way into his expression. "You and Ciran know me too well."

"*So* sorry. We must care about you too much not to guess what you're feeling."

Her mock sympathy caused the corner of his mouth to twitch, though his response seemed at least partly serious. "I don't think it's possible for you to care about me too much."

"You could join me," she suggested, one wet finger trailing up his strong forearm. "I could demonstrate how much I care close up. I know this sort of excess is a symbol of the repressive class, but these bath salts have made me all smooth and silky. It'd be a shame not to share that with the less privileged."

She supposed she'd laid it on too thick. Hattori rolled his eyes at her.

"Please?" she added in her most dulcet tone.

She had him then. "I thought you'd forgotten that word," he came back, peeling his thermal shirt up his fine torso.

The shifting of the muscles in his chest and arms were worth admiring. She did so until he stood and shoved down his trousers, his smile faint but aware of the effect his unveiling had. As he straightened, he was half erect—or half erect for him. His cock projected out horizontal from its exotic nest of curls, bouncing just a bit from his blood's pressure. Its skin was flushed and full-veined, its cap shiny. Impressed, and not wanting to spoil the moment, Kat tried not to laugh at the way he stepped into the steaming tub.

His movements were as careful as if the water were a vat of acid. Once his feet were placed beside her ankles, he supported himself above her on rigid arms. She noticed his erection was still stretching, thankfully undaunted by his concerns. One clear droplet welled from its slit.

Possibly no amount of awkwardness could prevent him from wanting sex with her.

"The water's going to overflow if I get in," he warned.

"There's a drain in the floor," she told him, feeling strangely protective because he didn't know. A life spent going straight from a rearing center into the guards was unlikely to include many creature comforts—not beyond what Ciran offered him, anyway. "You won't damage anything if it floods."

His knuckles whitened on the sides of the tub. "Maybe we should call Ciran in. He's used to this sort of thing. I've never been in a bath before."

All his insecurity was in the rueful words—not only about their disparate socioeconomic levels, but over the possible new developments between her and Ciran. Kat could tell he didn't want to be jealous. The way he fought what he must have thought a smallness in his spirit made her love him more than she could explain. Her secret pleasure at his jealousy she kept to herself. She shouldn't have needed it to prove he loved her.

Of course, she also shouldn't have left a handsome man in his state of readiness hanging.

"Let me show you how wonderful a bath can be," she purred.

The huskiness of her words did more to assuage his pride than anything. He sank to her, and half the scented water spilled out in one great wave.

The kiss he pressed on her was as heavenly as the bath. This was a luxury too: his taste, his breathing, the quickened thudding of his heart as her hands slid over his big body. She knew he loved her touching him. The caring she put into her caresses soothed more than his feelings. He shifted in the water, bringing the ripe tip of his erection to the soft meeting of her folds. That part of him was full and silky as it pulsed against her just there. The tantalizing touch on her clitoris pulled more sound from her.

"I love when you sigh for me," he murmured.

His hips canted forward, pushing his erection into her entrance, slow and easy. Her sigh transmuted into a moan. The gliding penetration took forever. Her neck arched, his length and thickness filling her in delectable increments. When he was completely in with his pelvis pressed hard to hers, she locked her calves behind his clenched bottom.

He was hers, and she was his—no matter if neither of them could be perfect.

"I love you," she said, and his eyes went momentarily all-black.

If he'd been a prince, this could have been a mating sign. As a pleasure reaction, inspiring it still felt marvelous.

"Kat," he said, his hand sliding down her side to get a grip on her thigh. His dark gaze searched his. "Don't ever stop saying that."

She would have laughed, except he was moving, rocking his long thick shaft smoothly in and out. He started gently, but that could only last so long. Both their sensual natures tended to impatience. Mere minutes passed before he was ramming into her.

"Too much?" he gasped—all he could get out.

She shook her head in quick negation and held onto him tighter. His thrusts were jabs of longing, his expression starting to twist. She loved how that made her feel but didn't want him to suffer, not when giving him what she thought he needed was so easy. The oil in the water made it simple to push two fingers into him from behind. He groaned, loud and grateful, as she found the little gland that piggybacked his prostate.

His kingmaster felt swollen, hotter than normal as she rubbed it through the smooth wall of his passage. He shivered, threw back his head, and came without spilling. The dry peak didn't satisfy him; the opposite, in fact. His hips hammered her so energetically in his climax's wake that she came twice in quick succession.

That rather shredded her control.

Feeling like she had to come again or die, she drove her pussy frantically up him until they both cried out at the concentration of wonderful sensations. His diamond hardness was a marvel she'd never get enough of.

"Yes," he snarled, his left hand clamped on her bottom while the right threatened to crack the tub with his grip on the rim. To her delight, he used that hold to lever into her harder. "Open for me, Kat. I want to fuck you up to your heart. Take me all the way into you."

She splayed one leg out of the tub to do it, which made him gasp for air and pump fervently. The water churned at his movements, somehow exciting her even more. She had just enough presence of mind to push harder over his kingmaster, to rub its whole length and width with her fingertips. The little bulge throbbed wildly under the pressure, Hattori grunted, his body going fevered all over.

"Fuck," he said. "More of that. More—"

He broke off and came again with a desperate sound, throwing his whole body into it. This was the big one for him. His thigh muscles were steel bands as he drove his cock inward to its very end and hers. The deep internal pressure was an uncontrollable switch for her. Fireworks exploded from her nerves, rolling out from her core in waves. She clamped on his hardness, crying out as her body worked itself over him, driven by needs she only half understood. He was the male for her, the conqueror her body had been born to accept. She couldn't even want to fight the match. The paroxysm he brought her to was sweetly violent, every involuntary ripple carrying its own dark pleasure.

Both of them were panting as the climax trailed into shimmering afterglow.

Hattori sighed and sank down on her, his brow resting on the pearl-lined rim of the tub as her trembling fingers combed through his hair. She pushed higher so his cheek could lie on her breast. That also made him sigh, though almost silently this time.

"Still sweet," he said sleepily, his words fanning her tight left nipple.

Kat indulged in a wry private smile, able to trace the compliment to its cause. Apparently, he thought princesses and sweetness were mutually exclusive.

"Sorry," he said, so maybe she and Ciran weren't the only ones with deductive powers. "I know it shouldn't bother me that you like nice things."

"I can't help where I come from, or that it will always be part of me."

"Neither can I."

Her hand paused in its slow petting of his head. "That's true," she said, her surprise that he had a point audible even to herself. "I guess we are who we are unless we decide to change."

"You don't need to change. I know you're not some snow princess who doesn't care about small folk."

Emotion pricked hot behind her eyes, evidence of how much she valued his good opinion. "Glad to hear it," she said lightly. "Not that you're small in any way."

She felt his grin stretch his face. Sometimes men were so simple. Since he was feeling pleased with himself, Kat decided it was safe to bring up what she'd observed. "You didn't ejaculate tonight. Is everything all right?"

"Fine," was his sleepy answer. "I don't think it's heat, if that's what you're concerned about. Sometimes my reactions are off kilter."

Kat was glad to hear it. Him going into heat on the verge of rescuing his brother would have been incredibly bad timing. Her hand slipped down to his shoulder, where it took less effort pet him.

"I should be fine for the mission," he added.

The nape of Kat's neck tensed. "You know you can't come inside with us, right? You looking just like your twin could give the game away."

The water sloshed as he sat up and stared at her. She didn't like that she'd surprised him. "Haro and I aren't identical."

"Even so, there must be a strong resemblance. Ciran and I need to go alone."

"No," he said and set his jaw stubbornly.

"What if something goes wrong? We'll need someone on the outside to rescue us."

"That's crap, Kat. Neither of you can—"

Ciran stuck his head in the door. "Watch the volume, you two. No need for the whole hotel to know why we're here."

Hattori flushed and lowered his voice. "I can go in disguise."

"And *that* wouldn't be suspicious."

"Kat."

"Hattori. We're talking about Imperial security. The sort of disguise we could scrape together would show up on their scans."

"She's right," Ciran said, causing Hattori to glare at him. "Your resemblance to Haro is stronger without your birthmark. You'll be more useful as backup."

"You be backup," he retorted belligerently. "I'm the best fighter."

"Kat's scheme depends on deception. Of the three of us, you're not even the second best liar."

Hattori's eyes shot daggers, though Kat suspected Ciran didn't consider his lesser talent in mendaciousness a flaw. Hattori opened his mouth to speak.

"I trust Ciran," she interrupted before he could argue. "For this particular purpose, I trust him more than you."

Hattori's eyes actually welled up, which truly made her want to apologize. She held back with an effort. The odds against them were long enough. Their survival depended on making non-emotional choices.

"I can lie," he insisted. She and Ciran raised their eyebrows in unison. Seeing this, Hattori's breath gusted out. "Fine. You two have more practice pretending not to feel what you do, which means you'll understand if *I* don't pretend I'm happy."

♦

Kat and Hattori remained in the bathing chamber after Ciran withdrew. They made love once more, very gently, almost all the way through. As sated then as they ever got, they pulled themselves out of the water with matching sighs.

Kat noticed Hattori forgot to be offended by the decadent pre-warmed silk guest robes.

When they emerged into the sitting room of the suite, they saw Ciran had ordered dinner from the hotel kitchen. A table had been set up, with a crisp white cloth and electric candles flickering prettily on it. Attired in his own silk robe, Ciran stood beside the display. He was elegant from head to toe, his bladelike features lending him an air of danger. If he'd still been a pillow boy, and she'd still been her old self, she'd have been tempted to hire him. He smiled faintly at her and Hattori, his expression as smooth as glass otherwise.

This is how he looks when he's hurt, Kat realized, and a second later: *We have to stop doing this to him.*

"Elk steaks," he said, lifting one of the domed black lids. Heat coils glowed in its inner curve. "I gave our sizes to the shopper. She seemed competent. I expect she'll find what we need."

Hattori's stomach rumbled as the smell of seared meat reached them. "Thank you," he said with more sincerity than he usually allowed to sound in his voice. "For everything."

Ciran looked at his friend, a wordless message passing between them. Hattori's fingers were linked with Kat's, but she didn't squeeze them. Let him focus on Ciran. Hattori had already given her more love than she'd dared hope for.

"No problem," Ciran said after the slight pause. "I imagine we're all sick of meal bars."

"Heartily," Hattori agreed.

They took their seats around the festive table. They were used to eating together. Kat shouldn't have been surprised if they did it comfortably today. But maybe surprise wasn't her emotion. Maybe she was recognizing how precious that comfort was.

Kat loved her father. She knew that even when he'd thought she'd tried to poison her younger sister, part of him still loved her. The rest of him was an old-fashioned Yama. He prized emotional dignity and control. One of the reasons she'd treasured her birthday teas was because, for that one meal, he'd let her see what was in his heart. *Your mother would want me to*, he'd say. Without Katrini Shinobi's memory between them, their interactions were both stilted and built on sand. Hattori and Ciran hadn't known her nearly as long, but she couldn't imagine either believing she'd murder an innocent girl for gain.

"You two are more my family than my family," she burst out.

The men turned their eyes to her. Hattori enveloped her hand in his. Understanding shone liquid in his gaze. The connection was as intimate as any they'd shared in bed.

Ciran was the first to lift his fork again. "As long as you're not thinking of us as brothers," he said dryly.

♦

Ever since they'd left Black Hole, the three of them had been traveling at night and sleeping during the day. It wasn't possible to reverse that pattern without effort. Because of this, they were dragging by the time they let themselves fall into the prince-size bed. Then, just a few hours later, Kat's body jerked awake. She lay on her right side, as did Ciran in front of her. The knuckles of her left hand rested on the silky skin of his back, as if she'd reached out to him in sleep. Behind her, the wall of heat she'd grown used to sheltering her was missing.

She pulled her touch away from Ciran, her sleep-fogged mind trying to decide how she should react.

"He's in the sitting room," Ciran said, his voice not sleepy at all. He rolled onto his back, his head turning toward her on the pillow. "I checked on him a little while ago. He was staring out the window, but he seemed all right."

Hattori was probably thinking about tomorrow, about whether he'd see his long lost brother or perhaps lose them. Kat didn't like the idea of him standing out there alone but hesitated to insult Ciran by suggesting she should check on him as well. In the end, she settled for stalling.

"I didn't hear you get up," she said.

Ciran rolled onto his side and touched her mouth with his fingertips. Their faces were a hand span apart. The glow from the Royal Arms sign shone through the window, revealing the motionless perfection of his features. "You were sleeping too hard to wake. You put your hand on me when I crawled back in. It was nice."

Her breathing changed. She didn't mean it to, any more than she meant her sex to go wet. Her left hand twitched, remembering how he'd felt beneath it: not just his back but the hot fullness of his cock.

Ciran was too observant not to notice her reaction. He smiled, slow but clear. "Thank you for that, princess."

"I'm not trying to complicate what's between us," she blurted out.

"Neither am I. No sensible man could mind you responding to him like that."

His flattery sounded as smooth and meaningless as any former pillow boy's might be expected to. Kat would have thought him unaffected were it not for the pulse she noticed throbbing between his collarbones. The telltale sign—and the absence of any other—made her wonder how often he'd hid his interest in having sex with her. She hadn't thought it possible for him to want her as strongly as he did Hattori. If he did, Hattori's preference for keeping her to himself must have been more uncomfortable than she'd known.

She didn't know what to say. Everything she could conceive of struck her as wrong. They stared at each other from their separate pillows: him calm and worldly, her feeling a smidgen gauche. In the end, Ciran took pity on her and spoke.

"I'm not sure how upset Hattori is," he said, shifting to a topic he must have thought safer. "I doubt I'll ever completely understand his bond with his twin. Perhaps you can. You treated your cousins with more affection than most Yama do their siblings."

"It's true I care for them, but I never felt what Hattori described to me: as if my heart were split between two bodies. Maybe ordinary Yama don't have that capacity."

"Maybe." Ciran's gaze was thoughtful. "I knew them both for a few months, before Haro was arrested. Watching them together could be unnerving. They'd walk in synchrony with each other, would mirror each other's posture and say words at the same time. When they fought as a team, no one could defeat them. Hattori told me they often shared thoughts as well."

A hint of wistfulness tinged his tone. It wasn't hard to guess Ciran wished he could read his friend's mind. That he also feared he wouldn't enjoy knowing what was in it was just as obvious.

Kat touched him, fingers squeezing warmth into his bicep as she tried to choose her words wisely. "Ciran, I'm not convinced what Hattori feels for you isn't serious. He may care more than he's aware of."

Ciran grimaced, perhaps doubting what she'd said or maybe in self deprecation of his wish to believe. "I know he cares, but not like he does for you. He needs you, and I want him to be happy. However much I . . . wish I meant more to him, I'll always be thankful our paths crossed. Before I met him, I was a daimyo's toy and then a daimyo's killer. Knowing Hattori made me more than most Yama get to be."

"You mean a person who loves another more than himself."

Ciran didn't deny it. "What I feel for Hattori is the closest I've come to understanding what family is."

She wondered if he realized she'd said nearly the same thing— that he and Hattori were more her family than her family was. Whether he did or not, he'd moved her. She kissed his brow and pushed off the heaped covers.

"I'm going to get him," she said as he looked at her questioningly. "We all need to sleep tonight. That's something we do better together."

8: WINTER PRISON

Reliable information about Winter Prison was hard to come by. Fortunately, nowhere in the Yamish world were bribes refused utterly, the size of the offers being determined by the trouble people could get into for accepting them. Ciran's former life as a pillow boy had given him an understanding of different classes—and the tokens of appreciation that would inspire them to abandon their principles.

For some, being bought a drink was enough to loosen their tongues.

It took two days of cautious maneuvering through the city's tired teahouses and rice wine bars, but he managed to arrange an interview for himself and Kat with the head warden.

The morning of the meeting he and Kat dressed with care. To prepare the ground before them, Ciran had dropped their cover story into ears he'd thought useful. Kat was Princess Mahalawi, rebellious seventh daughter of a declining royal House. Ciran became Ganden, the princess's rohn lover and right hand man. The business venture in which they were conspiring was so illicit, so dangerous and potentially lucrative that it was worth Ciran's life to hint at details. He was—just barely—willing to reveal that Winter Prison's warden was in a position to do them a favor, should he be interested in augmenting his coffers.

Chances were good that the mystery piqued the warden's interest as much as the promise of lucre. Yama of every class were lovers of intrigue.

The garments they donned were appropriate to their identities. Kat wore a cream silk tunic and trouser set, lined for cold weather and embellished as befitted a lesser royal with semi-precious jewels. Ciran wore rohn gray, but in good quality cloth and fit. As he studied his reflection in their suite's full length mirror, he thought he looked precisely like a business partner and bed-pet should.

Details like this mattered. Yama learned from the cradle to distinguish class nuances.

Hattori sat on the bed, watching them get ready with an expression he probably didn't know was ornery. He wore a fresh black coverall. It fit better than his old one, though his shoulders still strained the seams. Strangely, or maybe not, Ciran thought he looked beddable. As luck would have it, Kat also called to him more than usual. Unlike Hattori, Ciran adored her sleekly polished princess persona, the untouchability it implied increasing his attraction by a foolish degree. His cock gave a good hard leap as she smoothed the jewel-studded tunic down her torso.

He truly was going to go mad if he didn't find someone obtainable to lust after.

"I don't like this," Hattori said.

For a second, Ciran thought Hattori had read his thoughts. He suppressed a blush as he realized his friend was talking to Kat. "You don't know anything about this man you're meeting. Ciran couldn't even get his proper name."

"Ciran was being careful not to push too hard. I doubt the warden's identity is well known. If Winter Prison isn't supposed to exist, neither can its administrator. We'll figure out how to handle him as we go."

"It's reckless."

"It's necessary." Kat went to him and hugged him gently. "We're going to rescue Haro. Just concentrate on that."

"I can't lose you," he confessed, his arms coming around her. "I want Haro safe, but I'd never survive it."

"You won't have to. We're going to be all right."

He dragged his face across her shoulder, letting out a small pained noise. Ciran immediately wished he hadn't heard it, but his martyr's streak kept his gaze on the tender scene. This was his reality now. He'd better learn to face it. He told himself he only interrupted because they were out of time.

"We should go," he said. "Arriving late won't do us any favors."

Kat released Hattori and turned to him. Her lips were pressed together, the rims of her eyes gone red. The sight of her repressed emotions was more than Ciran could stand. He strode from the bedroom before Hattori could thank either of them again.

♦

Driving the snowskip through the dreary city with only Ciran for company felt to Kat strangely like cheating on Hattori. Ciran wasn't responsible for this impression. He sat beside her, composed and serious. The thought of everything he was risking—and for other people's benefit—drove her to speak impulsively. "Maybe I could do this alone."

Her heart clenched with dread the moment the words were out, for fear that he would accept. Ciran looked at her and then at the street ahead. The handful of skips they shared the space between the grimy buildings with were ancient compared to theirs. "You wouldn't be safe without me. Winter Prison is off the grid. We can't be sure how a female alone would fare."

"I just don't think you're profiting enough from this."

The look he sent her this time took longer to turn away. "You might be surprised what your safety means to me."

He sounded like he valued it for more than the sake of Hattori's happiness. Butterflies she wasn't sure what to do with fluttered in her stomach. It was all well and good to invite Ciran to join her and his friend in bed, to not want him to feel left out. This odd new jumpiness inside her was something else.

She cared for Ciran. She was in love with Hattori.

I'm grateful is all, she told herself. *And I admire Ciran's loyalty.* She needn't worry she was falling for someone who'd always put her second. Much as she admired Ciran, that was a brand of crazy she wasn't crazy enough for. Worse, it was a brew whose bitterness she'd already quaffed. Miry hadn't even had to fight to come first with Kat's father.

"There's the security post," Ciran pointed out, breaking into her thoughts.

Kat returned her attention where it belonged. The security post wasn't the compact blue and green striped booth she was accustomed to from the capital. Out here it was a plasteel bunker in a peculiarly threatening shade of gray. The turnoff it hunkered over was at least a mile from Winter Prison's walls. No visitor got closer without official permission. Two extremely dirty delivery trucks sat in line in front of them, waiting for security personnel to open the tunnel doors. An intertwined *W/P* marked the vehicles as prison property.

"Stay in the skip," Ciran said from the side of his mouth. "If it looks like I'm in trouble, take off as fast as you can and tell Hattori."

He put this in such a way that she couldn't argue. He stepped out when one of the guards beckoned him, his manner conveying the sort of boredom rohn in service tended to pick up. *I'm spiritless and dull*, it said. *No need to think of me as a threat.*

The guard checked Ciran's claim that they were expected on his handheld. Evidently, the prison's local network was functioning today. When the guard glanced at Kat, she made certain she gazed aloofly straight ahead. She kept her profile to him even after Ciran climbed back into the front seat. It seemed a good sign that the guard was sweeping them with a scanner for weapons and contraband.

"We're in," Ciran said. "They'll tag our car so the automated defenses don't fire on us."

Kat nodded without looking at him, watching a second guard slap the tag on their hood. She switched the skip out of idle as the heavy tunnel doors swung open. The specially engineered metal was at least three feet thick. Kat doubted explosives would do more than dent that barrier of doom.

It went without saying that they'd better not step wrong once it shut.

This happened soon and without fanfare. The passage that led underground to the prison was big, poorly lit, and smelled like an old sewer. Kat wished she had a mask, but the cold probably discouraged the smell a bit. The surface their skis bumped over was dirty snow compacted down to ice. Ciran muttered a curse in Human. Her concern over what condition they'd find Haro in worsened. Yama were notorious for keeping places they lived and worked spotless. This tunnel—in truth, this whole worn down city—didn't bode well for how Hattori's brother had been treated.

Neither she nor Ciran commented on their surroundings. Surveillance cameras tracked them every twenty feet or so, whirring to life as they passed. She had no doubt the equipment was wired for sound.

She wasn't happy to find security so tight, but it did reassure her that her plan had been their best option. Two lone men simply couldn't have broken in. As to that, an army would have had trouble.

The grubby tunnel ended at a huge subterranean loading dock. Kat and Ciran were ordered brusquely to leave their skip, which was driven off by another guard. Ciran watched it disappear down a dark passage.

"That's leased, you know," he said impassively. "We'll need it back undamaged."

He might as well not have spoken. The two armed guards who flanked them didn't react at all.

Kat estimated they were escorted another mile through a warren of narrow corridors that gradually grew cleaner and broader. When the floor changed from plascrete to shining marble, she knew they must be near their goal.

An atrium opened before them. Though not fancy by daimyo standards, the sudden increase in height and brightness jolted her nerves. Simple stone benches—all empty—were spaced between tall palms whose trunks stretched gracefully upward toward the dome's weapon-proof skylights. Color flashed high up, catching her attention. Some exotic bird had just flown to another frond.

She blinked, taken aback. What did it mean that this luxury was here?

She could only wonder as the guards led them across the circular space to a set of wide plasteel doors. Their matte black surface was enlivened with scrolling patterns in polished jet. The picture the inlay formed was not the prison's initials, but an ornate *O* twined with poppy flowers. The skin atop Kat's skull contracted.

This looked like House insignia to her.

One of the guards knocked on the panel. Receiving a response through his headset, he used his palm print to unlock the door. He leaned in to address someone they couldn't see.

"Sir, Princess Mahalawi and Citizen Ganden are here."

"Send them in," said a smooth deep voice—a cultured one, Kat thought.

They stepped into a room that could have been transported, object by object, from a palace in the capital. Silver gilding twinkled from columns and furniture. The white marble floors matched those of the atrium, and were overlaid with large colorful carpets. The walls were black plasteel like the doors. The same decorative family crest repeated over them.

The man who rose behind a broad silver desk was undeniably a prince. Royal blue garb aside, no nonroyal ever looked that haughty.

Kat realized she should have foreseen this possibility. Running a prison could be done for profit, just like anything else. If this was a House's business, some family member would be expected to keep an eye on it.

"Welcome, Princess Mahalawi," said the warden, a stiff little bow accompanying his greeting. He was an attractive man—tall and well formed with the long blue-black hair prized by royals, perhaps in his fourth decade. His eyes were sleepy, and his mouth looked as if it had been designed to pout. It wasn't pouting now. Beneath his very proper smoothness, the young prince struck her as sharply interested in his guests.

She bowed back more deeply than he had, willing to flatter him if it would help their cause.

"Shall we make ourselves comfortable in the sitting area?" he said, gesturing gracefully toward the space. "I admit I'm pleased to entertain a fellow royal. Civilized company can be a rarity out here."

"You're too kind," Kat murmured. "Might I know whom I have the pleasure of addressing?"

"Oh yes. Security. Sometimes I forget how that necessity hedges us. I am Prince Toper Ombino."

Kat had to clamp down her reaction. She hadn't recognized the prince—daimyo didn't all know each other—but she most assuredly knew his House. Avel Ombino, whose mating reaction she'd triggered prior to Miry exiling her to Ningzha, had tried to court her on her return. Fresh from her blissful summer with her guards, Kat had rejected him. At the time, mild appreciation for a male had seemed a poor substitute for joy. She'd let Avel down gently, but she couldn't doubt he remembered her.

The question was, had he discussed her with his male relatives?

Toper's manner gave her no clue.

Left with no choice but to play this out, she and Ciran followed Toper's suggestion to be more comfortable. They sat on opposing sofas, with Ciran beside her and the prince facing them. The leather upholstery was embossed with more poppy-entwined O's. Clearly, the Ombinos liked to remind people who they were. Regardless, the prince had manners. For the next quarter hour, he poured tiny cups of tea and politely brought up names of acquaintances they might share. Though she recognized quite a few, she explained that her family seldom left the provinces.

"Pity," said the prince, his sleepy eyes hooded. "Loveliness such as yours would set the Forbidden City upon its ear."

"You honor me," Kat returned, inclining her head exactly as expected.

She doubted either of them believed the compliment. They hardly needed to. This entire conversation could have played out in any salon in the capital, between any two royals. The only interesting thing about it was how Toper Ombino's gaze kept sliding toward Ciran. As a prince, he shouldn't have acknowledged a rohn unless he couldn't avoid it. Ciran hadn't spoken, nor done anything to draw him. He sat quietly beside Kat, lashes lowered, a decorous foot of space between them. Despite his stillness, Ombino was unable to control his eyes. The next time they drifted to Ciran, the dark forked marking on the tip of his tongue crept out.

Regardless of whether the prince knew Kat, he certainly recognized something in Ciran.

Ciran recognized it too. He shifted slightly and crossed his legs. Kat wasn't looking at her companion, so she didn't know what flirtatious signal he might have sent, but a flush swept up Ombino's neck. Fascinated, Kat watched the rosy color climb right onto his face. The prince's jaw fell open, and then he shook himself.

"Well," he said, yanking his focus back to her. He tugged his pearl encrusted tunic more firmly down his lean torso. Kat didn't think she imagined the increased elevation of the embroidered silk that overlay his lap—or the size of the erection that must be causing it. Ombino cleared his throat. "Perhaps we should discuss your business."

"My business is diamonds," she said bluntly.

She had his attention then, though talk of money likely wouldn't discourage his arousal. To her surprise, his nostrils flared when he looked at her. Was he attracted to her as well? She thought she'd pegged his preference, but perhaps he *was* suffering from a lack of royal company. If he were related closely enough to Avel for her biochemistry to tease his, this might account for him exposing his sexual interest so blatantly.

"Diamonds?" he inquired huskily.

Kat pulled herself back on topic. "We've found a previously unsuspected diamond-bearing pipe. Its location—which I'm certain you'll forgive me for not describing—puts it out of range of the cartel's spy satellites. If all goes well, our geologist estimates we'll be producing stones in the ten thousand carat range per year."

"Stones you'll want to sell on the black market."

"That would be preferable. The diamond cartel's hand can be heavy when it comes to price setting."

"Not to mention taking their cut of each sale." Ombino had relaxed back on his couch, the amused gleam in his eyes indicating he had experience with authority chafing. In all likelihood, he'd been banished here by his family for kicking out at their restrictions. He and Kat shared a moment of wry understanding, young royal to young royal, but Kat knew better than to build too much on it. The prince tapped one finger beside his thigh, the single sign of his ticking thoughts. "You do make me wonder how I, a lowly prison warden, might aid your enterprise."

"We need workers," Kat said, not bothering with indirection. "Skilled, strong, and completely under our thumb. Were we to hire miners through normal channels, word of what we're doing would get out."

Ombino's gaze cut to Ciran. "Citizen Ganden is your manager?"

"Among other things."

"We could use a dozen men," Ciran said, speaking for the first time. At the sound of his voice, the warden jerked before he could stop himself. Pretending he hadn't noticed, Ciran went on. "We're willing to bring their health up to par so long as their genetic baseline is sound. No one under six foot, no one predisposed to violence, and higher than average intelligence is a plus. Some of our machinery is complex. Naturally, we'll pay a premium for any candidates we accept."

Ombino was silent. He didn't ask how much they were offering. He must have known the sum would be astronomical. He looked at Kat, calculations flickering behind his smooth features. Kat waited, fighting the urge to fidget. Ombino surprised her by leaning forward over his knees, his previous indolence blown away. The flush was back in his cheeks again.

"Would you want to view them today?"

"That would be agreeable," she said.

He rose abruptly, the fall of his pearl-studded sapphire tunic not quite hiding the large arched ridge that swelled from his groin. Did his arousal explain why he was cooperating? Hormones often overrode royal males' good sense. If this were the case, was Ombino expecting to be paid in more than coin? Depending on how she viewed it, this was either extremely awkward or a stroke of luck.

"Excuse me," he said before she could decide how she felt. "I need to make a call from my private room."

His private room was accessed through a hidden panel in the black wall. As he slipped behind the rotating section, Kat caught a glimpse of viewscreens and control panels. Then she and Ciran were alone.

They raised eyebrows at each other but did not speak, aware that they were probably being watched. They didn't need to speak anyway. Kat knew they both were thinking this had been too easy.

♦

In less time than Ciran would have thought possible, prisoners were being led into the warden's grand reception chamber, shackled together in groups of five. Some were in better shape than others, but none could be called healthy.

Their dirty white jumpsuits were truly sad.

Using Humans he'd seen vetting slaves on holoshows as his example, Ciran checked them over. Though he tried not to wonder what was going on behind their dull eyes, he couldn't help thinking enforced labor in a mine might be an improvement in their lot. He saw bruises he knew would haunt him, injuries old and new. The notes he made a show of scribbling into his handheld would surely make for surreal reading. He began to worry he wouldn't recognize Hattori's brother. They'd stipulated conditions that would make him a candidate—his penchant for nonviolence being the biggest one. The problem was that many of the men were so worn down from their privations their own mothers might not know them.

The fifth group proved at least that fear unwarranted.

The hair on Ciran's arms began to prickle as the convicts shuffled through the door with their guards. Despite being constrained by ankle shackles, Haro's bearing set him apart. Everything about him recalled his brother—the line of his shoulders, the way his head turned to scan the room for threats. Haro didn't look good; he was gaunt and pale and disturbingly hollow-eyed. Even so, he was recognizable as himself—some small spark still flickering within his near starved frame. In that moment, Ciran understood why Hattori missed him so much.

Of all these prisoners, only his brother stood straight and tall.

Beside him Kat's aura flared, buzzing perceptibly at the edges of his own. Daimyo weren't as adept as rohn at reading energy, so Ciran hoped Ombino didn't notice. Plainly, Kat had identified Haro too.

He was in the middle of his chained line of five. Ciran forced himself to examine the two men before him and not to spend extra time on him. Hattori's twin didn't twitch as Ciran checked his eyes and teeth. When he turned Haro's hands gently back and forth, he saw three fingers on his right hand had been broken. The bones looked like they'd healed without being set by a physician.

"Squeeze," Ciran said, laying two fingers along the affected digits' base.

Haro stared at him, clearly not comprehending what he wanted.

"I need to test your grip," he explained, his voice almost but not quite normal.

Haro squeezed, his eyes slightly wide on Ciran's. His hold was stronger than Ciran expected. It was unlikely these prisoners had been told the reason why they were here, nor did Haro appear to remember Ciran from the few months they'd both resided at the Feng palace. Nonetheless, at some level deeper than words, Ciran knew Haro sensed something important was happening.

"All right," Ciran said. "That's fine."

Haro released the hold, then made a fist of the hand Ciran had tested. Ciran worked very hard not to draw attention to it by staring.

Letting Haro be led away again wasn't easy. His guards looked more like criminals than their charges, and would be returning him to who knew what conditions. For the sake of their plan, it had to be done. Ciran examined two additional gangs of convicts, careful not to betray that he'd already found what they sought. As the outer door sealed shut behind the second group, Kat called an end to the procession. "Thank you, Prince Ombino. We'll make our selection now."

The prince's brows lifted a fraction. "You are decisive. Shall we discuss terms?"

"Why don't you tell me how many workers this will purchase?"

Kat pulled a small black bundle from her trouser pocket. Seeing it, Ombino smiled faintly. "How nice. Barter is more entertaining than bank transfers."

The prince must have guessed he was about to paid in diamonds, but he had no idea the sort of diamond he'd see. Ciran could hardly believe it himself; they hadn't discussed beforehand that she would offer this. Offer it she did, however, and without obvious regret. When Kat set the bundle on the prince's desk and unwrapped the neatly tied black velvet, the 500-carat Katsu Blue twinkled like a sun.

The stone was as beautiful as he remembered; magical, really, imbued as it was with the Human cutter's odd genius. To see it was to want it, though the wanting felt dangerous. Ciran was a bit amazed Kat would part with it, but he couldn't fault her logic. Her prize possession made an argument no amount of credit could equal. Ombino gasped at the sight, one hand rising to his throat in unguarded shock. His other hand stretched out a moment later, hovering over but not touching the bright facets. Ciran read the prince's desire to possess the diamond as easily as he'd read his desire for him.

Unable to help himself, Ombino spoke breathily. "The emperor himself does not own such a treasure."

"Indeed," Kat agreed with her own slight smile. "I think it ought to buy us a dozen workers—and maybe one or two to spare."

Ombino blinked before turning to her with dazzled eyes. "It would buy you more than that . . . were it not for my knowing you only want Haro Yan."

◆

"Pardon?" Kat asked, her voice as wispy as his had been. Her brain spun with her attempt to figure out how he'd guessed. She and Ciran had been careful.

Her lack of composure allowed the prince to recover his. "Privacy on," he instructed the room's computer, then tapped his ear. "Hidden transmitter. I've had a servant watching you from a spy camera. Both your auras went supernova when Prisoner 2052 arrived. I find that as interesting as you using an assumed name."

Kat retreated one involuntary step, prevented from stumbling by Ciran's hand coming up to support the small of her back.

Ombino enjoyed that as much as his chance to show off his superior acumen. "I knew who you were the moment you showed up on our cameras. We have them all over town, you know. Even if I hadn't seen you on the vids after your arrest, my idiot cousin Avel showed me your holo often enough. Katsu Shinobi, the princess who got away. You've no idea how noble he thought himself for ending his pursuit once you'd turned him down. I expect he'll be feeling just as virtuous—and unmated—on his deathbed."

"If you know who I am . . ."

"Why did I let this play out? Maybe because you're not the only Yama I recognize." Ombino turned his body to face Ciran, his eyes glittering with more than victory. He looked to Kat like he was going into heat that instant. "You're Ciran Khosov. Muto Feng's pillow boy. I saw you across a room at the party for my twenty-first natal day. Muto had you escorting the wife of a cabinet member whose favor he was courting. You disappeared with her into a chamber for two whole hours. I never forgot the expression on her face afterward, like she'd never really been fucked before. I swore if I got the chance, I'd hire you myself. As luck would have it, you transferred to the guards days later. I'd resigned myself to missing my chance, but here you are."

"Here I am," Ciran concurred blandly.

The lack of encouragement didn't put off Ombino. "For six years, I've been left to molder here by my hidebound House. No princesses to sleep with. No men except untrained rohn. Heat would have driven me insane were it not for the jails' physician drawing off my kith every month. Unless it's happened to you, you cannot fathom how unpleasant a six-inch needle to the groin can be."

"I imagine you'd do almost anything to avoid it," Ciran said dryly.

"Almost." Ombino nodded more emphatically than he should have. A streak of red blotched either side of his neck, unmistakable sign of the glands activating there. Sadly, his lust-darkened eyes remained canny. "Lovely though your diamond is, Princess Kat, it doesn't persuade me to risk losing what freedom remains to me. For that, you'll have to sweeten the pot."

Though he addressed Kat, he drifted closer to Ciran, as if the other male were magnetic. The men' gazes locked together, Ombino's hunger facing off with Ciran's caution. Ombino's hand approached Ciran's chest like it had the diamond. Then, exactly as he had with the stone, he drew it back at the last moment.

"Tell me," he said. "Who is Haro Yan to you that you'd go to all this trouble?"

"What does it matter?" Ciran replied calmly. "You want me enough that you'll give him to us without knowing."

"I want you both," hissed the prince. "I want her juice on my penis. I want to ejaculate like a true royal. I want you to watch me screw her, and then I want to fuck you."

Ciran jerked back at his fervor. Ombino didn't seem to notice he'd provoked a response at last. He was too caught up in his fantasy.

"It's Fate," he went on, "that the pair of you is here. Finally, the universe is handing over what I deserve."

"You can't have her," Ciran said, startling Ombino and Kat too.

"She means that much to you?" the royal warden asked.

Rather than answer, Ciran set his jaw. Recovered from her surprise, Kat thought she understood. He was protecting her for Hattori. He thought his friend wouldn't be able to bear her having been with a stranger. Oh Hattori would understand why she'd done it; he was Yama enough for that, but understanding wouldn't factor into his more basic responses. They were bonded now—and not just physically. Whether or not they'd mate in truth someday, Kat felt like she belonged to him. Instincts too strong for him to fight would rebel.

If part of him was grateful, that would just deepen his turmoil.

"He has to take me," Kat said reasonably. "Once," she added when Ombino opened his mouth eagerly. "Ciran and I will work on you together. Willingly. With all Ciran's famous skills brought to bear. We'll empty you in one go. It will be an experience unlike any you've ever had. You'll be thanking us when it's over."

Kat hoped he would anyway. Ciran's erotic training was better suited for keeping this promise than anything she knew how to do. Fortunately, she'd judged the effect the promise itself would have. Ombino was jaded enough—and intrigued enough—that his mouth was hanging open, his breath coming in quick huffs. He rubbed his palms up and down his thighs, probably wishing it wouldn't have been undignified to grip his now immense erection.

"And the diamond?" he asked hoarsely.

Kat almost smiled. He really was a prince if he could ask that in his present condition. "The diamond is yours as well—once we have Haro safely out of here. You can trust us not to renege. It's in all our interest to leave you satisfied."

"Would you . . ." The prince swallowed, his nervousness suddenly as apparent as his arousal. "Would you be willing to tie me up?"

Kat glanced at Ciran, but his gaze was on the prince. She noticed her companion no longer appeared reluctant. Color had come into his face, and his breathing had deepened.

"The cabinet member's wife," he mused. "I tied her to a desk that night. You want to recreate her experience."

"She had marks on her wrists. She rubbed them afterward like they felt good."

The prince licked his lips, exposing his lamril, and Ciran smiled like a cat in cream. Kat read danger in the subtle curve of his lips. "We'll make you feel as good as her, your highness."

"You won't . . . take advantage? You won't hurt me when I'm restrained?"

"No more than you want us to," Ciran promised silkily. "As the princess said, we'll need your cooperation when this is over."

Ciran had understood some pain was desirable. The prince's countenance went as dark as plums. "Do it now," he burst out. "Both of you."

Ciran's gaze flashed to Kat. The heat in his eyes was shocking, black fire shooting straight to her soul. He wanted to do this, especially with her. She was thoroughly aroused then, wet and hot and unavoidably eager. No matter what that said about her, she couldn't deny it. Awareness of what was going on inside her enlarged Ciran's pupils, until the slimmest rim of silver was all she saw.

In that moment, wanting what they knew was wrong was a vice they shared.

"Get ties from the drapes," he instructed, his voice as rough as Ombino's. "I'll start undressing him."

The prince was already moaning as she obeyed.

When she returned, the makeshift bonds clutched in sweaty hands, the prince was naked. He stood in front of his big silver desk, hips braced back against its edge, knuckles white from his hold on it. His deathgrip might have been due to Ciran being on his knees before him, performing fellatio. Ciran's jaw was strong from years of practice, and he knew the force daimyo liked. That his special talent was appreciated was clear from the pleasure contorting the prince's face. Kat noted his body was very nice— lean and sinewy. It writhed helplessly at the bobbing of Ciran's head.

"Infinity," Ombino breathed, obviously overcome. "If you were royal and a woman, I'd marry you for this."

Kat couldn't keep her small laugh inside. "Stay as you are," she said when Ombino tried, unsuccessfully, to focus his eyes on her.

"But he—" Ombino shuddered as Ciran's mouth sank down him. "He can't draw my kith from me. I need to let go of it."

"We'll get to that," she said as confidently as she was able. "I'm going to tie your hands behind you."

His back was as attractive as his front, its muscles rippling as Ciran worked on him.

He gasped as she secured him, his excitement heightened by the light restraint. Kat wondered if today was the first time he'd ventured into this territory. He was young enough for it to be true. Bondage virgin or not, his skin quivered like a horse with a fly on it.

"Tie his legs as well," Ciran said.

This was too titillating. The prince cried out from no more than her pulling his feet apart, a necessary step for tying his ankles to the legs of the solid sterling desk. She was kneeling when she finished, close enough for Ciran's movements to brush her side. Ombino's new position exposed everything being done to him. She watched his painfully erect penis appear and disappear between the constricted circle of Ciran's lips. All royals' cocks were big, and the prince's was no exception. Though it didn't surpass Hattori's, it was redder. Its shaft curved upward, as if rut had it yearning for Ciran's mouth. Kat could hardly blame it. Ciran took its entire length, using the strength of his tongue to rub it, to leave it wet with saliva. His enthusiasm for his task couldn't be mistaken. He'd stripped off his shirt but still wore trousers, as if giving head were a sporting event he'd thrown his whole heart into. The whip marks she rarely noticed anymore stood out on his torso. They told a story that aroused her—that perhaps he'd learned to enjoy the upper hand by being forced to relinquish it himself.

When Kat laid her palm between his shoulder blades, he was perspiring.

He grunted—in thanks, she thought—but didn't stop what he was doing. For a prince in heat, Ciran's concentration was a mixed blessing. Being stimulated so forcefully had to be wonderful. Not being able to come, by contrast, could only torment him. A hard dry climax flung back the prince's head. Sadly for Ombino, its aftermath was more arousal.

"Please," he begged, forgetting his daimyo pride. He shoved his hips toward Ciran, going deeper into his mouth. His balls were heavy, the skin stretched tight around their month-long burden of seed. "Please let her suck me now."

Ciran pulled back and sat on his heels. The hump that rose from his groin was worth a double take. Distracted, but assuming it was her turn to contribute, Kat began to rise from her knees. Ciran stopped her by extending one arm in front of her.

The prince cursed at him, struggling against his bonds. "This isn't what you promised me."

"You like men better," Ciran said unperturbed.

"I like ejaculating," the prince snarled back. "She's the one whose essence matches mine."

"Ciran—" Kat began. She might not precisely want Ombino, but she was willing to uphold her end.

"Trust me," Ciran said to both of them.

"I want to spill," the prince insisted, his pout in evidence now.

"You'll spill in me."

"But—"

"In me, your highness. Fucking me like you've been dreaming about for years." Ciran stood and dropped his trousers, revealing the pale perfection of his fighter's physique. Usually, such symmetry was restricted to royals.

Not that the prince was appreciating the whole picture.

He moaned, unable to tear his gaze from Ciran's erection. Seeing this, Ciran stroked himself slowly with one hand, showing off his extreme stiffness. "You see how hard I am, your highness? How the tip of me swells so wide? Imagine how perfect my head will feel running over your kingmaster."

Ombino choked out a strangled sound. "At least let her kiss me. The kith glands in my throat are aching."

"No," Ciran said. "You're going to watch me kiss her."

Kat feared the prince would be angry, but Ciran's refusal seemed to wind him up—as Ciran no doubt had guessed it would. The prince's cock jerked higher, its bloated head now strafing his flat belly. "Please."

"Beg all you want," Ciran said blithely. "We both know you've been waiting your whole life for someone like me to take a firm hand with you."

He turned to Kat. When he'd stopped her from helping, Kat had sat back on her heels. Now Ciran's erection bobbed above her. He was harder than she'd ever seen him, his reddened glans shining with the fluid that wasn't kith but was hardly less interesting. Even as she watched, a fat drop squeezed out from the slit and rolled down.

"Kiss me, princess," Ciran ordered, one hand wagging the large tip at her.

Maybe Kat liked a firm hand too. Her pussy tightened and went molten as she kneed up and leaned to him.

He groaned as her mouth closed on him, pushing luxuriantly into the warm, wet clasp. The reaction delighted her. He'd been wanting to do this—maybe for a long time. His hands came to either side of her head, urging and guiding her. It had been a while, but she thought she recalled the spots he most enjoyed pressure on.

"Wetter," he rasped, his neck falling back. "Tongue me all the way up and down. I want . . . the prince to taste you on me."

She tongued him just for him, though it did spread her essence over his skin. She must have remembered what he liked well enough. He sighed as she sucked him, and squirmed, and drew circles above her ears with surprisingly gentle thumbs. He tasted sweet as pre-ejaculate leaked more copiously from him, his thighs beginning to tremble with pleasure. Kat caressed the heavy muscles, loving their combination of weakness and power. When she slid her hands up to cup his balls, he pulled away with a low, rough sound.

Kat hadn't noticed before, but the prince was panting from watching them.

"Now you kneel," Ciran said to him.

Given how he was tied, this was awkward, but Ombino was too eager not to comply. His knees sprawled wide as he succeeded, his wrists trussed behind his back. His prick curved up like a thick sapling, jerking like the blood inside it was going mad.

"Yes," he murmured as Ciran and his shining cock moved closer. "Give that beautiful thing to me."

Ciran gave and Ombino took, swallowing and licking at the same time. Kat knew the second the essence she'd left on Ciran took effect. Ombino and Ciran gave almost the same high-pitched cry as kith started spurting into the prince's saliva. The substance was a strong aphrodisiac, both for Ombino and anyone who contacted it.

"Fuck," Ciran swore, his hands suddenly claws on the prince's head.

The prince grunted as Ciran's next thrust surged forward—but not in objection. When he pulled back to Ciran's tip, he let the head pop free and laughed throatily. His lips shone with slick fluid. "Haven't felt kith before, have you?"

"Only . . . shit—" Ciran's answer was broken by the prince swallowing him again. His hips twisted violently to get closer. "Only a few times and . . . not for years."

Not since he was a pillow boy, Kat surmised, wondering if he could maintain the control he needed to get their hoped for results. Ciran seemed to have doubts himself.

"Kat," he said, waving for her to come to him. "This feels too good. Help me pull out of him."

She stood and helped him, and then they all were panting. The prince's eyes were completely black.

"You didn't have to stop," he said, sounding like it was a struggle to get the words out in order. Repeated shudders ran through his kneeling frame. "I would have enjoyed swallowing your seed."

Ciran leaned forward, braced over his knees, and tried to catch his breath. His cock stuck straight out from him and pulsed. "I'm the hardest I'll be now. That's better for fucking you. I'm going to take you while you take her your one time."

Ombino looked at her and then back at Ciran. Kat had less experience than Ciran with princes in full heat, but Ombino seemed pretty far gone to her. Evidently, he thought so too. "I don't think that's going to work. She's too good a match for me. If my cock so much as touches her pussy, everything I've stored up is shooting out. I'll want to stay in her until I'm empty. Ten men won't be able to drag me out."

Ciran smiled shakily. "You leave that to me, your highness."

The prince stared at him and then gave a short half laugh. "You're crazier than I am, but as you wish. I put myself in your expert hands."

He turned to Kat, giving her his full attention, his all-black eyes surprisingly warm. "Would you undress, princess? I'd be grateful for that honor."

The way he asked so respectfully made everything abruptly seem personal. What they were doing would have felt easier—and less wrong—if she could detest him. To sleep with Ombino and almost like him was a far worse betrayal of Hattori.

Ciran seemed to sense this. He reached out to rub her arm. She couldn't look at him. She was afraid to see too much in his eyes.

She bit her lip and then decided. "As you please, your highness."

Both men watched her as she disrobed. Her heart was racing by the time she finished, beating as hard in her contracted nipples as it did in her chest. Despite her arousal, the shyness she felt was uncomfortable.

"Princess," Ciran murmured.

He stepped to her and kissed her, intimate and deep, covering what she'd just revealed with his close embrace. His left hand caressed one breast while his right slid down to engulf her bottom. Squeezing it brought her tight against his erection.

"I want to dip this in you," he said.

She didn't know if she gave permission. He nudged her feet apart, bent his knees, and probed her folds open with his tip. Their eyes held—two heartbeats, three . . .

"Oh God," he said as he slid inside.

The Human exclamation seemed right just then, as did the rigid length of him entering her. His skin burned from Ombino's kith, lubricating his way as she grew wetter in response to it. It was strange to do this with them both standing, to know he only intended to wet his skin and not come. Not climaxing must have been difficult. He didn't dare thrust with speed, and his slow penetrations were rather a tease to her. She closed her eyes as he went gently in and out, savoring this in spite of her frustration. He was smooth and hot, and he hadn't been inside her in forever. The shape of him was familiar, but as exciting as if he were someone new. She suspected him being inside her now was going to make her miss him more later.

Maybe he felt the same. His grip on her bottom tightened, his throbbing tip pressing toward the end of her. Kat couldn't resist digging her fingers into his hair.

"Last time," he whispered, his breath hot beside her ear.

He rocked his farthest yet, straining to reach that place only Hattori had touched before. Her pussy tried to help, contracting to pull at him. She supposed that felt good around his penis. His groan as he withdrew did funny things to her heart.

When she opened her eyes, dazed from her own reactions, the prince was gaping up at them from the floor.

"You love each other," he marveled. "The way you touched . . . He was dying to spill in you."

A flush as hot as an oven swept up her cheeks. She suspected if she looked at Ciran, his face would have been as bright. Naturally, neither of them commented on Ombino's guess. What they did or didn't feel was too personal to share.

"What about you?" Ciran growled, his voice so dark and sexy it made her shiver. "Are you dying to spill yet?"

Ombino actually had a dry orgasm from hearing the question. He gasped, and strained, but nothing came from his engorged slit.

"Good answer," Ciran said with a soft chuckle.

He stepped into the space between Ombino and the desk. Before the prince could prepare himself, Ciran reached down to jerk him onto his feet. Ombino cried out, fear and anticipation mixed in the reaction. Ciran pushed his tied wrists higher behind his back, forcing his arms to bend, after which he wrapped his left arm around his chest. The fingers of his right cinched the base of Ombino's scrotum, the pressure tight enough to whiten both men's skin.

"That hurts," Ombino complained, squirming in Ciran's trap.

It might have hurt, but his erection throbbed crazily.

"It hurts just right," Ciran corrected. "You won't be able to ejaculate while I hold you, no matter how good being inside her feels. That's the secret to letting go all at once. You hold off and hold off until you're certain you're going to burst."

"At least free my hands."

"No," Ciran said with relish, nodding for Kat to come closer.

Ombino's eyes went a little wild as she approached. She thought the emotion she saw was panic until she realized he was simply more excited than she'd seen a Yama get. Too many of Ombino's fantasies were coming true at once.

"Will you fuck me at the same time she does?" he asked Ciran breathlessly.

"That's the plan," Ciran growled.

She had to climb Ombino, to support her weight on both men's shoulders. Ciran released the prince's chest to grip her bottom. Though she was strong enough to hold herself up, she was glad for the warmth of his hand on her.

"We take him together," Ciran said, looking at her directly.

The two bodies beneath her shifted, masculine muscles sturdy and damp with sweat. She knew Ciran had found his mark when Ombino began to tremble. She found her own shortly after. Ombino sucked in a breath sharply, his cock spurting kith as it came into contact with her cream. The release of the aphrodisiac was a mini-orgasm, designed to be maddening for both parties. The drenching made her clit itch for friction. It made Ombino swell fuller, the bulb of his erection pulsing hard as the spurt of heat came again, this time against her entrance. Ombino stiffened as if with a seizure, heaving so strongly Ciran struggled to keep him from spearing her then and there. All the while as they wrestled, more hot kith poured from him.

"Shit," Ombino gasped. His tip rubbed frantically against her, something Ciran couldn't prevent him from doing. "That feels too fucking good to believe. I don't—Fate—I don't think you're gripping my balls tight enough."

"Sorry," Ciran said, his other hand doing something she couldn't see.

Ombino made a sound like Ciran had truly hurt him. Whatever he'd done, the prince's kith did stop geysering. The cessation was too late for her pussy. It was burning to be taken. Her dismay at this made her realize her body was ready but not her heart. She didn't want this stranger inside her, even if she enjoyed it.

"Kat," Ciran said softly, seeing her hesitate.

His tone was kind. He'd done his best to protect her, to take most of this on himself. For his sake—and for Haro's—it was too late to turn back.

"Now," she said hoarsely, and drove her sheath down the prince's cock.

She came before reaching the end of him. Her body couldn't help it. Ciran shoved inward too, and Ombino began to cry. It took a moment for her to understand that he was weeping with ecstasy.

"Yes," he gasped between sobs. "Yes. Fuck me until I die."

They fucked him as long as Ciran had fucked the cabinet member's wife, two hours of unstinting sensual asault. Under the influence of his kith, Kat came too many times to count, but Ombino went even more. The dry orgasms were like repeated hits of a drug, each peak making the next seem more necessary for survival. He'd beg Ciran to let him spill in one breath, and then promise he could stand just a little more.

"I can wait for you," he swore to Ciran. "When you decide I'm ready to fuck you, I'll let it all loose in you."

Maybe Kat should have been insulted, but his determination to only ejaculate in Ciran excited her as much as his erotic agony. If a person could die from being denied release, the prince was ready to meet that end. When his oaths devolved into cries, Ciran pulled out of him with a tortured sound.

She saw at once that he hadn't come either; he was too hard and red to have allowed himself a climax. Her jaw dropped even as her gaze rose to his. He smiled ruefully at her silent question, so drenched with sweat it barely helped to drag his free forearm across his eyes.

She supposed he was waiting for something too.

"Climb off him," he said to her. "I can't release his testicles until he's not inside you."

Her pussy didn't want her to disengage. The prince's kith had increased its appetite for pleasure. She grimaced as she pulled free and stepped back onto shaking legs. The size of what she'd been bucking up and down amazed her. Ciran's fingers kept their stranglehold on his sac.

"Ready?" he asked Ombino.

The prince shook his head, his eyes screwed shut and his teeth sunk into his lower lip. He must have feared he'd ejaculate into the air if he was set free. He forced himself to take a few slow breaths.

"All right," he finally said. "I think you can let go. Just please don't touch me. I'm really close."

Ciran unclamped his hand cautiously. When nothing exploded, Ombino let out a lengthy sigh. His eyes blinked open and he looked down his own body. His gaze went round at the sight of his frenetically thudding balls. A reddened handprint was wrapped around their curves.

"You bruised me," he said softly.

His tone told Kat this wasn't a complaint. Ciran must have known it, because he didn't apologize.

"I'm going to untie your wrists," he warned. "Don't give in to temptation and rub yourself."

To Kat's surprise, Ombino shrank back from him. "Don't free me," he said, shaking so violently he could barely get the words out. "I want to fuck you so hard, I'm afraid I might injure you."

Ciran touched his shoulder, obviously moved by his concern. "It's all right. I'm as strong as a prince would be." Ombino shook his head, but Ciran nodded. "You can take me however you want to."

Ombino was unable to keep from moaning at that idea. Ciran undid the knots at his wrist, but left his ankles bound. Maybe he was being cautious, or maybe he didn't want the prince to lose the benefit of his predilection. He was panting again as Ciran finished.

Ciran bowed his head to him. "Would you like to fuck me now, your highness?"

His shift to subservience flipped a switch in the prince. The daimyo growled and grabbed Ciran, shoving him forcefully to the floor. Ciran caught himself on his hands and knees, barely having time to brace before Ombino was on him. He made a sound as Ombino dragged his cheeks apart and roughly penetrated, a muffled cry Ombino drowned out with a roar.

Considering the way Ciran's neck arched, Kat didn't think he'd hurt him.

Apparently, Ombino didn't like the way his bound legs were stretched. The heavy desk wouldn't move, so he yanked Ciran and himself back toward it, probably giving them both rug burns.

Then the prince started fucking him.

There was nothing elegant in the act. Brute strength and brute lust drove it, with no apologies for either. For the last two decades, Ombino had been fantasizing about having sex with the infamous Ciran Khosov—and who knew how long he'd obsessed over spilling into a man. Both impossibilities being fulfilled at once must have been overwhelming. Ombino grunted as he pounded into Ciran, tears again spilling from his eyes. He didn't lose his seed as soon as she expected, but it was soon enough. His grunts sped up, his pounding becoming more frenzied. Ciran's cheek fell to press the carpet, his face twisting with some private torment or ecstasy. Ombino looked as if he were trying to drive his prick up to Ciran's throat.

Kat couldn't look away; could scarcely catch her breath. Suddenly, Ombino uttered a long, strange cry. His torso reared up and his hips slung deep. Kat heard the curtain ties snap as both his feet tore free. His balls contracted so powerfully as he held himself deep in Ciran that invisible fingers appeared to be squeezing him. Kat knew he must be ejaculating, his muscles tightening to ropes at the evidently unbearable pleasure. The pinnacle wasn't brief. Ombino gasped as it continued, successive waves of orgasm seizing him. It seemed he was experiencing what they'd promised, letting loose in the space of minutes what normally took days.

A quarter of an hour later, Ombino groaned one last time. He rolled off Ciran with the last of his strength, collapsing on his back on the floor. His cock was as limp and wet as the rest of him. "Infinity take me," he gasped. "You two are geniuses."

Though Kat appreciated him including her in the praise, she was worried for Ciran. He lay face down on the carpet, palms up by his shoulders, flat on the tufted wool. Those palms curled into fists as she scooted closer, tremors still running through her from watching Ombino take him in that frenzy.

"Are you all right?" she asked, afraid to touch him if he was hurt.

His head came up in slow motion. The dark gleam in his eyes was alarming, it was so thoroughly carnal. "Lie down," he said harshly.

Her brain was too muddled to understand. "Lie down?"

"Yes," he said, pushing his upper body up on his arms. "Lie down and spread your legs."

Every scrap of heat that had ebbed from her sex flooded back twice as strong. "Ciran, didn't you come?"

"Shut up," he ordered. "I need you take me and not argue."

She shut up and sprawled back. He crawled over her like a cat, his cock so hard and red it must have been killing him. He kneed her thighs wider with a grunt and lowered his weight gingerly. His discarded trousers were lying by her head. He pulled a plastic packet from one pocket, which he tore open with his teeth. He handed her the specially treated antiseptic cloth that had been inside.

"Clean off my prick," he said, sounding like his teeth were clenched. "Just be careful not to rub it too much."

He awed her, he truly did. No man but he would have thought of this. She reached between their bodies to do what he'd asked.

She was careful, but his breathing still grew ragged as she touched him. His eyes didn't leave hers for one second, only threatening to close when she stroked the moist cloth over the parts of his penis that most liked her touching them. She liked touching them herself, their incredible heat and fullness seductive to her palm. Air hissed between his teeth, reminding her not to linger. Done then, she cocked up her knees for him.

He looked at her a moment longer. "I wish this wasn't going to be rough."

She smiled, the only response that made sense to her. A heartbeat later he smiled back, then took her mouth and sex in a single swoop.

The kiss ended first, because the intercourse part of the equation was too incredible. Ciran had to wrench his head back and gulp for air. Kat dug her heels in to intensify his thrusts, knowing gentleness was the last thing he needed now. He pounded into her almost as hard as Ombino had pounded him, crying out in wordless appreciation for how wonderful it felt to finally let loose the reins. In spite of being at his limit, he was quieter than Ombino, more accustomed to restraining his desires. If Kat's heart had its way, he'd never have to hide them again.

This was what she wanted, to always share this act with someone she cared about.

Something must have betrayed the wish: the way she moved or her expression.

"Kat," Ciran choked out, shortening his thrusts to go faster.

He rammed deep inside her, barely pulling out halfway. The tip of him caught a pleasure spot on her upper wall. Delicious sensations pummeled out from her core. Kat began to spasm, her fists tangled in his hair as she arched. He felt her go and he went as well, shoving desperately through her constriction with a sound an animal could have made. He spilled hard and long, so much seed releasing that she couldn't hold it all. Rohn didn't store emissions like royals did, but he'd surely been storing some.

"Oh God," he sighed as he finished, sagging carefully down on her.

That care he took broke her heart. She circled him in her arms, letting him know he could stay right where he was if he wanted to.

She kissed his cheekbone for good measure and hummed when he nuzzled her.

She knew holding him felt better—not to mention righter—than her conscience should have allowed.

9: OUT OF THE FIRE

They lay there after, incapable of moving, until the prince's computer dinged for attention. Grabbing the desk for support, Ombino hauled himself onto wobbling feet.

"You should get dressed," he said. "I may run this jail, but it's probably best no one has time to question my orders."

Kat's overworked heart thumped harder. This was it then. Hattori's twin was being released to them. Ciran sat up and helped her absently. He looked as dazed as she felt. "You're satisfied with your fee?" he asked.

Ombino's slight smile slanted. "You've more than earned your reward . . . even without that final show." He was stepping into his fine silk trousers, reminding Kat and Ciran they needed to do the same. "I'll arrange for a ride to meet you on the roof."

It seemed rude to doubt him, but Kat's questions must have showed on her face. Ombino slipped her diamond into his pocket and flat out grinned. "I'm a man of my word, princess."

Kat hoped his erotic glow would keep him honorable long enough for them to get away. Her anxiety lessened when he ushered her and Ciran through his private office to an elevator, one keyed to his retinal print. If he'd intended to betray them, chances were he wouldn't have come with them. As the capsule rose through the tube, he spoke into his handheld, issuing cryptic instructions.

The elevator stopped, its curving door retracting. Ciran tensed. Like her, he knew this would make a fine place for an attack.

No ambush came. Ombino stepped into the opening to look wistfully back at them. "If you're ever in this part of the world again . . ."

"Assuredly," Ciran said politely.

The prison roof—or at least one point of its star—stretched behind Ombino, windy and snow-swept. The early arctic dusk veiled the world in cobalt. A tall solitary male stood at the cold-whipped ledge looking out, not even a guard with him. The breadth of his back was eerily familiar.

Judging it wise, Kat spared a moment for Ombino. "We won't be returning," she said gently.

The prince's face rolled smooth of its faint yearning. "No," he agreed. "I'm sure that would be best for us all."

He retreated into the elevator, leaving them with Haro. Kat and Ciran approached him cautiously as he turned to watch them. He no longer wore his prison jumpsuit. Plain gray robes, thick with winter quilting, protected his thin figure. His head had been shaved like the rest of the prisoners, giving him a forlorn look. Some part of Kat wanted him to meet them halfway, but he remained where he was. Even without his participation, it wasn't long before they were near enough to see his eyes tearing from the cold.

"This is an aircar pad," he said without inflection.

His voice was so like Hattori's it squeezed her chest.

"Yes," Ciran said, clearly unsure how to proceed.

Kat put her hand on Ciran's back. The winter gloves she'd tugged on couldn't keep her from feeling his energy leap at the contact. It seemed the bond they'd formed today wasn't dissolving. "Your brother Hattori sent us to rescue you."

"Hattori?" For a second, she feared Haro didn't know who that was. His face pinched in confusion. "You two aren't planning to throw me off the roof?"

Kat didn't know which was more disturbing: that this was where his logic led him, or that the prospect of plummeting to his death didn't trouble him.

"We bought you free," Ciran said, reaching out to touch his sleeve.

Haro flinched like he'd been struck.

The whoosh of an approaching aircar saved them from more awkwardness. They drew back from the luminescent landing markings, allowing the vehicle to settle into a thin layer of snow. The disc-shaped flier was only big enough for four passengers. Dings pocked its plain black skin, visible even in low light. When Ombino said he'd arranged a ride, he hadn't meant a palanquin.

The lowering of the door revealed another surprise. She'd been wasting her thought power wondering how they'd rejoin Hattori. He turned out to be their pilot. Evidently, there'd been little about their group the prince hadn't uncovered. Had he known all along that Haro was Hattori's brother? Had he asked Ciran what they wanted with him because the average royal couldn't comprehend sacrificing for family or friends?

Hattori's eyes locked onto his brother, who also stared back at him. Though they'd told him Hattori was behind this rescue, Haro appeared stupefied.

"We have to go," Hattori said, hands tight on the opening as he leaned out. "The warden shut off surveillance in this sector, but the window for us to get in and out is short."

His twin shrank back like he was alarmed. Perhaps he was. After nearly twenty years in prison, freedom couldn't have been a comfortable concept.

Hattori's expression flickered in surprise and then hardened. "Now," he said. "We've literally got minutes."

Kat was prepared to grab his brother and force him in. In Haro's current debilitated state, she thought her royal strength might be up to it. Luckily, Ciran understood better than she did what was required.

"Prisoner 2052," he barked like a squad captain, "get in that transport now."

Haro's body stiffened, but he obeyed. He was up the ramp before Kat. He even offered her a hand in. Ciran followed right behind her, after which Hattori heaved up and sealed the door. He glanced at Haro, then swung without speaking into the pilot's seat. Tender reunions would have to wait until the danger was over.

◆

Hattori's half-royal brain calculated milliseconds as his hands raced in practiced patterns over the instrument panel. He'd paused too long on the roof at the astounding shock of seeing his twin again— a distraction he'd known better than to succumb to. However rich

158

Kat had made the warden, a stranger wouldn't lose sleep if they were killed.

Hattori grunted as they lifted off, his body doing things he didn't have time to think about. His fingertips were tingling, his face gone hot from what he'd noticed the instant his friends climbed inside.

Kat and Ciran smelled different.

They'd had sex with someone. . . and with each other. Instincts so deep Hattori was barely aware he had them goaded him to do something about that. He remembered learning on some vid that if a man's mate cheated, even without his knowledge, the competing male's lingering essence increased the first's sperm count—nature's way of helping the rightful mate reassert his claim. This didn't explain Hattori's sudden urge to screw Ciran through the floor. If he'd had two pricks at that moment, Ciran *and* Kat would have been in trouble.

Facial control in shreds, he grimaced and banked west into the wind. He didn't have time for hormonal surges—or whatever his reaction was. He had to get this craft out of here.

A pulse of white-blue light sizzled by his port window.

"Crap," Ciran said from the seat behind his right shoulder. "The automated defenses must be coming back online."

The decommissioned aircar had no shielding, no weapons, and a cranky booster engine—no doubt the reason the warden could hand it off to Hattori without sending up red flags. Speed was their best defense. With a silent hope that the first engine wouldn't stall, Hattori punched the throttle full forward.

A second plasma pulse burst where their stubby right wing had been.

Not bothering to curse, Ciran threw off his seat restraints. There was only one pilot bay, but he squeezed into it beside Hattori to watch the screens for incoming fire and help operate the controls. Hattori barraged him with quick instructions, knowing his long-time partner would understand the shorthand. Another bank of guns came to life on the prison roof, weapons targeting them from two directions now. He veered left and right, but their little craft shook with the nearness of the explosions. Ciran's aid wasn't optional. Evading the attack required two genetically tinkered minds.

Movement caught the edge of his vision, his brother rising to come forward.

"Stay where you are," Hattori snapped, too busy to turn around. "Protect the princess."

Kat squeaked as his twin pushed her to the floor and covered her with his body.

Tears Hattori couldn't control stung his eyes. Whatever Haro might have suffered, part of him remained the man he'd been.

He didn't have time for gratitude. G-forces shoved him without warning into his seat, the booster engine belatedly kicking in. The little ship shot forward like a greased bullet, the landscape blurring as the atmosphere protested their acceleration with a tooth rattling sonic boom.

Ciran's reflexes were all that prevented them from colliding with a mountain.

And then they skipped. Older generation fliers couldn't usually do this. The technology was new, and finessing the multitude of variables involved called for more computing power than they had. This junker, apparently, had a few tricks hidden underneath its ceramiskin. Disorientation from breaking light speed turned Hattori's brain upside down. The twilight blue sprawl of Winter Prison blinked out as if it had been a dream.

Maybe that warden *had* wanted them to escape. Maybe Kat and Ciran had given him extra reasons to feel beholden.

This was a thought Hattori didn't have the luxury of obsessing on. Instruments spun wildly as the aircar's computer tried to recalculate their position from a satellite that wouldn't speak to them. Simply looking out the window was little help. Snow-locked mountains surrounded them on all sides, lit by a crescent moon and a horde of stars. The sky was darker than it had been a moment earlier—pure black rather than indigo. At the least, they'd jumped to a new time zone.

Knowing they were past being tracked, Hattori slowed the craft to a crawl.

For a few hard heartbeats, the only sound was all of them breathing.

"Everyone all right?" Hattori asked, craning around in his seat to see.

"I'm squished," Kat announced, a slight laugh in it.

"Sorry," Haro said. He got off her awkwardly. Maybe both their knees were shaky. He and Kat only pushed up far enough to sit on the floor in the aisle. This was Hattori's first real chance to study his twin. His shaved head was strange, but his profile was so familiar Hattori's throat tightened. There was the little bump that differentiated his nose; here the scar on his jaw that he'd got in a sparring match. Hattori knew his brother's face better than his own, having spent more than half of his life with it. Perhaps sensing his attention, Haro's eyes flicked up to his and away. As they did, Hattori realized what was missing: their old mental connection. He didn't have the least idea what Haro was thinking.

He told himself it wasn't important. Haro was free and he was with them. That was what mattered now.

"Where are we?" Ciran had the presence of mind to ask.

"I'm not sure," Hattori answered. "There's too much interference to hook up with the satellite. Further east than we were, I'd say. And an hour or so later, unless I mistake the stars."

Ciran moved to a different view window to peer out. He nodded toward a line of mountains, a jagged stretch that rose higher than the rest. "That could be the Victoria Range. If it is, we're near Yskut."

Yskut was a Human country, which meant no radar and no advanced weaponry. Kat's big blue diamond had been cut in its capital, though he wasn't clear on whether she'd smuggled it to the cutter in person. Familiarity with the terrain would be an asset, but either way the people of Yskut looked more like Yama than most Humans, being mostly dark of hair and fair-skinned. Due to interbreeding with other populations, some even had gray eyes. Hattori's little group of escapees might be able to lay low there.

Hattori's twin wasn't thinking strategy. He was watching Ciran with his brow furrowed. "I know you," he said slowly. "You're Ciran Khosov. You showed up at Prince Muto's palace before I was arrested. We faced off on the practice mat a few times."

"That's right," Ciran said warily.

Haro stared at him some more. "You helped rescue me."

"Yes."

"You and my brother have become close."

"Yes," Ciran said, and Hattori sensed him fighting self-consciousness.

Kat must have sensed it too. She rose and offered her hand to help Haro regain his feet. Hattori's twin also stared at that.

"I'm sorry, princess," he said, swallowing. "I don't think I can touch you."

She'd been plastered to the floor beneath him half a minute earlier, but Hattori didn't think his brother's reluctance had much to do with logic. Kat was a woman and a patently gentle soul, two things that had been outside his experience for a while. He knew then that breaking his brother out of Winter Prison wouldn't be all there was to getting him back again.

"Take the controls," he said quietly to Ciran.

"Of course," Ciran said. "We'll circle a bit. See if we can pinpoint where we are."

Hattori nodded, unsurprised that Kat understood he meant for her to stay with Ciran. Pressure tightened in his chest as he left the pair together, those hormonal instincts protesting. He couldn't deal with them now. Haro had to be foremost in his mind.

Hattori lowered himself to the floor beside his brother, shoulder to shoulder, as they'd so often sat before. The aisle was narrow enough that the seat edges crowded them. Haro glanced at him sheepishly.

"Sorry," he said. "I feel like a cat who's been abandoned out in the street. I don't want to bite people, but I might."

Abandoned and abused was more accurate, but Hattori kept that thought to himself. "You're doing fine. You've been through a lot."

Haro's breath huffed out in what might have been a laugh. "I can't believe I'm here, that you're here. You look good, brother. You look strong."

Hattori supposed he did by comparison. "Soon you'll be strong too."

Haro nodded, his jaw clenched hard, his arms wrapped tightly around his shins. Through the place where their sides leaned together, Hattori felt his brother begin to shake.

"I'm nervous," Haro admitted. "I felt safer in prison."

Hattori put one arm around his shoulders, squeezing him closer. That Haro's muscles felt like boards didn't make him stop. It must have been the right thing to do, because his twin didn't fight the hold.

"You're safe," Hattori said, letting his cheek drop briefly to Haro's head. "All of us will look out for you."

Kat glanced back at him and their eyes connected electrically. Ciran turned a moment later. Something about both of them regarding him activated a circuit inside his body. The heat that flooded his face was just the beginning. Lust kicked through his groin a second later, his instant erection blotting out every thought. He literally itched with his need to fuck—the flesh of his slit afire, the gland within his anus throbbing like it was suddenly twice as large. Muscles he hadn't been aware he had shifted inside the crest of his prick, feeling both incredibly good and unnerving at the same time. With all his strength, Hattori held back a gasp.

Fortunately, the reaction subsided. As it did, he found himself hoping Haro couldn't read his feelings any better than he read Haro's.

◆

As luck would have it, the mountains Ciran had spotted were the Victorias—so named for the Humans' long-lived queen and empress. With very little debate, they agreed they should take their chance among the foreigners, at least until a better idea occurred to them. Kat claimed to have a contact in Prewtan she more or less trusted.

"I know it's difficult to be sure when it comes to Humans, but Benjamin DuBieren kept faith with me before. It shouldn't be hard to tell if he will again."

That Haro needed peace and quiet was obvious to everyone.

Ciran hadn't expected him and Hattori to fall into each other's arms, but even for Yama, their reunion was restrained. Hattori's eyes revealed his emotions—worry and wonder and gratitude. His brother mostly seemed to be trying to hold himself together. He was watchful of every movement, his own and others. Kat especially stiffened his barriers, though he watched her with as much fascination as unease.

Ciran didn't want to think how he'd react to a city full of females.

Because aircar technology was banned from being shared with Humans, they concealed the flier in an isolated cavern some leagues outside the capital.

The hike down the glacial mountains into the city was a cup of tea compared to their trek from Black Hole to Prisonville. Though the journey tired them, they reached Prewtan's outskirts around sunrise.

This was Ciran's first experience of the Human world, apart from what he'd seen on the HFC. Most of the popular adaptations—*What the Butler Saw*, the endless reruns of *Pride and Perspicacity*—were set in Ohram, Queen Victoria's home country.

Ciran's initial impression was that the snow caused the city to resemble the frosted cakes on *All My Weddings*. The architecture was different from what he was used to. It wasn't older; Humans were a young race compared to theirs, but because it was so grimy it seemed ancient. Unlike Prisonville, here the dirt appeared picturesque. Soot from centuries of coal fires emphasized arches and cornerstones, the film it left lending a poignancy to the murals painted here and there on facades. The streets were crooked and narrow, following no sensible pattern. Vendors with carts and horses constricted them even more, as did the men in overcoats and bowlers who strode purposefully along pavements. Work started early in this city, the bustle growing as they went deeper in. Ciran's ears were assailed by the sound of cobbles crunching beneath carriage wheels.

Though Humans had been given electric technology, the few powered vehicles they encountered appeared to run on petrol. Despite their inefficiency—and the chugging noises their engines made—the motorcars struck him as gorgeous: shining black beasts perched on precarious rubber tires with fancy silver grillwork on their noses. He saw one mired in a snowbank being towed out by a drafthorse. Ciran grinned like a maniac at the sight, an expression that for once drew no attention to him at all.

To his delight, he understood almost everything the people around them said. Learning Ohramese was useful for more than reading books. It was the near universal language of Victoria's empire.

"Fun, eh?" Kat said from beside his elbow. "The last time I was here, I spent most of a day gawking."

She was smiling too, though not as crazily as him.

"We'll need a place to stay," Hattori interjected, his eyes wide and cautious. "And somewhere to buy clothes that look more like theirs."

"I have some Human currency laid by," Kat said. "Enough to get us started."

Hattori was tired enough to let out his sigh. He didn't enjoy the princess constantly staking them. Kat rolled her lips together, her silver eyes sparkling with humor. "If it makes you feel better, your boots are worth six months' rent on the black market."

Hattori looked down at the battered things. "These boots?"

"It's the self-warming mechanism. And the fact that they use the motions of your feet as their power source. Prewtanese love taking apart clockwork."

"Isn't it illegal to sell it to them?" Haro asked unsurely. "Especially if you know they'll try to reverse engineer the science?"

"Absolutely," Kat agreed happily. "Which is why we'll only relinquish them as a last resort."

In the end, Hattori couldn't resist her glee. A smile broke through his worry as he clasped her face and looked down at her. "Where to next, my criminal mastermind?"

She stroked his cheek, and their expressions softened at the same time, the world disappearing for both of them. Hattori's eyes went dark, the rise and fall of his chest hastening. Ciran hurt less than usual to witness their bond, perhaps because his recall of Kat coming apart beneath him hadn't yet had a chance to fade.

Maybe that moment wouldn't have happened if they hadn't needed to save Haro. For that matter, maybe he shouldn't relish remembering it so much. Reliving those feelings was a little too close to gloating at his friend's expense, and that he certainly didn't want to do.

"We should get clothes first, I think," Kat said, the trace of huskiness in her voice folding his memories onto the present. "Then hot cocoa and a hotel, after which we'll see if Benjamin DuBieren will give me an appointment."

"Hot cocoa?" Hattori asked, seizing on the foreign term.

"Trust me," she said, "when you get your first taste of that, you'll never doubt Humans can be geniuses."

◆

They bought their clothes secondhand, something none of them had done before. Ciran was secretly elated to be the best bargainer, convincing the sharp-eyed, rickety old lady who ran the shop to trade one leg of Kat's gem-studded trousers for their purchases. Ciran hadn't imagined a living person could look so old. Yama simply didn't age the same way. He did not, however, let himself be fooled by appearances. If nothing else, Mister Dickens' *Big Expectations* had taught him elderly Human females were sometimes dangerous.

"These are real," he said, stroking the line of garnets around Kat's hem. He was holding up her ankle so the woman could examine them. "Look at the clarity and the color. You can resell these for quite a bit."

The ancient proprietress grumbled but gave in, her complaint that she wasn't a bloody jeweler amusing him. They left the cramped street-level shop with two changes of clothes apiece, appropriate undergarments, and even hats. If Ciran had known how to whistle a happy tune, he would have. He felt like he'd just starred in a scene from a favorite book. Though he knew Human emotions could transfer to Yama, he didn't think that accounted for his triumph.

In spite of everything, this was the best adventure he'd ever had.

"You might be having too much fun," Kat teased as he handed out brown paper and twine-tied parcels for the men to carry. "We're on serious business here."

"I got us a deal," he crowed, then paused as doubt struck him. "At least I think I did."

"You did well," Kat assured him. "Plus, I've still got one leg and a tunic left."

She smoothed the snug, corseted bodice of her Human gown to her waist. They'd all changed in the musty shop and were now transformed. Kat's dress was the nicest the shop carried, Ciran being of the opinion that she shouldn't appear second class. Kat looked scrumptious to him—cinched and bustled and pressed upward at the bosom. He wasn't the only one to find her fetching. As she worked to fill her lungs through the constriction, Hattori wrenched his gaze away, so piqued by the effect her inhalation had on her cleavage that he didn't dare look at her. Ciran smothered a laugh.

Sometimes his friend was *too* easy to arouse.

Garbed in their new-old disguises, the men followed Kat to an overheated café popular with local mothers and their offspring. The Humans were more colorful than Yama, and certainly more noisy. Their quick speech and dramatic gestures crowded the space enough for twice their number. A few of the pink-cheeked females caught Haro's curious eyes. Fortunately, he was too quiet to draw their attention back, even after sampling the hot cocoa. The drink was a hit with everyone but Hattori, who pulled a face at its sweetness. Haro made up for that by commandeering his brother's portion as soon as his own was gone. He didn't say a word before he did it, just pulled the cheap stoneware cup in front of himself. His assumption that he had the right seemed like a good sign, as did his behavior after the drink was gone. Sunlight streamed through the plate glass window by which their small table sat. When Haro turned his face to it and closed weary eyes, every one of his companions—Hattori included—had to smile as they looked at him.

His enjoyment of this simple pleasure, however controlled it might be, spoke eloquently to all of them.

◆

As relieved as Hattori was to be gone from Prisonville, he'd had less frustrating days. True to form, Kat found the priciest lodgings the city had. She chose a two bedroom residence on the upper floor of a luxury hotel, complete with dining chamber and wraparound balcony. Fully furnished, the penthouse's painted ceilings sparkled with chandeliers, its parquet floors softened by hand-loomed carpets. The wood-burning fireplace in the "grand salon" was at least six feet tall. When Hattori pointed out it might be wise to conserve their funds, Kat lifted her brows at him.

"This is hardly the most expensive place I could find. Hand manufacture isn't as rare in Human lands. Besides which, if I chose somewhere reasonable, we'd all be uncomfortable. Those sort of rooms are unlikely to have electrical power or updated plumbing—and please don't try to convince me you'd rather wash up in a bucket."

Hattori wouldn't have been eager, but he'd have been willing. He nearly said so . . . except it seemed childish.

"Is the second bedroom all right with you?" she asked Haro.

Haro glanced at Hattori, probably wondering exactly what the arrangements between the three of them were. "It's fine," he said. "Everything here is fine."

His hands were clenched by his sides, so *fine* wasn't precisely what he was feeling.

"You'll get used to being free," Kat said compassionately. "I expect it just takes a bit of time."

"Yes," Haro agreed with a jerky bow. "I'm sure you're correct, princess."

Ciran snorted at his politeness, which made Haro startle like a spooked pigeon.

"Sorry," Ciran said, lifting his hands, palms out. "Just trying out some Human habits. Why don't you and Hattori get settled while I accompany Kat on her errand?"

Hattori actually felt a growl rising in his chest. The reaction shocked him sufficiently that he managed to hold it back. It made perfect sense for Kat and Ciran to go together. They both were fluent in the local language, and Haro could hardly be left alone.

The problem was, Hattori really wanted to be alone with Kat, to rip open her tight new clothes or maybe just throw up all those skirts. Even thinking about her lacy petticoats and knickers hardened his prick painfully. He could fuck her against the wall while she wore them. He could tie her to the "king" size bed, as they called it here. Sadly, his imagination wasn't cooperating with his fantasies. A picture flashed through his mind of Ciran kissing her madly in the hallway, as soon as the door was closed.

The growl he'd held back before started to rumble.

"Are you all right?" Ciran asked. They stood in the foyer, and he was adjusting his Human tophat to the precise angle actors wore them in holoshows. His fingers were so graceful, so long and clever that Hattori's prick strained to breach his zipper.

Imagining those fingers buried in Kat's pussy didn't improve his mood at all.

"I'm fine," he said, snarling it. Unable to stop himself, he leaned closer to Ciran's ear. "Don't forget who she belongs to while you're alone out there."

Ciran jerked back and gaped at him.

Hattori spun away before his friend could demand if he'd lost his mind. Ciran had never given him cause to think he'd try to steal his mate's affections. Whatever had transpired with the prison warden had to be a part of a bribe. Despite the shame that pricked Hattori, he didn't apologize.

He strode away from the door even as Ciran and Kat went out. The palatial sitting room/salon with its wall of partitioned windows seemed a fine spot to pace. Given how old and faded its hand-woven carpet was, he might in truth wear a hole through it—damage Kat would no doubt be ecstatic to pay for. His body burned with each step, his cock hard as iron inside his new silk-lined wool trousers. That lining shifted over him in a caress, both infuriating and pleasing him. It took a couple passes up and down the room for him to notice his brother in the doorway, watching him gravely. Haro stood in review posture. He hadn't relaxed enough to lean against the lintel.

Hattori had to stop pacing them. He couldn't worry his twin.

"Do you need something?" he asked Haro.

Haro shook his head. "She loves you, brother. So does Ciran, from what I can tell. You deserve to be valued by both of them."

Hattori didn't know what to say. He felt vaguely embarrassed, though he wasn't sure for what. He thought of telling Haro that he and Kat were bonded, that she was able to bring him the releases he'd so often despaired of in the past. That seemed too personal—and like rubbing salt in wounds. His brother wouldn't have had a woman in two decades.

"I received the food and the blankets you arranged," Haro said. "In case you'd wondered."

"I got the notes you sent back."

"I couldn't write much. Very little mail left the prison. We inmates knew it was monitored."

"I treasured every word," Hattori said.

Haro smiled at him, the soft curve of his mouth holding all the sweetness Hattori remembered. Haro shouldn't have been born a Yama. A Human monk, perhaps, in a monastery devoted to good deeds.

"I'm hungry," Haro said. "Do you suppose the princess would mind if we discover what Human room service consists of?"

"I'm certain she'd be pleased," Hattori answered acerbically. "Kat enjoys supplying others with sustenance."

♦

Because she suspected Ciran would be entertained by it, Kat took the horse drawn trolley to the diamond district on the east end. Ciran looked handsomer than seemed fair in his Human clothes— and so excited by their surroundings he could scarcely contain himself. His eyes went everywhere: to the gaudy advertising on the trolley panels, to the storefronts, to the ragged children hawking newspapers from corners. They were magic to him, and he was magic to her. Her heart ached to realize it. She didn't see how this tangle could unravel well.

She didn't mean to ask, but something inside her had to know. "What did Hattori say to upset you at the door?"

Ciran looked at her, startled. "Nothing. I think we've all been on edge lately."

He was lying, but she didn't call him on it. She didn't have time to. The narrow marble-faced building she remembered was coming up on their right, the one with *DuBieren* chiseled in block letters beneath the elegant pediment. She tugged the cord for the conductor's bell, recalling too late that Ciran would have liked doing it.

"This is our stop," she said. "We go down the stairs in the middle of the car."

"Allow me," Ciran said, making sure he reached the door before her. With courtly ease, he lifted her off the final step, setting her on her feet out of the worst of the slushy snow.

"Too much?" he asked, noting eyes on them.

"Only a little. You're very dashing by Human standards. Those women are probably wishing they were me."

"Jolly good!" he exclaimed, jumping at the excuse to use the phrase.

His inward preen at her compliment couldn't be mistaken, which made her laugh to herself. Her affections didn't care that she'd never come first with him. Not finding him charming really was impossible.

♦

Benjamin DuBieren wasn't the cutter who'd created the Katsu Blue, but he'd founded the diamond dealing firm that employed the man. DuBieren's specialty was designing jewelry, making his family name a byword among Humans for glamour. Kat had heard the mere sight of the trademark DuBieren black velvet box could cause the females of his race to lose their breath.

Being Yamish and unused to such artistry, Kat knew she was many times more susceptible.

This may have been the reason Benjamin had taken a shine to her. She'd nearly fainted the first time she saw one of his necklaces in a shop window. Benjamin had been coming out the door and had caught her elbow to prevent her collapse. They'd struck up an acquaintance and then a sort of friendship, which Kat hoped she wasn't hanging too much on. Her plan today was to speak to his secretary and request an appointment. To her pleasure, the female guardian of his gate asked if she and Ciran would like to wait. No more than five minutes passed before the patriarch himself emerged into the outer room.

Her old acquaintance was a tall portly man with a neatly squared salt and pepper beard. Tiny spectacles—which he liked to polish—balanced on a larger nose than most Yama could dream of. Despite this prodigy, his brilliant smile made him beautiful. To her relief, he was smiling now.

"Princess Katsu!" he exclaimed, enfolding her in the Human-style welcome she'd never quite grown used to. "What a sight for sore eyes you are! I hope this visit means you've been released from your unfair banishment—and with a handsome man come to meet me too!"

He pushed her back to the end of his arms and wagged bushy brows, probably a millimeter from designing wedding bands. For such a sharp businessman, he was ridiculously romantic.

"This is my friend, Ciran," she said. "I hope you haven't forgotten I prefer you to call me Kat."

"Indulge an old man," Benjamin scolded. "How many princesses do I know?"

He was pumping one of Ciran's hands between both of his as he said it, treating the younger man to a wink as well.

"I expect you know quite a few," Ciran said, recovering from his surprise. "Given what you do for a living."

Their host laughed with great motion and volume. "Human only," he confided, one finger laid beside his great nose. "Katsu is the single demon princess I have the honor of calling friend."

"I hope you still consider it an honor when I explain why we're here."

Benjamin took one look at her wry expression and grew as serious as he'd formerly been jovial. "Trouble," he said, his canny eyes narrowed. "Why don't we go into my private office and break out my thinking cap. Miriam, sweetie, no interruptions while we're in there and no mentions to anyone that the princess is here."

Since Miriam had the look of one of his numerous daughters, Kat expected he'd be obeyed.

♦

Benjamin's thinking cap was a supply of twelve-year-old Jeruvian brandy. He poured snifters of the strong liquor all around, then sat back in his worn leather chair to cradle his own. The quiet she'd been surprised from the first to find him capable of made it easy for her to confide in him, especially when he listened with such obvious affection. He wasn't connected to her except by business, and yet he treated her as warmly as his daughters. Kat didn't tell him everything, but she did share more than she expected.

When she'd finished, Benjamin set down his brandy to tap his fingers together and think for a few minutes. His golden watch chain gleamed on his snug black vest.

"You have a conundrum," he said at last. "You need cash now and possibly a way to support yourself, longer term. New identities would be helpful, either here or somewhere else. As long as you're living incognito, protection could become an issue. Keeping secrets has a tendency to make people vulnerable."

"I know it's a lot to ask for your counsel on."

Benjamin waved his hand in dismissal at her apology. "I wish my relatives would come to me like this. I volunteer advice, and they accuse me of bullying." He removed his little glasses, leaning forward over his desk to polish them with a handkerchief. His posture was more informal than a Yama would have displayed, but Kat found it no less endearing because of that. "I have the rough you left me for safekeeping. I'd be happy to buy those stones from you; they're very good quality. Before I make you an offer, however, I'd like to propose a different sort of business arrangement."

"How different?" Kat asked, unable to keep caution from tightening her voice.

Benjamin smiled, a strong glint of business savvy joining the fondness in his eyes. "My proposition would require some daring, but it could solve more than one of your problems, and for a farther stroll down the road."

"All right," Kat said warily. "Both my ears are open."

◆

The old man could have been Yamish to have come up with such a plan. His proposition was devious, barely legal, and had the potential for huge profits. Ciran wondered if a fiscally adventurous princess like Kat would be able to resist it.

She gave Benjamin no decision before they left, just a promise to consider what he had said. As she pulled her gloves back on and stepped with Ciran onto the hand-shoveled pavement, her pretty face was thoughtful.

Sensing she wasn't ready to return to their rooms, Ciran stopped and turned to her. "You trust that man. You told him a lot."

Maybe her new outfit was affecting her. Her rueful shrug was nearly a Human one. She looked up the building they'd just departed before she spoke. "Once a year on my natal day, my father behaved like him, with warmth and smiles and an affection I couldn't possibly mistake. The rest of the time, he was a proper self-controlled royal sire. I know Benjamin probably drives his daughters crazy, but there have been moments during my exile when I wished I could trade places. I expect I should know better. Human openness has a way of disarming me."

"Maybe your trust is founded. He'd be trusting you as well in this enterprise."

Kat regarded him with a purse-lipped smile. "I suspect Benjamin DuBieren loves business gambles. In that trait at least, he could be one of us."

Ciran nodded. He'd been thinking the same thing. A trolley approached them, clanking on its rails, but he didn't move toward it. "Do you want to tell Hattori?"

He'd hesitated to ask, because his own motivations weren't clear to him. Did he like the idea of keeping Kat's secrets a bit too much? He knew he liked the closeness that had grown between them lately.

Kat let out a careful breath. "I wouldn't mind more time to think about it. And to decide how to spring it on Hattori. I know he was hoping I'd left my past behind."

"Humans believe in revenge," Ciran ventured to observe. "Almost all they do on *All My Weddings* is get even."

The comparison surprised her into laughing. "Well, if it's good enough for *All My Weddings*, it certainly—"

She stopped short, her hand clutching his coat sleeve tight enough to wrinkle it. "Do you feel that?"

"Feel what?"

"Someone watching us. All the hair on my nape stood up."

He looked around casually, returned to being an assassin in one heartbeat. He was better than royals at reading energy, but in this instance that wasn't an advantage. The Humans who shared this busy street with them were radiating such a dizzying array of emotions that opening his other senses made the noise impossible to sort through. The swiftness with which their feelings infected his drove him to shut them out. Keeping a level head seemed more important.

"I don't see anyone out of place," he said, uncertain he'd spot the signs in this alien land. "Did the energy feel familiar?"

Kat was upset enough to wrinkle her nose. "I don't know. Possibly it was nothing. Like you said, we've all been on edge."

On edge or not, Ciran wasn't going to dismiss her feeling. Their enemies were too dangerous for that.

10: HEAT

Haro opened the door to their lodgings while Kat was still fishing for the key in her secondhand reticule. His appearance drove her grumblings about Human "conveniences" from her head. Though his expression was as impassive as before, to Kat's eyes he looked worried.

"My brother is in the living room," he said.

Kat interpreted this as a request that they go to him—and probably a warning that something was amiss. She shed her gloves and coat along the way, thinking guiltily as she tossed them onto a chair that it wouldn't be awful to have a servant to hang them up. Though Benjamin would pay fairly for her stones, the proceeds would only support the four of them for a while. If she accepted his alternate proposition, they'd be able to afford staff. She thought she'd proved she wasn't lazy back in Black Hole. Surely princesses were allowed to want some luxuries.

Ciran was a step behind her as she entered the grand salon. Hattori had thrown open two of the terrace's window doors. Chill wind gusted inward, making sails of the sheer curtains. The moment he turned to face them, Kat knew he wasn't feeling the cold.

Hattori's eyes were black pools of lust. Two streaks of red climbed either side of his neck, the swelling of his kith glands visible from across the room. A far larger swelling rose from his groin, testing the expansive powers of the wool. Hattori had already torn off his waistcoat and unbuttoned his white dress shirt, leaving his big chest bare to the icy air. The gooseflesh that swept his muscles didn't lessen his appeal. Despite her sympathy, Kat's body throbbed at the sight of him.

"It's so bad," he grated out as if reluctant to admit it. "Worse than it's ever been. I don't know why it's come on me like this. I feel like I'm going to kill someone if I can't have you this second."

"All you ever have to do is ask," Kat swore, hurrying across the carpet to him. "I'm always here for you."

He met her in the middle, his big hands gripping her upper arms. Heat rolled off him like a furnace as he pulled her up to her toes. He swallowed, then groaned, clearly dying to kiss her and release the aphrodisiac from his mouth. Kat heard the door latch behind them open. As he'd done so many times recently, Ciran was withdrawing.

"Don't," Hattori growled, already panting from her nearness. His fingers shifted their grip as his night-black gaze left hers to find Ciran. "I need you too. All I can think about is fucking the pair of you."

Ciran's intake of breath sent a hot chill skimming down Kat's spine—as hot as the declaration that inspired it. Ciran shifted uncomfortably. "Hattori . . ."

"I mean it, Ciran. I'm sorry if it bothers you, but my body can't stand the thought of not taking you as well."

"You're sorry if it *bothers* me." Ciran let out a ragged laugh.

"Please," Hattori said, because Ciran still wasn't moving. "Please come here and kiss me." He wrenched his gaze back to Kat. "That's all right, isn't it?"

"It's more than all right," she said throatily. "It's perfect."

Emotions he might not have understood crossed his handsome face. None of them had time for questions. Ciran was there, and Hattori was urging his friend to him with a steely hand wrapped behind his neck. They both groaned as their tongues battled, the kiss instantly open and wet. Kat saw a world of difference between this kiss and the ones Ciran had given Ombino. His heart was in this, his passion and his love and his pent-up hurt. The broken noises he made were hungry for more than sex, though that was in there as well. Kat could hardly fail to perceive his longing, given how desperately close Hattori's other arm was holding her.

Now that he had them, he wasn't letting go.

"God," Ciran moaned, breaking free long enough to speak. "You taste delicious."

Hattori's kith was spilling for him, their genetic profiles close enough for Ciran to trigger it. Hattori kissed him again, pouring the aphrodisiac into him. He couldn't seem to stop doing it, and Ciran was soon writhing against him, one leg levering around his hip so he could grind their cocks together. Between his heightened drive for sex and Hattori's kith, and Ciran was as agonized for relief as the other man.

It was a good long time before either of them came up for air.

"Touch me," Hattori begged when his mouth was free. "This itching in my prick is driving me insane."

Kat wasn't sure it mattered which of them complied. Ciran's hands met hers at the stretched out front of Hattori's trousers. Together they fought the unfamiliar fastening open, with Ciran somehow managing to caress her fingers at the same time. Hattori groaned as his huge cock fell free. Kat caught and clasped the thick heat of it, her hold as firm around his hardness as royal strength could make it.

"You know, princess," Ciran breathed, "in my old profession, you could make a mint off a grip like that."

Hattori squirmed like he was trying to fuck her hand.

"Yes," he said. "Please suck me."

His lust-fogged mind must have been sending him pictures she hadn't hinted at, but the suggestion was fine with her. She'd never felt as eager as when she dropped to her knees on the soft carpet. His massive erection jerked up and down like it was alive. His kith was running by itself, lubricating that rigid pole. She wrapped both hands around the shaft, her thumbs pressing inward hard as she drove them side by side up his strut. A coin-sized inflammation underneath his glans took her by surprise, though maybe it shouldn't have. If the redness was what she suspected, he was entering the most advanced form of rut. This was a stage mated royals didn't always experience; it depended on how closely matched they were.

If Hattori's royal whip was awakening, it was no wonder this heat felt different. Curious, because she'd never seen this phenomena outside of royals-only erotic vids, she stroked the swelling with the pads of her thumbs. The reddened flesh protected an extra sexual organ, one meant to lock male and female together when it uncoiled. Hattori cried out as she compressed it, his hips twisting so violently he nearly pulled his cock from her hold. She thought she'd rubbed him too firmly for comfort, but this wasn't the case.

"There," he said, shoving his shaft back into her hands. "*Harder.* That's where I'm itching worst."

Kat thought she knew the cure for that—at least a temporary one. She took the swollen head of him in her mouth, laving him with wetness and pulling hard with her cheeks. Hattori's groan of thanks was lost in Ciran's throat, who he was kissing frenziedly again. Oddly pleased by this, Kat continued to stimulate his power spot with her tongue. Kith jetted repeatedly from his slit, the bliss of the mini-ejaculations causing him buck and moan. He tasted spicy and just a little sweet, her head beginning to spin at the aphrodisiac flooding her.

It was hard to think as it hit her bloodstream. Her own body was on fire, her clit a little coal tucked between pulsing folds. Needing more of everything she was feeling, she sucked his shaft deeper. She'd always been a bit orally fixated, but the silky throbbing feel of him in her mouth was unbelievably pleasurable. She loved working him over, no matter how hungry the rest of her was.

The hoarse curses that came from him were the best praise she'd ever heard.

"That feels too incredible," he groaned. "I can't make myself make you stop."

She didn't want to stop. She yanked down his open trousers, craving him naked: a trembling, sweating warrior above her. She butterflied the tip of her tongue back and forth across his slit, knowing he'd also be itching there. Hattori gasped a second before a hard orgasm ran through his cock, the intensity of the contractions causing his shaft to ripple within her mouth. No seed came out with the climax; he hadn't yet reached that stage—which meant the pleasure reaction would mostly madden him. Sure enough, he thrust more deeply into her mouth, instincts too strong to fight compelling him to seek more orgasmic sensations. Her own body's extreme arousal probably saved her from choking.

She was too avid not to want all of him.

"I can't stop," Hattori panted, his hips surging in again. She hadn't thought it possible, but his cock was harder, like steel pulsing against her palate. "I need to be inside you. Ciran, help me pull free of her."

This was what Ciran had asked her to do with Ombino. The parallel drenched her pussy, which hardly needed to be wetter. Ciran let go of Hattori and moved behind her.

"Lie down," he said, pulling at her shoulders until she released her prize. To her amazement, his voice was rougher than Hattori's.

"Throw up her petticoats," Hattori said, need deepening the order. "I'm going to take her just as she is."

Ciran flung up her skirts and dragged off her knickers. No less quick to action, Hattori knelt between her legs. His hands rubbed his thigh muscles restlessly, his prick thrusting up from his groin like a length of stone. Even as she watched, he gave in to temptation and squeezed his balls. His neck arched back with relief at the self-massage, the force he used to loosen his stored up seed almost frightening. He wasn't simply squeezing his scrotum, he was stretching it out as well, uttering primal sounds that were very animal.

"Let me," Ciran said, laying a calming hand on his fisted ones. "I'll rub you, and you can go down on her. She smells too good not to have a taste."

Hattori moaned, seeming to agree but not ready to let go of himself yet. Reduced to simple thoughts, he stared between her splayed legs at her no doubt glistening pussy. This seemed to excite him further, his palms and fingers compulsively squeezing his testicles. She had no curls to obscure his view of her sex, but she couldn't be shy when she witnessed what the sight of it did to him. His nostrils flared as he scented her, the flush that stained his cheeks darkening. His eyes were so glassy they swum with stars. His lamril swept his upper lip in the universal signal for appetite.

"I want that," he said, forming words with difficulty, "but I'm nearly out of patience. Rub me hard so I'll have some time with her."

Kat's vagina spasmed, the idea of him wanting to focus on her almost too much to take in. When he forced his hands to release his balls, she shuddered right along with him.

He lowered himself to her like he was genuflecting. She felt his hot ragged breaths on her intimate flesh and then two strong index fingers sliding up her creamy folds. The way he parted them separated her clit from the rest of her, a treasure he wanted to examine all by itself. As he tugged away the flesh that surrounded the little organ, it stood out and pulsed harder. His finger pads pushed around its sides, causing her to gasp at the heightening of sensation along her nerves.

"You're so pretty here," he said, then moaned at something Ciran had done to him.

Kat struggled up on her elbows to see. Ciran was behind him straddling his hips, one arm flexing strongly as his fist tugged Hattori's cock. His grip was tight on that kith-oiled skin, giving what must have been a delicious twist when it reached the reddened circle under the flare. This, she suspected, was the trick that had made him moan.

However good he felt, Hattori didn't like her attention straying. His eyes narrowed. "You need to forget everything but me."

All the threat took to fulfill was him putting his mouth on her. He had her full concentration then, having locked his lips around her clitoris while his tongue and cheeks tugged it rhythmically. Kat decided he had a gift for sexual directness. Not about to ask him to delay, she grabbed his head and rocked closer, more than ready for a climax. His intent didn't seem to be to give her one. Instead, he painted her with his kith, teasing the burning substance under her clit's soft hood. Her folds were next and the first few inches of her sheath. Every swipe of his tongue felt incredible, teasing her to the aching edge of explosion without quite sending her over. Kat began to thrash beneath him, in some danger of damaging his ears with her grip on them. It didn't help that Hattori's own hips were jerking, the taste of her essence unavoidably increasing his urge to copulate. Ciran had trouble holding him, though he seemed bent on keeping Hattori's cock as pleasured as possible.

That kind of dedication had to produce results. Hattori made a strangled noise against her and came with a long shiver.

The second dry climax spelled the end of his self control.

He wrenched his head from her hands, kneeling up with his thighs spread wide under her bottom. Her hips he took in a hard tight grip. As she looked up his gorgeous body, his expression was like nothing she'd ever seen. He was in a state of arousal beyond speaking. The passion his face conveyed was fierce, a single-minded determination to possess her. He swung her upper body up with ease, the speed of the motion stealing her breath. She caught herself on his huge shoulders, trembling with uncontrollable eagerness. He made her feel feminine and helpless, at his mercy for the satisfaction of her desires. She shouldn't have liked that, but her breathing came so quick and shallow her corset didn't hamper it. Liquid heat ran from her, her pussy twitching and aching for his entry.

Her hands were shaking too badly to help him find his way. He needed his own fingers to position the broad hot tip of him at her gate. The moment those age-old puzzle pieces kissed, one giant spurt of kith flooded hotly into her from him.

His body was making certain she'd welcome what was coming.

His eyes shut with killing pleasure. His lips moved, maybe whispering her name or just cursing. The curve of him felt huge against her, perhaps too big to take. Kat wasn't sure she cared. Blood rushed in her ears as his hands tightened on her waist. His muscles gathered, he sucked a breath, and then his hips drove monumentally upward. He pulled her down him at the same time, grunting with urgency and effort. With both their bodies under his control, he filled her so quickly she barely had time to adjust. Fortunately, she'd been ready, her passage too wet and greedy to resist him. Now that he was all the way in her, the pressure was wonderful—the heat and thickness and the sheer length of him. With no effort whatsoever, he pressed that tender spot she loved deep inside. Its nerves felt extra sensitive today, starving for the stimulation only he could offer. She almost came from his entry, but before she could, he began to thrust.

She felt as if she had to redefine ecstasy. Instead of coming, her body jumped to a new level of suspense, one she wasn't certain she'd live through. Each ferocious upward stroke of Hattori's penis hammered that excruciating sensitivity inside her, feeling better than anything real should have been able to. She gasped for air, tears squeezing from her eyes. Her inner muscles tightened as the paroxysm she was desperate for drew closer. She needed it more than she'd thought she could anything. She writhed from the hips, trying to go even harder than he was pulling her. A moan she didn't recognize as Yamish broke from her throat as the climax began to crest.

It slammed her sex like a speeding train. She bit his shoulder at its intensity, helpless to stop herself from acting like a wild creature. Hattori didn't protest. He squeezed the breast that had bounced free of her décolleté, roughly thumbing its tight nipple. His own utterances were little more than snarls, rising in volume as her pussy clenched on his pistoning. Though she couldn't doubt he relished what they were doing, she also sensed he wasn't getting quite what he needed. He shuddered as two more dry orgasms tore through him, the climaxes hitting with barely a pause between.

The effect this had on his already racheted up libido made him throw back his head and roar with frustration.

"Ciran," she gasped.

Ciran was already moving, scarcely needing her to give him his cue. Of the three of them, only Hattori had any doubt he'd be given whatever he required. He was letting out sounds of pain as he strove for more friction.

"Shh," she said, stroking his contorted face. "Ciran's going to take you now."

Hattori needed to slow his motions to let him in, a goal directly opposed to his instinct to keep powering into her.

"I can't," he panted as he lowered her back and shoulders onto the floor. Having her beneath him meant he could pump into her harder, which his body immediately took advantage of. He groaned with pleasure at the increase in stimulation, though he had to know it wasn't a good idea. "Fate, I'm going mad."

Ciran must have decided force was the best solution. He grabbed Hattori's hips, shoved his pelvis all the way into Kat, and then stopped him from moving by the simple expedient of leaving his entire weight pressed on Hattori's back.

Trapped though he was, Hattori squirmed inside her, his cock desperate for its previous motions to continue. The center of his shaft was swelling, unmistakable signal that he could in fact become more aroused.

"Do it," he demanded hoarsely of Ciran. "Shove inside and fuck me before I throw you off."

That he'd be able to accomplish this was apparent. Hattori had more muscle mass and a lot of motivation. Ciran took him at his word. He used one hand to unzip himself, spat on his palm for lubrication, then eased himself into place.

"Hold onto your hats," he said, which must have been a Human expression. For Hattori's sake, Kat hoped it meant he was going to take him hard.

Hattori groaned the moment the other man began entering. His body twisted, but he didn't try to throw him off as threatened. Maybe how good Ciran felt sliding in helped him control himself. When Ciran's tip reached his kingmaster gland, Hattori's cheek dropped to hers with a blissful sigh. The sound repeated as Ciran's hips settled into a steady roll. His motions were firm and smooth, not as hard as they could get but hard enough for now.

"Don't stop," Hattori found breath to moan. "Please keep doing that."

Ciran's eyes crinkled with amusement as his silver-blue gaze met hers. In that moment, their goals were completely harmonious: to give Hattori pleasure and—in doing so—experience it themselves.

This is how it's supposed to be, she thought. *The three of us together.*

She tried not to let her fear that it couldn't last ruin it.

◆

Ciran was an erotic genius. Hattori never should have doubted he could soothe the madness inside of him. He writhed with enjoyment as his friend shoved his cock across the heat of his anal gland, finally scratching the itch that had been building there since he'd picked them up on the prison roof.

Each of Ciran's thrusts slung him into Kat's body, and that was a pleasure too. Her nipples strafed him like hot pebbles, making him wish he could reach them with his mouth.

Right then, he had more longings than he could satisfy.

Of course his penis was itching too—most insanely on the spot where Kat had rubbed and sucked it. He didn't know how she knew to do it, and right then he didn't care. The slippery fist of her pussy was his salvation, the pressure he could exert when his length reached the end of her. There was an area of extra heat in her there, at the culmination of her passage, that sent a teasing tingle straight to the itchy spot each time he pushed the surfaces together. Doing this was a compulsion he couldn't fight. Though he didn't mean to insult Ciran or—Fate knew—interfere with what he was doing, he realized his pelvis was rocking ever more insistently into her, the sensation of those places knocking each other too crucial not to keep up.

He groaned as his body made him do it harder, the sound tinged with his regret. Ciran kissed his shoulder, his palms sliding gently up his tense back muscles.

"It's all right," he said, his own voice rough with sensual enjoyment. "I'm in you now. I'm helping. You do whatever your body needs."

Hattori didn't deserve for Ciran to be so kind. He could feel how hard Ciran was, how much he was savoring being able to touch him again. Ciran was in love with him. There was no denying it any more. Hattori had to be the most selfish Yama ever. He couldn't even be sorry that Ciran cared for him; he was too grateful for what it made him do.

He moaned as Kat reached past him to stroke Ciran's face. As long as he was around to participate, his body thought this was arousing.

"You should see your aura, princess," Ciran murmured, a soft laugh squeezing out between jostled breaths. "You're glowing from head to toe."

If she was, Hattori wasn't the sole reason. *It's more than all right*, she'd said. *It's perfect.* Fair or not, selfish or not, the three of them made up this whole.

"Kiss me," she said to Ciran. "I want to feel your energy too."

She said it like she wasn't convinced he'd want to, but Ciran laid that idea to rest. "Princess," he said, "never doubt I welcome the chance to share these pleasures with you."

Kat gave a soft, small cry, craning up as Ciran was craning down. As their mouths met and fused together, Kat's movements changed. Her reactions to Hattori's thrusts grew slower, more undulating and yet still deep . . . more like Ciran's, to be truthful. Jealousy brushed his ego but blew away before it dug in. Ciran and Kat's attraction to each other simply felt too good to him. Their auras billowed through his like erotic seas, hot and sleek and silky as their energy currents caressed his. His body couldn't decide which pleasure to strain toward; so much was being given him.

In the end he had to surrender, had to trust them to get him where he yearned to go. Sighs issued from him all by themselves. Soon he was thrusting like Kat and Ciran: slow, deep, hard, every inch of heat sliding lubriciously over and into his partners' complements for it. The itch in his cockhead intensified, the strange, fluttering sensations inside its flesh. He moaned at this, but his suffering was delicious. He found himself grinding into Kat at the end of each penetration, taking extra seconds to rub the worst itching against her there. No matter how hard he pushed, she clutched him and pushed back. The fact that Ciran did the same to his kingmaster overwhelmed him with pleasure.

Part of him wanted to continue like this all night, to weep with longing if that's what it came to. His body, however, had its own agenda.

The change started as a tingle at the tip of his cock, much like the ones he felt each time he ground his sweet spot hard into hers. The tingle didn't ebb as it usually did. It grew stronger, and larger, sweeping up his prick with alarming speed. The wave spread so fast it swallowed him. His sweet spot stung then, his skin trying to split open. He didn't decide to jam himself into Kat with all his might; his muscles did it for him. To resist was impossible; to even attempt to spelled destruction. He needed to be that deeply inside her, needed to connect their bodies so they'd never separate. Even with all his strength brought to bear, their connection didn't feel tight enough.

"Push," he gasped to Ciran, and Ciran did, squashing flesh he'd thought too hard to flatten into her cushiony wall. Only then did he feel like he was far enough into her. Now all he had to do was stay like this forever.

Kat was embracing him with her thighs and arms when the place beneath his glans opened. He gasped and cried out rawly. Something was uncoiling from him, a tensile snake of flesh that felt like it was all nerve. Lightning bolts of sensation, truly too sharp to bear, streaked through him as the thing wriggled.

"It's all right," she crooned next to his ear. "This is supposed to happen."

It was good she hugged him so tightly. He was trembling like a leaf. The thing was seeking something inside of her, whipping blindly between her soft, hot walls. She made a throaty sound, so he guessed the pleasure-pain had her in its clutches too. The whip curved around him, as thick as her smallest finger sliding up his wet cockhead. Inches had brought him ecstasy before. Now millimeters did. The whip found her hotspot and burrowed in. Nerve met nerve, binding one to the other. Signals overloaded like an exploding star.

The orgasm wasn't hers or his. It was both combined. He didn't always perceive auras, but the dancing luminescence was unambiguous, and only the start of the fireworks. Fierce contractions ripped through his penis, rising up from deep in his groin, a devastating accompaniment to the clenching of her pussy. Still he strained farther inward, that mysterious extra appendage thrumming where it locked to her. More sensation spiked at its vibration. The first bursts of seed streaked from him, creating a delicious loosening in his spine.

"God," Ciran gasped, his thrusts speeding up. The acceleration reminded Hattori he had another pleasure center, now being pounded in a frenzy by Ciran's cock.

Kat liked this as much as he did. Her back arched, fingernails pricking into his skin.

"I feel him inside you," she panted. "I feel what he's doing to you."

He hadn't known anything could excite him so ferociously, certainly not in the middle of his current firestorm of ecstasy. Pressure gathered in his balls as Ciran's strokes took on yet more urgency, his groans of longing indicating how close he was. Red flashed across Hattori's vision, the sensations in his kingmaster too acute to process. When he felt Ciran go with a violent shudder, everything in him cut loose.

He'd been ejaculating, but now his testicles contracted dramatically, wanting to empty faster than they were able to. He'd never come in one go when he was in heat, but his body seemed to be attempting it. Semen rocketed from him in thick hot waves, rioting through and over the other delights of his orgasm.

This, at last, was release at its most basic.

His mind went *ahh* as groans rumbled lavishly in his chest. He came and came and his urethra still squeezed out more. Each time he thought the flood was stopping, that little whip of flesh vibrated and sent him rolling over the edge again. It sent Kat as well, oscillating the buried cache of nerves it had locked onto. Her pleasure kicked more thrills through him, until a lifetime of climaxes seemed to be packed into one sex act. Every guard he could have erected against wallowing in them succumbed. When Kat petted his shoulders, even his skin tried to come.

He couldn't have been more physical, but he'd also never been less. His emotions were realer than he'd ever felt them, deeper and stronger and completely independent of anything Kat and Ciran did. He loved *to* love, that transcendent part of his being asking nothing in return. Love itself was his greatest pleasure, stripping him naked in a place of absolutely safety.

The impression was so warm, so joyous and comforting, that he had to sigh when it slipped away.

He was on his back and couldn't remember how he'd gotten there. Kat was sprawled atop him, her slender, half-clothed body rising and falling with his hard breathing. Ciran lay face down beside him, his warm damp side leaning against his. Kat was more than damp, she was drenched, especially her sex. He had a strong suspicion her new garments were ruined. For once, the waste couldn't bother him. The evidence that he'd claimed her gratified his primitive nature. Given this, he was startled to discover his right hand shoved into Ciran's trousers, cupping his left butt cheek—a gesture of ownership, if ever there were one. As his orgasmic euphoria faded, it occurred to him that leaving his hand there might be misleading. His fingers couldn't have cared less about his scruples. They tightened on Ciran's rear, relishing its firm give.

"Mm," Ciran said, turning his head to sleepily nuzzle his shoulder. "That's what I call a royal orgasm."

With an inward jolt, Hattori realized Ciran's hand was under Kat's crumpled petticoats, giving her bottom the same appreciative attention his hand was giving him. For some reason, this made him pull his hold away.

"Fine," Hattori said, his voice ragged from groaning. He cleared it and went on. "Since neither of you is surprised by what happened, perhaps you could fill me in."

"The prince's whip," Kat mumbled into his pectoral. "A sexual organ only royals are supposed to have. I guess your tinkered genes made you princely enough."

Hattori would have spoken, but Ciran chose then to groan and roll into a more comfortable position. He ended up with his head pillowed on Hattori's chest next to Kat's. How good the pair felt resting on him had him fighting a squirm.

"There are theories," Ciran said, his fingers playing gently along the sensitive inside of Hattori's lolling thigh. "One of the more popular is that the whip intensifies a mated couple's emotional bond—Yama being a trifled stunted when it comes to intimacy. Another claims it improves the chances of conception. As you might or might not know, princes sometimes have trouble hitting the mark, as it were."

The thought of Kat having his child made his chest tighten. Infinity knew she'd made a sweet mother. Possibly his heart had started beating harder, because Kat patted the ribs above it. "Don't worry about that. Odds are good it won't happen the first time. Royals don't get pregnant that easily."

"I'm not worried. I'm . . . I'd be incredibly happy to father a child with you."

Kat's head lifted from his chest. "Really? You'd be happy?"

"And honored, of course." Inexplicably, this made Ciran and Kat laugh. "Why is that funny?"

Kat's smile was soft. "Sometimes you are the dearest man. You don't have to be honored. You being happy is actually better."

"You're a princess. Not being honored could be taken as disrespect."

Kat laid her head back down, probably to hide the smile he could feel curving up her mouth. "Apparently, Citizen Hattori, you're prince enough for me."

"Prince," he muttered, knowing he was anything but. The sheer well being in his body didn't allow for grumpiness or guilt. He stretched beneath his two warm burdens, sighing as joints popped and realigned pleasurably. His shoulder ached where she'd nipped him, but he didn't begrudge the pain.

If he'd marked her, she'd done as much to him.

"You two need to shower," he said.

"*We* do," Kat repeated, a hint of a laugh in it.

He couldn't fault her humor. He supposed he wasn't daisy fresh himself. Nonetheless, he went on stubbornly. "Ciran still smells like another man."

Kat sat up to look at him. "You smelled the warden on us?"

Since he was no longer holding her, Hattori laid his forearm across his eyes. "I knew the moment you got into the aircar. But please spare me the details. I know you only did . . . whatever it was for Haro."

He sensed Kat and Ciran exchanging glances. Then Ciran sat up as well. "You can smell him on me now?"

"A bit," he admitted. "And I don't like it, so please humor me and wash up."

There was a pause. Ciran pushed to his feet. Kat stayed sitting long enough to lean down and kiss his cheek. "Join us if you want," she invited.

"Too tired to move," he declined, though it was more than that.

He owed them a chance to be together, if that's what they wanted. As replete as his body was, this might be one of the few times he didn't resent it.

◆

By Human standards, the bathing chamber was luxurious. Clean as any "demon" could demand, it was tiled from floor to ceiling in slightly cracked black and white porcelain tiles. Candles stood in sconces in case the power went out, but to Kat—and probably to Ciran—they appeared romantic. The size of shower stall was generous, the water pressure unpredictable but generally strong. The dual brass fixtures suggested there'd be spray enough for two.

"No drying tube," Ciran observed as he looked around.

"The towel rack is heated."

"Ah," he said with a little nod.

"This really is the best technology Humans have."

He turned and smiled at her. "I'm not complaining, Kat."

He hadn't used that soft tone with her in a while. Kat couldn't help if it made her blush. Also unhelpful was the fact that his fingers were unbuttoning his sweat-dampened, sharp-collared shirt. Only Hattori had been naked when they made love. Inevitably, Ciran noted her interest.

"Oh princess," he said. "You gratify me more than you know."

"Should I leave?" she asked, suddenly nervous.

"Do you want to?" He must have taken out his corrective lenses, because his eyes were once again different shades. He tugged his arms from his sleeves, but she couldn't look away from his face. The color in his own cheeks was darkening, the message in his eyes very male.

"You want more sex?" she asked a bit breathlessly. "Even after what we did?"

His mouth took on a sardonic twist. "I'm afraid quantity usually matters for me, no matter how good that first orgasm is. Plus, Hattori's kith has me a bit . . . keener than usual."

He spread his palms to indicate his erection, which pushed out his half zipped trousers. Kat swallowed without thinking.

"How often does Hattori truly satisfy you?" Her cheeks blazed hotter, her impulsive question assuredly impolite. Ciran received it calmly.

"When he's in heat, he almost always does," he said.

Almost always. And only when he was in heat. And that had been before Kat showed up again.

"That isn't right," she blurted.

Ciran shrugged and smiled gently. "I'm responsible for myself, princess."

She thought that over, but somehow it still seemed wrong. "Would you like to take me in the shower?" she asked. She twisted her hands together, unsure of herself around him—though apparently without cause.

"Yes," he said simply. His smile then was broad and beautiful. It made her smile in return and reach behind herself for the ties to her snug corset.

"Let me help you," he offered.

She turned to let him, wondering how it was that she loved him a little less than Hattori, yet could speak to him more frankly.

Maybe I love him differently, she thought. The idea caught her imagination. She had time to mull it over. Even with Ciran's aid, her laces were a tangle.

"I'm surprised Hattori noticed my smell," he said as he worked on them. "We cleaned off the worst of it before we left the warden."

Kat sensed this wasn't casual conversation. "Maybe we didn't clean off enough. I think scenting Ombino triggered the emergence of his flagellum. People say infidelity can amplify hormonal reactions. His genes may have decided he'd been doubly cheated on."

Ciran grunted, then let out a Human curse. "Brace yourself. I think I need to rip these laces."

He used his strength to snap them, enabling the back edges of her undergarment to spring apart. Kat drew in a delicious breath.

"Better?" he asked, surprising her with his husky tone.

She turned, looked into his face, and went sultry from head to toe.

"Did you think I lied about wanting you, princess?"

"Kat," she said. "Please call me Kat tonight."

"Push the rest of those things off you, and I will."

She pushed them off with a laugh that might have surprised him both. Naked, she stepped backward into the shower, spinning the hot water spigot without looking away from him. The tripping risk was worth it. His gaze sizzled up and down her, the action of his lungs noticeable now.

"Better catch up while the hot water lasts," she teased.

He shucked free of his trousers with flattering speed, seeming at a loss for clever responses. His eyes gleamed as he backed her toward the tiles. When her shoulders hit them, she gasped without meaning to.

"Kat," he said with a small male smile.

Instead of grabbing her, he stepped back to lather himself, letting her enjoy the sight of the suds sluicing down his tall, tightly muscled form. His nipples were tight pink points, his arms a beautiful assemblage of hard curves and graceful lines. The hand that held the soap wended toward his groin. Both sets of long fingers found occupation there, showing off his ripe cock and balls even as he got squeaky clean. He rinsed himself with equal thoroughness, not bothering to ask if she liked what she saw.

She had eyes, after all, and she was a female.

Then, with a smirk she couldn't deny he'd earned, he hiked her up onto him.

She'd known her body had remained soft and wet, but not that it was hungry for more pleasure. Ciran's strong, smooth entry enlightened her. She shivered as he slid into her, and again for the lunge that slapped her buttocks against the tile.

His assured hands felt wonderful gripping them.

"I'll be quick," Ciran promised as he pressed inward a fraction more.

She wanted to tell him he needn't hurry on her account, but as it happened, her body enjoyed his haste. They came in tandem following a fierce and intent minute of forceful strokes. Ciran used no fancy pillow tricks to make love to her. He was simply driving straight to the goal. His first orgasm lasted long enough for her to imagine he'd needed it.

"Okay," he panted next to her ear. "I'll just want a few more now."

It sounded like he thought he was imposing. Kat turned her head on impulse, catching his mouth for a soft deep kiss. He joined it after a startled second, then moaned and hiked her a bit higher. She tightened her calves on his waist, wanting him to know she liked his enthusiasm. Possibly he was beyond worrying. He was sucking hard on her tongue when she pulled away.

"A little slower next time," she requested.

His eyes were dark with lust but smiling. "Your wish is my command, princess."

He came in her four more times, the last capped by a relieved groan.

"Better?" she asked, deliberately echoing him.

He cupped her face as her legs slid down him. "Much. I haven't felt this good in a while."

Probably she should have left this comment alone. Ciran certainly meant her to. He pulled her forward into the lukewarm spray, lathering a crisp brown sponge in preparation for soaping her. She didn't stop him. She knew by now he liked cosseting the people he cared about. Also strong in her awareness was that he probably wanted to cleanse his scent from her. Making Hattori jealous wasn't a goal he'd pursue.

For better or worse, that knowledge was what unlocked her mouth.

"Ciran," she said, touching his chest so he'd look at her. "Sometimes you have to ask for what you want before you can get it."

"Sometimes it's better not to ask for what you can't have."

"He loves you."

"I believe you." Ciran's eyes dropped a moment before coming up again. The look in them was determined but not, she thought, for the right reason. "He's uncomfortable about wanting me. He'd rather just want you."

Kat made a fist she tapped lightly on his breastbone. "Uncomfortable or not, he wants you—and maybe more than wants. You smelling like Ombino is the reason we're in this shower. That tells me there are a few things our mutual lover doesn't want to face up to."

"Doesn't that upset you?" Ciran blurted.

Kat considered this, trying to be unflinching as she examined her own heart. "Other things upset me more. Seeing you hurt, when that strikes me as unnecessary, might be the biggest one."

Ciran shook his head. He looked like he wanted to debate this, but she guessed they were both out of frankness then.

Because they were, Kat evicted Ciran from the bathing chamber so she could do private things. When she emerged, feeling much refreshed, the long hallway to the larger of the bedrooms was empty. Resigned to making her way there alone, she stuck her head into the open door of the grand salon—just in case Hattori was still there.

He wasn't. His brother sat on one of the spindly gilded sofas with his knees drawn up, his profile turned to the dark windows. She couldn't help wondering if he'd heard them having sex in here earlier.

"Haro?"

He turned his haunting, hollowed-out face to her, one bare foot returning to the floor hastily. He might have been a deer about to take flight. "I am well," he said haltingly, once he'd identified the voice as hers. "Just . . . appreciating my freedom."

Including the freedom not to be asked how he was every five minutes. Not sure if she should, Kat took one step into the room. "I wish I knew how to make this easier on you."

"Thank you, princess. Your kindness makes you a fit mate for my brother."

Amusement bubbled up in her at the way he'd worded this. Clearly, Haro had no issues about a royal being too good for his sibling.

"I'll leave you now," she said with a slight head bow. "Please try to sleep. I'm sure rest would be restorative."

He nodded back without speaking. He might not be the same man he'd been before, but his years in prison hadn't robbed him of his manners.

When Kat reached the bedroom, Ciran was sitting on the mattress edge, watching Hattori slumber like a tree felled. Decision unfolded inside her. Kat dropped her robe and climbed into the middle of the piled up blankets. With a jerk of her head and a raised eyebrow, she invited Ciran to snuggle behind her.

He accepted, his robe a warm slide of silk against her. Its breast pocket bore the monogram of the Prewtan Grande, the hotel that managed their residence.

"Good night, princess," he murmured.

"Sleep well, Ciran," she returned.

She hugged herself to Hattori's body. Deep within her the sense unfolded that much was right with her world—not everything, perhaps, but surely enough for happiness.

"You did it," she whispered as softly as she could. "You brought us all to safety, together."

The rest of them might have played their parts, but it was Hattori's unswerving will, his sense of what ought to be for the people he cared about, that was the driving force. When Ciran wriggled closer and gave a sigh, Kat let herself sink into slumber without a qualm.

11: OATH

Haro shook the three of them awake just a few hours later. He lay quieting palms across their mouths, though Kat suspected only she would have been foolish enough to speak. Though no lights were on, a silver half moon hung in the snow-frosted city's sky.

"Someone is on the balcony," Haro said so softly he could barely be heard.

"Staff?" she asked, trying to match his tone.

The brothers both shook their heads. They were right of course. Humans weren't *that* different. Any hotel employee would have knocked on the door. Ciran also knew this. He'd left the bed to pull on his trousers. Though the pants' construction was unfamiliar, he zipped them without a sound.

"I'll get the princess to safety," he said. "You and Haro handle the intruder."

With that, they weren't three men anymore. They were a trio of fighters, a team who knew each other's specialties.

Hattori drew a small black bag from beneath the bed. Weapons lay inside it, which she assumed he'd picked up in Prisonville. Ciran chose a plasma pistol, tucking the dark gray muzzle into his waistband at the small of his back. That done, he held his hand out for her to come with him.

Kat didn't want to go. She knew Ciran could protect her, but in her bones she wanted to stay with Hattori. If nothing else, the biological bond between them made being close to him feel better.

Hattori placed a warm hand on her shoulder. "Ciran will keep you safe. Let Haro and I do what we're good at."

What they were good at was moving in absolute silence. She hadn't let Ciran tug her more than two steps away when the room began to feel uninhabited. There were no sounds of respiration, no flickers of movement, just a dark and apparently empty space.

Though their seeming disappearance stirred a shiver, she told herself it was a good thing. With luck, they'd ambush the intruder.

As she tried to keep up with Ciran—and to be even half as quiet—she very much regretted she was naked. Fleeing danger felt far more perilous with her private bits hanging out. To her relief, when they reached the end of the unlit hall, Ciran passed his robe to her.

She put it on more quickly than she'd ever put on anything. She started to whisper *thank you*, but he held up his hand. She saw the men a second later—but just barely. There were two of them, dressed from head to toe in formfitting black, like members of the death squads less scrupulous royals sometimes kept on their payrolls. Slits in their cowl-like headgear exposed their eyes, which they'd blackened with greasepaint. The only reason Kat spotted them was that the walls of the entryway were eggshell. One man moved toward the door, as if intending to open it. Ciran gave her a silent signal to stay.

The noise of something crashing back in the bedroom jerked the assassins' heads around. Without a millisecond of hesitation, Ciran exploited their distraction to launch himself at the closest one.

When Kat said *launched*, she meant it. Ciran leaped through the air as if the black-garbed man was a pool he was diving for. His target fell as he hit, knocking the second over in the process. None of the men took long to recover. Heartbeats later, the three were fighting feverishly—more wrestling than punching, though there was some of that as well. Evidently, the assassin code forbid them from yelling during a fight. Aside from a bit of grunting and the sound of bodies scuffling and thumping against floor, the battle was strangely hushed.

Kat debated pushing on the electric light, then decided she'd better not. Hattori had treated this intrusion as an attack on her. If these men knew she was right there, it might make Ciran's job harder. She winced as she recognized his grunt. From the streak of motion she could pick out, one of his opponents had just landed a flying kick.

Determined to do something, she eased a decorative brass urn off the console table she'd crouched behind. The knickknack was small but heavy. When a black-garbed body hit the wall beside her, she rose up and smashed its brow. Once again, her royal strength was useful. The body moaned, crumpled, and didn't stir again. Her victim's removal from the fight energized the others. Ciran was wrestling more fiercely with the remaining man, as if the struggle were reaching some mutually agreed upon climax. Locked together, they rolled into the arch to the dining room, in which squares of moonlight stretched. Ciran's opponent grabbed something that had been left inside: a coil of thin rope, she thought. The next time he rolled on top, he got its bundled length against Ciran's throat, jamming it into his windpipe with all his might.

No, she thought. She still held the urn, though it was slippery with blood and other things. She gripped it tighter, stepping forward on shaking legs.

Before she could swing, Ciran flipped upward like his spine was a spring. His next move was too fast for her eyes to follow, but it spun his opponent around the other way. Like lightning, Ciran dropped the man's own looped rope around his neck. Ciran was choking him from behind, tightening the coil until the man's knees gave way. Ciran let him sink to the floor soundlessly.

He took half a second to catch his breath before darting to the door.

"Stay," he hissed when she would have joined him.

She remembered one of the men had been moving to open it. Maybe they'd been planning to let more attackers in. And maybe those reinforcements were out there now. A flash of cool blue light distracted her from the thought. The strobe had come from the vicinity of the bedroom, suggesting someone had used a plasma gun. When she looked back, Ciran had his in hand, though the weapon was tricky for fighting in close quarters. The shooter was too apt to vaporize himself. With his free hand, Ciran grabbed the doorknob. He twisted it and flung the door open, simultaneously dropping to one knee in a shooting stance.

No new death squad members burst in from the corridor. Somewhat anticlimactically, a dirty linen cart sat outside, sheets trailing out from its canvas bin. Ciran checked the hallway and the bin. Then he shut the door again.

He didn't have to tell her that rolling cart could have concealed her dead body.

Her reaction to this prospect didn't have a chance to sink in. Right then, every hair on the back of her neck prickled, much as it had outside Benjamin's building. She spun to face the stillness that seemed to be rolling up the hall. No more crashing sounds came up it, no more flashes from plasma guns.

Her throat felt as if her heart were stuck inside it, its chambers pumping too wildly to let her breathe. If Hattori had been killed, she wasn't certain she could go on. She'd been getting by in Black Hole, congratulating herself on her ability to survive. When he'd come back to her, her life became more than existence. Despite the dangers they'd been facing, loving him—and being loved in return—had reminded her what joy was.

Her gaze flew pleadingly to Ciran. He measured her with his eyes, taking in the solid little urn with its smear of gore and her deathly tight grip on it. She knew he understood what she was wordlessly asking. No matter what Hattori would have preferred, they couldn't abandon their beloved.

"All right," Ciran said quietly. "We'll go back and investigate."

♦

Hattori wouldn't have wanted to predict how his brother would react in combat. Not only was Haro's physical strength in question, he'd been sentenced to Winter Prison for defying orders to kill people. This battle was in defense of himself and others, but that didn't guarantee good results. This being so, Ciran taking charge of Kat had been welcome. To Hattori's relief, Haro's willingness to fight was soon established. His brother was actually quicker than he remembered, each counterblow as precise as a laser strike. Haro was left to finish off their opponents but, everything considered, that was a small complaint.

He didn't have a choice but to end the intruders' lives; they were going for the kill. Six men in total had converged on the main bedroom, creeping along the wraparound balcony to get there.

Haro had only heard one, because the rest had been scaling the building. Their targeting a chamber where a princess would sleep couldn't have been an accident.

This strike was designed to take Kat out.

Fortunately, their skills were inferior to the brothers'—which probably explained why they'd brought a plasma gun into play.

Hattori was pleased he hadn't had to draw his. Haro had disarmed the shooter and was now tying him to a chair with his own climbing rope. The man was the sole survivor of his companions. Hattori didn't object to him being kept alive. He was almost certainly the squad's leader. Questioning him might provide useful intelligence. Less satisfying was Kat and Ciran's unexpected arrival. No matter how plucky Kat could be, five violently dead assassins weren't a fit sight for her to see.

"Sorry," Ciran said, understanding the look Hattori shot him. "It got too quiet back here."

Once he'd apologized, there wasn't much point in getting mad. The danger was over, and Kat seemed unharmed. Hattori took a quick inventory of Ciran's wounds—mostly nasty contusions, none life threatening that he could see. Kat's worst injury appeared to be her shock at the room's condition, which was very close to destroyed. The huge carved bed was upended, two windows shattered, and a long smoldering burn mark charred a good six feet of the inlaid floor. Her eyes widened at the sight of a severed foot resting on its side in a pool of blood.

Hattori had almost forgotten swinging his fighting sword through that ankle. At the time, the leg it was attached to had been unleashing a lethal solar plexus kick.

"Um," Kat said, when she'd finished taking this in. "Are you two all right?"

His response was ridiculous, but Hattori couldn't help smiling at her concern—and her lack of hysteria. This woman was the bright beating heart of him, his complement and his match in so many ways. Biology didn't matter. He'd have fallen for her no matter what.

He didn't want to think about losing her again.

"We're fine," he said. "A few burns and scrapes. We'll both be healed in no time."

Their prisoner seemed to believe the tenderness in his voice called for a snort of derision.

Kat turned at the sound and regarded him. Her response was not what Hattori anticipated. She went still, one hand rising to the base of her throat.

"Pull off his hood," she said.

He saw no reason not to do as she asked. When he did, a vaguely familiar head of black braids emerged.

"Hello, Kat," the man they belonged to said.

"Longsheng," she breathed before Hattori could summon up the name. Her face flushed with sudden anger. "You tried to seduce my cook!"

Longsheng's lips stretched wide but not in a Human smile— more like a animal baring teeth. "What makes you think I didn't succeed?"

Kat surprised him by letting out a growl. "I thought you were my friend. I pled your case to Rya. And all the time you were working for my stepmother!"

Longsheng's slitted eyes showed how pleased he was with himself. "The best spies are likable," he observed.

Kat's facial muscles went tight with rage, but she controlled herself. Hattori couldn't have been prouder than when she ignored their prisoner's baiting and turned to him. "He outfitted my initial trip to Prewtan, got me currency and supplies and probably planted a tracker in my sled. That's how he knew to lay in wait for me here. He was hoping I'd show up again."

"You really should have left a body," Longsheng couldn't resist scolding. "A witch like Miry Shinobi wasn't going to be satisfied with a few pints of frozen blood in a sunken truck."

His words started Hattori's mental gears turning. If Longsheng hadn't *known* Kat would reappear, if he'd been waiting in this Human city on the off chance that she'd turn up, he might not have informed Kat's stepmother of his activities. His fellow assassins hadn't been much better than second rate. If he'd hired them on his own credit, and his own initiative . . .

Miry Shinobi might have no idea they were here.

Ciran was following the same trail. "Kat sensed him watching us yesterday, when we ran her errand. Whether he spotted us before that, I couldn't say."

So had Longsheng contacted his employer with the news? Did the Human telegraph make that possible? Yskut was close enough to magnetic north to suffer the same interference as diamond lands. Portable transmitters could connect to the Yamaweb, if it was operative, but transmitters with sufficient power were costly. Regardless of whether he had one, Longsheng might have been waiting until he had Kat in hand to demand the price on her head. He wouldn't have wanted to risk disappointing a dragon lady like her stepmother.

The problem was how to get him to answer truthfully. In their present circumstances, Hattori wouldn't shy from torture, but that wasn't always reliable. Many Yama had gained fame for speaking falsehoods under duress.

"I'll question him," Haro volunteered.

"*You* will." The words of doubt came from Ciran. Hattori was too busy trying to lift his jaw.

"This should be good," Longsheng drawled. "The pacifist brother questioning me."

Haro's gaze didn't waver from Hattori. Either he was who Haro felt most comfortable interacting with, or no one else's permission mattered. Hattori suspected the truth was a bit of both. Haro had held up well in the fight, considering his aversion for killing. Now, however, he was looking pasty around the gills. Without immediate danger to occupy him, the strain was starting to tell.

"I'll know if he's lying," Haro said, a hint of earnestness in it. "I sharpened my ability to read people while I was away."

"While you were away," Longsheng mocked. "That's one way of putting it."

If Longsheng remained this chatty during his interrogation, they might indeed learn some things. Already they knew he was aware of Haro's identity. However close or distant his business relationship with Miry, she'd entrusted him with that.

"He's all yours," Hattori said to his brother. With a subtle flick of his eyes, he signaled Ciran to move closer. That much backup Haro ought to have.

For nearly a minute, Haro simply stared down at Longsheng, his eyes steady and thoughtful. Predictably, his subject sneered in response, but as the perusal lengthened his rope-bound body coiled with tension.

Even for a Yama, Haro was being unusually self-controlled.

"How long ago did you contact your employer?" he asked at last.

The question relaxed Longsheng. He pushed one shoulder against the chair's upholstered oval back so that he was lounging. "Wondering how many hours you have before you're dragged back to jail?"

Haro couldn't hide his flinch. His jaw tightened once before he went on. "What name did your parents give you?"

"Kiss. My. Ass."

"That is not your name. Please answer truthfully."

"Long . . . sheng," he said, making it sound dirty. In case they missed his implication, he cut his eyes to Kat. When her brows went up, he licked his lips lasciviously. He made certain the fork of his lamril showed.

Hattori shouldn't have let this childish ploy get to him, but his hand fisted anyway, ready to strike their prisoner if he said another word.

"Longsheng is not your name," Haro said, unaffected by his display. "What name was entered in the Registry at your birth?"

His harping on this surprised their prisoner enough to blink. He recovered his derision a breath later. "Maybe I'm not in the Registry."

Haro's hand lashed across his face so swiftly it shocked them all. For a hanging second, Longsheng stared at him with his mouth agape—all his guards and posturing gone. The cheek Haro slapped was red.

"Never mind," Haro said. "I'm not interested anymore." Clearly off balance, Longsheng shut his mouth as Haro studied him. "Did you notify your employer that you found the princess?"

This time Longsheng answered more cautiously. "Maybe I did. Maybe I didn't."

Hattori realized he was trying to decide which answer gave him an advantage.

"Which is it?" Haro asked calmly, as if he hadn't just struck Longsheng hard enough for one eye to be swelling shut. "I'd like to help you, but I can only do that if you tell me the truth."

Longsheng gawked at Haro like he'd gone off his rails, and Hattori couldn't swear he was wrong. He'd never seen his brother behave like this before.

"I'd like to help you," Haro repeated. "Did you tell anyone we were here?"

"I prepared a message," Longsheng said slowly. "If anything happens to me, it will be sent automatically."

Haro's fighting sword was tucked in a sheath that secured it behind his back. He drew it and held it in front of him. It was a simple weapon—double-edged black plasteel with a rubber coated pommel and hilt. Long favored by fighting men, it would never catch the light, make attention-drawing noise, or require powering up.

Haro ran his thumb along the barely bloodied blade. "Until tonight, I hadn't swung one of these in years. It's interesting how quickly muscle memory returns."

His tone was mild, not a ghost of a threat in it. Nonetheless, perspiration popped out on Longsheng's upper lip. "I didn't lie. If I don't deactivate my transmitter by a preset hour, Miry Shinobi receives the news that you're here."

This could have been true. Yamish minds tended to devise failsafe schemes. Longsheng's understandable nervousness made it difficult for Hattori to get a read on his honesty. He couldn't tell if his brother fared better. Haro was treating their prisoner to another of his long stares.

"Look," Longsheng said. "All you have to do is pay me for my silence. *She's* got plenty of credit. More than enough for a man like me."

"Her name," Haro said, "is Princess Shinobi."

"Fine." The sweat on Longsheng's face glittered. "I didn't mean any disrespect. The princess can pay me and you can all get on with your lives. I know you don't want to kill me. You didn't kill my men even when they attacked you."

Haro lowered the sword. His eyes were sad, his face serious. Evidently, Longsheng thought this meant his argument had gained ground. "You won't be sorry," he said. "You have my oath you won't hear from me again."

Before anyone could stop it, the black sword blurred up and spitted him, sliding neatly between two ribs. The weapon had pierced his heart. Blood gushed from Longsheng's mouth, but he didn't have time to scream. His death rattle was short and wet. When his head fell forward, his body sagging in the ropes, they all knew he was gone.

For one long moment, everyone was speechless.

"I'm sorry," Haro said into the pause. "He lied about keeping silent if we bribed him. And about the preset message. He didn't tell anyone he saw us. Once I'd established his baseline for truth or falsehood, the deception was as clear as day in his micro-reactions."

"As clear as day," Ciran repeated.

"Good liars learn to control their auras, because that's what most Yama read. But we also have tiny muscular 'tells' that give us away, involuntary responses that stem from primitive structures inside our brains. I've yet to meet a Yama who can suppress them."

Haro's words seemed perfectly rational, despite being pushed between clenched teeth. His body, by contrast, was shaking violently. Blood stained the front of his thick gray robes, in part from the earlier fight. He looked down at the smears and spatters as if unsure how they'd gotten there. Very gently, Ciran took the sword from his hand. Haro's fingers needed to be eased off the handle before he would let go.

"It's all right," Ciran said. "You did what you had to."

Surprisingly, Haro caught Ciran's arm. "I couldn't go back to prison. If he'd just wanted to kill me . . ."

"You saved us too," Ciran assured him. "The princess is a good person. She didn't deserve to be killed by those assassins."

"You're right," Haro agreed in relief. "That man wasn't innocent."

"Maybe you'd like a shower," Kat suggested. "Cleaning up always makes me feel better."

He didn't appear to take her soothing as an insult, though she could have been addressing a troubled child. "I would like that," he said. His brow furrowed. "Do you think there are enough towels?"

She assured him there were plenty, all of them thick and warm. When she returned from escorting him to the bathing chamber, her expression was deliberately smooth.

She didn't want Hattori to know how concerned she was.

His emotions felt like they were melting. He opened his arms to her, and she stepped to him, pressing her cheek to his upper chest.

Holding her, stroking her tousled but silky hair, felt indescribably wonderful. Ciran watched them from a foot away, his face as unreadable as Kat's had been.

"Thank you for protecting her," Hattori said roughly.

"I'd protect anyone you loved," Ciran responded.

Hattori could tell he meant it. Kat's hands shifted on his back, giving and taking comfort from their closeness. Ciran's statement seemed no surprise to her. When had his old friend become so noble? Hattori wondered if he were capable of Ciran's selflessness. Would he have protected anyone Ciran cared about? Or to be precise—if Kat gave her heart to another male, would Hattori risk his life for him?

He wasn't convinced he would, and maybe that made Ciran the better man.

None of us know what we'll do until we're tested.

The words didn't feel like his. He knew Kat and Ciran considered him a good man, a respect he wanted to live up to. Could other people's love make a person better? He sensed himself on the verge of grasping a vital truth. Ciran was still watching, the calmness of his expression mesmerizing him. Hattori's heart beat faster, something electric passing between him and his friend. It felt like the connection he shared with Kat, a tug of spirit to spirit and heart to heart. Still looking at Hattori, Ciran laid his hand on Kat's shoulder. Kat didn't seem to mind. Her cheek rubbed Hattori's chest as she let out a pleasured sigh.

Hattori didn't know what might have been said if a loud banging on the suite's front door hadn't shattered the moment.

A Human voice called out a demand.

"It's the hotel manager," Ciran translated. "He's demanding we open up."

Kat pushed back from Hattori, her mouth rounding in dismay. "Another guest must have complained about the noise."

She glanced around the shambles of the bedroom, at the bodies and the blood and the burn that went through the carpet to the floor. These things wouldn't be possible to hide in a reasonable amount of time.

"I'll hold off our visitor," Ciran said. "You carry the two dead bodies back from the foyer."

"*Two?*" Kat said in a shocked voice.

Ciran grinned wolfishly. "Yes, princess: two. You didn't leave your man breathing any more than I left mine."

♦

Ciran had always had a knack for deceit, but even he hadn't known he could be such a good actor.

He delayed the manager long enough for Hattori to haul the dead men to the bedroom—and to pop in the Human-style contacts he'd had the amazing foresight (if he said so himself) to purchase in addition to the set that turned his eyes one color. The difference between Yamish and Human irises wasn't obvious unless you looked for it. With the other lies he had to juggle, Ciran was grateful not to worry about that. He spent a few more moments pulling on a clean white shirt, preferring not to offend the Human's modesty. Dressed then, he was ready to play victim.

He'd already composed a story inside his head. Not knowing what had been heard by the other guests, or how much evidence they'd be able to destroy, the fiction had to include a slice of truth.

"Thank God you're here," he was able to exclaim as he steered the short and dapper manager into the undamaged sitting room. The man introduced himself as Pierre LaForte, which his shiny name badge confirmed. His tidy clothes and upright carriage said he took his dignity seriously. Deciding a display of respectfulness would smooth his path, Ciran gestured for him to sit. "Did you know an assassin sneaked past your hotel security? Our bodyguards took care of him, but if they hadn't been so quick, the Prewtan Grande might have had a dead princess on their hands!"

To Ciran's delight, the little man perked up at the mention of royalty. Though he expressed a decent amount of horror for their ordeal, his black waxed mustache—which Ciran was fascinated by—twitched with interest.

"Your said your wife is a princess?" he tacked on at the end of his condolence. Ciran fought a smile at his hopeful tone.

The manager's assumption that he and Kat were married sank in belatedly. Rather than contradict him, Ciran pursed his lips modestly. "My wife is one of a number of princesses. Her family hails from the Silver Islands, where virtually every rock has a royal line."

The manager nodded sagely, as if familiar with the ins and outs of the hoi polloi. "And the origins of the assassin?"

"Sent by relatives, I expect. You wouldn't believe the politics in some of these small principalities."

"But the princess is safe and sound?"

"Oh yes," Ciran said. "Just frightened and resting. You know how women are."

The manager, whose legs were rather short, squirmed on the edge of the couch cushion, his body language telegraphing discomfort as clearly as Haro had claimed Longsheng's did. "If I could speak to the bodyguards," he suggested delicately. "You understand I have a responsibility to look into the matter. Our other guests aren't accustomed to these sorts of disturbances."

"Certainly," Ciran said, glad the little man wasn't mentioning the police. Then again, a fancy hotel might not want the scandal calling them could entail. "I must warn you, our employees are foreigners. Very loyal, but with scarcely ten words of Ohramese between them. Shall I have them pop round your office tomorrow? Say around noon?"

Ciran's favorite comic character on *What the Butler Saw* was Lord Breckenbottom, an aristocrat who bullied his fellow Humans with the sheer force of his sense of entitlement. Though Ciran knew the manager wanted to talk to Haro and Hattori immediately, thankfully Lord B's tactics worked as well in real life as on the HFC. The hapless manager rose when Ciran did, his face betraying his reluctance to accept his dismissal—and his lack of knowledge on how to avoid it.

"Thank you," Ciran said as he guided the flustered man back to the foyer. "I know the princess will be grateful for the consideration you're showing her."

He bowed to the manager, who was then obliged to bow back. After that, getting rid of him was a simple matter of opening the door.

"He's gone?" Hattori asked, sticking his head out the bedroom into the hall.

Ciran nodded, weariness hitting him. Hattori knew him well enough to interpret it.

"Don't keel over yet," he advised dryly. "I'm pretty sure the hotel will find this incident easier to overlook if we get rid of the bodies."

Ciran expected that was true—especially since he'd only admitted to there being one assassin. If he'd revealed there'd been eight, their patronage might have seemed less desirable.

◆

Kat didn't argue when Hattori informed her she wouldn't be on body disposal duty. Though her stomach was strong enough, some jobs she'd rather be spared. There was plenty of clean-up in the suite anyway—which Hattori and Ciran might not have realized.

While they trundled the corpses off to who-knew-where in the abandoned linen cart, Kat tiptoed down the corridor to find a cleaning supply closet. She'd observed the white-capped and aproned maids during her previous stay, and believed she knew what the various solutions and applicators did. Her Yamish clothes were more sensible for the task, so she changed back to them. Considering the jewels had been removed from one trouser leg, she'd hardly need the outfit for public wear.

The work kept her from dwelling on the fact that she'd bashed a man's head in.

She'd swept up the broken glass and had sponged most of the blood from the watered silk wallpaper when Haro made her jump by appearing silently at the door.

He looked around at the aftermath of the battle he and his brother fought. His gray robes were damp where he'd run cold water over their bloody spots. As if to reassure himself they were gone, one hand idly patted the darker patch. The patting stopped as the chair Longsheng had died in caught his attention. Immediately, Kat wished she'd cleared it away first thing. He shuddered when he wrenched his focus from it to her.

"You could use help," he said.

His tone was calm, his eyes intelligent and clear.

"I could," Kat admitted, dragging one sleeve across her hot forehead. "Cleaning isn't really my forte."

"I scrubbed a lot of floors when I was in jail. Some of them were bloody too." The twist to his mouth suggested this might be a small joke.

"I'd happily bow to your expertise," she said.

They worked quietly side by side, saving what they could of the room's décor and discarding what they could not. At the least, whoever Kat paid to make repairs wouldn't think they'd entered a butcher shop. When they'd done what they could, Haro helped Kat tip the big carved bed back onto all four feet.

To her amazement, the rumpled sheets were free of rips or blood. She almost opened her mouth to exclaim over it, then realized this might be insensitive. Haro was staring at the bed, his expression opaque to her.

"Your energy is a bit like his," he said.

"Like your brother's?"

He nodded. "I feel calmer when he's close by."

His words put Kat in mind of a confession. "I'm sure he and Ciran will be back soon."

He grimaced. "It doesn't matter. I can't— I need to stand on my own two feet."

"You will. You can't expect that to happen right away."

He turned to sit on the end of the restored bed. He looked at his hands, which he'd rested palm-up on his thighs. His skin was wrinkled like hers was from the cleaning. "Soap and water," he murmured.

She suspected he was thinking about the kind of stains they *couldn't* remove.

She sat tentatively next to him, careful to leave a few inches between them. She hadn't forgotten how he'd reacted to the prospect of touching her on the flier. His head was lowered, his respiration suddenly ragged. A drop of water ran down his cheek and onto his collar, leaving a new dark spot. When a second followed and then a third, Kat knew he was crying.

"Don't tell him," he said throatily. "I don't want to worry him."

Kat might have said many things, but none struck her as helpful. Instead, she handed him a clean washrag to blow his nose. He did so noisily.

"I swore an oath," he said, "that I wouldn't kill again, not even to save my life. For twenty years, I kept that promise, and in a place where people murder each other for an extra serving of burnt rice stew."

"You probably saved my life," she pointed out.

He shook his head a few more times than he needed to. "I killed that man because I couldn't stand the thought of going back to Winter Prison. To be given a taste of freedom and then have it snatched away was too much for me."

"I think I understand a bit. I survived without Hattori for a long while. When he came back into my life . . ." She shook her head almost like he had. "I knew I never wanted us to live apart again."

Haro nodded and mopped his face, tears still trickling slowly from his eyes. She should have been embarrassed. Crying openly was considered scandalous for Yama. In spite of this, all she could think was maybe his tears needed to come out. Maybe they would lighten his burden. Hoping this was true, she put her hand very carefully on his upper arm. The tightness of the muscles underneath his sleeve pricked at her sympathy.

Hattori's brother was on guard against everything in the world.

"Your oath was important to you," she said. "Maybe you should grieve for it. I just don't think you should let breaking it break you."

The sound of the suite's door opening traveled down the hall. Hattori and Ciran were returning. Though Haro must have recognized their voices, his body stiffened like a board. "Please," he said huskily to Kat.

"He'll worry no matter what I tell him," she said. "I suspect that's the nature of being a twin. In fact, it might be the nature of being him."

Haro blew out a resigned breath. "All right," he said, rising to his feet. "I'm going to wash my face."

He managed to slip out without crossing his brother's path. When Hattori reached the bedroom, he was alone. He looked utterly exhausted—and filthy from head to toe. He and Ciran must have found somewhere to bury the unfortunate assassins. He let out a low whistle to see the extent to which the room was restored.

"Haro helped," she said. "I think he might have a future in janitorial science."

Haro was too weary to be amused. "Was he all right?"

Kat took a moment to consider. Their people prized emotional control, weeping hardly being viewed as an indicator of mental health. In this case, however, she wasn't sure it was a bad thing.

"I think he's a little better," she said at last. "I also think it might be a while before *he's* ready to believe that."

12: THE NATURE OF THE BEAST

It wasn't Hattori's nature to sit and wait, but for the present Fate gave him little choice. Earlier, he and Haro had endured a necessarily brief interrogation by the hotel manager, during which Hattori discovered he'd picked up more Ohramese than he thought.

He hadn't enlightened Mister LaForte. Being presumed to be ignorant muscle was in their best interest.

That hurdle cleared, he and Haro sat in the grand salon, awaiting Kat and Ciran's return. The pair had gone back to the secondhand clothes seller, to exchange more of Kat's dwindling supply of gems to pay for the suite's repairs. Hattori found this errand uncomfortable on so many levels he could hardly keep to his chair. Though pacing was a strong temptation, he'd promised himself he'd exercise more control.

"These Human 'newspapers' are written very simply," Haro commented from the couch, flipping the page of one. "With the translator on Ciran's handheld, I'm puzzling out quite a bit."

Hattori grunted, happy his brother had found this distraction.

"I could read aloud to you," Haro offered, "if you'd rather not study on your own. The others are behaving as if we'll be here for a while."

In spite of his good intentions, Hattori pushed to his feet. "Go ahead," he said when his brother tipped his head inquiringly at him. "It's good to hear your voice again. I'm sure some of the words will sink in."

He stood by the window, keeping an eye on the foreign city and managing not to pace while his brother read. He hadn't lied. Haro's voice was a comfort. The sun was as well, sparkling off the ancient seeming rooftops and square bell towers. Kat and Ciran were out in those streets somewhere, maybe laughing at a café over their shared love of hot cocoa. His body tightened with a combination of sullenness and lust. He should have been bigger than those reactions. He should have been more like Ciran.

Kat was doing everything she could to reassure him—though her knowing he needed it bothered him. They'd made love on their own after Ciran and he returned from their grisly errand. His heat was over, but sharing that quiet closeness had spread peace through more than his blood and bone. He was certain she felt the same. She'd fallen asleep almost at once afterward. He should have dropped into unconsciousness with her. Instead, he'd lain there for half an hour, staring at the shadows of the winged babies who'd been painted on the ceiling. Finally, he'd padded here, to find Ciran curled on the couch sleeping. Hattori had sat cross-legged on the carpet, watching him slumber. He hadn't moved even when Ciran's eyelids rose. He'd stared into those sleepy two-tone irises, not tiring, not embarrassed, just knowing he felt better when he did. After a few minutes, Ciran's soft mouth had curved.

"Miss me that much?" he'd teased.

Which was when Hattori realized it was true. Infinity knew he loved Kat, more than he loved himself. Their bed simply didn't feel right without Ciran.

"If you're waiting for an invitation, you have it," he'd said gruffly.

Ciran had swung onto his feet as Hattori rose, following him to the bedroom without a single smart comment. Kat hadn't awoken at either of them climbing up beside her—no small marvel considering the fright she'd experienced there earlier.

Now Hattori ran one hand down the terrace door's sheer white drapes. Even in sleep, Kat recognized both of them.

"You could view this as your genes doing you a favor," Haro broke into his thoughts to say.

"What?" Hattori asked, more to stall the conversation than because Haro's comment was off topic.

Haro's eyebrows said he knew this perfectly well. "Your genes have picked both of them for you, and as a result, it's impossible for you to deny you care. We Yama place a lot of weight on being the superior race, but maybe Humans handle a few things better."

"Don't let Ciran hear you say that. He'll fall in love with you next."

"He won't," Haro said as seriously as if Hattori hadn't been being droll. "He isn't fickle. He's given his heart to you to keep."

"And you know this because of your new expertise in truth telling?"

Haro closed his newspaper and set it aside on the couch cushion. "I know a lot of things about you, perhaps the most important being that you want each of them to love you best. Apparently, you're suffering some guilt over that."

"I should feel guilty," Hattori retorted. "What I want from them isn't fair."

Haro gave a surprising shrug. "Who said life is fair? They do love you best and, from what I can tell, I'm not sure you can change their minds. Maybe you should just be grateful."

This wasn't a debate Hattori had expected to be having with his brother. "How do you know this?" he burst out.

"Why shouldn't I know? We're still twins."

"You can read me through our old bond?"

"Of course." Haro squinted at him. "Are you saying you can't?"

"No. I thought . . . I thought you had extra mental guards up, because of what you went through."

Haro sat deeper in the couch to consider this. "Perhaps it's an effect of mating. Perhaps your ability to connect has switched itself to her. And to him, I suppose."

"Are you saying you know everything I've been feeling?"

Haro laughed at his tone of horror, looking boyish for a moment. "Well, I didn't know the messages only ran one way. I assumed you were aware of my emotions too." He wiped his hand down his mouth, obviously still amused.

"It isn't funny."

"If you knew how long it's been since I found anything humorous, you wouldn't begrudge me."

"I'm sorry. I shouldn't have gotten angry. The last thing you need is my problems piled on top of yours."

"Hattori." Haro's scold was fond, his gaze too bright to look away from. "Do you honestly think you have to be perfect before you deserve to be loved?"

Hattori's eyes burned, but he refused to give in to tears. "I see how it is. Twenty years in prison and suddenly you're a jailhouse philosopher."

"Maybe a little," Haro admitted with a ghost of a smile. "I had plenty of time to contemplate the truths of the universe."

The strange black telephone jingled on its half moon shelf, cutting off whatever response Hattori might have come up with. He picked it up gingerly. "Hello?" he said in hopefully intelligible Ohramese.

A Human voice issued from the end he held nearest to his mouth. "I'm calling for Princess Katherine. Mister Benjamin DuBieren is here to visit her."

By this time, Haro had risen and was listening with his ear next to Hattori's. For a heartbeat, the warm reality of his presence shocked. His brother, the part of him that had been missing for two decades, was truly here—not a dream or a memory. Unaware of his thoughts, Haro turned the talking apparatus right end up and spoke. "Princess Katherine has errand. Mister DuBieren would waiting like?"

Mister DuBieren did waiting like. Five minutes later, Hattori and Haro went to answer his knock. Hattori's curiosity concerning this trusted associate from Kat's past had been colored with suspicion. To find an old man with a neatly trimmed salt-and-pepper beard and a belly that strained his waistcoat relieved Hattori more than his pride was comfortable with.

The man's brown eyes widened behind spectacles whose thin gold wires perched on an impressive nose. It seemed Haro and Hattori weren't who he'd expected to be greeted by. "How many gentlemen does Princess Katsu travel with?"

This was a question only a Human would have been direct enough to ask. Benjamin DuBieren didn't seem particularly abashed to have let it slip.

Hattori offered a shallow bow. "I am Hattori and this is my brother Haro. You met our friend Ciran earlier."

"You speak our language," Haro observed.

Mister DuBieren blushed modestly. "I'm not as quick to learn as you Yama, but I do my humble best. I must confess your people have been a fascination of mine since I was a boy of ten. To discover a whole new race has been secretly sharing the same planet—well, let me tell you, it captured my imagination like nothing else!"

If Kat's associate had been ten when Yama were discovered, he was barely past fifty now. Yama didn't reach middle age until they'd lived a few centuries. No wonder Humans were emotional; their passions had to fit a much shorter span of years.

"Please come in," Hattori said, hoping he'd concealed his thoughts. "Haro and I believe we've figured out the workings of the electrical teakettle."

They tramped together to the snug pantry, which contained a "hotplate" and a receptacle for the kettle's plug. Mister DuBieren must not have spent a lot of time in such rooms, because he looked around the space almost as curiously as they originally had. Hattori concluded wealthy people seldom did their own cooking— regardless of their culture.

"I expect you deplore our modern teabags," DuBieren said as Haro dropped a pair into the brewing pot.

"You've had Yamish tea?" Haro asked politely.

"Once," he said wistfully. "It was exquisite."

Hattori carried the silver tray of tea things back to the grand salon, where they sat awkwardly.

"I'll play mother," DuBieren offered. This turned out to mean he would pour. Hattori found himself wanting to ask Ciran if he'd known that already. It was the sort of linguistic quirk he delighted in.

DuBieren filled the cups, took a sip of his own, then sat back in his spindly chair. "I imagine you're wondering why I've shown up on the princess's doorstep."

They were, though it wasn't their way to press

Luckily, DuBieren wanted to explain. "I have a friend on the hotel staff. Many of my clients who come to this city stay at the Grande. I like to keep abreast of what concerns them."

By *friend*, Hattori understood he meant informant. "I'm sure that's good sense on your part."

DuBieren smiled. "It's good business sense, though in this instance my reaction to the news was more personal. My friend assured me Kat was unharmed in last night's attack, but it disturbs me that her enemies have struck at her here. If ever there were a time for her to be in a fiscally sound position, it's now."

Hattori's brows lowered before he could master them. Whatever Benjamin DuBieren was angling toward, he didn't think he'd like it.

Haro leaned forward beside Hattori on the couch, possibly picking up a wisp of his thoughts. As he had so often before Muto Feng tore their paths apart, he took his brother's interests as his own. "You're kind to be concerned, Mister DuBieren."

"Please," he said, "call me Benjamin. And I'm not trying to be kind. I'm trying to keep Kat safe. That girl is a stone of the first water—and a stellar mercantile mind. Please talk her into accepting my proposition. I know it would benefit us both. If the lion is stalking you, the best thing really is to beard it in its den."

The lion he spoke of could only be Kat's stepmother . . . which would make its den their home country. A muscle began ticking next to Hattori's eye.

"She's still exiled," he pointed out, ignoring the involuntary nerve misfire. "Imperial edicts aren't easy to get around."

"Pfft," said DuBieren, an expression Hattori wasn't familiar with. "With my backing, she could pay off any number of bureaucrats."

"You are Human, Mister DuBieren. Powerful among your own people. Ours might be more challenging to manipulate."

"I know my quarry. Your race is brilliant, dangerous, and absolutely jelly when it comes to Human-created art. Caruso gave one concert in the Forbidden City, after which all similar performances were banned. I know why that was, Mister Hattori. Emperor Songyam, the supposedly supreme ruler of all your icy hearts, burst into tears before the first act finished.

"The jewelry I and my firm design are the equivalent of Caruso's arias—just composed of diamonds and fine metals. My people spend fortunes to possess them. Yours would—and could—pay twice as much, except the protectionists in your government won't allow me to sell to them. Only Yama can do business on your soil, and who better than a princess to approach the likeliest customers? If Kat were to serve as my representative, with a commission on every sale, she'd be ten times as wealthy as Miry Shinobi within a year."

Hattori had the pieces assembled then—the truth of the errand Kat hadn't seen fit to share with him. She'd never intended to leave her royal past behind. She was going to wade right back into the mess they'd risked so much to save her from. She was going to put revenge above the love they'd been lucky enough to find.

The ticking in his temple became a throb.

Haro placed a restraining hand on his arm. Hattori didn't need it. He felt every bit as icy as their emperor was supposed to be.

"Thank you for coming," he said, startling Benjamin DuBieren by rising from the couch. A hint of a growl crept into his voice. "I promise you, I shall discuss this with the princess."

♦

Kat and Ciran's business had gone well. Not only had they obtained the funds they needed, they'd gotten a referral for a carpenter who could replace the burned floorboards. Their problems weren't solved forever, but they were fine for now. They celebrated by purchasing a satchel full of meat pies and a warm loaf of gingerbread. They'd feast on the food together—and hopefully please Hattori that it cost less than room service.

Kat felt like she'd been with a lifelong friend, sharing activities they enjoyed. It would have been relaxing if Ciran hadn't been able to put more eroticism into a single smile than most Yama could convey with their whole bodies.

He'd gone out of his way to remind Kat of that today.

Their time alone in the shower seemed to have spurred a change in him, the results of which she was seeing now. Despite the wariness this inspired, she and Ciran were laughing as she turned the key in the door.

"You're back," Haro said, the tension in his voice cutting short their merriment.

Hattori's brother stood in the hallway outside the grand salon. Hattori himself emerged as she peeled free of her closefitting coat and gloves. His thick black hair was unusually disordered, as if he'd been tugging it with his hands. He looked at her without speaking, muscles clenched in his jaw. His silver eyes were icy—and made to

218

seem more so by the flush that rose to his cheeks. The vein in his nearer temple was beating visibly.

A matching pulse started ticking in Kat's throat. She fell back a step without meaning to, bumping into Ciran. She'd never seen that look on his face before.

"Don't," Haro cautioned, touching his brother's arm. The contact drew her attention to Hattori's fisted hands. "Don't say things you'll be sorry for."

Hattori snarled, the sound impossible to call by a nicer name.

"Hattori?" she asked unsurely.

He seemed unable to bear her voice. He spun away and strode stiffly to the bedroom.

"I'll take the packages," Ciran said. "You'd better talk to him."

She glanced at Haro, but his face provided no clue to what the problem was. "Fine," she said, hiking her impractical Human skirts up a few inches. "I'll go."

She hoped her stalk down the hall had some dignity, but forgot to worry when she found Hattori. He was gripping the back of a dark wood chair that provided seating for a delicate vanity. It wasn't the chair Longsheng had died in, but if he weren't careful, he'd ruin it just as thoroughly. He pushed his considerable weight into it as his lungs went in and out like bellows.

It wasn't the time to notice, but the tailored trousers showed off his legs marvelously.

"Are you ill?" Kat asked—perhaps hopefully. Ordering her feet past the doorway required more nerve than she expected.

Hattori's head swiveled to face her. "I'm not ill. I'm furious."

"If this is about me and Ciran spending the morning together . . ."

Hattori straightened with a short hard laugh. "This isn't about my jealousy, though I certainly thank you for thinking me so childish. This is about your plan to let DuBieren help you go after your stepmother."

Kat's stomach gave an unpleasant lurch. "How did you find out?"

"I hardly think that matters. What I want to know is are you insane? Do you even care that you could get yourself killed? No matter how rich DuBieren could make you, Miry Shinobi is no one to mess with."

"Maybe I'm no one to mess with," Kat retorted, her temper rising at his tone. Though her decision regarding DuBieren hadn't been firm, defending it came naturally right then. "Maybe I've had enough of being chased from my rightful home for crimes I didn't commit and having killers sent after me. I'm not weak, Hattori. Maybe it's time I stopped running."

Hattori let out a roar and spun toward the wall, his right arm and shoulder uncoiling a punch that smashed a crater straight through watered silk to plaster.

Kat gasped and still found herself short of air. "Longsheng came after you," she said, refusing to let fear—or breathlessness—silence her. "Miry's man would have killed us all. I *have* to take the fight back to her."

Hattori shook pieces of wall from his fist, his knuckles now bloodied. His lip curled in disdain, but at least he appeared calmer. "You *have* to," he repeated. "Even though she doesn't know where you are. Even though, given sufficient time, she might be convinced to write you off as dead."

"You're telling me might be is good enough for you?"

"I'm telling you I don't think revenge is worth losing what we have. I should have known what meant most to you when you leased this place. Fuck, I should have known when you showed me your precious blue diamond. You always meant it to fund your comeback. You never intended to live as anything but a princess."

His voice was cool, but she heard the hurt in it. "I would live like a pauper," she said, "if I actually believed we'd be safe that way. Surely you see I'd only be doing this for us!"

He didn't respond. He zipped the black carryall she'd only half noticed sitting on the bed. Her chest contracted as she realized it was packed with his clothes.

"You're leaving?" she gasped as he slung its strap over his shoulder.

"I wish," he said bitterly. "The truth is I'd follow you to the Human hell, if that's where you wished to go. I'll protect you no matter what. I'm just not going to live like your play-husband anymore. From now on, I'll sleep on the couch."

"I didn't tell Benjamin *yes*," she begged, panicked to get through to him. "Before Longsheng came, I was only considering his offer because I didn't know how else to take care of everyone."

Hattori had been walking toward her, on his way to the door. At her words, he stopped in front of her. "The fact that you believe you have to take care of everyone means you're not thinking of me as someone you can count on."

"I do!" she cried. "I do count on you."

"For my sword arm, princess? For a body to warm your bed?"

"I love you," she said miserably.

If anything, his face grew graver. "I know you do, and you may not realize right this minute how deeply I value that. The problem is I need you to trust me in *all* the things that matter to both of us."

Kat was trembling too hard to speak—and didn't know what to say anyway.

"You should have told me," he went on. "Rohn or not, you should have treated me as your equal."

She'd stepped far enough into the room that she wasn't blocking the doorway. If she had been, he'd have brushed her on his way out. As it was, her hands were pressed tight against her mouth, holding in pleas she didn't dare let out.

She didn't think she could stand it if he ignored them again.

He didn't shut the door behind him. He just slipped out noiselessly. Kat trudged to the end of the bed and sat, struggling not to fall apart. She shouldn't have had to worry about this. They both knew he was her mate. In all her life, no one had loved her as selflessly as he did. If he cast her off, where would she find the strength to care about anything? She knew this might be the most pathetic question she'd ever asked herself, but she couldn't will it away. Her heart felt like it was being ripped from her chest.

When Ciran entered, worry written across his face, her tears burst out like a storm.

"I meant to tell him," she sobbed. "I swear I wasn't trying to treat him like a child."

"Of course you weren't." Ciran sat beside her to rub her back. "No one could mistake Hattori for anything but a man."

His words made her cry harder. They came from his good heart, not her own. As her breath hitched uncontrollably, she recalled her father yelling at her after she'd been accused of attempting to poison her stepsister. *How could you?* he'd demanded. *How could you do such a thing?* As badly as that hurt, it hadn't savaged her like this. Then she'd held back her tears. Then her knowledge of her innocence bolstered her.

Now she might be guilty as charged.

"I don't think I like Human-style drama," she announced, trying to be funny even as her eyes leaked tears at a frightening pace. "It's very uncomfortable."

Ciran gave her a little squeeze. "Certainly from the inside it is."

"I've probably got little specks of their emotions stuck in my aura. We were around them for hours today."

"Oh princess, as much as I love you, I'm not sure you ought to blame this tempest on them."

He was right, naturally. She took the folded handkerchief he offered and blew her nose. "I hate being in the wrong."

Ciran's smile had never been so soft. "That sentiment isn't exclusive to princesses."

She put her head on his chest, letting his patting soothe her until she stopped sniffling. Then she sat up and squared her shoulders. "Is he still in the apartment?"

"He was headed for the balcony, last I saw."

She began to rise, but he surprised her by catching her mouth for a slow, penetrating kiss. His fingertips brushed tingles along her jaw even as they kept her face turned to his. Oh he was a lovely kisser, his technique the perfect foil to his interest. When he released her, more than her cheeks were warm.

"Be sure I get credit for this," he said.

"Credit?"

One corner of his mouth tipped up. "For not jumping at the chance to claim his place in your bed."

He had a talent for knowing the right thing to say. "You'll get no credit from me," she teased back. "I know whose blanket you most want to share."

His expression flickered, but he didn't deny it. She left him shaking his head at her. The warmth in his eyes—part affection, part attraction—went a long way toward shoring up her courage.

♦

Courage wasn't easy to hold onto when you'd just told the only woman you'd ever loved you weren't going to sleep with her—especially when you knew she had options. Ciran's feelings for Kat aside, they'd only met because Miry had been trying to head off a match with another prince by shipping Kat to the provinces. If Hattori were gone and Kat succeeded in winning back the daimyos' good graces, she could have those options again.

He fought not to shudder at the chill that skipped down his spine. Now wasn't the time to give in to fear.

With his hands locked together behind his back, he looked out over the sunlit metropolis. Not by accident, he stood on the end of the balcony farthest from their bedroom. A frozen river snaked between the low buildings of Prewtan, its surface smoothed to allow sleighs and skaters to traverse it. The latter sport was a draw for Prewtan's children. Even from a distance, he heard their excited gales of laughter as they raced each other or took a spill. The colors of their hats and scarves stood out brightly against the snow. Those primitive knitted garments wouldn't warm them like Yamish winter wear, nor were their little bodies as resilient his people's. For one odd second, he found himself wanting to protect every one of their red noses.

He and Kat might have had a child someday.

"Hattori."

His heart leaped into his throat at the sound of her saying his name. He told himself to stand firm, that he didn't need to be perfect in order to be treated the way he was asking for.

"Kat," he said, turning to face her.

Her hands were twisted before her breasts, her figure simultaneously neat as a pin and uncomfortably alluring in her corseted light blue gown. "There's something else I need to tell you," she said.

This didn't strike him as promising, but he bowed his head for her to go on.

Kat pulled in a fortifying breath. "I traded my blue diamond to the warden for Haro. It was the only bribe I knew he wouldn't refuse."

It hadn't been the *only* bribe, or she and Ciran wouldn't have left that prison reeking the way they had. The color that bled into Kat's cheeks betrayed that she recalled this.

"Maybe some of what you said was right," she went on hurriedly. "I did think of that diamond as my ticket back to my rightful place in society. Maybe I felt insecure without it, and that influenced me to take Benjamin's offer more seriously."

"You could have told me you'd traded it," he said.

"I thought if you knew I'd used it to buy your brother's freedom, you'd believe you owed me."

"Kat, I—"

"You don't owe me," she broke in fiercely. "Haro's life is worth more than a chunk of stone, and not just because you love him and I love you. No matter what happens between us, I'll always be grateful I had it to give. What I'm trying to say is, I've always been aware that there are . . . inequities in our positions, due to the classes we were born to. It didn't occur to me that by shielding you, I wasn't showing you enough respect."

This was more of an apology than he'd expected from a royal. The hint of primness in her tone said she thought so too. If the stakes hadn't been so serious, he'd have smiled. Since he couldn't, he heaved a sigh.

"You know there's a difference between shielding my feelings and making decisions that put you into harm's way."

She did know, because she bit her lip. "Sometimes I just can't stand it," she confessed. "I pretend I can because I have to, but sometimes I think about what Miry got away with, and I want to explode."

Tears trembled on her lower lids, clearly not the first that had welled tonight.

"Oh Kat," he said, stepping to her so he could wrap her up in his arms. She clung to him, and it felt like he hadn't held her in a long time.

"I'm sorry," she cried out against his shoulder. "It's me who's the childish one."

He stroked her hair, his cheek pressed to the top of her head. "You're not childish. Most Yama would want revenge for what you suffered. I just want you to see that the cost of seeking justice might not be worth it. You lost your inheritance, Kat: money and position. If a chance for happiness isn't more valuable to you than that, then all we have between us is an accident of genetics."

Her arms tightened on his back, but she didn't speak. He kissed her temple, hoping he hadn't pushed too hard. One thing he'd said wasn't quite the truth. No matter what she chose, more than his genes wanted her. After a minute, though he didn't ever want to let go, he let her ease back from him.

"All right," she said. "I'll make you a deal."

"A deal," he responded, the back of his neck tensing.

"As long as Miry doesn't find us, I won't go after her. I'll turn down Benjamin's offer. I . . . we'll find another way to build up security."

The set of her mouth was too resigned to make him happy. "You're sure, Kat? I meant what I said. I'd never let you go after her alone. I'm not even—" He cleared his throat. "Chances are, it might not be possible for me to resist sharing your bed."

"You have to know I want more from you than sex. I want us to be equals, to learn to rely on each other. I also want your brother to have the peace he needs to recover. That can't happen if I pursue Miry."

"You wouldn't be able to see your father before he dies." He hadn't wanted to remind her, but it was only fair.

Kat let out a quiet sigh. "I know. I think I needed that more for my sake than his. I wanted one last chance for him to see me as innocent. And who knows how strong his desire to reconcile really was? I doubt it would take much softening on his part to put Miry on the offensive." Her lips twisted ruefully. "My father loved me and my mother, but he never did have the strongest spine."

Hattori took her face between his hands. Because he'd grown up without parents, he knew he couldn't completely understand her sadness.

"I love you," he said, wanting her to have this truth. "Nothing you do can change that. Not going after Miry. Not falling in love with Ciran. I'll love you with all my heart as long as I draw breath."

Her lips parted in surprise. "You think I'm in love with Ciran?"

"Yes," he said, forcing himself to say the words. "I would be if I were you."

Her palms lay flat on his chest, the thudding of his heart bare to them. "Here's the thing," she murmured. "I'd be in love with him if I were *you*."

◆

Kat watched her implication hit him, muscles tightening in his face.

"I'm sorry if I've misread your feelings," she said. "I just don't understand why you wouldn't keep both of us if you could. Ciran is wonderful."

"You . . . you wouldn't be hurt by that?" he stammered.

"I care about him, and maybe my heart is greedy. I think—" She stopped, wanting to choose her words carefully. "If I'm not going to shield you, I have to tell the truth. My heart enjoys loving both of you. Maybe I ought to feel guilty, but instead I feel bigger. You come first with me. I won't lie to you about that, but—given a choice—I'd let him inside the bond we share. Really inside, not waiting on the fringes."

He touched her face, his eyes searching hers. "I hate myself for needing you to love me best."

She went onto her toes to put their eyes closer to level. "I'd rather you didn't hate yourself for anything."

He made a sound, a rush of air that could have been self-mocking.

"I'm glad you love me best," she added, her arms twined behind his neck. "Mostly, though, I'm glad you love me at all."

He didn't smile in answer. Her words struck too strong a chord in him. His arms tightened on her waist as his head lowered.

Then he was kissing her.

He'd never taken her mouth so softly, his tongue as gentle as it was intimate. Calculation wasn't in him; his technique came from his soul. It spoke to her in ways no one else's kisses could. They understood each other. They'd bared their hearts and their love hadn't been destroyed. It was a stroke of fortune no Yama would have bet credit on. Knowing this, he kissed her like he would never stop. A sigh of relief and pleasure had her sinking into him.

Hearing it, he lifted her off her feet onto the hard heat of him. His hand was tight around her bottom.

"I need to be inside you," he said.

She needed that too, and gave her answer by turning her head to kiss him more hungrily. He already held her weight, but suddenly her back was shoved into the cold stone facing of the building. He rolled his erection between her thighs, the big ridge rubbing deliciously. Kat moaned at his strength as he trapped her against the wall. Her skirts didn't permit her to lift her legs, and she was desperate to. Her body wanted him to fill it, to jam that hardness into the heat and tenderness of her sex.

Irrational though it was, fighting and making up had made her want him more.

She wasn't alone in the reaction. Groaning, Hattori tore his mouth free of hers. "I could take you right out here in daylight."

"Me too," she said breathlessly. "More than once probably."

He cursed, muttering about her stupid corset driving him mad. He eased his weight back enough for her to slide down him onto her feet, a journey that left him panting and maybe a bit harder. To her surprise, he didn't yank her toward the bedroom.

"Ciran," he said, squeezing the fingers she'd wound between his. "We need to talk to him. We need to see if he wants the same things we do and go forward from there."

"He'll want them," she assured him, "and then we're all going to have fun."

Hattori's eyes flashed darker, not going black but approaching it. "I love you, Katsu Shinobi, more than I'll ever be able to prove to you."

She twitched her brows, because they both knew precisely how she would let him try. Hattori laughed shakily.

"Come on," he said, tugging her after him by the hand. "Let's get this show on the road, as the Humans say."

♦

Ciran forced himself to stay in the bedroom after Kat left. Even when he heard her and Hattori's footsteps approaching, he didn't retreat. Their husky voices told him where their rapprochement was leading, but that was irrelevant.

It was time to ask for what he wanted, time to demand it or find a way to move on. If that interfered with their peacemaking, so be it.

They entered the bedroom through the doors to the balcony. He was lying on his back with his ankles stacked and his hands locked tensely on his stomach. He told himself no Yama in his situation could have pulled off true calm.

"Ciran," Hattori said in surprise. "We were just coming to find you."

Ciran pushed up to sit. Hattori's cheeks were flushed with desire, which he ordered himself to ignore. "Good," he said. "There's something I need to say."

Hattori blinked and shot a glance at Kat, whose hand he was holding. "All right. We'd be happy to listen."

Kat pulled free to bounce onto the bed with Ciran. He didn't mind, though he hadn't expected it. When she hugged him from behind and laid her cheek on his shoulder, his vocal chords eased a bit.

He was as ready as he was going to get.

"I love you," he said directly into Hattori's eyes. "Not just as a friend but with all of my heart and soul. I know that doesn't surprise you. What might is that I've come to believe you might feel the same for me."

Hattori didn't flinch, though he was crimson now. "I do," he said simply.

"You do?" Ciran knew he shouldn't have been startled, but the words came out anyway.

"Yes." Hattori tugged the bottom of his waistcoat, the nervous gesture more Human than he could know. "I love you just as you described loving me. You've become important to my happiness, and as more than a friend. I'm sorry I fought admitting it. Part of me thought it would be better—or simpler—to just love Kat, but that part of me was wrong."

Ciran's mouth worked as he tried to take this in. Evidently, suspecting someone loved you wasn't the same as hearing it.

"I love Kat too," he blurted unstrategically.

Hattori smiled, much of the redness receding from his face. "I know, maybe better than she does. Kat and I . . . we want you to be a real part of what we share."

"Yes," Kat agreed, her arms tightening around him. "No more running away when things get interesting."

"But you hate that we're attracted to each other!" Ciran exclaimed to Hattori.

"I don't hate it," he said. "It makes me feel insecure. It doesn't stop me from wanting you—sometimes even more. I love you both enough to try to get over it, or to live with it, if that's the best I can do. You deserve to be loved by each other as much as you're loved by me."

The clamp of his jaw was stubborn, as if he were trying to convince himself.

"Hattori . . ." Ciran said, not liking that idea.

"Stop arguing," Kat cut in. "If we wait for all of us to be perfect, we'll never be happy. None of us can guarantee we won't ever be hurt or jealous. What's important is that the love we share now, without even trying to do better, is head and shoulders above what most Yama can dream of. Fate gave us an incredible gift. I, for one, would like to hang onto it."

The lump in Ciran's throat wouldn't let him speak. Kat squirmed around him to stroke his face. "Trust me," she said, "I know how good being loved second best by you is."

"Shit," he said as the moisture in his eyes overflowed.

Kat laughed and kissed a fat tear away. "Of all of us, you should enjoy crying. I can hardly think of anything more Human."

"I just—" He swallowed and tried again. "I feel so lucky!"

Kat hugged him, and Hattori joined her, embracing him from the other side. That truly made him dissolve, which amused the others.

"All right," he finally said, drawing his sleeve determinedly across his tear-streaked face. "I'm done with that now."

"Sure?" Hattori joked. "We could get you a glass of water to replenish."

His eyes were affectionate. Knowing how deep that affection ran caused Ciran's emotions to take a turn. His penis hardened in a breath-stealing surge, slapping against his zipper. The impression he always had—that no amount of sex would be too much—suffused his body.

"Time to make up," he said, for once not doubting he had the right. "And this time is for me. You two are going to do what I want."

Kat inhaled sharply, then thought better of speaking. Her gaze shifted to Hattori, who'd begun breathing more deeply. Seeing this stiffened Ciran's cock the one bit more it took for its skin to sting.

"What do you want?" Hattori asked softly.

Ciran didn't have to think. The answer was ready. "You naked and her in her corset. I'm going to take you one at a time, and the other is going to watch." He let his eyes run over Hattori's substantial trouser bulge. "I'll take you first, I think."

"Me."

"I know how it cranks you up when I pleasure her. If I'm feeling nice, I'll let you have me afterward."

"If you're feeling *nice.*"

Hattori crossed his arms in annoyance, but his face had gone pink again. Ciran smiled, confidence spreading headily through him. "Better start undressing before I change my mind."

Hattori hesitated, but he did it. Satisfied, Ciran took Kat in hand. She didn't protest anything, eyes wide as he turned her by the shoulders to unhook the back of her pale blue gown. He peeled the fine wool away without ceremony, focused on unveiling the garment that lay beneath. When he reached it, the laces of her corset weren't tight enough for his purposes.

"Suck in," he said a second before he yanked.

Kat gasped, and heat coursed through his body as he retied the knots. Her shape was always slender, but the corset squeezed it into an hourglass, her hips and breasts curving out from her tiny waist. Stripping her lacy knickers down her legs displayed their graceful length and exposed her tight bottom. *Tempting* wasn't the word for how she looked to him. No matter what she believed, as he knelt behind her, he wasn't convinced she was second best at all.

He rose to enjoy the slight advantage he had in height. Cinched by the boning, she looked as fragile as a Human female, though she was nearly as strong as him. He remembered taking her in the shower, holding her against the tile as he pushed and pulled his cock through her slick passage. She was wet now, the scent causing his fingers to curl with greed. Rather than explore her directly this early in the game, he palmed her round bottom. She was cushy there and resilient—just feminine enough to push his switches. She shivered when he dragged his lips up her vertebrae. Unable to resist, he caught her vulnerable earlobe between his teeth.

"I was too easy on you in the shower," he said.

She turned to face him, cheeks flushed, pretty mouth soft and red. Arousal had enlarged her pupils, which he couldn't deny exulting in. The tightness of the corset pushed up her perfect breasts, the row of ruffles at its top cutting across her nipples. If she breathed any harder, he suspected they'd pop free. Behind him, Hattori let out a low pained sound.

"Pretty, isn't she?" Ciran asked.

"Yes," he agreed in a husky tone.

Kat leaned closer, other things on her mind. "Could I tie him up for you?" she whispered.

Ciran had planned on directing the coming events himself, but this idea slammed through him with the force of a runaway maglev car. Back when he'd been a pillow boy, bondage had been one of his favorite requests to fulfill. Maybe Kat had realized that from their experience with the warden. She licked her lips, the elegant shape of her lamril peeking out wetly. The primal signal shook his resolve.

When Ciran responded, his voice was hoarse. "You won't interfere with what I'm doing?"

"I'll try not to," she answered. "I really like touching both of you."

He almost smiled, but he was too aroused. He stepped back from her, one finger up to warn her to stay where she was.

Then he pulled off his clothes.

He knew how he looked, that even men who didn't desire men would spare him a second glance. Hattori was raw power hammered into flesh, graceful in his way but not like Ciran was. Ciran's body was spare and lean, the clean lines of his muscles, of his proportions, as pleasing to the eye as a carved statue.

At the moment, he was also extremely hard, his erection pulsing full and straight from the hairless plane of his groin. His balls were tight but heavy, like they hoped what was coming would be more satisfying than usual. He wanted that so badly it alarmed him. Kat's attention locked on the picture his penis made. When her tongue swept over her lip again, a bead of excitement welled warmly from his slit.

"No," he rasped before she could ask to kiss it away.

He knew her too well. She laughed breathily and slid her gaze to Hattori. From the corner of his eye, Ciran saw he was naked. Kat's brows shot up at the condition she found him in.

Ciran didn't think he was prepared for that visual. Hattori's extravagant erections tended to break his concentration. Not wanting to surrender the upper hand, he handed Kat a silk tie from one of their lounging robes.

"Secure his wrists," he said.

"That bit of silk won't hold him. He's strong enough to rip it."

"He'll have to keep himself from trying. He ought to be able to. His heat isn't riding him."

"You could let me hold his hands. I'm strong, and it would remind him that you're in charge."

"I'm right here," Hattori growled. "You don't have to pretend I'm not."

Ciran turned and braced to take in the sight of him. As always, his naked gorgeousness was a blow—the breadth of his shoulders, the sweat that sheened his contracted muscles, the exotic fuzz of hair at his chest and groin. He was a gigantic sexual god, his cock as big and ready as Kat's reaction to it implied. If Hattori had been impassive, the picture he presented would have aroused. Instead, he was utterly alive, utterly involved in what was happening. Far from being repelled by their talk of bondage, his diaphragm jerked in and out above his very excited cock. Seeing it, practically tasting it, Ciran's nerves prickled all over.

"Get on the bed," he said gutturally.

He received another thrill when both his lovers obeyed.

"On your back," he ordered Hattori. "Kat, you sit at the headboard."

She sat with Hattori's head on her folded calves. "Hands," she reminded as he tried to get comfortable.

He gave them to her, his gaze seeking Ciran's warily. She wrapped her fingers firmly around his palms. "Do you want the tie as well?"

Hattori shook his head and swallowed. His erection lay on his belly, beautifully thick and long, the blood that pumped through it causing it to bounce slightly. His muscular legs were sprawled, his knees moving restlessly up and down on the soft covers. When Ciran smiled, his heavy testicles twitched upward.

Ciran didn't say a word. He didn't want his friend to be self-conscious. Not yet ready to join the others, he opened his personal bureau drawer to dig out a cinnabar-lacquered flask. Hattori tended to travel with extra weapons. Ciran's preparedness was broader.

"That's Dragon oil," Kat exclaimed.

This was the name of the exclusive brand, developed—so legend ran—by a former empress's pillow boy. It lasted like no other lubricant, the feel of it on skin extraordinarily silky. Some claimed it heightened sensitivity as well, which Ciran thought might be true. He crawled onto the mattress with the flask in hand, sitting on his heels to one side of his captive audience. Near enough to touch but prevented from doing so, Hattori clutched Kat's fingers as Ciran broke the seal on the cap.

"I've been saving this," he said, "for a special occasion."

Hattori's gaze followed his motions. "I could help you with that."

Ciran was pouring a coin-sized puddle into his palm, the fragrance of sandalwood and vanilla immediately wafting out. He capped the flask and set it aside. "Thank you," he declined. "I'd rather do it myself."

Once his palms were oiled, he proved it. He massaged his cock with sensual thoroughness, rubbing it, pulling it, until every swollen inch of it shone. Touching himself felt good, a starter course to the feast to come. Best of all was the way Hattori's eyes ate up his caresses. Encouraged by the attention, he didn't neglect his balls or the little slit where his precome was seeping more speedily.

Hattori licked his lips just as Kat had done earlier.

"Your turn," Ciran said, his voice gone understandably husky.

Ciran rubbed the oil with equal diligence over his partner. Hattori's strong hips flexed at the slow and pleasurable pressure.

"Fate, Ciran," he moaned. "Your hands . . ."

"Like them?" Ciran teased, bending for just a second to tongue his glans.

Hattori cried out and shoved at him with his hips. Unable to resist, Ciran accepted the mute entreaty to stimulate his tip. He gave his friend two minutes of the sweet treatment, sucking him, licking him—but only on the crest—until his spine appeared to be melting.

He let go so he could clamber between his outspread legs.

Hattori looked up at him unsurely. "Shouldn't I be on my front for this?"

Ciran shook his head. He was on his knees, his weight still not lowered or stretched out. He wanted Hattori looking in his eyes when he came. This should have been simple to explain, but suddenly he could not.

"You want us to rub swords," Hattori said with dawning comprehension. "Face to face. That's what the oil is about."

Ciran tried to read what he felt about that, but the only emotion he saw was calm.

"Do it," Hattori said decisively. "I want to feel what that's like with you."

It was a kind of heaven—without the winged cherubs. Once Ciran let his weight sink, the warmth of their well oiled flesh, the different shapes of their aroused pricks sliding against each other, created an amazing intimacy. Neither could mistake the other for anything but a man. Their penises precluded it, their balls and their hard hipbones. Pleasure climbing, Ciran shoved one hand under Hattori's ass and wrapped the other on the carved headboard.

His arm crossed Kat's shoulder to reach the wood. She kissed the bend of his elbow, a secret sweetness between them. He didn't have a chance to do more than register the frisson it sent up his nerves.

Hattori was reacting to his new strategy.

"Yes," he hissed at the increase in pressure and rubbing speed. He cocked one hairy leg around Ciran's, his ferocious strength squeezing him closer still. His neck arched atop Kat's calves as a torso-long shudder rolled up him. Though he wasn't spilling, it looked like an orgasm. Possibly the quirks associated with his heat hadn't subsided completely. Toward the end, he ejaculated one hot spurt. His body strained then, but no more came. Probably no more would without Kat's cream on him.

To Ciran, this was more arousing than he'd ever be able to explain.

He waited until Hattori's head came back down, panting almost as hard as if *he'd* climaxed. Hattori's lashes rose lazily. He'd enjoyed his half-release. His eyes were fully black with pleasure.

"Can I go?" Ciran asked, his own cock aching terribly. "Will you come again with me if I do?"

"Try me," Hattori purred.

The low dare ran through his bloodstream like lightning. "Open the oil," he rasped to Kat. "I want more on my palm."

She poured it for him, her eyes unexpectedly gentle when they met his. He knew she was excited, because her pupils were bigger than normal.

"This is for you," she said, agreeing with his earlier claim. Then she grasped Hattori's hands in hers again.

The muscles in her arms were taut; she was genuinely restraining him. Hattori realized it. He tested her grip with a tug, then let out a gasp as she withstood his strength. He could break free if he wanted, but he'd have to work for it. He wasn't used to being physically controlled, even partially. To judge by the way his cock jerked, her hold was heightening his passions.

"You'd better hurry," Hattori warned, his tone breathy. "I'm having trouble not trying to pull free."

Ciran kissed him until he moaned, both their tongues battling. When his own impatience burst its limits, he put his freshly oiled hand to its intended use.

"Fuck," Hattori cursed, his big body lifting Ciran as he writhed. Ciran was squeezing the thickened shafts of their pricks together, his thumb on his side, his fingers wrapping Hattori's.

"Now rub my sword," he said throatily.

His hand kept the friction tight as they hitched and gasped against each other in hard small jerks. The sensations they created were twice as strong as before. Their swollen veins added texture, the flared rims of their cockheads. The whorls and calluses of Ciran's palm provided charms they both could enjoy. The Dragon oil smoothed it all, allowing them to go faster and faster with their heads thrown back and their hips grinding. Ciran dug his knees down into the covers as Hattori's leg clamped him wonderfully closer.

Hattori grunted, his veins pulsing noticeably wilder in Ciran's grip. "Go," he said through gritted teeth. "I want your seed spurting over me."

Maybe he liked this because of his own limitations regarding when he could spill. Whatever the cause, he didn't look like he'd last much longer. His eyes were screwed shut with impending pleasure, and Kat's knuckles whitened where they gripped his sweaty hands. Hattori was holding her just as tightly—as if she were a lifeline against drowning in ecstasy.

"I want it," he repeated, his all-black eyes opening. "I want to feel you come."

Determined to make this happen, he changed the slant of his hips so that their balls were squashed together. The feel of that was too much. Ciran gasped, trying to hold back the leaping pressure of

235

orgasm. He felt so good. He wanted to sink into those black eyes and never climb out again.

"Now," Hattori ordered, his voice grating.

The flood inside Ciran crested—huge, hot, forcing out his ejaculation in volcanic streaks of bliss. A swallowed sound broke in Hattori's chest. He was climaxing too, groin jamming against Ciran's as the convulsion took hold of him.

Two more gushes from Hattori joined Ciran's eruption. Hattori's groan made him crazy. He came harder, hotter, loving that Hattori had spilled for him . . . but not completely.

The intensity of the release weakened him. He dropped onto Hattori's chest only to be wrapped in his big warm arms. Kat had released his hands. Overwhelmed and still twitching with aftershocks, Ciran gasped desperately for air.

"There," Hattori said, mouth warm against his hair. "There."

Ciran relaxed as he didn't think he ever had in his life, plummeting into sleep so swiftly the end of the world couldn't have prevented it.

When he woke he'd been turned over onto his back. His head was in Kat's lap where Hattori's had lain before, but that wasn't the most noteworthy change in his conditions. Pleasure rolled through his cock in waves. Hattori was bent over him sucking it. He had a great mouth for oral sex: big, warm, with a strength of suction that more than made up for any lack of subtlety. Ciran wasn't the only one with a fetish for other people's erotic suffering. Hattori must have been fellating him for a while—and not let him come. Ciran's cock was so hard, so tender and sensitive that the pleasure it was receiving hurt.

He groaned at the strafing of Hattori's tongue, his pelvis pushing instinctively deeper as his hands tangled in thick black hair.

Hattori was too strong to be forced into anything. In order to bob up and down, he'd braced his weight on Ciran's quadriceps. The press of his palms restrained him as he freed his head and sat up. Perhaps to take the sting from stopping, his thumbs stroked Ciran's trembling inner thigh muscles.

Hattori's smile threatened to draw tears to his eyes again. It was the smile of someone who loved him, someone who knew and accepted his worst foibles.

"You can sleep through a lot," his old friend observed.

Ciran couldn't prevent his hungry squirm. "Sorry I missed the build up."

"That wasn't all you missed. I got Kat warmed up for you."

When Ciran turned his eyes upward, she did indeed look like someone had been at her. Her hair was tousled, her corset had been removed, and the tips of her breasts were delectably red and sharp. The left was circled by a distinctive kissing bruise. She blushed as he noticed it. "He didn't let you come either."

"No," she confirmed, one side of her mouth slanting. "He can be very bossy when he wants to."

Ciran would have paid good money to watch the holofilm of that.

"Move away," he said to Hattori, authority returning. "And keep your distance while I finish what you started."

He began at the top, jerking Kat to her knees for a kiss. She liked a little force, the same as Hattori did. Ciran kept his mouth soft and his hands hard, clamping her tight against him until she trembled.

Then he laid her back against the covers.

"This is for me," he repeated, triumph coursing through him as her teeth caught her lower lip.

He kissed her neck, her shoulders, the slopes of her satiny breasts. He rolled her budded nipples like candy against his tongue. When she squirmed, he slid one curved finger into her hot wet sheath.

"Ciran," she gasped, her nails pricking his shoulders.

The finger was there to calm her and perhaps to tease as he nipped a path from her breastbone to her stomach. He smoothed his other hand down her leg, a light whispering caress designed to wake the nerves in her lower limbs. She was a beautiful instrument to play. Her toes curled hard as he drew his touch along the arch of her foot. While he did, he watched her pussy where his finger disappeared into her. His stimulation of the meridians on her foot had fluid welling silkily from her.

Hattori must have seen her response from the edge of the mattress where he'd been banished. His groan of reaction made Ciran's cock throb as much as Kat.

He curled his penetrating finger just enough to make her pelvis twist around it. "I'm going to be in you here, princess. Pumping hard and fast and as deep as my prick can go. First, though, you need to be wetter."

She tried to say his name, but he'd put his mouth on her pussy. He meant to give her exactly what he'd given Hattori: two concentrated minutes of oral expertise. She was simply too much fun to play with to curtail the exercise—her taste, her pulse, her hard little swelling against his tongue. She couldn't control herself as well as Hattori, no doubt because she had less practice. The helpless mewls she let out excited him. Wanting more, he pushed her right to the edge and backed off.

Then he did it again.

"Ciran," she gasped. "Please."

Hearing her beg was a whip his lust truly could not withstand. He stopped, panted, and crawled up her. Her calves slid up his sides like magic. The combing of her fingers around his scalp was enough to make him shudder. He suspected his eyes were as dark as hers.

"Come in me," she whispered. "And please let it be as many times as you want."

Her request was a near twin for Hattori's. She wanted him to release in her, to mark her with his essence. Her pelvis shifted angles, causing the throbbing tip of his penis to touch the sleek wet heat of her folds. He jerked, then worked himself between her labia until his friction-loving crown found her gate. She didn't push herself over him, but he could tell she wanted to. His cock went so rigid he might not have come at all.

"Kat," he purred, his mouth lowered to her ear. "I'm going to pound you right through this bed."

She shivered, and his cockhead tingled a warning that it might want to do what he'd promised quite literally. It didn't matter. Tonight, no demand was too excessive for him to make. She and Hattori had put themselves in his hands.

That realization galvanized him. He thrust and their hips collided with the first stroke, both of them crying out. Ciran came at the end of the second, but without lessening his desire. The chance to take all he wanted was too much of a charge. He powered through the slight fading that tended to overtake him at the end of an orgasm. This was only two releases, and he did best with five or six. Kat came herself, her contractions bringing him back to full hardness. Grateful, maybe even giddy, he bent one of her legs up around his shoulder so he could drive into her more deeply.

Her head flung back and she groaned, telling him he was hitting her favorite spot.

"This is where he gets you," he panted. "This is where that big cock of his reaches. This is where his prince's whip hooked you."

She gasped and flooded him with wetness, too aroused by what he was doing to answer. His cock felt huge, but he knew its signals. This time it could stand more excitement before it exploded. He took advantage and went at her harder.

She cried out, high and wild.

"Ciran," Hattori cautioned, probably alarmed by his vigor.

"She's . . . all right," he got out, kneeling now with both hands boosting up her rear. This allowed him to concuss his glans more precisely against her most sensitive area. "If you saw . . . how hard you take her when you get going . . . you'd know she adores this."

Kat reached for Hattori's hand, groaning and arching as he clenched it in support. She hadn't gone over yet. Like Ciran, it was going to take more for her this time. Ciran relished that more than he could say.

"This is how much I want you," he growled, each word shaken by a new thrust. "This is . . . how much I love you."

Her dazed eyes opened, black with pleasure and liquid with emotion. He was looking down at her, her lovely body splayed before him. She was so beautiful and abandoned that awe at his own good fortune slammed him with a force equal to his lust. This wonderful, generous, brave woman wanted him.

His desires aroused her, whatever shape they took. The imminence inside him sharpened. He understood what Hattori felt: that she *had* to belong to him. He could share her . . . but not right then. Right then, he needed to put his stamp on her in the most personal way he could.

He knew the instant she began to peak. Her back bowed and her pussy tightened deliciously. Heat swelled in his prick as the flush of orgasm stained her breasts. The sight triggered him, pure delight kicking his gonads into unstoppable action. They went together, his body seizing its chance to fulfill his private vow. Seed jetted from him at such length and with such power that it was like a dozen climaxes wrapped in one. He shot until he overflowed her, the fusillade of delight seeming unending. She held him through it, coming tightly around him.

"God," he gasped when the bliss finally receded, no exclamation but the Human one sufficient. "Kat."

She collapsed warm and soft beneath him. "Mm," was all she troubled herself to say.

He laughed with what oxygen he had left and relaxed his weight on her.

"You'll squash her," Hattori said.

"Mm-mm," Kat managed to deny. "You too, please. So my side won't get cold."

He grumbled under his breath, but arranged himself next to her with his head sharing her pillow. Almost as warm as they were, his hand rose to stroke Ciran's hair. The gentleness of the motion was hypnotic.

"You'll put me to sleep again," he warned.

Hattori snorted but didn't stop petting him. "Like it matters. I saw how hard you came that last time. You're done for now, my friend."

"Night hasn't even started," Ciran protested. He was smiling against Kat's cheek, his muscles and joints as warm as if they'd been taken apart and oiled.

"Don't worry," Kat said just as sleepily. "There'll be more nights for us all."

13: AFTERGLOW

"What do you suppose this character means by 'shiver me timbers?'" Ciran asked.

"Well," Kat said, "if timbers are a ship's framework, they're probably a metaphor for the pirate's bones. If he says his timbers are shaking, he could mean that he's afraid."

Ciran frowned at her theory. He sat at his prized junkshop desk beside the fire in the grand salon, his current manuscript stacked in two tidy piles to either side of a ruled ledger. He liked writing his translations in longhand, claiming this put him in an authentic frame of mind. Kat had a sneaking suspicion he just enjoyed buying Human pens.

"Saying he's afraid isn't very colorful," he griped. "People ought to read these stories in their original language if they want to experience their full charm."

"If every Yama spoke Human, you wouldn't have a business."

This comment came from Hattori, who was sprawled on the couch with his head in Kat's lap, lazily reading the newspaper.

"True," Ciran said, preening. "Nor would I be this household's biggest breadwinner."

"You don't get tired of saying that, do you?"

Ciran grinned at his friend. "Not even a little bit."

With Benjamin DuBieren's aid, he'd set himself up as a translator and smuggler of Human novels for the Yamish black market. The lower class's appetite for the proscribed stories was apparently limitless, and Ciran suffered no pangs of conscience at profiting from it. By contrast, depriving his precious Human authors of their labors' fruits was anathema to him. Benjamin and his co-conspirators at the publishers had devised a method by which writers could be paid without anyone knowing where the money had come from. Benjamin took his cut as well, but only—as he liked to say—what the "man upstairs" would approve of. He called Ciran his "D flawless demon translator."

The adventure involved in running the under-the-table trade kept him from reminding Kat—at least too often—that he still hoped to employ her.

When he did bring it up, she reminded herself that happiness was the best revenge.

"What about a footnote?" Haro suggested. "Then you can explain all about the shivery timbers."

Haro sat in a leather wingchair chair next to the marble hearth, seemingly doing nothing but being still. These days he worked for Hattori, who'd convinced the Prewtan Grande's manager that not only were Princess "Katherine" and her retinue the furthest thing from trouble, but that his hotel couldn't truly claim to be grand without a competent head of security. Even Ciran had been impressed by Hattori's persuasive powers, not having known he had it in him.

"That might work," Ciran said in response to Haro, "but footnotes interrupt the flow, and this particular scene is especially action-packed."

"You'll think of something," Kat said, having seen him solve stickier conundrums. In truth, he rarely took anyone's suggestions except his own—ironic considering how much he liked working with them as sounding boards. Fortunately, none of them minded. They understood the appeal of gathering here together.

They also enjoyed watching Ciran's spirits bloom. These last six months had been the best of Kat's life, but no one could deny Ciran was radiant. Given his position in their trio, Kat hadn't expected that.

Hattori smiled up at her as she played idly with his hair, his expression echoing the contentment she felt inside. They all wore Human-style contacts outside the suite. Since Hattori's shift had ended, his eyes were his own again. Their gleam promised contentment was only one of the emotions they were sharing. Like her, he was looking forward to enjoying Ciran's bloom in their bed tonight.

"Coo-coo-coo, " Ciran teased, because he thought they were acting like lovebirds.

"They're wondering why you're so happy," Haro explained, his ability to read them uncanny.

"Well, why wouldn't I be?" Ciran said. "They both love me more than they realize, plus I have the added advantage of always being a slightly forbidden treat."

"An obnoxiously egotistical treat," Hattori corrected without looking away from her.

Haro laughed, a sound they didn't often hear from him. When the others shifted their gazes, he was leaning back in his chair, his hands draped loosely on its arms, his eyes closed without tension. Day by day, as their time in Prewtan unfolded, he'd grown calmer. Tonight he looked peaceful. Ciran wagged his brows at Kat and Hattori, seeing the truth as easily as they did.

Picturesque though it was, the crackling fire didn't matter. Their joy was the warmth Hattori's brother was basking in.

THE END

ABOUT THE AUTHOR

Emma Holly is the award-winning, *USA Today* bestselling author of more than twenty romantic novels, featuring vampires, demons, fairies and just plain extraordinary ordinary folks. She loves the hot stuff, both to read and to write!

If you'd like to know what else she's written—with demons and without—please visit her website at: http://www.emmaholly.com. She also runs monthly contests and sends out newsletters. To receive them, sign up on the contest page on her site.

If you enjoy your heroes with a little something extra, do try *Hidden Talents* and *Prince of Ice*.

Thanks so much for reading this book!

An excerpt from HIDDEN TALENTS

available in ebook and print

Werewolf cop Adam Santini is sworn to protect and serve all the supes in Resurrection, NY— including unsuspecting human Talents who wander in from Outside.

Telekinetic Ari is hot on the trail of a mysterious crime boss who wants to exploit her gift for his own evil ends, a mission that puts her on a collision course with the hottest cop in the RPD. Adam wants Blackwater too, but mostly he wants Ari. She seems to be the mate he's been yearning for all his life, though getting a former street kid into bed with the Law could be his toughest case to date.

CHAPTER ONE

Dusk settled over the city of Resurrection like a blanket of bad news.

That's me, Ari thought, flexing her right fist beside her hip. *Bad news with a capital B.*

This wasn't just whistling in the dark. Ari had been bad news to some people in her life. To her parents. To every teacher she'd had in high school. *You'll come to no good*, they'd threatened, and she couldn't swear they'd been wrong. Certainly, she hadn't turned out to be a blessing to Maxwell or Sarah. Because of her, Max was in the hospital with too many broken bones in his arms to count, and Sarah was God knew where. But at least Ari was trying to change that. At least she was trying to be bad news to people who deserved it.

To her dismay, Resurrection, NY wasn't what she'd been led to believe when she'd looked it up on the internet.

She stood on the crest of a weedy hill outside the metropolis, her presence hidden by the deeper shadow of a highway overpass. She'd been expecting a down-on-its-luck backwater. Storefronts stuck in the seventies. Maybe a real town square and a civil war battlefield. Instead, she found an actual cityscape. The skyline wasn't Manhattan tall, more like Kansas City. Few buildings looked brand new, but many were substantial. They formed a grid of streets and parkland whose core had to encompass at least five miles. This was definitely more than a backwater. Resurrection reminded her of city photos from the early decades of the last century, when *skyscraper* meant something exciting. What could have been a twin to the Chrysler Building stuck up from the center of downtown, reigning over its brethren.

Finding the Eunuch among all that was going to take some doing.

You have to find him, she told her sinking stomach. If she didn't, she and her very small gang of peeps would be looking over their shoulders for the rest of their lives. At twenty-six and thankfully still counting, Ari had endured more than enough hiding. She was stronger now. She'd been *practicing*. Henry Blackwater, aka, the Eunuch, wouldn't know what hit him.

"Right," she said sarcastically to herself. She'd be lucky if she got out of here alive.

But faint heart never vanquished fair villain. Ari knew she'd been born the way she was for a reason. Maybe here, maybe soon, she'd find out what that reason was.

CHAPTER TWO

No one messed with people who belonged to Adam Santini. Unless, of course, the person messing with the person was also Adam's relative.

"You. Ate. My. Beignets." To emphasize his point, Adam's irate cousin, Tony Lupone, was bashing his brother's head against the squad room floor.

Since Rick's skull was made of sterner stuff than the linoleum, he laughed between winces. "What sort of cop—*ow*—eats beignets anyway?"

"Your faggot brother cop, that's who. Your pink-shirted faggot brother cop who's whupping your butt right now."

Amused by their exchange, Adam leaned back against Tony's cluttered desk. The precinct's squad room was a semi-bunker in the basement. A mix of ancient file cabinets and desks were balanced by some very revved-up technology. Grimy electrum grates on the windows protected them, more or less, from things that went bump in the night outside. The hodgepodge suited the men who manned it better than most workplaces could. Rough-edged but smart was the werewolf way. At the moment, Tony was so rough-edged his eyes glowed amber in his flushed face. His big brother could have defended himself better than he was, if it weren't for his rule against hitting his siblings.

"Ow! Lou!" he complained to Adam. "You're supposed to be my best friend. Aren't you going to call off this squirt?"

"You're the one who ate his fancy donuts."

"All dozen of them!" Tony snarled, his grievance renewed. "I brought them in to share."

"Shit," said long-haired Nate Rivera, Adam's other cousin, once removed. "Now *I* want to whup you."

Considering even-tempered Nate was growling, Adam judged it time to end the wrestling match. "All right, you two. Enough. Rick, I'm docking your next paycheck for the price of his beignets. Dana, if you'd be so kind, raid the coffee fund and pick up another batch for tomorrow night."

"None of which *you're* going to enjoy, Mr. Pig!" Panting from the exertion of trying to give his brother a concussion, Tony rose and pointed angrily down at him. "You can choke on your damned donuts."

Wisely, Rick remained where he was while his little brother stalked back to the break room, where his heinous crime had been discovered. The dress code for the detectives was casual. Rick's gray RPD T-shirt was rucked way up his six-pack abs. His concave stomach didn't betray his gluttony. His fast werewolf metabolism saw to that.

"My head," Rick moaned, still laughing. "Come on, cuz. Give your beta a hand up."

Adam sighed and obliged. None of his wolves were small, but Rick was six four and all muscle. Even with supe strength, Adam grunted to haul him up. "Some second you are. You had to know this would cause trouble."

"I couldn't help myself. The box smelled so good. Plus, he was totally obnoxious about bringing them in for everyone."

"So you knew you were stealing food from my mouth?" Nate interjected, not looking up from his paperwork. "Not cool."

"He's sucking up. Ever since he came out, he's been—" Rick snapped his muzzle shut, but it was too late.

"Uh-huh," Nate said in his dry laid back way. He'd spun around in his squeaky rolling chair to face Rick. "Ever since he came out, your brother stopped being a butch-ass prick. In fact, ever since he came out, he's been the nicest wolf around here. You don't like that 'cause you're used to being everyone's favorite."

"Crap." The way Rick rubbed the back of his neck said he knew he was in the wrong. Being Rick, he couldn't stay dejected long. A grin flashed across his handsome olive-skinned face. "Can't I still be everyone's favorite? Do I have to turn gay too?"

"I don't know," Nate said, returning to his work. "So far only gay boys bring us good breakfasts."

Seeing Rick's private wince, Adam patted his back and rubbed. Touchy-feely creatures that werewolves were, the contact calmed both of them. He knew Rick was still working on accepting his little brother's big announcement. Werewolves were some of the most macho supes in Resurrection, a city that had plenty to choose from. Adam knew Rick loved his brother just as much as before. He suspected Rick was mostly worried Tony would end up hurt. Being responsible for policing America's only supernatural-friendly town made the wolves enough of a target. Turning out to be gay on top of that was as good as taping a target onto your back.

"Tony will be all right," Adam assured his friend. "Everyone here is adjusting to the new him."

Rick rubbed his neck once more and let his hand drop. Worry pinched his dark gold eyes when they met Adam's. "They're pack. They have to love him."

Adam didn't believe this but wasn't in the mood to argue. Plenty of folks endowed being pack with mystical benefits. Some were real of course, but as alpha, Adam wasn't comfortable relying on magic to cement his authority. He thought it best to actually *be* a competent leader.

"Boss," Dana their dispatcher said. The young woman had her own corner of the squad room. Apart from its cubby walls, it was open. Banks of sleek computers surrounded her, each one monitoring different sectors of the city. The sole member of the squad who wasn't a relative, Dana was the most superstitious wolf Adam had ever met. Anti-hex graffiti scrawled across her work surfaces, the warding so thick he couldn't tell one symbol from another. How they worked like that was beyond him. Despite the quirk, Adam took her instincts seriously. Right then, she didn't look happy. Her silver dreamcatcher earrings were trembling.

"Boss, we've got a suspected M without L in the abandoned tire store on Twenty-Fourth."

M without L referred to the use of magic without a license. Adam's hackles rose. Jesus, he hated those. "Who's reporting the incident?"

"Gargoyle on the Hampton House Hotel." She touched her headset and listened. "He says it's a Level Four."

Adrenaline surged inside him, making his palms tingle. Gargoyles were rarely wrong about magical infractions. While the strength levels went up to eight, four was nothing to sneeze at. Thumb and finger to his mouth, Adam blew a piercing whistle to get his men's attention.

"Suit up," he said. "We've got a probable ML on Twenty-Fourth."

"Don't forget your earpieces," Dana added. "I'll help coordinate from here."

Adam's men were already loping to the weapons room. "Load for bear," he said as he followed them. "We don't know what we're in for."

∞

Resurrection, New York couldn't have existed without the fae. For nearly two hundred years, it had sat on an outfolded pocket of the fae's other-dimensional homeland, *in* the human world but only visible to a special few.

Those who wandered in from Outside found it less alien than might be expected. The founding faeries had used the Manhattan of the 1800s as their architectural crib sheet. Since then, the bigger apple had continued to provide inspiration. Immigrants especially liked to recreate pieces of their native land. Resurrection had its own Fifth Avenue and Macy's, its own subway and museums. Little Italy still flourished here, though—sadly—its theater district was as moribund as its role model. Adam was familiar with the theories that Resurrection was an experiment, created to see if human and fae could live peaceably as in days of old. Whether this was the reason for its existence, he couldn't say.

The only fae he knew were exceptionally tight-lipped.

Whatever their motives, Resurrection had become a haven for humans with a trait or two extra. Shapechangers of every ilk thrived here. Vamps were tolerated as long as they behaved themselves. The same was true of demons and other Dims: visitors from alternate dimensions who entered through the portals. If a being could get along, it could stay. If it couldn't, it had to go. And if the visitors didn't want to go, Adam and the rest of the RPD were just the folks to make sure they went anyway.

The job fit Adam better than his combat boots, and those boots fit him pretty good. He loved keeping order, protecting the vulnerable, kicking butt and cracking skulls as required. The only duty he didn't like was apprehending rogue Talents. Sorcerers were trained at least, and demons who went dark side were generally predictable. Talents were the wild cards in an already dangerous deck. Their power was raw, depending not on spells but on how much energy they could channel. That amount could be a trickle or a mother-effing hell of a lot.

The previous year, a Level Seven Talent who'd gotten stoned on faerie-laced angel dust had taken down the six-lane Washington Street Bridge. Just popped it off its piers and let it drop in the North River. If the bridge's gargoyles hadn't swooped in to save what cars they could, the loss of life would have been astronomical. Adam still had nightmares about talking the tripping Talent into surrendering. If tonight's incident ran along similar lines, he might need a vacation.

Along with the rest of his team, Adam clutched the leather sway-strap above his head. Nate was driving the black response van because no one else dared claim the wheel from the ponytailed Latino. They all wore body armor and helmets, plus an assortment of protective charms. Their rifles leaned against the long side benches between their knees. The guns could fire a range of ammo, both conventional and spelled. Rick, who had a knack for effective prayer, was quietly calling on the precinct's personal guardian angel. Sometimes this worked and sometimes it didn't, but even the atheists among them figured better safe than sorry.

"God," Tony said, tapping the back of his head against the van's rattling wall. "I hope this isn't another thing like the bridge."

"Amen," Carmine agreed. The stocky were was the oldest member of their squad, the only one who was married, and—yes— another of Adam's cousins.

Before he could smile, Adam's earpiece beeped.

"You're four blocks out," Dana said. "The gargoyle is reporting another series of power flares. Still nothing higher than a Four."

That was good news. Unless, of course, the Talent was warming up.

"Okay, people," Adam said. "Watch your tempers once we get inside. Be safe but no killing unless you have no choice."

He didn't warn them against hesitating. Given their inbred hair-trigger werewolf nature, hesitating wasn't an issue.

∞

The defunct tire store sat on a small parking lot between a very well locked print shop and a transient hotel. Apart from the hotel, which wasn't exactly bustling, the area wasn't residential. A cheap liquor outlet on the corner drew a few customers, but the main business done here after dark was drugs. Most of the product filtered in from the human world. Since this was Resurrection, some was also exotic. If you knew who to ask, you could score adulterated vamp blood or coke cut with faerie dust. Demon manufactured Get-Hard was popular, though it tended to cause more harmful side effects than Viagra. Every EMT Adam knew had asked why they couldn't get GH off the street. All Adam could answer was that they were doing the best they could.

Policing Resurrection couldn't be about stamping out Evil. It had to be about making sure Good didn't get swallowed.

The reminder braced him as he and his team ran soundlessly from the van onto the buckled and trash-strewn asphalt of the parking lot. His scalp prickled half a second before a soft gold light flared around the edges of the boarded-up back windows.

Adam had answered previous calls to this location. The rear section of the tire store was where vehicles had been cranked up on lifts for servicing. Fortunately, there was plenty of cover for slipping in. Unfortunately, lots of flammables were inside. Adam took the anti-burn charm that hung around his neck and whispered a word to it. That precaution seen to, he hand-signaled Rick and Tony to split off and block escape from the front exit.

This left Adam, Carmine and Nate to ghost in the back.

The flimsy combination lock on the door to the service bay had been snapped—probably magically. Adam and his two detectives ducked under the low opening. Inside, the scent and feel of magic was much stronger, the air thicker and hotter than it should have been in autumn. A male voice moaned in pain farther in, standing Adam's hair on end. Without needing to be told, Nate peeled off to the right. Adam and Carmine took the left.

Scattered heaps of tires allowed them to creep up on their goal without being seen. One bare bulb dangled from a wire, lighting the far end of the garage. In the dim circle beneath it, the Talent had her moaning victim tied to a plastic chair. The sight of her stopped Adam in his tracks. Christ, she was little. Five foot nothing and probably a hundred and small change. She looked to be in her twenties and wore the kind of clothes street kids did. Ripped up black jeans. Ancient T-shirts that didn't fit. Her oversized Yankees jacket had its sleeves torn out and was decorated with unidentifiable small objects. Her hair was a shade of platinum not found in nature, standing in white spikes around her head. A swirling red pattern was dyed it, as if her coiffure were her personal art project. What really got him though, what had his breath catching in his throat, was the clean-cut innocence of her face. Outfit and hair aside, she looked like a tiny Iowa farm girl.

It made his chest hurt to look at her. The part of him that needed to protect others wanted to protect her.

Knowing better than to trust in appearances, Adam shook the inclination off. He tapped the speaker fixed into his vest with the signal for everyone to hold. The victim was still alive. They could afford to take a minute to discover what they were up against.

As they watched, the girl lifted her right hand. Pale blue fire outlined her curled fingers. Her already bloodied victim shrank back within his ropes. He was some kind of elf-human mixblood with long gray hair. He was a lot bigger than the Talent, but that didn't mean their fight had been fair. Despite the elfblood, he didn't give off much of a magic vibe. A near-null was Adam's guess. His run-in with the Talent had left damage. He looked bad: both eyes swollen, bruises, shallow cuts bleeding all over. Though he seemed familiar, as injured as he was, he was hard to identify. Even his smell was distorted by blood and fear.

"I can do this all night," the Talent said in a voice that was way too sweet for a torturer. "Or you can tell me where to find the Eunuch."

Carmine and Adam came alert at that. This was a name they knew too damn well.

"Lady," said her bloodied victim. "I have no idea who you mean."

The girl closed her glowing hand gently. The man she was interrogating arched so violently he and the plastic chair fell over. He screamed as blood sprayed from a brand new cut on his chest. Carmine started forward, but Adam gripped his shoulder.

"Wait," he murmured. "That cut was shallow. He's not in immediate danger."

Carmine shook his head but obeyed. When the man stopped writhing, the girl drew a deep slow breath. With no more effort than gesturing upward with one finger, she set man and chair upright. Despite the situation's danger, something inside Adam let out an admiring *whoa*.

"Clearly," she said, "you think you ought to be more afraid of your boss than me."

"Lady," panted the injured man, "*everyone's* more afraid of him."

The girl's lips curved in a smile that had Carmine shivering beside him. Admittedly, the expression was a little scary. For no good reason Adam could think of, it made his cock twitch in his jockstrap.

The Talent spoke silkily. "I'm glad we've established you know who I'm looking for."

Adam expected her to cut him again. Instead, discovering her victim did know the Eunuch inspired her to up the ante on her torture. The blue fire she'd called to her hand now began gleaming around her feet. She was drawing energy from the earth—and no piddling amount either. Her glowing hand contracted into a fist, and her victim's face went chalky. Adam was pretty sure she was telekinetically squeezing his beating heart. Unless she was really good at medical manipulation, she was going to kill him.

"*Go*," he said sharply into his vest microphone.

Even in human form, werewolves weren't slowpokes. What went down next was textbook perfect. Adam and his men were on the Talent so fast she didn't have a chance to shift her attack to them. Nate got her nose squashed down on the oil-stained floor, then snapped electrum plated cuffs snug around her wrists. The cuffs were charmed so she couldn't break them, no matter how powerful she was. The Talent struggled, then cried out as Nate yanked her roughly onto her feet.

He dropped a depowering charm around her neck for good measure. Immediately, the energy-charged air settled back to normal. The girl gaped at the enchanted medal, then straight up at Adam. Adam's heart stuttered in his chest. Her eyes were a breathtaking corn-fed blue, her lashes a thick dark brown. The twitch she'd sent through his cock morphed into a throb. Carmine shot him a look of surprise. Adam fought an embarrassed flush. The smell of his arousal must have gotten strong enough to seep through his clothes.

"'bout time you showed up," the girl's victim huffed. "This bitch needs to be locked up."

Carmine flipped up his face shield and turned to consider him. The man flinched back, obviously wishing he'd refrained from complaining.

"Aren't you Donnie West?" Carmine asked. "'Cause I know we've got a handful of outstandings on your drug dealing ass."

"Uh," said Donnie, abruptly recognizable under his bruises.

"That's what I thought," said Carmine, and let out his belly laugh.

Through all of this, the Talent's eyes moved from one of them to the other, taking in their gear and their guns and getting wider by the second. When Rick and Tony caught up to them from the front, Tony's upper canines had run out and his amber eyes were glowing. The girl sucked in a breath like this shocked her, though a partial change when younger wolves got excited wasn't uncommon.

"What the—" she said before having to swallow. "What the hell kind of cops are you?"

Still holding her from behind, Nate's slash of a mouth slanted up in a devilish grin. "Well, what do you know," he drawled. "Looks like we've got ourselves an Accidental Tourist."

CPSIA information can be obtained at www.ICGtesting.com
Printed in the USA
244644LV00002B/228/P